F.G. KEEL

The Ring Eternal

First edition

This book was professionally typeset on Reedsy.
Find out more at reedsy.com

The Ring Eternal

F.G. Keel

Part One, Chapter One

2011

I will not cry today, Hannah silently resolved as she settled quietly on the weathered bench. This decree had become her daily mantra ever since her husband's sudden passing, at least after those miserable first few months. She allowed herself the space to grieve and leaned, or more accurately, stumbled, head-first into suffering. But now, eleven months later, it was a fragile oath that always ended up broken.

"Grief can evolve into a ravenous beast, and the more you feed it, the more insatiable it becomes," Hannah's therapist recently warned her. "It's a necessary process, but when you allow it to linger on like this, it can and will consume you."

She'd gone from being grief-struck to eventually becoming grief-stuck. So, she tried to tame the beast the best way she knew how: by visiting all the places that had made her happiest. And no place brought her more joy and inner peace than this idyllic spot overlooking the rolling hills of Lake Hollywood Park. There was a darker side to her strategy since this was also the place where she'd met her husband, Van.

The problem was that there were very few places in Los Angeles that were not haunted by his presence. That's what ten years of sharing your life with someone means; their shadow looms over every space. But optimistically, she kept coming back to her refuge, hoping its sway of serenity would one day return.

She slowly inhaled the crisp air of this clear, gentle winter day and forced herself to gaze down at the tree-lined lake. *I still cannot believe I am a widow. They're supposed to be old women, like grandmothers, close to the end of their lives. But here I am—only thirty-eight—and I'm a goddamn widow.*

She lowered her head and blinked away her nascent tears. Before Van's death, she seldom reflected on her age. He had this mystical way of making her feel comfortable, even in her own skin. But in his absence, she now felt every day of those thirty years like they were twofold.

As the sun peeked out from behind a billowy cloud, she briefly considered taking one of her anxiety meds but decided against it. Instead, she took stock of herself, as she'd become wont to do since Van's passing.

What does someone in the prime of life do when they've lost their soulmate, the partner who all future plans not only included but were centered around?

She paused as the sunlight washed over her like a comforting embrace, then continued her rumination. *I still have at least half my life ahead of me. I have a successful career, and I'm in great shape*, she mused, trying to break her spiraling routine. *Okay, more like decent shape right now. It's not like grief is the best motivator to eat right and work out.*

There was that word again: grief. In an effort to attenuate its power, she'd dubbed it her constant companion. A constant, unbidden companion that would wax and wane but never abate.

She scanned the half-empty park, her mind desperately seeking any kind of distraction, like an overstimulated child searching for repose. The crowd was surprisingly light for such a picturesque midwinter Sunday. The majesty of the day was not completely lost on her, with deep blue skies surrounding the radiant morning sun, currently bathing her in its halo of warmth. It was panoramic, even for Los Angeles, where most take anything sublime for granted.

It really is a beautiful day. Or, as Van might have said, "a resplenday." The image of her late husband floated to the surface of her mind. To banish it back down, she concentrated on the mint green water of the lake, thirty yards in front of her. The water was placid, as if in awe of the scenic atmosphere, which was in direct contrast to her turbulent soul.

Never has a mood been so conflicted with a setting, she mused as she watched a squirrel scamper up a eucalyptus tree. *How long will I have to endure—* Her thoughts were interrupted by an attention-grabbing voice.

"Oh, believe me, he knows what'll happen. I made damn sure of it!" a young woman exclaimed to her gaggle of followers as she punctuated her sentence with a shrill laugh.

Hannah's attention was involuntarily drawn to the source of the disturbance, and she glanced to her left at the new denizens invading her personal sanctuary. Seated in the middle was an attractive blonde woman in her mid-twenties, wearing pink hot pants with a black crop top. She was the type of person who only wore summer clothes regardless of weather or season and commanded a perpetual spotlight. Flanking her were two similarly dressed drones, perched on a bench about fifteen yards away, parallel to Hannah's.

"If he expects me to put up with that kind of shit," the queen bee continued, "then it's going to cost him."

As the drones buzzed their agreement, a different voice wafted over from Hannah's right. "There's an indoor voice, an outdoor voice, and then there's megaphone voice over there."

She flinched back in her seat and whipped her neck around to find a man dressed in khakis and a navy-blue button-down shirt standing at the other end of her bench. She quickly regarded him before meeting his smirking gaze. He had ash brown hair and hazel eyes and appeared to be in his late twenties or early thirties.

"Sorry, didn't mean to startle you," he said, as his smile faded.

Hannah's face went slack as a wave of familiarity nearly knocked her over. His voice was softly melodic and eerily intimate. Not only his voice, but his build and even his smile reminded her of Van. *Stop it! Quit letting your subconscious gaslight you,* she chided herself.

Then she remembered something else her therapist had told her: "Everything and everyone will continue to remind you of Van until you are ready to let go and move forward." But knowing this did nothing to lessen the impact the stranger had on her already delicate, maudlin state.

The man must have noticed the tears welling in her green eyes because he took a step back. "I'm sorry; it was stupid and rude of me to just, I don't know, interrupt you like that."

Hannah finally found her voice, unsteady at first but recovering, and shook her head. "No, no, you didn't do anything wrong. I was just in my own world, I guess."

"When I'm done with him, he'll end up calling me mommy," the woman on the adjacent bench cackled.

"I hope it's a world without the cannon mouth over there," he whispered, nodding to the obstreperous woman as another clamorous roar of laughter rang out. "Why are some people so clueless as to how their voice dominates a room? Or, in her case, a whole park."

As he glanced over to the other bench, Hannah studied him once more, doing another round of cerebral comparison. Whenever she swore she saw someone who looked just like Van at the grocery store, in a restaurant, or simply driving by, her therapist assured her it was completely normal and told her to concentrate on the differences instead of the similarities.

So, she took a mental snapshot of this stranger and examined it. He was probably around thirty which made him twenty years younger than Van, much thinner, sans his half-rim glasses, and completely clean-shaven. When they made eye contact again, she said, "This might sound sad, but I don't know if I could imagine a world without any self-absorbed people. My imagination isn't that vast."

"I guess even dreams have limits," he chuckled. "My roommate calls folks like that NPCs."

He also has a mild Southern accent, she noted, then asked, "NPC? Is your roommate in the military?"

"No, but he does play a lot of *Call of Duty*," he replied. "NPC is a gamer term that means non-playable character. He thinks anyone that he doesn't know is simply here to either give him information or be an annoying obstacle." He nodded to the other bench and added, "Case in point."

"That's an interesting philosophy, I suppose," she said as she glanced back over at the three women and wondered what their lives were like. Were they truly blissful, or, like her, were they simply struggling to get through each day?

"I don't know if it qualifies as a philosophy. It's more like a geeky joke."

Or a way to dehumanize someone, she thought, but said nothing.

"I'm Greyson, by the way. Greyson Caden Squires," he said nervously. "I don't know why I just told you my full name like this was a job interview."

This jolted her off that dark path of obsessing over her late husband. "Or like America's Most Wanted," she teased. "Pleased to meet you, Greyson Caden Squires. I'm Hannah."

"Let me guess, your last name is Palindrome?" Greyson joked. After a moment of awkward silence, he said, "You know, a word that's the same whether you say it forward or backward."

"I know what a palindrome is," Hannah smirked and once again thought of Van.

"Sure, I bet you hear that all the time."

She shook her head and muttered, "Not as often as you'd think."

"Mind if I sit down for a minute?" he asked tentatively.

She nodded and inched over, even though she was already close to the edge of the bench. "Be my guest."

"So…" he hesitated, then blurted out, "You come here often?"

She glanced over and noticed his sheepish grin. She could read that he was nervous, which automatically disarmed her to some degree.

"Sorry, you know the old myth that says your first answer is usually correct? Well, that may be true, but what I've come to learn is that my first question is usually wrong and also kinda corny," he confessed.

She smiled back. "It's okay, actually; I come here all the time." She turned her gaze toward the water. "This is probably my favorite place in the whole world. I—" She stopped herself before saying, "met my husband here," and continued with, "I've been coming here my whole life. It's like my private hideaway from the world."

"I can see why; it's so tranquil. Except for the occasional shriek squad or awkward person intruding on your haven," he said, motioning over to the gal group and then to himself. "Even though we're in the middle of LA, it feels like we're, I don't know, in a galaxy far, far away."

She just nodded as he continued, "Not that I'm overly familiar with this area; I've only been here a couple of months."

"What brings you to the city of angels?"

"I wanna be an actor. You know, be the next Ryan Reynolds," he replied quickly, as if rehearsed.

She glanced back at him as he chuckled. *He really could be Van's younger brother.*

"Don't look at me like that," he said, and she panicked for a moment as if he had read her mind. "Everyone always looks, I don't know, mortified when I make that joke. I used to think it was because it's a tired cliché, but now I'm wondering if I should be taking it more personally. Like, people are freaking out because I have the audacity to compare this," he said, pointing to his face, "to Ryan Reynolds."

"Don't worry, it's the former. I don't even know who that is. I assume he's an actor."

"Yeah, he hasn't done any blockbuster films, except maybe *The Proposal.* He does smaller movies like *Waiting*, *Definitely Maybe*, and *Adventureland.*"

"Ah," she hummed, "I'm not super into movies."

His face widened exaggeratedly as he said, "How is that possible? Here we sit in the shadow of the Hollywood sign, and you're not into movies. That's like living in Paris and not caring a whit for fashion. Or living in New York City and not being a foodie. Or living in London and not being obsessed with good manners."

She had to bite her tongue on her stock answer that her husband isn't into movies, so by default, neither is she. Van's major complaint was that there hadn't been anything new or original in years. She banished that memory and replied, "The entertainment industry is more than just movies."

"You're not wrong."

"So if you're not here to be the next Burt Reynolds, why are you here?"

"Ryan," he corrected with a laugh. "I came here for a job. I recently started at Crastino Industries."

"Let me guess, you're helping to build an artificial neural network-based superintelligence system for the defense department?"

"Heyyy," he said while holding up a hand like a teacher who'd just caught a student running in the halls. "I thought you didn't like movies, and here you are effortlessly lobbing *Terminator* references at me."

"I never said I didn't like movies, just that I'm not obsessed with them like some people," she responded, nodding at him.

"Fair point. No, I am not building Skynet. I'm—" He paused for a moment, then said, "Well, not really supposed to talk about it, but I'm working on a project to develop, in layman's terms, what would be called teleportation."

"Oh, so you're like Jeff Goldbum in *The Fly*?"

He shook his head and said, "Not like that. I can't talk about it, though. I signed an NDA when I was first hired, so you know what that means. I could tell ya..." he said, letting his voice trail off.

"But then you'd have to kill me?" she finished playfully.

He feigned shock. "Heavens, no. I could tell ya, but then I would get sued by my employer. It's not like I work for the CIA or anything. Let's just say it's avant-garde physics. We are trying to turn science fiction into science fact. And I can't believe I'm telling you any of this," he said, shaking his head.

"Don't worry, your star tech secrets are safe with me," she assured, but once again was haunted by a memory of Van, who'd been a science professor at the University of California, Malibu. Her body tensed as a chill ran down her spine.

"Let's turn the beat around. What do you do? And please do not say you work for Google or something."

"No, nothing like that. I'm a TV producer."

"Oh, this explains the animosity toward film. Anything I've seen?"

"For the last nine years, I've worked on *Baking for Dough*."

Recognition slowly dawned across his face, and he asked, "That baking competition show with that model, what's her name?"

"Azalea."

"Yeah, that's her. I always found it kinda oxymoronic that a model would host a baking show. You'd think it would be called *Binge and Purge,* or maybe *Boot and Rally,*" he said, chuckling at his own joke until he detected gravity in her expression.

"She and I came up with the show together. And she's my best friend."

"I'm sorry. Guess I should host a show called *Boot in Mouth.*"

"It's okay; we've heard it all before, especially when we were pitching the show."

"Still, I need to think before I step into conversational quicksand. But you said 'worked,' as in there won't be a new season?"

"Nope, we've been officially canceled," she said flatly, and saying it out loud like that made her a different shade of wistful. She peered over the lake and asked, "Do you ever think that if you could just figure out one aspect of your life, everything else would magically fall into place?"

"I know exactly what you mean. I've been so preoccupied with a work problem that it's getting dangerously close to obsession level. It's like, if I can just solve it, I'll finally prove myself."

Hannah nodded. "That's the reason I came here. I need to figure out my next career step. I have an idea for a new show; I just need to sort out the details," she said, knowing it was the truth yet very much a lie at the same time. Feeling a touch of guilt about the minor deceit, she balanced it with naked honesty. "I tend to come here when I need solace or am trying to work something out. I call this my reflecting spot."

"Reflecting spot, I like that," he said, gazing at the calm water. "I guess I was looking for a pensive place. Not only did I come here for a job, but also to kinda get away from a..." The playfulness drained from his voice as he paused for a beat. "A situation. I was in a long-term relationship that wasn't exactly healthy. Thing is, it's pretty much the only relationship I've ever been in, so there's that too."

He sighed, then glanced over at the now empty bench. "Wow, I can't believe I didn't notice that Thundermouth had left."

"Yeah, the Jeep girls took off a couple of minutes ago. About the time you were making fun of my best friend."

Greyson's face went flush. "Again, sorry about that. And about unloading all this on you. It's just that I haven't met anyone since moving here with my brother. And he, well, he's tired of this story. Plus, it isn't exactly his area of expertise."

It's not really mine, either. At least not anymore.

"Wait, what's a Jeep girl?" he asked, turning back to the vacant bench.

"Oh, you know, the blonde-haired, blue-eyed, golden-skinned sorority girl who always has a bikini on under her clothes and either drives or rides around carefree in a Jeep with the top down," she explained. *Basically, the polar opposite of me.*

"Ah, I do know the type," he said quietly, looking down. "I was kind of hoping a fresh start would be just the cure for a dysfunctional relationship, but it's taking a lot longer than I'd hoped."

"How long has it been?"

He hesitated for a moment, then said, "We've been broken up for several months. Even before I got the job offer here." He unconsciously pointed at the ground in front of him and went on. "I've been here maybe seven weeks. Guess I thought the change of scenery would be an instant cure-all, but it's not getting any easier."

"Don't worry; what you're going through is completely normal. You're still detoxing, so to speak. A couple of months is not a lot of time to get over a long-term relationship, especially a preliminary one. Even with a change of venue."

He smiled and said, "You make it sound like a court hearing."

She returned the smile. "All relationships can be a trial sometimes."

"Staying with the legal theme, ours was a court of errors almost from the start. Someone who marries their high school sweetheart might make a great story for a dinner party, but I'm not sure whether it's practical. I mean, who we are at sixteen isn't who we'll be at thirty. Hell, it's not even who we'll be at twenty. How are two people supposed to grow that much together? I don't think it's healthy to want the same things as you grow older that you did as a teenager," he said, then looked at her like he was hoping to discern a sliver of understanding.

She felt his gaze and froze for a moment as if she'd been called upon by a teacher who'd caught her daydreaming. It had been so long since someone had sought out her counsel that she'd almost forgotten how to respond. *God, I hope giving relationship advice is like riding a bike.*

"I'm sorry; I don't know what came over me. I usually wait thirty minutes after meeting someone before unpacking my failed love life," he joked. "You know, so I don't get mouth cramps or whatever."

"I think that's an old wives' tale," she replied. "It's okay, though; I was just thinking it's been a minute since I dispensed any post-relationship advice."

"Maybe this can be your next show. Randomly go up to strangers here and hit them with some crazy, serious life crisis and see what they come up with. You can call it 'Amateur Park Bench Analysis' or something."

She shook her head. "That just rolls off the tongue, doesn't it?"

"We can workshop the title."

She turned to him and asked, "Deflections aside, you do know most high school sweethearts don't end up together for the very reasons you stated, right?"

He looked away and muttered, "I guess, but I still feel bad. You know, like a failure."

"Which is a natural reaction to a breakup. Shows that you're not a sociopath."

His gaze caught a cardinal flying over the lake. He followed it across until he lost it in the trees, then said, "That's the hardest part. It's knowing all this and still not being able to do anything about the emotional part. It's like my brain is texting my heart all these salient points, but it's getting left on read."

His affectations reminded her so much of Van that a shiver raced down her spine, forcing her to turn away. Luckily, his attention was still lost in the trees on the other side of the water. She took a few deep breaths to try to calm her suddenly pounding heart.

While she composed herself, he stood up abruptly, glanced at his watch, and said, "I better get going. Thanks for indulging my melodramatic ramblings; you've been extremely helpful. I swear, I'm not usually such a sinkhole of emotions." He added a half-smile to punctuate his last sentence.

"No worries. I don't charge for the first session anyway," she teased. "But seriously, just give yourself a little grace and some more time. I promise you'll be fine eventually."

He nodded and said, "Thanks again. And good luck with your new show." Then he offered a brief wave as he walked away. As she watched him stride down the path, Hannah realized she felt surprisingly better after chatting with Greyson. Better than she had in a long, long time.

Chapter Two

Hannah surveyed the overcrowded restaurant and spotted Tanya nestled in the back of the outside patio. She strolled through the throng, dodging scurrying employees like a heroine in a zombie film. She opened the door for a server laden with entrées and drinks, then stepped onto the patio.

"OMG, you're that famous model, Azalea, right?" she squealed as she lightly clapped her hands. An older, balding man in a black and white striped shirt at the table next to them leered over.

Tanya looked up in surprise, then sneered, "Late and sassy, that's not a good look on you." She then turned to the gawking man and said, "You on break from Foot Locker?" causing him to scoff and look away.

Even seated, Tanya Holt appeared statuesque. Standing, she was a hair under 6' 1" with ebony skin and a wiry frame that could wear any outfit and make it look regal. Today, she was dressed in a simple yet elegant white blouse with black capris. And this season's hairstyle was a tapered scarlet pixie cut.

"Sorry about that. I mean, the late part," Hannah said as she dragged a chair out and plopped down. "I was at the park."

"Of course you were. Always a glutton for punishment."

Hannah nodded to the almost empty basket of bread between them and mumbled, "Better than being a glutton for gluten."

Tanya cracked a tiny smile. "That's your fault for making me wait."

Hannah shrugged, then said, "You know I don't go there to punish myself. It's just, it's where I've always felt the most at peace."

"I know, but it's been almost a year. And right now, that place is more haunted than the Amityville house. Every time you go back there, it triggers you. I'm just saying to move forward, you might not want to keep revisiting a place so overloaded with nostalgia."

Hannah brushed her off and asked, "Do you know what you're going to get?"

"I'm going to get through to you, babe. One way or another," Tanya said with a smirk.

Hannah looked up at her friend, who wore her concern on her sleeve and forced a return smile. "I don't just go there to revisit the past. Sometimes I go to think about work. You know, my future. Our show isn't just a side hustle for me."

After Tanya replied with a shrug, Hannah added, "I, uh, actually met someone there today."

Tanya's worry quickly transformed to shock as she uttered, "You're fucking kidding, right?"

"Okay, maybe not met someone as in met someone," Hannah explained, emphasizing the last two words, "But I did talk to somebody."

"A boy?"

"A boy makes it sound kind of inappropriate."

"You know what I mean," Tanya shot back.

"He was of the male persuasion."

Before Tanya could reply, they were both startled by a server who appeared to manifest from thin air. "Are we ready to order?" the tired server droned.

"I'll have the kale salad," Tanya replied, not taking her eyes off Hannah.

"Yeah, I need some more kale in my life; I'll have the same," Hannah said, then surrendered her menu.

After the server vanished back into the ether, Tanya leaned forward and demanded, "Tell me everything."

Hannah briefly replayed the day's earlier event in her head, then said, "I was sitting on my bench—"

"Moping," Tanya interrupted.

"Not moping," Hannah defended, then caught her friend's dubious expression and gave in, "Okay, fine, moping. Then this guy just appeared out of nowhere."

"This sounds more like one of those *Saw* movies than a Hallmark romance."

"He wasn't wearing a hockey mask."

"That's *Friday the 13th*, but points for trying."

"Can I finish, please?" Hannah asked, and after Tanya raised her hands in an apologetic gesture, she continued, "There was a squad of boisterous Jeep girls sitting next to me, and he strolled up and casually mentioned how annoying they were, and then we just, you know, started chatting. It was sweet. And the weird thing was..."

Hannah paused, trying to frame her next sentiment. Impatiently, Tanya repeated, "The weird thing was..."

She glanced down and said, "He reminded me so much of Van. He looked like he could be his younger brother. And he even sounded like—"

Tanya cut her off again, "Honey, we've talked about this. It's completely normal for you to see and hear Van in other men. And to be honest, most white LA guys look and sound the same."

"He's not from LA. He had this cute Southern accent."

"Whatever. Remember that poor PA a couple of months ago? You freaked out and stormed off when he asked you something about the next segment."

"I know, I know. It's just, I was daydreaming, and suddenly there's this man badgering me like I'm the director. It startled me, that's all."

"You told me that you thought he was Van for a moment," Tanya reminded her in a soft voice.

"I was thinking about him and wasn't expecting..." Hannah paused and slowly exhaled for a moment, then continued, "This wasn't like that. Or any of those other times."

"You told me your therapist said it's very common after the loss of a loved one to see their features in others. Hell, you even said our set designer David suddenly started reminding you of Van, and we've known him for years."

Hannah nodded. "I know, but that was a while ago. When it was still so fresh."

"And to meet this guy on the very same spot you met Van… that's gotta be a double shot of emotional transference."

"I guess," Hannah reluctantly agreed. "His voice and some of his mannerisms did make me think of Van, but the weird part was it didn't trigger me like it had those other times. I can't explain why."

Tanya smiled and said, "Maybe it's that you're finally—" She hesitated for a moment, then finished with, "healing."

Hannah shrugged. "It was a nice conversation. He did most of the talking. Poor guy is trying to get over a bad breakup."

"So, what did this poor guy look like?"

"Ryan Reynolds," Hannah whispered without thinking.

"Are you fucking kidding me? Please tell me you got his number, his address, blood type, mother's maiden name, and social security number."

Hannah shook her head as she laughed. "I'm just joking. I don't even know what he looks like."

"You sure he wasn't wearing a hockey mask?"

"I mean Ryan Reynolds, not Greyson."

"So Captain Mysterio has a name. Does he possess physical features to go along with this name, or was he a disembodied voice?" Tanya asked playfully.

"He's about six foot, with brown hair and hazel eyes. He's probably, I don't know, close to thirty. He just moved here for a job at a tech company."

"I haven't seen this much dancing around since the last Shakira video," Tanya sighed, then spoke slowly and deliberately, "Was he cute?"

Hannah immediately thought, *Very cute, borderline full-blown handsome*, then scaled back her reply to, "I guess you could say that. I didn't, you know, sculpt his face out of clay or anything like that."

"But you did talk to him, and for that, I'm proud of you. And I can totally see that little sparkle in your eyes when you described him, so I know there's still hope for you yet," Tanya said with her personalized Cheshire grin.

"What does that mean?"

"What it means, honey, is that you might finally be getting out of this life limbo that you've been stuck in for the last year. You might even be ready to get out there, and you know, date," Tanya said, making air quotes around the word date. "You don't have to be a lonely spinster at the ripe old age of thirty-eight. There might be a gentleman caller in your future—maybe this Greyson dude. Shit, you may even get laid."

She'd said the last sentence so loudly that Hannah embarrassingly glanced around while trying not to look like she was embarrassingly glancing around. Then she shot Tanya a scowl that said, "Shut it."

"Don't look at me like that. Birds do it, bees do it, even elderly referees do it," she said, nodding to the man at the table next to them who was looking over again.

"When I first met Van, it was one of those rare occasions where we clicked instantly, almost as if we'd known each other in a previous life. That's how I knew he was my soulmate. And that's how I know there aren't going to be any gentleman callers now or ever," Hannah declared, repeating what she'd been resignedly telling herself since his death.

"That's nonsense. Even if soulmates were real, who's to say you can't have two? Or two dozen? I mean, I was sure my Lexus was the one car for me, then I got my BMW last year, and, well, it was love at first drive."

"Not the same," Hannah objected while shaking her head.

"Look, I understand. Thinking like that makes life so much less complicated. But you're just being faithful to a memory."

"It's more than anything you've been faithful to," Hannah teased.

Tanya pursed her lips, then shot back, "Oh, it's like that. Well, I bet Van's up there in heaven right now getting it on with, like, Marilyn Monroe."

"Uh, I don't think people have sex in heaven."

"Then what's the point in going? Sounds more like the other place," Tanya said, motioning downward with a finger.

Hannah laughed as her salad suddenly landed in front of her. "We will not be continuing this conversation later," she said and unraveled her fork from its napkin restraints.

Chapter Three

"Where the hell have you been?" Nolan shouted from the couch as Greyson strolled into the living room.

It was a familiar scene; his roommate was deeply enraptured in the latest *Call of Duty* game. The room was sparsely decorated, with a worn red sofa underneath a curtainless window on one side and a wall-mounted flat-screen TV on the other. A second-hand hazelnut coffee table sat in between.

"Good afternoon to you, Sergeant Scarpulla."

"What? Shut up, man," Nolan hissed without taking his eyes off the fifty-five-inch screen. He was gyrating in his seat like he was being attacked by fire ants instead of animated Nazis.

"I was just at the lake," Greyson said as he sank down next to the man he considered his brother.

Nolan Scarpulla was a muscular, squat Irish-Italian fellow with short black hair and a somewhat Neanderthal face. He was wearing his favorite gray sweatpants and a stained In-N-Out Burger tee that he proudly bought on the first day they arrived in Los Angeles.

"You want in?" Nolan said, nodding to the controller on the cushion next to him.

"Naw, I'm good."

"What lake?" Nolan asked, then accidentally elbowed Greyson in the arm.

"Watch the people's elbow there, Rock. You're getting a little too into the game," Greyson said, inching over to the corner of the couch. "It's the Hollywood Reservoir."

"Is a reservoir a lake?"

"It's an artificial lake, usually created in a river valley by a dam."

Nolan made a loud snoring noise, then said, "Okay, Mr. Wikipedia, I'm sorry I asked. What the hell were you doing there?"

"I went for a little hike, *Mom*," Greyson said, stressing the insulting last word.

"I just worry about you, is all. My little boy all by himself in the big, bad city," Nolan replied in a falsetto voice.

"I actually kinda met someone," Greyson said as he watched Nolan's avatar blow up a tank.

"But whattttt?"

"Maybe not like met, more I talked to a…" Greyson paused, searching for the right word. Girl made her seem too young, woman too old, and lady made her sound like a character in a *Bridgerton* novel. He finally said, "Sheila," in his best Australian accent.

"She hot?"

"Why is that always the first thing you ask?"

Nolan shrugged and said, "Don't blame me, dude, blame society." He then motioned to a Carl's Jr. flyer on the coffee table with a model in a bikini trying to look sexy while cramming an overstuffed hamburger into her mouth.

"Well, apparently society finds it acceptable to have a percentage of starving children, so maybe shoot for standards that are above societal."

"Whatever dude."

While his friend continued to take out German soldiers in some very creative ways, Greyson pictured Hannah sitting there on the picturesque bench and thought, *Okay, she was definitely attractive, but that's not why I stopped to talk to her, right? No, there was something else that drew me to her. Something like gravity or maybe kismet that I couldn't explain to Nolan even if I wanted to.*

Nolan interrupted his pondering and asked, "You get her digits? Or were you too much of a gentleman to take it that far on a first meet?"

Greyson scoffed and just shook his head.

"Why the hell not, Grey? Best way to get over Ansley is to get under someone else," Nolan said, laughing at his unoriginal joke.

Greyson winced at the mention of his ex and said, "It wasn't like that. We just talked."

Nolan made another exaggerated snoring noise. "Dude, only you can make meeting a new prospect sound so hopelessly boring. Is she at least single?"

Great question, Greyson thought as he just shrugged.

Even though his attention was still fixed on the TV, Nolan sensed his friend's response and huffed, "Was there a ring?"

"I forgot to check."

"Jesus Christ, you are such an amateur," Nolan chastised. "Now, can I ask what this respectable female looks like? You should at least know that."

"She's probably around 5'5", maybe. I don't know because she was sitting the whole time. She had auburn hair and these enchanting green eyes that you could lose yourself in."

"Boobs?" Nolan asked as he put his hands out a couple of feet in front of his chest briefly before returning to the game.

"Yes, she had boobs, ya troglodyte. I did mention she was female, right?"

"At least as far as you know," Nolan said with a wink. "If you didn't get her number, did you at least get her name?"

"It's Hannah."

"Hannah Montana?" Nolan uttered, then snorted.

At least I didn't say that. "I didn't get her last name; it wasn't a job interview."

"Then how do you ever expect to see her again?"

"She did say she goes to the park a lot," Greyson said, then added almost to himself, "She was remarkably easy to talk to."

"Well, there you go. Just stalk the park and boom, another chance encounter."

"Thanks for the tip, but I'm not going to stalk her," Greyson replied, feigning disgust.

“I said stalk the park, not the girl. You need to understand the subtleties of hooking up with someone.”

“Since when are you studying to be a *court* lawyer?” Greyson quipped.

“I’m studying to be an ass-whipping lawyer, and you’re about to be my first case,” Nolan grunted and, without looking, quickly reached over and smacked Greyson in the arm.

Greyson responded by knocking the controller out of Nolan’s hand, causing his character to wander aimlessly into enemy gunfire. “What the fuck, man?” Nolan barked.

“See what happens? Mess with me, and you get a bullet shower.”

Without leaving the couch, Nolan reached down and swiped the gamepad off the floor, then sneered, “I’m glad you missed your chance with this girl, who’s probably your soulmate.”

Greyson rolled his eyes. “Oh, come on, man, grow up. Soulmates aren’t real; that’s just the mass media trying to sell you an unrealistic and unattainable version of love.”

“Well, aren’t you the Grinch who stole Valentine’s Day? Remind me not to let you give a toast at my wedding to Megan Fox.”

Greyson shook his head, then said, “Who knows, maybe I’ll find a reason to go back. I mean, it was a beautiful area with great views.”

“Screw the views; you need a woman. You always say you’re ready to move on from Ansley, but it’s like you still have both feet rooted in the past.”

“I have enough on my plate with work right now. I don’t know if I even have—”

“See, you got more excuses than LA’s got mini-malls, dude,” Nolan interrupted.

A brief image of Hannah sitting next to him smiling flashed into Greyson’s mind. “Okay, I’ll go back next weekend and see if she’s there.”

Nolan grinned and proudly declared, “One day, I’m gonna turn you into a real guy.”

“Keep telling yourself that, Geppetto,” Greyson said as he got up and shuffled off into the adjacent kitchen in search of lunch.

Chapter Four

Hannah sighed when she saw her sister's red Audi parked behind her mother's SUV. *Great, this just went from a family duty to an excruciating chore.*

In the past few years, she had made it a point to stop by and visit her mother weekly, yet she seldom looked forward to it. She purposely chose Mondays, knowing that it would be inconvenient for her younger sister, so she could avoid the double barrel blast of criticism and comparison that came externally from her mother and internally from herself.

Why is it always a competition with Jenna? I have a successful career and marriage. Well, at least I had both. She got out of her car with a sense of dread weighing in the pit of her stomach like an anchor.

She ambled up to the porch, and before she could reach for the door, it flung open. Her sister almost jumped into her arms and exclaimed, "Oh my God, Hanni, it's been way too long!"

Jenna Ackerman-Rader was wearing a button-up plaid pinafore dress with a pleated almond blouse that hung from her lithe body like it was still on a hanger. Her golden hair cascaded over her shoulders, and she looked ready for a board meeting, even though she hadn't worked since her first pregnancy. And after her second child two years later, the odds of her ever going back were slimmer than winning big at keno.

As she hugged her sister back, Hannah noticed more than a whiff of Beyoncé

Heat. "Yeah, it's been a while."

"Not since just after the funeral, bae. Christian and I have meant to come over, but with the kids and work, we've just been so freaking busy," Jenna said, then finally released Hannah. "You're lucky. I just stopped by to borrow Mom's Blendtec. Mine broke, and I'm hosting a little gathering next weekend. You should come." Her last sentence came off as a throwaway remark, akin to, "We should do lunch."

Before Hannah could even process the invitation, Jenna added, "Although you won't really know anyone. But there will be tons of people in the biz, so maybe you can make some new contacts."

It's like a stream of consciousness invite, Hannah thought. "Who knows, maybe I will."

"Super! It's this Saturday, around seven-ish. It's a semi-formal, semi-casual thing."

"I guess they're not mutually exclusive," Hannah mumbled.

Jenna ignored the quip and said, "Oh, but you can wear anything you want, of course. Just make sure it's, you know, nice." As her final caustic word hung in the air, she then turned and led Hannah into the house.

When they walked into the ivory kitchen, they were greeted with, "Both my girls under one roof. And it's not even my birthday."

The famous Hester Ackerman was leaning against the massive kitchen island with a wine glass in her hand as she regarded her two daughters behind a pair of browline eyeglasses like a drill sergeant sizing up a pair of hapless new recruits. She was dressed in an A-line plum-colored dress and looked more like Jenna's older clone than her mother. She was one part Mary Stuart and two parts Martha Stewart.

Suddenly, Hannah felt underdressed in her simple yellow cotton sundress. Then, she silently admonished herself, *This is a family gathering, not Project Runway.*

What made Hester famous and relatively wealthy was her early 90s hit show, *Mother Knows Brett.* She played everyone's favorite matriarch in the comedy, which lasted six seasons. It was about a man-child in his twenties who was perpetually trying to find love, a career, and his place in the world, all while still living with his overbearing mother. No one seemed to care that the actor playing Brett was only ten years younger than Hester, who was in her early forties at the time. C'est la Hollywood.

"Hi Mom," Hannah said as she strolled over and pecked her on the cheek. It was almost as if she were bumping into a longtime friend who had gotten lost among the years. Hester may have been a dazzling, if somewhat domineering, mother on the small screen. But in real life, she was more laissez-faire with a sprinkling of passive-aggressive judgment.

Through the years, she'd left the heavy lifting to the nannies: the changing of diapers, the bathing, and the dreaded midnight feeding. She was far too busy playing mom for the whole nation. To Hannah and Jenna, she had been more like the aunt who would show up now and again, offering gifts along with dubious wisdom and advice like a Pez dispenser necking out empty calorie pellets.

"Good to see you, darling," Hester said, then raised a glass in a mock toast right before taking a large sip.

"I just invited Hanni to my event on Saturday," Jenna declared as if it were the White House State Dinner.

The gathering just escalated into an event in the space of one minute, Hannah mused, causing herself to smile unconsciously.

Jenna noticed Hannah's grin and boasted, "It definitely will be a blast. I'm not saying it's going to be the social gathering of the year or anything. That's for others to say and, more importantly, write." She ended her brash statement with a wink towards her mother.

"You're going?" Hannah asked her mom.

Hester swirled the rest of her wine in her glass and said, "I'm going to try and pop by." She always fancied herself far too important to ever give an iron-clad guarantee about where she would be and what she would be doing at any given point in time. She was more like a force of nature who answered only to her own whims.

Hannah and Jenna had scores of personal disappointments in their youth to back this up. Hester had missed a myriad of birthdays, school plays, sporting events, and entire summer vacations due to the rigors of her celebrity life.

She'd even missed Hannah's high school graduation, which Hannah had unsuccessfully tried not to be upset over.

Now that her fame had faded like a dying star, she was a lot more reliable, much to Jenna's delight. But being the older and somewhat jaded sibling, Hannah had to fight off indifference and resentment like a burned-out college student battling exhaustion. So, Hester's nonchalant "try and pop by" now translated into "be there with bells on."

"Hate to borrow and run, but I've got to go pick up Neil and Simon," Jenna announced as she cradled the blender and headed for the door.

"It was good seeing you. Give my love to the boys," Hannah offered to the figure sweeping through the kitchen.

"Don't forget, next Saturday at around seven," she replied and was out the door before anyone had a chance to object.

"Why doesn't anything start at a clearly defined time? It's always around, about, or ish, which really means don't show up for at least an hour after the nonspecific time frame," Hannah wondered out loud.

"Do you want a glass of wine?" Hester offered, which was her usual answer to a question she didn't quite understand the point of.

Hannah nodded. Hester moved behind the island and grabbed a hanging glass from the wooden rack. As she poured heavily, she asked, "So, how are you doing?"

Before Hannah could answer, she continued, "I know I ask you that every time you visit, but I am your mother. It's my duty."

It's funny how you feel the need to remind me of that fact, Hannah thought, then quickly banished it away, along with the accompanying bitterness. "I'm fine, really. I took your and Tanya's advice and finally packed up all of Van's things."

This revelation made Hester smile proudly as she handed Hannah a glass of Merlot. After topping off her own glass, Hester said, "Oh dear, you should've called me. I would've come and helped so you didn't have to do it alone."

Hannah wanted to say, "I'm used to it, Mom," but instead went with, "It wasn't that big of a deal. It was mostly his clothes, which he didn't have a ton of."

She pictured their shared closet and how he only had a small rack and an old dresser that they'd picked up from an antique shop in the valley. She remembered searching the house for anything that was solely his and being surprised by how little she found. He didn't even have the ever-popular man cave and thought the very notion was ludicrous. Like their life, everything was shared.

There was a framed wedding photo taken on the outskirts of some wooded area hanging in her home office that she hadn't the heart to take down. Everyone who knew him was well aware of his complete disdain for having his picture taken. He had a litany of reasons, the most famous of which was that he always ended up ruining any picture by making an unintentionally goofy face. He was truly a dinosaur in this burgeoning age of social media.

"He really didn't leave very much of a spousal footprint, at least physically," she said wistfully.

"What dear?" Hester asked as she sat down on the stool next to her daughter.

"I mean, there wasn't a lot that was, you know, just him," Hannah said, stressing the word *him*. "All our furniture was either mine or we picked it out together. He didn't have anything from his childhood, since all of that was lost in a fire while he was away at college. He used to say, 'I collect experiences, not things.'"

Hester nodded and said, "Yes, he was unique in that way. All of my husbands loved accumulating possessions. Almost as much as I loved claiming them in the divorces," she joked, then added soberly, "Except for your father, of course."

Hannah gave a solemn nod at the mention of her dad. Ben Ackerman had died in a car accident thirty-three years ago when Hannah was five and Jenna was just a toddler. Hannah had hazy recollections of a bear-like, jovial man lifting her into the air that felt more like dreams than actual memories. He and her mother had been married for five years at the time, so their relationship still had a sense of freshness to it. They'd met at a mutual friend's Christmas party while she was a struggling actress, and he was a budding financial advisor with a large bank.

"I do know what you're going through," Hester said as she placed her hand on top of Hannah's.

"I know, Mom," Hannah said as she looked at her mother and fought back unwelcome tears.

After a few moments of stillness, Hester said, "So, any traction on your next show?"

Just like Mom. We can't linger too long in the emotional realm before she switches to a more familiar zone, Hannah thought, then replied, "Nothing so far. Tanya and I have a meeting with some Food Network execs next week. We just need to refine the pitch for the new show."

And by refine, I mean develop.

Hester smiled and quickly shifted into a more comfortable, pseudo-agent role. "I'm sure whatever you two have cooked up will knock their socks off. But just be careful—having one hit under your belt doesn't always ensure future success. Sometimes it can hurt more than help."

"I will," Hannah said, understanding that she was again speaking from experience. After Hester's show ended, she was branded with the label "sassy, overbearing mother," which never seemed to wear off. The only work she was offered was basically the same role on a few TV movies or pilots, which she turned down on principle.

The only way she managed to stay in the public eye was to keep getting married and divorced, which she did a total of four times in the span of fifteen years. Now once again single, she finally accepted her epithet and agreed to the role of a sassy, overbearing grandmother in a series of moderately successful Christmas movies.

"You know, Jenna and Christian may be able to help you. As producers, they've got a lot of contacts. I'm sure they'd love to help you get back on your feet," Hester suggested as if they were one single being.

He's a producer. The only thing she's ever produced are children, Hannah corrected in her head as she took a sip of her wine.

"Maybe ask them at the party this weekend."

"I will," Hannah repeated absentmindedly as her attention was drawn to the floor-to-ceiling windows showing off the backyard's perfectly manicured lawn. The pastoral scenery caused a tiny thought in the back of her mind to whisper, *I wonder where Greyson is right now.*

Chapter Five

"Listen up, newbie, you better dot your t's and uncross your eyes because the big boss is coming to town," Tsai announced as she swept into the office. Tsai Ruan was Greyson's mentor/friend at Crastino and five years his senior, in both age and work tenure. She was dressed in blue capris and a tropical print blouse, with her long raven hair pulled back in a ponytail.

"Fuck-shit," Greyson said, smashing down the space bar on his laptop several times.

"It's okay, Grey; I didn't mean to get your panties in a bunch. Dr. Greene's not that bad," she assured as she flopped down into the chair opposite him. She pulled her laptop from its bag and carefully placed it on the clear glass desk.

"It's not that," Greyson huffed. "I thought I cracked the 2001 conundrum. I'd been working on it all morning, but the simulation I just ran basically blew up cyberspace. I feel like an abject failure."

Tsai lifted the screen on her laptop. "Relax, dude. Quit being such an electron. You've only been here a couple of weeks. Everyone's tried and failed with that problem. Even me, and I'm the most brilliant person you know. It's like a rite of passage; you think you're going to come in and be the one who pulls the sword from the keystone. Then, after a while, you'll stop being stuck in the past and concentrate on more important things. That's what Elden told me."

Greyson nodded at the mention of her fabled mentor, Elden, who'd recently left to start his own company. Even though he'd never met the man he replaced, Greyson respected his work and hoped to meet the legend behind the myth someday. "It just feels like the answer is on the tip of my tongue, kinda like the title of a song whose partial lyrics are stuck in your head."

"I can name that solution in three terms," Tsai snickered. "Give it up; if I can't crack it, some other Wahoo definitely can't." She was one of the few people he knew who had not only confidence but also the skill and talent to back up her swagger. They'd met on Greyson's first day and instantly hit it off, to the point where he felt at home in his new surroundings by the end of his shift. And they'd become friends by the end of the week. He'd felt extremely fortunate that he'd been assigned as her office mentee. Or her padawan, as she liked to call him.

Trying to solve the 2001 conundrum had been his daily morning ritual. It was like a secret quest he assigned to himself immediately after hearing about the massive and mysterious energy spike that almost ended Project Gateway before it really began. Although he wouldn't admit it, Greyson felt like this was the only way to show everyone, especially himself, that he truly deserved his position here.

"I guess. I just hate unsolved mysteries," he mumbled as he pushed back from the shared desk.

"What? I loved that old show. Robert Stack was hot."

He wrinkled his nose as if she'd opened a bag of burnt popcorn, which she was apt to do, and said, "Eww. Just, eww."

"What can I say? I have a thing for older gentlemen in trench coats. It's the only type of guy I'd go straight for," she joked. "Anyway, did you even hear what I said? El Jefe is down in the labs today, making the rounds."

El Jefe, or as it was stenciled on his top-floor office door, Dr. Tyson Greene, was one of the founders and current CEO of Crastino Inc. Born and raised in Chicago, he received his doctorate from Stanford in the early 1980s. When he started the company in 1995, he was one of the youngest Black CEOs in American history. Now, he was a fifty-five-year-old icon with a laundry list of accomplishments. One of his proudest, Crastino Inc., was a Fortune 500 company with a reputation that rivaled Google and Microsoft.

"Oh, shit biscuits," Greyson muttered as his heart rate spiked. He'd been with the company for nearly a month but had yet to even lay eyes on Dr. Greene. Or, to use his more prominent and infamous name, El Jefe. Dr. Aarón Vicario, Crastino's other co-founder, and second-in-command, playfully gave him the sobriquet. And it was soon adopted by everyone.

Tsai glanced at her suddenly pale mentee and asked, "You gonna be okay? If you need to throw up, you can use the restroom down the hall."

"I'm not going to throw up," he shot back. "It's just that Dr. Greene is kinda like a hero to me."

"Oh God, not you too," she said while shaking her head. "Trust me, he's just a man. He puts his pants on one leg at a time. Although he probably does it a lot smoother and with more panache than anyone else. On second thought, if anyone has figured out a more optimal way to dress, it would be him."

"You're not helping."

She shrugged. "You sure picked the wrong day to dress like a Denny's server."

He glanced down at his black polo shirt. "What? The dress code says collared shirts, and anyway, half the people here are wearing either a Star Wars or anime t-shirt."

"Calm down. I'm just fucking with you, dude."

He looked up and asked, "Why did I get cursed with an evil office partner?"

"Just lucky, I guess. But seriously, are you sure about that hair? Do you squirrel away a lifetime supply of Aqua Net or something?"

Greyson lightly patted the top of his head. "It's styling product, thank you. Not everyone was blessed with thick, luxurious hair."

A sharp knock on the door interrupted their banter. "Hope I'm not intruding," a burly gentleman wearing a charcoal gray suit said as he entered.

Dr. Greene stepped in and nearly filled the office with both his size and reputation. Greyson and Tsai had to crane their necks up to meet his gaze. He was a towering figure, standing just over 6'4", wearing thick glasses and dark hair with hints of white sprinkled around like spring snow on a mountaintop.

"No, no, not at all," Greyson said as he sat up straight in his chair.

Dr. Greene glanced over to Tsai and said, "Hello, Tsai. How's it going?"

"Fine, another day, another brilliant breakthrough."

"And you must be Greyson Squires. I have been looking forward to meeting you," he said as he turned to Greyson and swiftly assessed him. "You're not exactly what I expected."

What the hell does that mean? Greyson thought but simply nodded like he expected that reaction.

As if reading his mind, Dr. Greene said, "I just mean you look a lot younger than I thought you would. But at my age, everyone looks a lot younger. Sometimes, it feels like I'm working with a bunch of teenagers." Then he waited for a beat and added, "Maybe you should grow a beard."

"I had a goatee once but quickly realized that was a mistake," Greyson replied, then instantly regretted his nervous overshare.

"I just wanted to stop in and say hello," Dr. Greene said as he took a step back toward the doorway.

"It was nice to meet you, sir," Greyson said, and he automatically brought his hand up as if to salute, then at the last second turned it into a clumsy wave.

"Sir?" Dr. Greene said in near disgust. "Please, just call me El Jefe."

"Seriously?" Greyson asked.

Tsai and Dr. Greene chuckled as he said, "No, I'm just kidding." Then he turned to Tsai and said, "Your suggestion to use gravitational energy on the converter was brilliant."

"That's why you pay me the medium bucks," she replied with a grin.

Dr. Greene turned, then paused as he reached for the door. He glanced back at Greyson and said, "Oh yeah, if you don't mind, I'd like to take you to lunch. A kind of welcome-to-the-team gesture. You free next week, say Wednesday?"

"Well, yeah," Greyson mumbled, then added more assertively, "Sure, of course."

"Great, I'll email you the details. Or at least, someone will," Dr. Greene said, then looked over at Tsai and added, "Have a great rest of the day and do something extraordinary for me." He punctuated the sentence by closing the door.

After a pregnant pause, Tsai turned to Greyson and exclaimed, "A welcome to the team lunch; what the hell?"

Greyson's surprise quickly turned to perplexity as he asked, "What? Is that not a normal thing?"

Tsai leaned back and peered out the glass wall of their office to ensure Dr. Greene was gone. "It's not a thing at all. In the 1,989 days that I have been here, I've only eaten with him five times. And those were end-of-year celebrations with all the department heads and their direct reports."

"Maybe he started it recently."

She shot him her patented "be serious, dude" expression, then said, "And no one's ever mentioned it? I don't think so. We may be exceptional at maintaining corporate secrets, but we're horrible at office gossip."

"Okay, maybe he's starting it now."

She ignored his comment and, almost to herself, muttered, "There's nothing particularly special about you. I mean, your grades were excellent, but so were everyone else's here."

"You do realize sound travels." Then, his eyes widened as he asked, "How do you know what my grades were?"

"I'm the one who vetted you. Duh," she replied dismissively, then slowly glanced around the sparsely decorated office and continued, "You have no prior work experience to speak of—"

"Hello, I was an assistant manager at Blockbuster," he interrupted.

She lightly bit her bottom lip as she thought for a moment. "I can see no reason why El Jefe would want to have lunch with you."

"Thanks for the motivational speech, Tony Robbins."

She frowned at him and said, "Calm down. I don't mean anything pejorative by it. You're a great worker, and surprisingly, you've actually pushed the project forward in the short time you've been here. But why one of the most remarkable and accomplished minds of our time wants to meet with you is a brand-new conundrum."

"It's probably my shirt. He wants to know where I got it," he teased, then asked, "Should I be honest and say TJ Maxx?"

She slapped her hand on her forehead. "Oh God, I'm going to have to pick out your clothes for this, aren't I?"

"I think I can handle it."

"Well, I expect a full report."

"Yes, my master," he said in a passable Darth Vader impression. Then he turned his attention back to work and tried to ignore Tsai's stress-inducing query.

Chapter Six

The weekdays breezed by, and the weekend briskly arrived, like a plane making a steady touchdown on a runway. When Sunday came, Hannah found herself back in the park, but this time with a medley of emotions playing in her head. As she strolled down the pathway, the usual sense of mournfulness made its way to the front of her heart.

Relieved to see her bench empty, Hannah rotely took a seat and briefly admired her favorite vista. She could almost hear Van's voice whispering in the wind about how, even on a cold and dreary day, this was still a billion-dollar view. Then, she closed her eyes and slowly exhaled while murmuring to herself, "Okay, no tears today," just as the memories of their life together tried to flood her mind.

My days have become such a vague routine. It's almost like I'm living in a kind of suspended animation. I start each week off by visiting my mom and then wind up ending it here. The weekly trips to see her mother had started years ago at the suggestion of her therapist. It was a way not only to heal their relationship but also the residual scars of her childhood.

A gust of cool wind whipped her hair to the side as if casually vying for her attention. *It's going to be spring in a few weeks, and then it will be a year. One whole year of life without Van. How do you commemorate the anniversary of a loved one's death?* She tried unsuccessfully to fight back the tears welling up in her eyes.

"Oh, stop it," she breathed. brushing the moisture from her eyes. "Van is gone and there—"

"Hey, fancy meeting you here," a voice said, casually interrupting her melancholy.

She jumped, then turned toward the voice in a moment of discombobulation. She put her hand up above her eyes to block out the winter sun, almost expecting to see her late husband smiling down at her. After a brief moment, she recognized both the voice and the man it belonged to, standing at the side of her bench.

"I'm sorry, did I startle you again?" Greyson asked, suddenly sounding concerned. "I didn't mean to; I was just exci…" He paused for a beat, then continued, "Exercising. And I spotted you over here and wanted to say hi."

"It's fine. I was just sitting here contemplating, per usual. Like I said, I tend to come here more often when I need to sort things out. My husband used to call this my musing bench," she said, still disoriented.

Greyson let out a short breath, slowly glanced around, and said, "A musing bench on a reflecting spot. I think I get it." His reply was just a tad extra peppy, like he was trying to overcompensate for something.

"I mean, it is my favorite place in the world," she said with a somber smile.

"I remember," he said, as he focused on a couple jogging along the path in front of them.

As he was distracted, Hannah dared a glance at his profile. *He looks so much like*—an echo of Tanya's voice interrupted her thoughts, saying, *Oh girl, you've got to cut that shit out. Stop comparing every man you see to your spousal paragon.*

Just as Greyson was orchestrating a farewell, Hannah asked, "Would you like to join me?"

He swung his attention to the empty place on the bench and said, "You sure? I know that musing is a single-player game."

Hannah nodded and said, "I have been thinking far too much since his death. I could use a little time outside my own head."

Greyson paused as if weighing her offer, and then said, "I'm sorry for your loss."

"We met right here almost eleven years ago," she confided, then turned to her left and pointed to a parallel bench fifteen yards away. "Actually, it might have been that one. It's funny how the minor details get blurrier with the years."

Greyson leaned forward following her gesture as she continued, "That's why I'm usually lost in my thoughts, or, I should say, my sorrow, whenever I'm here now. This has turned from my happy place into my grieving spot."

"How long has it been, if you don't mind me asking?" he said.

"Almost a year," Hannah replied, as her attention drifted towards the pond like a leaf on the wind.

"I'm so sorry."

She softly exhaled and felt a modicum of alleviation. "No, I'm sorry. I honestly didn't mean to burden you with all that. I just…" She couldn't finish her sentence and only shrugged.

"Hey, quid pro quo. It's only fair, since last time I unceremoniously dropped all my issues on you like you were some porter at a train station. I probably sounded like an immature, whiny neophyte."

She turned to look at him and, with a half-smile, said, "No, it's not an adversity competition. It was actually a pleasant distraction." When she saw his eyebrows arch, she realized how that sounded and quickly added, "Not that your pain is something pleasing to me. I'm not a sadist or anything."

"If I squint hard enough, you do kinda sorta resemble the Marquis de Sade. Especially around the eyes."

"And you're about to resemble Rocky Balboa after going a couple of rounds with Mr. T," she shot back with a scowl that quickly evolved into a grin. "Especially around the eyes."

Greyson held up both hands as if in surrender. "Whoa, just kidding. I hope you don't solve all your problems with violence."

She chuckled and said, "Honestly, I don't know where that even came from. I promise you, I'm not a violent woman."

"I believe you," he said, then made a show of scooting to the other end of the bench. "But you know what they say: behind every jab lies the pain of truth."

"They must love to paint in broad strokes. But to be honest, I only saw the first *Rocky*, and that was years ago. But he did fight Mr. T, right?" she asked. Greyson replied with a nod. "Good. I know how you movie fanatics scrutinize all references down to the most minute detail."

"Don't worry, you got instant cred with me from that Goldblum reference last week. I'll admit, I do love me a good *Rocky* flick. They might be cheesy and formulaic, but I grew up watching 'em," he said excitedly. "On the negative side, they ruined the sport of boxing for me. The first real boxing match I watched was so boring compared to any of the ones from *Rocky*. It's similar to how *Happy Gilmore* ruined golf."

"I've never been into watching sports on television. Now, seeing a Dodgers or Lakers game in person, that's a blast."

He kicked a small rock down the slope onto the paved walkway, then said, "I'm not much into sports, either live or on TV. I think the closest pro sports team where I grew up was a minor league baseball team, and that was over an hour away."

"Where was that?"

"Williamsburg, Virginia."

"I've always wanted to go there. I have this idyllic vision of everyone wearing colonial garb churning their own butter on a charming wraparound porch," she said, then quickly added, "Then I remember the slavery part, and that fantasy quickly sours."

"It's funny how people always want to consign the heinous parts of the past to oblivion. It's always just the good old days, ignoring the fact that, to many, those were some of the worst of times. But as long as they were happy, who cares about the rest of the world?"

She sensed his sudden gravitas in his tone and wondered if there was something else behind it. Or was she merely projecting? He glanced back over at her and forced a smile. "Sorry, didn't mean to get so dark on you like that. It's just... growing up in a place so fixed on a certain point in history makes you weary of that kind of existence. Of course, then I think of my situation with my ex and can see why it's easy to get stuck in the past. My roommate likes to say, 'People looking back tend to miss out on what's in front of them.' I'm pretty sure he got that from a meme."

Hannah thought about her own situation and said, "I can understand how the siren's call of the past can prevent you from moving forward." After a brief pause, she added, "A little too much, I suppose."

Her words seemed to draw him out of his narrative. "Let's get back to the future; any movement on your new show?"

"What?" she murmured, as she was jarred from her meandering thoughts again. "Oh, yeah. We have a meeting next week about it, but the idea's still kind of coalescing. As in, I have an idea, just no clear strategy on how to execute it."

He put his palm out and quickly motioned his fingers back and forth as he said, "Pitch it to me. Maybe I can give you some feedback."

She shook her head. "No way. I told you, it's still…" she said, pausing to think of the right word, then settled on, "simmering. It's not ready for a taste test."

"Not to brag, but I have the palate of a small child, so I can be the perfect beta taste tester."

She considered his offer for a moment. *I've only talked about it with Tanya so far; maybe an outside view might be useful. Plus, it's always better for me when I talk things out.* After a brief sigh, she reluctantly agreed, "Fine, but no judgment. This is my second child, so to speak, and even though it's still in the womb, I'm very protective of it."

"Okay, there's a lot to unpack in that analogy, but we can save that for later. Just think of this as an ultrasounding board."

"Yeah, this whole dialogue has taken a hard right towards Weirdsville."

He nodded in agreement and then opened up both hands in a "let's hear it" gesture. She crinkled the side of her mouth for an instant, then said, "We still want to do a competition, but this time with first-year culinary students set at their school. This way, we could spotlight each school and its surrounding community, featuring cuisine distinctive to the particular region. The prize could be a year's tuition or something to help them begin their career."

"Wouldn't they already be pretty good at whatever dish they need to make?"

She exhaled audibly, then said, "I told you we haven't worked out *all* the kinks."

His voice enlivened, like a snowball rolling down a frosty hill. "What if you handicapped them somehow, like took away a key ingredient or appliance or whatever? Force them to try and make the signature dish in a new way. Maybe even healthier."

She looked at him and squinted. "You know, that's not the worst idea."

"Oh my God, you could call it '*Fake It Till You Bake It*.'"

"I'm not so sure about that one," she chuckled.

"You should do something for March Madness, like have the winners from each school compete in a tournament for the season finale."

"Tanya already suggested something similar to that."

He frowned and asked, "Who's Tanya?"

"Sorry, Azalea. Her real name is Tanya Holt. The name Azalea started out as a joke in high school, us trying to pick the most pretentious but believable name for a model. Then it became a sort of nom de plume when she started submitting pictures or went on casting calls. You know, so her mother wouldn't find out. She was dead set against the idea of her daughter being a model. She nearly retched every time someone told her, 'Your daughter's so beautiful she should be a model.' Which, of course, happened all the time."

"Why wouldn't she want her to be a model?"

"She didn't want her to be exploited. Plus, there is, or at least was that whole infamous model lifestyle. You know, the whole sex, drugs, and anorexia. When Ms. Holt finally found out..." Hannah trailed off while shaking her head.

Greyson waited a few moments, then asked, "What happened?"

"Do you remember Desert Storm?"

"Kinda. I was in elementary school, so I wasn't exactly reading Newsweek or anything."

God, he's so young. Or maybe I'm so—she quickly stopped herself from going down that road.

"Desert Storm," he prompted, trying to restart the conversation.

"Sorry. That's what we called Tanya's mom's reaction because it happened around the same time as the Gulf War. But after plenty of screaming and crying, she finally caved, with the caveat that it wouldn't affect school. By that time, the name had stuck, and her career quickly took off."

"So, what's the next step for our show?" he asked with a smirk.

Hannah looked at him sideways for a moment, then said, "Tanya and I pitch *our* show to some execs at Food Network. They have the right of first refusal."

"They'll love it. It's fresh and fun."

She just smiled and thought, *Fresh was the current show. This is more like day-old.*

"I also have an interesting meeting next week," he said. "Or this week, I guess. I always forget if Sunday ends the week or starts it."

"That is the eternal question," she said, briefly staring off into the distance as if pondering the meaning of life. She then looked back at him and added, "But I think here in the U.S. it starts the week. At least that's what my phone tells me."

"If you can't trust your phone, who can you trust?" he said with a grin. "Of course, that would remove Sunday from the weekend. Or maybe it's like Schrödinger's cat; it's both the end of one week and the beginning of the other."

She shrugged and said, "Tell me more about this meeting. I assume it's work-related and not you pitching a reboot of *Two Guys, a Girl and a Pizza Place*."

His eyes widened. "So, you did know who Ryan Reynolds was."

"I may or may not have Googled him. The funny thing is, I used to watch that show. I'd totally forgotten about it, though. But, back to your big meeting."

He held up a finger like a teacher about to issue a warning to their class. "I didn't say big meeting. It's probably more midsized. It's with my boss. Well, big boss. Big, big, big boss," he said while flattening his hand and moving it up an imaginary ladder with each "big."

"I hope you don't body-shame your supervisor to their face."

"Not big like that, big as in the man's not only our CEO but a freaking living legend," he said with reverence dripping from his tone like an ice cream cone on a hot day. "Do you know who founded Crastino Industries?"

"Steve Jobs."

"Think bigger."

"Bill Gates."

"Closer, but still not big enough," he replied, and then after she gave him an "I give up" look, he proudly announced, "Dr. Tyson Greene."

"Okay, I have heard of him. I know he's a big deal in the science and tech fields, so congratulations. What did you do to earn the honor?"

Greyson looked down towards his feet and replied, "Now, that's the million-dollar question. My mentor, Tsai, asked the very same thing, and neither one of us could figure out a good answer. He just blew into our little office like El Niño, introduced himself, and then asked me out to lunch." Then he muttered to himself, "El Jefe Niño."

"Maybe it's a welcome to the team deal."

"I said the same thing, but Tsai seemed to think it was unprecedented. And that makes me nervous as hell."

She reached out and gently patted his arm. "You'll be fine. I have a little experience with meeting a celebrity in my field of work, and it's never as bad as you fear. I once had dinner with Gordon Ramsay."

He rolled his eyes. "Oh God, that lurid Brit on TV? I bet he screamed at the server, threw hot sauce in all the cooks' eyes, and then burned down the restaurant, all while cackling like a madman."

"I had a similar impression in my mind before meeting him, but he was actually pretty casual and subdued. Granted, he did make one or two snarky comments during the meal, but overall he was, dare I say, gracious."

"So, he didn't even make a busboy cry? Was he possessed by an angel or something?"

She laughed and shook her head. "Point is, people are people. Whether they are maniac chefs or scientific legends. He's probably talking to his wife or whoever right now, telling them that he's got this upcoming meeting with one of his young and brilliant, albeit a touch neurotic, employees."

He shot her a skeptical glance, and she said, "Okay, maybe not. I don't want to come off sounding like a mother, but just be yourself."

Greyson quickly turned away. "You're probably right," he mumbled softly.

Again, she sensed a subtle change in him, almost like a barometric pressure drop in his mood. She wondered what was going on in that cute little head of his and had to resist the temptation to ask.

After a short exhale, Greyson said, "Full disclosure, I was hoping to run into you here. Not in a creepy, stalky way; I just wanted to thank you for listening to me last weekend."

"I didn't really do that much."

"It was a lot more than you're giving yourself credit for," he said, then glanced away again. "Back in college, like about ten years ago, a man saved my life. And I mean that literally. I never even got the chance to thank him."

She leaned toward him almost instinctively and asked, "What happened?"

"It was back during my freshman year when I was still getting acclimated to the area and, of course, the workload. So, there I was heading—I don't know, somewhere—in a hurry, not paying attention to my surroundings. You know, like most college kids. My mind was laser-focused on a paper I had to finish that night when I got to a crosswalk right as the sign turned to walk. Without even looking, I stepped off the curb and nearly into a box truck running a red light. Before I got too far, this dude grabbed me by my collar and yanked me back. I ended up tripping over the curb and smacking my head on the pavement."

Hannah put a hand to her mouth and uttered, "Ouch."

Greyson nodded as he continued, "Maybe he was afraid I'd sue him or something because he pretty much hit the ground running right after I hit the ground. I never even saw him. I was out cold for a minute or two, and when I woke up, some lady told me what had happened."

"Sounds like you had a guardian angel, and it was a divine and dash situation."

He grinned as he briefly tilted his head upward. "So, after that day, I vowed to always say thank you to anyone who helps me. Maybe you didn't save my life, but you probably saved me a couple of thousand bucks in therapy."

"I think we're pretty much even now."

After a long pause, Greyson turned to Hannah. "I still owe you one. I was thinking as compensation, maybe I could, I don't know, take you out to dinner or something?"

His proposal hung in the air for a moment, like an unfurled flag waiting for a gush of wind. Hannah tried to quell the sudden butterflies fluttering in her stomach while considering the proposition. *What do I even say? It's been so long since anyone's asked me out. Probably not since Van.* Then she remembered an incident with a reptilian director at a wrap party several years ago and visibly winced.

"I'm sorry. I shouldn't have been so presumptuous," Greyson apologized.

He's so adorably cute. But this is all happening too fast. Finally, Hannah said softly, "No, it's not that. I'm more than flattered, but right now, I'm not ready for something like that."

"I understand," he said in a sympathetic tone that tried to conceal his disappointment.

Hannah stole a glance at Greyson, and something deep inside of her sprang up like a half-asleep lawyer suddenly jolted into action and objected, *Don't let him go!* So, she offered him a smile and said, "But I really enjoy talking to you. What if we made a sort of arrangement to meet here again this time next Sunday?"

Like a man precariously hanging from a ledge being thrown a rope, Greyson quickly grabbed onto her offer. "I would very much like that. Let's just hope it doesn't rain on our arrangement."

"It never rains in Southern California," she sang.

"Don't tempt fate," he warned. "If you say the word never, my bad luck will ultimately reply, 'challenge accepted.'"

"I don't know if you've heard, but here in California we have this new thing called an umbrella."

"Ella, ella, eh, eh, eh," he chanted.

"Ah, you have heard of it."

He gave her a sly grin, then stood up and said, "I do always like to end with a song. Then, I can leave 'em wanting less."

"It was good seeing you again," she said with an accompanying wave.

"Likewise. Have a wonderful week and good luck with the pitch," he replied, offering a sincere smile alongside his farewell.

"Thanks, and I hope to see you next weekend."

As he turned and walked away, she overheard him say, "Definitely. Same bat-time, same bat-channel."

Chapter Seven

Wednesday morning came far too quickly, and Greyson was nowhere near ready for his close-up with Dr. Greene. That morning, he tried on all three of his suits and even a couple more business casual outfits before settling on his go-to for big occasions: a navy pinstripe suit with a white button-up and his lucky burgundy tie. *I feel like James Bond,* he thought as he regarded himself in the bathroom mirror. *Now, if I only had his boundless confidence.*

He strolled out of his bedroom right into a wolf whistle. "I thought you were going to work, not some hot date with Natalie Portman," Nolan teased from the couch. He was wearing red flannel house pants with a tight-fitting Under Armour t-shirt.

"I wouldn't be half as nervous if I were. I told you, I have a meeting with my boss," Greyson replied as he turned into the kitchen. He opened the refrigerator, knowing exactly what was in it yet hoping that a bounty of food had somehow magically appeared overnight.

"Is that the guy who's going to perform your sex change?" Nolan mumbled with a mouth half-full of Kashi Cinnamon Crisp.

Greyson ignored the prehistoric jest and snatched up a capsule of Greek yogurt. As he peeled the lid back, Nolan said, "I'm just joking, dude. If you bring him to my restaurant, I'll make sure to hook y'all up."

That might work if I were in high school and taking out my crush from English class, but I don't think free breadsticks and soda would impress one of the greatest minds of this or any generation. "Thanks, but Dr. Greene's already picked the place."

"Your loss. Listen, I came up with a brilliant idea yesterday at work."

Greyson started shaking his head even before the idea was spoken. Nolan was notorious for his "brilliant ideas" that were either already in existence or not remotely feasible. "Fart-proof pants!" he declared as if he were confidently answering a BuzzFeed quiz.

"And how do you propose to make them fart-proof?"

"I don't know. That's your department. You're the scientist. I just come up with the innovations; it's up to someone like you to come up with the solution."

"The solution to butt pollution," Greyson said, causing both to giggle like fifth graders.

"Come on, man, it's a great idea. Maybe you can even develop some kind of rear muffler for the sound too."

When Greyson didn't reply, Nolan said, "I know you love the idea. Sometimes, I even astonish myself. This is why I'm usually the smartest one in the room."

"The only time you're the smartest one in the room is when you're the only one in it. And that includes pets, too. Even pet rocks."

"Don't be such a cock sock," Nolan sneered, then unmuted the TV and went back to devouring his cereal.

"Hey, speaking of rocks, where's my rock garden?" Greyson asked, pointing to the cluttered coffee table.

"Oh, I threw that in the trash," Nolan replied nonchalantly.

"Why?" Greyson asked, his voice and eyebrows raising simultaneously.

"Calm down, dude; it's just a pile of rocks. It was getting in the way."

"It wasn't just a pile of rocks; it was *decor*," Greyson insisted. When Nolan just shrugged, he knew this was a lost cause. "Why would you throw them in the trash? Why not just take them outside?"

"Oh sorry, I didn't know where the nearest rock quarry was to set them free. Anyway, they were indoor rocks; they wouldn't have made it out there in the wild." Nolan's matter-of-fact answer caused Greyson to snicker again.

In between the puerile banter and bites of yogurt, Greyson calmed his nerves by taking several deep breaths. He tried to will his body not to sweat through his suit before even getting to work. He forced one last spoonful of yogurt in, then returned the half-eaten container to the fridge and shuffled out the door with the simple valediction, "Later, dude."

* * *

"What, no tux?" Tsai teased Greyson as he entered the office.

"My anxiety is all the way up to eleven. Please tell me this will be okay," he said as he collapsed into the chair with a brief sigh.

"Relax, newbie, this isn't that big of a deal," she white-lied. "You do look adorable, though, almost like a high school senior going for his yearbook picture."

"I feel like a cross between Woody Allen and Piglet," he huffed. "Why can't I be more like my roommate? That guy's got more self-confidence than anyone I know. It's like Muhammad Ali and Ferris Bueller had a baby."

"And what does your roommate do for a living?"

"He's a server."

She rolled her eyes, then placed a hand on top of her screen and said, "You work for one of the most prestigious companies in the world and are about to have lunch with an actual historical figure."

"You're not helping."

"I'm just saying, El Jefe wouldn't give you the time of day if you didn't deserve it."

Greyson's entire face widened. "Wait, did you just say something nice to me? And without even a hint of derision."

She quickly flung a half-used pad of sticky notes at him. After ducking, he said, "There she is."

"What time's your big date?" she asked, returning her attention to her computer screen.

"The confirmation email said to meet him at Sanderlin's at noon," Greyson said as he booted up his laptop.

"Ah, the waiting is the hardest part."

He stared at his reflection in the darkened screen. "How's my hair look?"

She peered at him over her screen. "Are you kidding? Your hair has looked the exact same every single day since you've been here." Then she tilted her head and added, "I sure hope you didn't tip your stylist at Super Cuts too much."

He ignored her snarky remark and ran his hand gently over the top of his wavy, high fade. "I don't know; it seems a little off today."

"Short hair problems," she scoffed. "Actually, grow it out, and maybe we can talk."

They both went quiet as they focused on their work. At least Tsai did. Greyson tried his best, but his mind kept running lunch with Dr. Greene simulations, exploring every possible topic of conversation, from his work on Project Gateway to how to survive a zombie apocalypse.

* * *

Several hours after his least productive morning at Crastino, Greyson strayed into the restaurant and tentatively stepped up to the hostess stand. "Do you have a reservation?" the hostess asked in a manner that made it sound like an assumption. She stood on a raised platform in front of the dining room, like a haughty gatekeeper to haute cuisine.

Greyson sheepishly glanced behind her and said, "Yes, but I'm a little early. I can just wait in the—"

"Name?" she interrupted with a bark.

"Squires," he mechanically answered, then corrected himself, "I mean, it's under Dr. Tyson Greene. But he's probably not here yet. I'm a little early. I wasn't sure where this place was since I've never been here. You see, I moved here not that long ago. From Virginia."

While Greyson rambled on, the hostess turned to a young man dressed in the standard black pants, white shirt, and charcoal tie, pointed to a board, and handed him a menu. Then she turned to Greyson and announced, "Ryan will take you to your table."

Greyson stepped back in surprise, then drifted behind the nimble Ryan, following him through the maze of tables and epicureans. He scanned the lively room and was impressed with both the food and the patrons. Everyone seemed genuinely delighted to be there.

This is a nice place; I bet Hannah would—he started to think, then remembered her polite yet devastating rejection. Then his anxious mind's antibodies attacked the sanguine thought like it was a virus.

His brief dejection morphed into consternation when he reached a booth and saw Dr. Greene sitting there reading a menu like it was the New York Times. *Oh shit, am I late? Did the email say 11:30?* he worried as Ryan waited for him to sit down.

Dr. Greene lowered his menu and glanced up. "Ah, Mr. Squires, welcome. Please have a seat."

Greyson slid into the booth across from him, received the menu from Ryan, and watched him scoot away, wondering what to say. Before he could even formulate a response, Dr. Greene said, "Mind if I call you Greyson?"

It's almost like God asking permission to call you by your Christian name, he thought and simply nodded.

"Good. And you can call me Tyson."

This isn't happening. This is one of those out-of-body experiences that's halfway between a dream and reality.

His brief self-hypnosis was snapped when Dr. Greene asked, "Are you always this chatty, or is the restaurant not to your inclination?"

"I'm sorry, Dr. Greene, I'm just a little out of sorts right now."

"Please call me Tyson."

"That's part of it, though. It's kinda like calling your parents by their first names," Greyson blurted out. "Not that you're my father or anything. Okay, bad example."

He paused for a moment, trying to collect his thoughts, which seemed to be scattering to the winds like a litter of kittens. Dr. Greene waited patiently as he finally continued, "I guess it's more like running into your favorite high school teacher the summer after graduation and them saying, 'Oh, you can just call me Bob now.'"

Dr. Green replied with a half-smile as Greyson explained, "It's just, I've looked up to you for so long as a her… ole model." There was a slight hiccup between the unintentionally merged words hero and role. "It's going to take a minute or two million to get used to this dynamic," Greyson admitted as he waved his hand back and forth between them.

"They do warn against meeting your her-ole models," Dr. Greene said, which helped to chip away at some of the tension on Greyson's side. Dr. Greene tilted his head down as he regarded Greyson over the top rim of his glasses, almost like a mentalist sizing up their next patron.

Greyson unconsciously gripped the menu like it was a stress ball. *Why do I feel like I'm about to have my fortune told?*

Dr. Greene slowly glanced back down at the menu, as if just remembering it was there, and said, "Maybe we should figure out lunch, then we'll worry about appellations."

"Good idea," Greyson agreed, wondering if there was any room in his angsty stomach for food.

As Dr. Greene perused the menu, Greyson stared openly at the intimidating figure across from him. *I cannot believe I am sitting four feet from the Dr. Tyson Greene. I wish I could go back in time, find the eighteen-year-old me, and tell him about this.*

"What are you thinking?" Dr. Greene asked.

Greyson exhaled, then said, "Just imagining getting into a time machine and going back to tell my younger self about this whole meeting, or, uh, lunch deal."

Dr. Greene chuckled, then said, "I mean, what are you thinking about ordering?"

"Oh shit," Greyson blurted, then quickly glanced back at the menu. "Chicken wrap, I guess."

"Good taste. That's what I was eyeballing."

As if summoned by the talk of food, a server suddenly appeared with two glasses of water and then took their order. After she left, Dr. Greene said, "You probably shouldn't do that, you know."

A confused expression dawned across Greyson's face. "What, order the sauce on the side?"

"No, go back in time and meet yourself. And when I say shouldn't, I mean couldn't. As in, it's impossible."

"You mean the grandfather paradox?"

Dr. Greene shook his head. "Not exactly. We're not speaking of killing a progenitor. But of you going back and giving yourself future knowledge. It's simply not possible."

Greyson made a steeple with his hands. "Yeah, I'm well aware. I'm a bit of a time travel… let's just say enthusiast, so I know there's only one direction to go."

"Forward," they both said in unison.

Greyson had to repress the somber reason why he was such an authority on the theory of time travel to focus on the present conversation. "It's odd hearing one of the greatest scientific minds use the word impossible. Doesn't physics at least allow the possibility of going back in time? As in, we can't unequivocally rule it out."

"Correct," he replied, slapping a hand down on the table as if adding an exclamation point. "I'm not saying journeying into the past is an absolute impossibility. But unless you have a memory of meeting your future self floating around somewhere in your head, we can definitively say it didn't happen. So yes, you can go back in time and meet your grandfather, at least theoretically. But of course, you can't kill him before he sires your mother or father."

"Hopefully, not both." Greyson chuckled.

Dr. Greene ignored the jest and said, "And you can't go back and meet yourself without remembering such an indelible event."

"Unless I wore a disguise or looked completely different and never revealed who I was. I mean, who's to say that elderly man who came into my video store and asked me if I'd recommend *Twelve Monkeys* wasn't my future self?"

Dr. Greene lifted his thumb to his chin and, absentmindedly, began scratching. "Now, that's an interesting notion."

"But it's all just science fiction."

"Most science facts start out as science fiction. Especially recently. We have to dream it—"

"Before we can do it," Greyson cut in, finishing the doctor's famous quote.

Dr. Greene gave him a nod as Greyson continued, "That's pretty much the crux of Project Gateway, isn't it? To take the science fiction around wormholes and make it a reality by using them to move something from point A in space to point B instantaneously."

"Spacetime," Dr. Greene corrected as he nudged his glasses up the bridge of his nose. "But yes, precisely."

"And your discovery of microscopic wormholes was the game changer. Before that, they were just theoretical objects. While everyone was busy scouring outer space for evidence of a galactic Einstein-Rosen bridge, some even suggesting they were the same as black holes, you found them in the quantum realm."

"I should get you to edit my biography."

"Sorry, I just wanted a chance to say thank you. You know, for your contribution to humanity."

"You and humanity are most welcome," Dr. Greene replied with a mischievous smirk. "And thank you for working on my little project. Finding the wormholes means very little until we figure out a way to pump enough energy into them in order to make use of them in the realm of general relativity. That's where I'm counting on folks like Tsai and you."

Greyson's eyes darted to the table beside them for an instant, then said, "Can I ask you something?"

"Depends on what the something is, of course."

"It's about the 2001 conundrum. I've been working on it a little, and I figured if anyone had advice, it would be you," Greyson said and paused to gauge Dr. Greene's reaction. Since it was neutral, he just went for it. "What do you think caused the energy anomaly?"

"I hope you're not wasting too much time on this," Dr. Greene said, with a trace of admonishment.

"No, of course not. It's more of a side project I do when I have free time," he lied, instantly regretting broaching the subject. "I've already been warned about spending too much time on this by, well, pretty much everyone. I'm just surprised no one else is even bothering with it. That unprecedented spike of energy seemed to come out of nowhere and without explanation. And since the energy signature is still unknown but certainly in the ballpark of what we need, it's—"

"A mystery," Dr. Greene interrupted. "One we absolutely researched exhaustively after it occurred. But none of my best and brightest have come up with any theories that actually hold a charge, so we chose to focus on the questions and problems we can solve."

Greyson leaned forward and said, "But you've got to have a theory."

Dr. Greene exhaled quietly, then said, "I only have guesses. But this is the wrong kind of hole, my friend. It's a rabbit hole, and I am only interested in wormholes."

"But according to the records, which are surprisingly incomplete and cursory at best, everyone stopped working on it shortly after it happened."

Now it was Dr. Greene's turn to lean over as he whispered, "Okay, so you want the inside scoop, huh? The truth behind the conspiracy."

Greyson matched him in demeanor and tone. "Of course."

"Okay, Mr. Squires, the real truth is…" Dr. Greene paused, and he quickly scanned the restaurant, then continued loudly, "We don't know. And that's it. We did every test and every calculation that we could think of and came up empty. So, I chose to focus on moving the project forward and stop wasting my resources on a MacGuffin hunt."

I think you mean snipe hunt, Greyson thought, then said, "It's just weird. It's like if Scotland Yard stops looking for Jack the Ripper shortly after his last murder. Why would they do that unless they knew something the public didn't?"

"Are you suggesting that I also know who Jack the Ripper is?"

Before Greyson could answer, the server interrupted the confab with their lunch, derailing its momentum. The talk during the meal was brief and centered around the quality of their food.

* * *

After refusing dessert and sending the server off to retrieve the check, Dr. Greene said, "The main reason I asked you here today was to get your assessment of Project Gateway."

As Greyson patted his napkin around his mouth, he could almost feel his anxiety flipping the switch on his sweat glands. *What could I possibly say to him about his pet project that he doesn't already know? This is why I need to prove myself by solving the 2001 conundrum.*

"I am looking for an outsider's perspective if you will, since you are the newest member of the team. Everyone else has been on this for years, so sometimes they lose focus on the forest and can only see the trees," Dr. Greene explained.

Greyson carefully folded and laid the napkin on his empty plate the way one would place a flag on a casket. "First thing, it's probably the most important project on the planet right now. I'm serious—if we can figure out the energy issue, we could basically save the Earth."

"The energy issue, as you so diplomatically put it, might not be solvable."

"I respectfully disagree. We have successfully moved electrons through the gateway. Granted, it's just several feet across the room, but still. In spacetime terms, a couple of feet might as well be a million miles. I think we are an equation away from turning that electron into a shipping container. So, a by-product of working on this could be solving the world's energy problem as well."

"The world doesn't have an energy problem. Energy is all around us," Dr. Greene said while waving his hand in a large semicircle. "It's one of the most plentiful items in the universe. What the world has is a people problem. People who are invested and entrenched in outdated forms of energy are what's preventing us from fully utilizing superior forms."

"Yeah, historically, people do tend to be more a part of the problem than the solution."

Dr. Greene folded his arms and leaned back. "I've been working on this project since its inception, well over a decade ago. And yes, it was a breakthrough when we first moved electrons across the room, but at the expense of so much time, effort, and, yes, money. I worry that it might be people like me who are holding it back. That I might be part of the problem. This is why I'm thinking about stepping back and turning the project over to the next generation of talent."

Greyson didn't bother masking his shock, to which Dr. Greene held up a finger and continued, "I will still be involved, but I need to take a more laissez-faire management approach while allowing folks like yourself the freedom to be innovative."

"You can't leave the project; we need you. Probably now more than ever!"

"I didn't say I was leaving the project. No, I doubt I could ever disengage fully. Like I said, we need fresh eyes and minds to overcome the same problems that have plagued us over the years. I just fear that, right now, I might be doing more harm than good. I need to put more trust and autonomy into the team that I mostly handpicked."

Greyson wondered if that meant he'd been one of the chosen few by his idol when Dr. Greene, as if reading his mind, said, "Tsai's the one who recommended you. That's why we made her your mentor."

He was both flattered and disappointed at the same time. "She's been a great mentor, that's for sure."

Dr. Greene nodded. "So, basically, what I'm saying is that I'm turning the keys over to you. And by you, I mean the entire team."

Baffled by this turn of events, all Greyson could think to say was, "I'm sorry, but why are you telling me this? I'm the most junior member of the team. Shouldn't you be informing the project heads?"

"I've told Aarón, of course, but that's it so far. I'd appreciate it if you kept this to yourself. I'll be announcing it to the whole team in a couple of days," he replied, then looked at Greyson for a long moment.

Dr. Greene's expression gave Greyson the feeling that he was holding something back. *God, I hope he's not terminally ill or something*, he couldn't help but wonder.

Finally, Dr. Greene said, "I guess I just wanted to get to know you a little. Since you are the future of this project, I wanted to meet the newest godparent I'm leaving my brainchild with."

"I hope I passed the audition."

Dr. Greene shook his head. "It's not like that. Trust me; I'm sure you'll accomplish great things. Just keep doing what you're doing, and don't let anyone, not even me, deter you. I believe in you."

And with that, Greyson knew the lunch was over. As they both got up from the booth, Greyson said, "It was an honor meeting you, sir," then immediately regretted it. *Lord, I sound like Oliver Twist asking for more, please.*

Dr. Greene extended his hand and said, "The pleasure was all mine."

"I'm just disappointed I won't get the opportunity to work with you," Greyson said, trying to make up for his awestruck moment.

Dr. Greene smiled and said, "I would have enjoyed that as well." After they shook hands, he added, "Who knows, perhaps we'll get to work together some other time."

Chapter Eight

"Bitch, I'm home," Tanya called out as she swung open the front door. She strolled into the modest ranch house and found Hannah seated in her office, busy on her laptop. "Where's my dinner, woman?"

Hannah finished a sentence, then looked up and replied, "Toxic masculinity is the one thing that's not a good look on you."

Tanya collapsed into a navy-blue loveseat opposite Hannah's desk. "What are you working on, honey? Please tell me you've finished the pitch, and I can turn my ass around and go home."

The March sun peeked through the blinds, quilting the room in ambient light. Hannah's home office was a simple rectangle, with her desk stationed in front of a wall of built-ins. The shelves were crowded with all manner of books and housed several awards positioned directly over Hannah's head, almost like a crown. The only pieces of furniture were a cherry wood L-shaped desk, a timeworn, high-back brown executive chair, and the loveseat.

"I'm getting there. I just need some of that Azalea magic to smooth out the rough edges."

Tanya swiveled, leaned back, and lifted her long legs over the end of the couch. "Honey, I'm the talent. I don't do rough edges."

"If you wanna keep on being the talent, then you will do these rough edges, my dear. I have most of it, and Greyson gave me an idea—"

Tanya perked up and said, "Whoa, whoa, whoa. You mean Greyson, as in the mysterious park guy? When the hell did you see him again? And where? And why were you talking to him about our new show?"

Hannah fought back a smile and said, "I randomly ran into him again at the park the other day. And the show just came up in conversation."

Tanya shot her a skeptical glare. "You randomly ran into him? This is LA; you don't randomly run into anyone here. Was it the same time and place?" She didn't bother to wait for an answer and said, "Yeah, he's totally stalking you."

"No, it wasn't like—"

Tanya cut her off again. "I don't mean the bad version of stalking—the oily skin and hair creeper who's positioned outside your bedroom window with a camera. I'm talking the rom-com kind. You know, like that scene with the dude holding up the boombox that makes all the girls swoon."

"Okay, he did admit he came there hoping to find me."

Tanya leaned back and pointed at her as she sang the word, "See?"

"But it wasn't anything so romantic or lascivious; it was just to say thanks," Hannah said, then thought about the invitation to dinner, and this time couldn't prevent a mile-wide smile.

"You say not lascivious and then immediately grin like you guys snuck off into the woods and knocked boots."

"I don't think anyone's said knocked boots for at least a decade."

"I'm bringing it back," Tanya declared. "Seriously though, to paraphrase Soulja Boy, 'he thirsty.'"

"Can we please get back to the pitch?"

"No, tell me more about this innocent, pseudo-coincidental encounter."

Hannah thought back to the meeting on Sunday and pictured Greyson standing there, bathed in the sunshine like a Greek god. *Oh shit, am I—*

"You look like you are a smitten kitten," Tanya said, derailing Hannah's train of thought.

She shook her head and casually said, "No, come on. I was just trying to remember what we talked about. He thanked me for offering advice on getting over his ex, told me about a big work meeting with his boss that was coming up, and I told him I was working out the details for our next show. That's it."

"So, what was your shiny new boy's suggestion?"

"He suggested we remove a key ingredient from whatever the groups have to make. That way, they would have to come up with a substitute, and we could end up with some interesting and even different finished products. Or we could handicap them by taking away a common appliance."

Tanya looked to the side and hummed. "Okay, that's not a *bad* idea."

"That's what I said."

"I'm starting to like this dude. You remember what happened the last time you met a tall park stranger?" Tanya asked with a wink. "Are you planning on another serendipitous meeting anytime soon?"

Hannah considered white lying for a moment, just to avoid Tanya turning it into more than it was, or is, or even could be. But she knew her friend would see right through any deception. "Okay, he did sort of ask me out."

Tanya jumped up in her seat. "But whaaat?"

Hannah lifted her hands and made a slow-down gesture. "Just to thank me."

"Oh sure, I've heard that one before. Come up to my room; I just want to say thank you. In bed."

"I said no, though."

Tanya shook her head in disappointment. "Guys will only try so hard before moving on to the next conquest… consort… concubine… whatever."

"I did tell him—"

"Contessa," Tanya cut her off. "If you're not going to go out with him, why do you keep bringing him up?"

"If you'd stop interrupting me, I'll tell you. God, talking to you is like fencing."

"Touché," Tanya said with a wry grin.

"I suggested we meet at the park this Sunday. That's it."

"At least tell me you are planning a picnic or some other white people soirée like that."

"I said no to a date, so I am not going to try and turn this into…" Hannah paused to consider her actual reason for declining to meet with him outside her comfort zone. Finally, she said, "Into something I'm not ready for."

"I get it. Baby steps," Tanya said, her face brightening. "There's no rush; just let this either grow or wither naturally. You're actually playing it smart. Reel him in slowly, so your bait looks more enticing."

"You're mixing your metaphors like an amateur bartender."

Tanya shot her a *shush* look. "But you be careful, 'cause who knows? This guy might be a serial killer or something."

The fleeting thought, *He did tell me his full name,* popped into her head like a camera flash. She dismissed it with a snicker and asked, "Wait, what the hell is my bait?"

"You know," Tanya said, then mimed the curves of a woman with her hands. "All that fun stuff in between."

"Are you sure you're not a dude deep down inside?"

"Just 'cause I know how they think doesn't make me one of them. I just see 'em for what they are. Men are like junk food; even though I know how bad they are for me, I still crave them."

"What about all the women you've gone out with? What are they?"

"They're more substantial, like main courses. I guess it all depends on my mood—do I want a snack or a meal?"

"It always comes back to food with you," Hannah giggled. "But men aren't all bad."

Tanya tilted her head to the side and said, "Maybe not, but I feel like my main problem is that I'm looking for a partnership, and most men out there are looking for ownership."

"I know it's tough, but you just have to keep trying. It's like the lottery; you can't win if you don't play."

"I am playing. Both sides even. I'm just not as fortunate as you are. Not all of us are lucky enough to meet Mr. Right." Tanya paused as her words acted like a sudden drop in temperature. "I'm sorry, honey. It's just for me, dating has always been more like poker. You bet, raise, and bluff through the relationship until you either go all in or fold. And I have always folded. You won huge on one of your first hands. Whereas me, I'm on a twenty-year losing streak."

"I wouldn't say that. You've had some…" Hannah hesitated as she searched for the correct descriptor and said, "productive couplings." She immediately knew it wasn't the best word choice, but Tanya's history with relationships was more like Cecilia Tallis and Robbie Turner than Allie Hamilton and Noah Calhoun.

"Productive couplings?" Tanya repeated, her eyes smiling. "You make it sound more like a business venture than a relationship. Look, I get that I have issues with relationships, mostly with the male persuasion. I'm not completely clueless. But having a shitty-ass dad will do that to a person."

Hannah nodded. "Yeah, you know I've had a couple of wretched stepfathers, so I get that."

"At least your mom would get out once things started going bad. My primary male role model was a lying, cheating son of a bitch. But since my mom could only work part-time, she was stuck with him until I graduated from high school. By the time we got away from that human compost, the damage was already done. To both of us."

Hannah pictured Benjamin "Benny" Holt, who, by all accounts, appeared to be the very model of a modern major gentleman. At least on the outside. He was charming, kind, and hilarious to anyone outside his immediate family. But behind closed doors, he quickly turned surly, malicious, and verbally abusive.

Even now, Hannah regretted being fooled and thinking so highly of him, right up until the day Tanya confided in her about who her father truly was. Tanya had caught him with another woman when she was only twelve, and her father nefariously manipulated her into keeping his secret for years. One woman quickly became two, then three, and so on. When she could no longer bear living under such a sword of Damocles, she finally told her mother.

It was the kind of conversation no child should ever have to have with an adult, let alone a parent. What surprised Tanya was her mother's lack of surprise. Her mom was painfully honest about their situation; they couldn't afford to live on their own in LA, at least not anywhere decent. So, they bided their time and suffered his many indignities until they could finally move out and on. It was the main reason Tanya dove headfirst into the world of modeling.

"I remember," Hannah replied, recalling those extended, lachrymose sleepovers.

"No one warns you when you're young that men like my father are way more common. But I'm not about to make the same mistakes as my mom. That's why I refuse to settle for anything less than the best," Tanya said with a smirk, then added, "The problem for me has been whether it is a male or a female, I keep finding either average or almost good enough. I need some of that Hannah serendipity."

Hannah just shook her head at her friend's good-natured taunt. "I know how rough it's been for you. I'm the one who's always there through the tears and the tantrums. And I realize how fortunate I was with Van. That's part of the reason why I've been so reluctant to try again. You only get one soulmate. Yours is still out there somewhere. But mine…" she said, looking down as a tear fell down her cheek, "he's gone now."

Tanya swung her legs back to the ground. "Honey, don't say that. Look at it more like our show. It's ending in the spring, and sure, it was an amazing adventure. But now we're faced with a choice. We can either say that's that, close the book on our careers, and just retire into crazy cat lady oblivion. Or we can move on to the next chapter. We don't know if it will be better or worse; just that it'll be different. And sometimes, that's enough."

Hannah nodded solemnly. She'd had different incarnations of this conversation for months, but maybe it was the timing, or maybe it was her mindset because now she was ready to listen. "Speaking of work, we really need to get back to it. The meeting will be here before we know it, and right now we have a good idea but not a fully baked one, pardon the pun."

Tanya just nodded, as if she were a judge, saying, "I'll allow the change of topic." As they went to work on the details of the new show, Hannah's phone buzzed with a text.

"Is it him?"

"No, he doesn't have my number. It's Jenna."

"What does the wicked baby sister want?"

"She's not wicked," Hannah tried to disagree as she read the message. "Okay, she's kind of wicked. She's asking if I will make extra hors d'oeuvres for her party next Saturday. Not bring but make. Fuck, I knew I should've told her I was busy."

Tanya looked at her with disappointed eyes. "After all these years, how do you not have a rotating list of 'I'm busy' excuses at the ready?"

"Wait, are you doing anything next Saturday?"

Tanya shook her head. "Sorry, I have a root canal in the morning, a wake for my aunt in the afternoon, and tickets to see *The Lion King* in the evening." She waited a beat, then clapped her hands together. "And that's how it's done!"

Hannah shot her the helpless puppy eyes until she clenched her jaw and said, "Okay, fine, I'll go with. But only if we drink ahead of time."

"I love you," Hannah beamed.

"I know," Tanya replied curtly.

As they transitioned back to work, Hannah couldn't completely arrest the random thoughts of Greyson that would pop in and out of her head like summer lightning. In fact, she was beginning to welcome the distraction.

Chapter Nine

Sunday came nonchalantly like it was accustomed to doing for all those not of the cloth. It was a golden pre-spring morning and the sun played hide and seek behind a parade of billowing clouds. Everyone appeared to be out basking in the radiance of nature.

Hannah was mildly annoyed when she found her favorite bench occupied. *Of course, on the one day I really needed it to be vacant, an old man had to claim it for his napping spot.*

She found an empty bench several yards away and quickly secured it. It had the same view, but not the sentimentality, which she decided was probably for the best. She glanced over at the elderly man, who wasn't napping but reading the paper, and silently wished him well.

She hoped that Greyson could find her, then laughed at herself. *Jesus, stop acting like some schoolgirl who is obsessing over every little detail that could ruin her dream da*—she stopped herself and whispered, "It's not a date."

Seconds after her mantra was lost to the wind, she noticed a young man strolling several yards down the sidewalk. She couldn't help but wonder if it was Greyson as she tried not to gawk. She directed her attention down toward the water, which allowed her to check her side view and monitor his progress.

Once he passed the antiquated reader, she knew it was him. As she side-watched him advance, the thought, *He even walks like Van*, invaded her mind like a germ.

"Good morning," he said from the pavement. "May I approach the bench?"

His words took a moment to register as her body tensed due to her sudden fight-or-flight reaction. She closed her eyes and forcibly exhaled as she told herself that this was just her grief rearing its overwrought head.

"Hey, you alright?" he asked, his carefree tone quickly oscillating to concern.

Finally, she opened her eyes, met his gaze, and offered him a weak smile. *Might as well be truthful* echoed in her head before she said, "Yeah, sorry. I sometimes get these kinds of emotional flashes. I've come to call them griefquakes. It's a sudden pang to the heart almost like a brain freeze. Any tiny thing can trigger them. Early on, they'd put me in a mourning spiral that could last hours or even days, but lately, they're gone after a moment or two."

"I know what you mean," he replied, sounding more like he'd responded instinctively instead of astutely.

Hannah looked to the empty space on the bench and said, "Please join me," while wondering if he truly understood. As he parked himself next to her, she could tell he was hesitant to continue down this verbiage path, so she softly probed, "Have you lost someone?"

She waited patiently as he appeared to glance off into the ether of the past. "This is definitely not the way I wanted to start our conversation," he replied.

Another cluster of wordless beats passed, but this time Hannah waited. Finally, he said, "When I was thirteen, my mother was murdered."

Hannah unconsciously gasped, then placed a hand gently on his shoulder. "I'm so sorry."

He just nodded. "You know, growing up, it was just the two of us. The two of us against the world. She didn't have any family; her parents died in a car accident when I was two. And there were no aunts, uncles, or cousins; no giant family support system that every other person seemed to have."

"And your father?" she asked delicately.

"Gone before I was born. From what she told me, it was one of those whirlwind, youthful romances that ended abruptly when she got pregnant."

She couldn't help but be reminded of her own father's sudden death but stayed silent. At least for now. *I don't want this to turn into another "top the tragedy" competition that so many people fall into.*

He breathed out audibly, then said, "I was spending the night at my best friend Nolan's house. He's my roommate now. While I was busy playing video games and secretly watching R-rated movies, someone broke into our house and shot my mother."

He wiped away a tear as he continued. "The cops said she must have awoken and just, I don't know, ran into him as he was searching for something to steal. I should have—" He stopped as his voice cracked. He took a long, deep breath, then slowly let it out. "I should have been there to protect her."

"I don't think there would have been much a thirteen-year-old could have done," she assured.

"I know. Everyone's pretty much tried to explain that to me. But still, I should have been there to at least try. They never even caught him. The bastard took my mother from me and got away with it," he said, wiping away a silent stream of tears.

"It's not your fault," she said, trying to draw his gaze to her.

He must have instinctively felt her lure as he turned to face her. "The thing is… it was my fault. The report said he got in through my bedroom window, which I left unlocked. It was summer, and I often slept with my window cracked. Even after several warnings from my mom about letting the AC out. So, yeah, I was responsible for it." Now the tears were a flowing runnel.

Without hesitation, Hannah said firmly, "That still doesn't make it your fault. You were a kid and way too young to be responsible for the welfare of your mother. A child shouldn't have to take on the burden of responsibility for a tragic event like that. It's not fair to blame yourself. There's only one person to blame, and that's the person who committed the crime."

Greyson looked down and nodded. "I hear you, and I recognize there's truth in what you're saying. But a part of me will always blame myself." He sniffed hard and once again wiped at his face. "Anyway, since I had no one, Nolan's parents took me in. He and his folks stood by me through it all, treating me like I was part of their family. Without them, I don't know what I would've done."

"I'm so sorry," Hannah repeated. It was all she could think to say.

He took a minute to compose himself, then said, "Yeah, me too. A couple of months after it happened, I got obsessed with time travel. Guess I wanted a way to not only go back and save her but to right my atrocious wrong. I consumed every theory and story on the subject. I felt like an addict desperately searching for anything that would numb the pain. That's pretty much what led me down the path to science. Thanks to good old Uncle Albert's theory of relativity, I learned that time travel is, in fact, possible. The problem is that you can only go in one direction—forward. So, by the time I got to college, I had to give up on my fantasy of finding a way back to that fateful night and focus on more practical physics."

He paused as a butterfly floated near the ground in front of him. Hannah watched him stare down as if he were observing the end of a memory play out. *I can't imagine the guilt he must feel,* she thought. She longed to assuage his remorse but knew there was nothing she could do. Recent personal experience had taught her that particular lesson.

The ambient noise of the park filled the conversational void until he said, "I'm sorry I dropped all that on you. It was probably the worst icebreaker ever."

"I know how hard it is to share something so personal, so thanks for trusting me with it."

"Thank you for listening," he replied, then added, "and again, not charging me for it."

"It's the first rule of tragedy club: don't bill for tragedy club."

He shifted in his seat like he was unconsciously trying to force a change in his demeanor. "So, where do we go from here? Hopefully to a topic a little more cheery, like maybe *Schindler's List, Old Yeller,* or *The Diary of Anne Frank.* Fun fact: My roommate first thought it was called *The Diarrhea of Anne Frank.* At least, that's what he claims."

She laughed in spite of herself. "He sounds like a charming man."

"You have no idea," he said, with an exaggerated eye roll. "But he's like a brother to me and has been the one person I could always count on. You really have to… I mean, maybe you'll meet him someday. Not that I'm proposing we should do the whole meet the family thing. Just that, you know, maybe we'll run into each other outside this park. Wait, you don't live in the park, do you?" He turned around and cast about as if trying to locate her possible domicile.

She laughed again. "No, I live in a modest house."

"Not that I am making light of homelessness. I mean, it's a serious issue. I realize no matter what's happened, I've still been quite fortunate compared to others," he rambled. "Sorry, talking about my mom has thrown me off my game."

"You could tell me how the meeting with your boss went."

"Well, he's not exactly my boss. He does run the company and all that, so technically, he's everyone's boss." He flattened his hands and rotated them over each other, simulating a ladder, as he continued, "But there are like four layers of management between us. Anyway, I think it went fine. It was weird, though; he told me he was stepping away from the project I'm working on. Which is his baby, really. It was as if he wanted to say hello and goodbye at the same time."

"So, he wanted to meet you and let you know he wasn't going to be a part of your project anymore?"

"Kinda. He did say he wasn't totally leaving, just not going to be a part of the day-to-day activities, I guess. We all work on different components of the project right now, so it's not like we're this huge team that all huddles together in some enormous room. We're more separated into pods. The whole team does come together quarterly to share findings and progress, unless, of course, something big happens. I just haven't been there long enough to take part in that yet."

She was intrigued, almost more by what he wasn't saying than what he was. Van had been a self-described run-of-the-mill physics professor, so she had a basic understanding of science along with a natural interest. "And this is the super-secret teleportation project?"

He quickly turned and faced her, as if momentarily forgetting that he'd confessed that during their first encounter. "I can't believe I told you that. Can we pretend like I never mentioned it? I could get into a lot of trouble."

"Who am I going to tell?" she said, while sporting a mischievous grin.

"There are literally thousands of people in this city that you could tell, and soon after, my goose would be cooked. Or, to use your parlance, baked."

"I see what you did there."

"Seriously though, Dr. Greene said I was the second person he told. The question is, why would he tell me? He didn't even know me before our meeting, and I've only started working on the project a few weeks ago."

"I don't know; maybe he was practicing with you. Sometimes, it's easier to divulge something personal to a stranger than to someone you're close with."

He nodded. "That does make sense. It was like a beta test. Or a dress rehearsal."

"Sure. And it was a 'two birds with one stone' deal. Meet the new guy and let him know the big news first. That way, he could get to know you a little, gauge your reaction, and work on the best way to break the news to everyone else," she explained, then added, "The news of him transporting off your teleportation project."

It was his turn to smile at her sly wordsmithing. "We probably should stop calling it that; it's somewhat misleading."

"I know what he should do. Gather everyone into the room, make his big leaving announcement, then step onto the pad and just beam away."

He laughed this time. "It's not like that at all. Teleportation is where atoms are disintegrated in one place and then reassembled in another."

"So, how are you doing it then?"

He exhaled in a huff and, after a prolonged moment, said, "Fine, but this stays in the park, got it?"

"Cross my heart," she said while pantomiming it.

"Yep, that'll hold up in a court of law," he said, then once again peered around the park.

"Don't worry, there's no one out there with a spy microphone or anything."

"We are working on a way to open an Einstein-Rosen Bridge. Better known as a wormhole. We have two machines, one called Lilith and the other Eve. We've entangled key particles in these machines so that one can act as an entrance and the other as an exit. Or vice versa. So, instead of having all of your atoms disintegrated and reconstructed, we open a portal at each point that folds space," he explained, as he pointed his index fingers at each other, then slowly brought them together. "So you can simply travel from one point to the next instantaneously. Like taking a shortcut through space."

"And you're close to accomplishing this?" she asked, not bothering to mask her enthusiasm.

"Close is such a relative term when talking about folding space. Without completely shredding my NDA, we can do it with microscopic particles like electrons. But anything larger takes energy levels that we don't currently possess." He glanced away as he added, "And honestly, may never reach. At least on a large enough scale to be practical."

"But you don't really believe that, do you? Otherwise, why bother working on it?"

He turned back to her and nodded. "Maybe I'm an eternal optimist, but yeah, I think it's very possible. We'll need to figure out a better way to harness the energy we know about, whether it's solar, nuclear, or even gravitational. Or discover a new energy source. But I think—no, I know it's attainable."

"Maybe you'll be the one to solve it. That's why he wanted to meet with you."

He shook his head. "Sure, I'm the person who'll succeed where everyone else on the planet—and we're talking about some of the most exceptional minds in the field—has failed."

"You never know," she said, then pointed to his head. "I bet there's a brilliant idea or two swimming around in there."

"I'm glad one of us thinks so. To be honest, sometimes I feel like I don't even belong there. Like I'm a fraud who's one misstep or failure away from being exposed."

Hannah had to fight an instinct to reach out for Greyson's hand. Instead, she simply said, "I do know what you mean, and it's quite common. I felt like that for almost the entire first season of the show. I hate to sound like a self-help book, but you just have to believe in yourself. Or at least fake it till you make it."

"Or fake it till you bake it."

"That's still not going to fly for a show title," she said with a laugh.

"Speaking of, how did your meeting go? Did they give you a three-season order?"

Hannah quickly reflected on the meeting and couldn't help but compare it to her initial one for *Baking for Dough. God, that feels like a lifetime ago. I guess, in some sense, it was.*

"You still there?" he asked as he waved a hand.

"Sorry, just thinking about how different it was from the first time I had to pitch a show. I guess that's what a decade of experience will do for you."

"So, it went well?"

She fought back a smile. "I'll just say that it was promising. They did agree to show a pilot."

"Holy cats, that's fantastic! Congratulations."

"Thanks. But it's just the first step. Now the real work begins."

There was a slight pause as the flow of their discussion hit a momentary hitch like a kayak briefly getting caught on a snag in a river, which allowed Hannah a small window to glance over at Greyson. *Minus the self-doubt, he reminds me so much of*—she started to think, then forced herself out of her head and blurted out, "What are you doing on Saturday?"

"Not much, just working on my *Gilmore Girls* fan fiction. Why?"

Hannah coughed out a laugh, then explained, "There's this party. Or, I guess, it's more of an event. Hell, I don't really know what to call it. My sister is throwing this thing for her Hollywood friends and acquaintances."

His eyes lit up like a pair of searchlights at a big movie premiere. "Where is it?"

"Malibu," Hannah said, and immediately recognized his starstruck gaze. She allowed him to fantasize for just a moment, then doused his euphoric flame. "Don't get your hopes up; her husband, Christian, is a mid-level producer, so we're talking more backroom insiders than red carpet stars."

Hannah could almost see his visions of A-List celebrities being replaced with anonymous set designers and script doctors as he said, "It's not like I was imagining sitting around playing Pictionary with Matt Damon and Ben Affleck or anything like that."

"Sure you weren't. I know that look."

His pitch inadvertently went up an octave as he defended, "What look?"

"That pre-awestruck look someone gets when they think they have a chance to hobnob with a celebrity."

"I gave no such look, plus I would never hob a celebrity's nob. Okay, possibly Ryan Reynolds. Maybe Denzel Washington, but that's it," he joked and glanced away. "But if there was the impression of a look, then it was merely based on the excitement of seeing where *The Big Lebowski* was filmed. And of course, the celluloid classic, *Malibu's Most Wanted*."

"The laddie doth protest too much, methinks," she replied in a faux British accent. "But back to the actual party; it's going to be an awkward affair at best. I thought maybe you would want to suffer through it with me."

"You do know the word suffer has more of a negative connotation, right?"

She smiled coyly. "Now that I think about it, there will be one celebrity there I can introduce you to."

"Meryl Streep? Tom Cruise? Halle Berry?" The excitement in his tone rose with each guess.

"There's that look again," she said with a grin. "No, Azalea. That should offset some of the torment, both mental and physical, that my sister's parties can inflict. And you can bring this infamous roommate of yours."

"If the whole TV show producing thing doesn't work out, you should consider going into advertising," he teased.

"I just want to keep your expectations realistic. Jenna's no Jay Gatsby, that's for sure. It's probably going to be uncomfortable, pretentious, painful, and maybe even give you nightmares for the next couple of months," she warned ominously, then, in a much perkier voice, added, "But you're welcome to come."

Greyson sat up straight and said, "That's without a doubt the worst party invitation I've ever heard. But it's also the only party invitation I've received since moving here, so how could I say no?"

"I did say painful, right?"

"Twice now. I gotta say, the more you try and instill fear in me about this get-together, the more intrigued I become."

"You say that now, but you might think differently when you have to sign a waiver to get in."

"What's a little waiver between friends?" he said. "Is there only one house in Malibu, or are you going to give me the address?"

"Well—" she hummed.

He cut her off with, "Don't tell me. You are going to plant a series of clues all over LA, and I have to find and solve them to discover where this Hollywood Inquisition is located, like in *The DaVinci Code*."

"You do love movies, don't you?" she said while shaking her head. "Give me your phone." As he reached into his pocket, a tableau of introducing Greyson to Jenna, Christian, and her mother caused a brief panic to course through her nervous system, but she quickly doused that anxiety flame. *That can be Saturday's worry.*

Greyson unlocked and surrendered his device. She thumbed her info into his contacts and returned it. "Text me Saturday, and I'll send you the address. That way, if something comes up or you change your mind, you have an out."

"I'm too morbidly curious to miss it, so I think it's safe to say I'll be there. That is unless the chance to get a Sriracha enema opens up."

Hannah winced and mused, *There's an excuse I bet Tanya's never used.*

"Too much?" he playfully asked.

"I honestly don't know which would be worse. Just text me. Either way, we'll definitely have something to talk about next Sunday." She got up and casually drifted down to the pathway.

Greyson watched her slowly fade into the surroundings, like the memory of a pleasant dream.

Chapter Ten

The next day, Hannah was back to her weekly routine, but with a pinch more verve. She and her mother were sitting on her back terrace, enjoying a bottle of dry Furmint. The cobblestone patio was in the shape of a heart that pumped into a well-maintained but seldom-used pool. The rest of the backyard was filled with a plethora of idyllic landscaping that created the illusion of their own private Eden.

They had just finished lunch, in her mother's own words, "…under the glow of the only star bigger than me." As they stared out at the topiary shrubs, Hester said, "I love springtime in LA. It's so optimistic and rejuvenating."

"It's technically not spring for another week."

"Oh pish posh! Here, spring replaces winter faster than an ingénue replaces a seasoned veteran."

After a prolonged moment of quiet, Hannah glanced at her mother and wondered what she was thinking. It was a common occurrence; Hester's stoic expression was as mystifying as the Mona Lisa, but she knew never to ask. Any inquiry would always be met with the same curt remark: "It's impolite to try and impose on one's private contemplations."

Instead, she tried a different avenue of connection. "Are you still planning on going to Jenna's party on Saturday?"

Hester turned and regarded her behind the Jackie Ohh sunglasses. "Is that this Saturday? I had completely forgotten."

"I'm bringing Tanya and..." Hannah trailed off, wondering if this was the best time to bring up Greyson.

"And whom, dear?" Hester asked nonchalantly, trying to mask her interest.

Hannah shook her head dismissively. "Oh, just some guy I met in the park." Somehow, talking to her mother about him made Greyson seem more real.

Hester tilted her head until their eyes locked, then said, "Oh really?"

"Oh really" was another famous Hester-ism. Spoken offhandedly, it meant, "Please tell me every single detail without me having to appear overly inquisitive." And as with most things, it was a passive-aggressive power play intent on reminding all involved who the most important person truly was.

Hannah hesitated to continue. The awkwardness of being open with her mother piled onto her steady grief and the emerging guilt she felt from her excitement towards Greyson. She forced out a nonchalant sigh, then said, "I met him at the park a couple of weeks ago. He's a scientist at a tech company here."

Hester simply continued to stare at her, which translated into, "You have my permission to continue."

So Hannah did. "We were talking yesterday, and I sorta kinda invited him to Jenna's thing. He and his roommate."

"Did you clear this with your sister?"

Hannah nearly laughed at the question. Jenna's events were always an avalanche of industry people, all jockeying to be seen and heard without appearing like they were trying to be seen and heard. Hannah and Van had attended several where they never even got the chance to speak with either Jenna or Christian. Each party had the usual suspects, along with an entirely new horde of parasites. It was a social function playbook indirectly passed down from Hester.

But Hannah knew her mother's decorum would require permission to bring someone outside their inner family circle. So, that meant Tanya was fine, but anyone else would need consent. At least if it were Hester's party.

"Not yet. I planned on texting her today," Hannah lied.

"That's good. Anything less would be discourteous," Hester warned, then switched subjects and tones. "So, he's a scientist?"

"Yes, he's working on some top-secret project." Then, without thinking about it, Hannah blurted out, "He reminds me a lot of Van."

Her last sentence hung in the air like a cloud of pollen, quickly coloring everything under it. Hester looked over at the nearly artificial blue waters of the pool and said, "That's not surprising. If you live long enough, you start meeting the same people over and over."

Hannah looked at her with confusion until she said, "When you lose someone who was basically your whole world, you tend to see little things about them everywhere and in everyone. I remember after your father passed, everything reminded me of him. Especially you."

Hannah's eyes widened at her mother's admission. Hester rarely spoke about Hannah's father, and this was a stunning revelation. Part of her resentment toward her mother was that she seemed to have forgotten all about Ben Ackerman. Throughout her childhood, Hannah pined for stories, details, hell, even the minor idiosyncrasies of her father—anything to help her connect with the fading memories of her dad.

"Oh, don't sit there slack-jawed. Of course, you remind me of him; you have his green eyes and blithe demeanor. It's probably why I..." Hester paused as if carefully wording her remark, "I threw myself into work. Being around you right after losing him was too painful."

Imagine losing your father and then your mother's attention, Hannah thought but remained silent.

As if reading her mind, Hester said, "I know pulling away from you was wrong, but I was very young and didn't know how to handle the whole wretched situation."

And just like that, another verbal bombshell dropped out of the sky. Hester Ackerman just admitted she was wrong. A small but significant part of Hannah's life had been spent trying to prove her mother wrong about something. It was like her personal Holy Grail quest. Every time she felt she'd been close, Hester would change the subject, and her goal would vanish in a proverbial wisp of smoke.

Once freed from the sycophancy of adolescence, every child seeks to find the faults in their parents, like a home inspector rigorously examining a house for structural flaws. It becomes a game of one-upmanship where you compete for your identity and independence. Maybe it's driven by a natural familial rivalry, which certainly shaped her and Jenna's relationship.

Now, with her prize before her, Hannah didn't feel triumphant. It was more like an emotionally pyrrhic victory. On top of that, the natural instinct to appease her mother kicked in, leading her to say, "It's okay, I understand."

Hester sniffed in quickly, then said, "The point is it's only natural to see traits and dispositions in others, especially if you have feelings for them. But it's all just an illusion, and you shouldn't let it color how you see him. Or the world."

Hannah hadn't felt this close to her mother since she was a small child. *I can't believe I'm sitting here getting advice—really intimate and emotional advice—from my mom. I've dreamed of this moment for as long as I can remember.* The flash flood of emotion caused her to reach out and grab Hester's hand.

Hester turned back towards her in surprise, as if she'd been suddenly pinched, then lightly squeezed Hannah back. "I can just sense a change in you. Almost see it. I've been so concerned about you this last year, especially knowing what you've been going through, that I guess I'm just relieved. And a little proud; you seemed to have avoided my mistakes. Maybe if I attend Jenna's event, I can meet this scientist," she said with a smile.

"I'd like that," Hannah said, slowly letting go of her mother's hand.

As the conversation waned, they quietly relaxed in the glow of the daylight, both feeling rejuvenated and serene. Hannah closed her eyes while cherishing their brief but deeply felt connection, hoping it would flourish.

Chapter Eleven

"What are you grinnin' about?" Tsai asked as Greyson bound into the office. "Jesus, one lunch with El Jefe, and you think you're the chosen one."

"Am I grinning? I hadn't noticed," he replied, as he promptly took his seat opposite her.

As he pulled out his laptop, she asked, "You did tell me everything about that meeting, right? You're not holding anything else back, are you?"

He shook his head. "I told you, Dr. Greene asked me not to say anything until he formally announced it."

"Secrets don't make friends." She paused and gave him an appraising look. "So, if it's not that, did you win tickets to Nickelback or something?"

"I don't like—" he started to answer, then realized he was walking right into her taunt trap.

Before he could formulate a proper retort, she asked, "Did you finally find someone to play pickleball with?"

Her dig caused him to chuckle, despite himself. "You know, you're like an office bully. I should start calling you Cameron Donovan," he said, without thinking.

"Who dat?"

Greyson paused for a moment, as if trying to remember the title of a song, then said, "He was the bully that tormented me all through junior high. It's funny; I haven't thought about him in forever."

"What's funny is how we always refer to our bullies by their first and last names."

"Yeah, that's true. I guess it's to distinguish them from the familiarity of our friends."

"Bully should be a relationship term like uncle or cousin. That way, you could just refer to him as 'Bully Cameron.' And I could reply, 'Ah yes, I had a Bully Courtney, Bully Heather, Bully Ashley, and Bully Jessica.'"

Greyson's jaw went slack. "Seriously?"

Tsai shrugged. "It was a long time ago." Then she pointed at his face. "Back to your mouth twinkle. Let me guess, you scored an all-expenses-paid camping trip to Crystal Lake?"

"No, I met someone at the park, and she invited me to her sister's party."

"Does this mean I don't have to hear about 'what's her name' anymore?" Tsai asked, using her personal code for his ex, Ansley.

"I don't talk about 'what's her name' a lot," he replied, then quickly added, "Do I?"

"Let's just say if this party invite is real, maybe I can go ahead and cancel your intervention."

Greyson beamed from across the desk. "Oh, it's real, alright. Her sister and husband are Hollywood players."

"Okay there, Don Wannabe, keep in mind she's inviting you to the most public of places: a party. And not just a party, but an LA party, where she has complete home-field advantage. This is less a date and more an audition."

"Aren't all dates basically auditions?"

"Yeah, but this is more like an open casting call where she's safely judging you from the back of the auditorium. A real date is more of a closed audition. You know, a one-on-one tryout," Tsai explained, then zinged him with, "So don't go planning on showing her the fifty shades of Greyson afterward."

"You LA people and your obsession with the entertainment industry."

"I am not an LA person," she said with heavy disdain. "I was made in Taiwan, then moved to Austin with my parents when I was but a youngling."

He smiled at her joke. "Why did you pick this city?"

She regarded him as if he'd asked how much she weighed. After an uncomfortable few seconds ticked by, she said, "Unlike you, I can't just live wherever I want."

"Sure you can; it's a free country."

"That's the second-biggest lie they teach you in school, right after 'you can be anything you want to be.' But being an Asian lesbian immigrant, there are only about five or six places here where I can live comfortably. And as it so happened, LA was the closest to Texas." Then she waved her hand and said, "Can we get back to your date?"

Greyson thought about Hannah's invite, then recalled one of the last things she said, *You can even bring this infamous roommate of yours,* and tempered his excitement. "I never said it was a date."

"Backpedaling already?" she asked, then partly turned her attention back to her monitors. She had four spread out on her side of the desk, and she could toggle between them and Greyson like a blackjack dealer watching several different players.

Greyson reconsidered the entire situation. It was Hannah's sister's party, which meant it was a very public event. Her best friend Tanya would be there, and Greyson was told he could bring Nolan along, reducing any chance for covalent bonding to absolute zero. The most likely outcome would be an awkward and lackluster evening filled with meaningless small talk, ultimately leading him down disappointment street.

After examining the upcoming evening without the rose-colored glasses, he tried not to let his sudden disenchantment show. "Not backpedaling, more like recalculating my expectations."

She offered him a terse smile. "Sorry if I poured cold water on your fervid presuppositions."

"No worries; better to be demoralized now than later. This way, I can anticipate a more realistic probability."

"Jesus, dude, now you sound like the nerdy Ghostbuster."

"Spengler," he automatically replied.

"Who's obsessed with the entertainment industry?" she shot back. "Look, all I'm saying is you have a naive heart. You pretty much wifed-up your high school sweetheart, who, from everything you've told me, sounds a touch sociopathic. I just don't want you jumping out of the blonde into a fire engine redhead."

"Hannah's not a redhead, but I get your point," he replied with a nod, then added, "And Ansley's not really a sociopath."

"Whatever you say, but in the spirit of feminism, don't ever make the mistake of thinking a woman can't be as ruthless and self-serving as a man. We're just better at hiding it."

"I believe you," he replied as she put in her earbuds, signaling the end to the conversation.

Greyson pretended to focus on his own screens. But he couldn't quite shake Tsai's subtext, which he was partly responsible for. He'd given her his side of the story about his first relationship, but with time and distance, he was gradually becoming aware of some of his own shortcomings.

Tsai bringing up Ansley was like a mental detour sign, forcing Greyson down a contemplative path. Hannah and Ansley were like opposite poles, the former being empathetic, sagacious, kind, and witty, while the latter was impetuous, narcissistic, and abrasive, but also funny. It seemed the only common denominator was a sense of humor, although Ansley's was more unsophisticated, sometimes mean-spirited, and occasionally spiteful.

He imagined both in a stand-up comedy classic western showdown using microphones instead of guns. Hannah donning the white hat as opposed to Ansley's black one. The absurd notion caused him to smile and shake his head.

Of course, Ansley didn't start off as a villain. At first, she was gracious, friendly, dazzling, and, to be completely transparent, fetching. Especially to an introverted, socially awkward, and to be completely transparent, horny teenage boy. She was the quintessential cheerleader debutante, and he was the stereotypical science geek.

They met in math class during their junior year, as the alphabetical gods smiled on him and placed her with the last name Smith in the seat in front of him. From there, the ostensibly clichéd nerdy boy helping the popular girl with her classwork began to play out. What broke this trite model was that she was merely feigning not understanding trigonometry in order to have a legitimate reason to be slumming with someone several rungs below her station.

The truth was, she had just been not only dumped but humiliated by her basketball star boyfriend. In the midst of her despair, she found solace, which slowly developed into attraction, in her shy, gawky, yet unassumingly brilliant quasi-tutor. He was the antithesis of her ex, which, although she'd never admit it, meant he was a safe rebound. Their friendship quietly blossomed into a romantic entanglement that neither could ignore nor control. And as with most youths, their intensifying attachment dominated their lives.

Things began to change in college as they were both growing up and apart. She gradually stopped being awed by his intellect and shifted more toward resenting it. She was no longer charmed by his eccentricities, and their relationship became contentious and taxing. That, in Greyson's mind, is when Ansley morphed from a supportive partner into a passive-aggressive adversary.

He was not entirely blameless, as his insecurity and social awkwardness became less charming and more wounding. His one true failing and regret was not being able to see things from her perspective. He often equated his inability to understand her to staring at the sun with a naked eye, which didn't help his cause.

He saw the writing on the wall in grad school but made the fatal mistake of soldiering on for a myriad of reasons. The most important and, conversely, the worst one was that he didn't want to hurt her. Even though he knew he needed to rip off the proverbial relationship band-aid, he lacked the fortitude, so he chose the coward's way out.

When he believed they'd reached an organic finale to their romance—his new job offer and relocation to California—he told her this would be an opportune time to take a break and try to figure their lives out independently. He knew she'd never move that far from her family since she was a Southern girl through and through, so there was only one possible outcome.

Deep down, he realized he was avoiding conflict, but he misappropriated a Sun Tzu quote and told himself, "If a battle cannot be won, do not fight it." So, in his mind, they would be over and without any messy estrangement. After he finally confessed to Nolan about his break-up scheme, his friend quoted their favorite line from *Billy Madison*: "I award you no points, and may God have mercy on your soul."

Those last couple of months in Virginia were the most acrimonious. The adage, "You never truly know someone until you try to passively break up with them," was never more accurate than with Ansley. She was no fool and recognized his strategy. In her mind, she was not about to give up on ten years of intimacy, along with an undertone of relationship high-handedness.

Everything that was dysfunctional about their relationship in those last few years suddenly amplified, as if he accidentally turned the toxicity up to broil. Her subtle manipulations of impugning his worth became overt. Their relationship escalated from a cold war into a nuclear one overnight. No longer his girlfrenemy, as Nolan liked to joke, she was now his openly hostile antagonist.

Those final few weeks were a long and arduous battle of the specious "you're nothing without me," both on social media and in real life. Greyson had to at least consider her accusation since she'd essentially replaced his mother as the most important female in his life. It was a calculated attack on his incessant self-doubt, based on the fact that she knew all of his weaknesses and understood exactly how to exploit them.

During this vitriolic and stressful period, he finally got his master's degree. His collegiate career lasted a total of nine and a half years due to his having to work several part-time jobs to bear the academic expenses. That, along with his underlying fear of change. The postgraduate degree was his proudest achievement and one he'd secretly doubted he'd ever attain.

Nearly coinciding with his graduation, he'd gotten the job offer with Crastino Industries. His first instinct was to share this exciting news with Ansley, but he knew she would only taint his exhilaration. So, he spent his first Christmas alone, sequestered in anticipation, quietude, and melancholy. Then, in January, he and Nolan packed up for the promise of a new life in California. With a mountain of insecurity and a leaden heart, he departed for Los Angeles.

Chapter Twelve

The day of the party was a fairly hectic one for Hannah since she was charged with making "back-up" hors d'oeuvres that, in all likelihood, would literally go to waste. Jenna tended to overplan and delegate duplicate responsibilities to others. This ensured that there was always an overabundance, which Van had called "squandered extravagance."

According to Jenna, she'd gotten most of the planner genes, which automatically assigned Hannah the role of doer. Of course, Hannah knew this was merely an excuse. Contrary to popular belief spread mostly by themselves, masterminds are capable of working just as hard as laborers. Not that Jenna was lazy, but her visions always overreached her laboriousness. And more often than not, they were left to Hannah to finish and clean up.

Even though she was three years younger, early on in their relationship, Jenna assumed the mantle of boss when it came to where they would go or what they would do. She exhibited the classic younger sibling inferiority complex that Hannah recognized early on without actually knowing its clinical term. So, she suffered her tantrums and domineering behavior with the patience of a mother, which gave her the illusion of control.

That meant Jenna often got her way, and without a true mother to set and enforce rules and boundaries, she became marginally spoiled. But not to the point of absolute obnoxiousness. Deep down, Hannah blamed herself, even though cognitively she knew that was unfair. She was not Jenna's parent, nor should she have to bear that burden. But since Hester was seldom around, the onus fell on her anway.

Hannah finished the final touches on her sun-dried tomato basil roll-ups with a proud smile. *Hey, at least I know these will get eaten,* she thought as she nudged the dish into the fridge. *Tanya and I could probably take this whole plate down ourselves.*

She tried to remember the last time she'd made them, and then the memory of Van's last birthday flooded her mind like a tsunami. He hated parties almost as much as Jenna loved them. He was so much the opposite of her small family, including the iterations of stepfathers.

He'd definitely resent having to go to Jenna's thing tonight, that's for sure. But still, he would've indulged me and made the best of it. Which meant we'd huddle together and make fun of everyone else.

When a partner dies, there's so much more to it than the loss of a loved one. What gets overlooked are the more banal absences. The person who would take out the trash, run to the store and pick up much-needed cold medicine, remember to change the water filter, and could always be counted on to accompany you to any function, even your sister's insufferable parties. There's the literal emptiness in your life where your partner once resided, such as on the other side of a bed, couch, or table. Partner can mean "part of," and it's this part of you that is ripped from your essence, a void in your soul that can never be filled, that no one understands.

Unless they, too, have experienced it.

Hannah found herself pulled into her office and staring at their wedding photo, as if in a fugue state. The black 8 x 10 frame was home to one of the few pictures she had of Van. Not only did he have an aversion to gatherings but also the camera. "We both know what I look like," was his other favorite retort whenever she would try to cajole him into a Kodak moment.

He even managed to resist the burgeoning of social media in the 2000s. For the most part, he lived an analog life with a very minimal online presence. The only place one could find him was on the University of California, Malibu's faculty and staff webpage. Except for their relationship, he was the archetypal self-contained man.

As she stared down at his image, a little voice in the back of her mind began to sound off, almost like a smoke alarm. *You've done your five minutes of mourning. Now, it's time to return to the living present.*

She feared her grief had become an addiction and decided to treat it as such, like a smoker slowly reducing their nicotine intake until it reached zero. She was currently trying a progressive approach to getting over Van's death, where she'd allow herself a daily number of minutes of lamentation. Once that time was up, she would force herself out of her head and into the waking world. At least until the next day.

Nothing else had worked, and desperate people call for desperate measures. At first, she expected grief to be more like the flu, starting rapidly and agonizingly. Then, it would gradually lessen with the passing weeks, until one day you wake up, and presto, you're all better. You're back to the old you.

Unfortunately, that's not what her experience had been like at all. It was almost dizzying how quickly she became Van's life partner in crime and entwined. But that part of her was gone forever. And as time crawled on, nothing really got better. If anything, it stayed the same, as if suspended in time like a boat moored for a prolonged winter. In moments like these, she felt as lonely as in those first few excruciatingly painful weeks.

Time to dig out of this black hole of despair. She delicately placed the photograph back on the bookshelf and purposely marched out of her office.

"What else can I do?" she mumbled to herself as she stood in front of her office doors and cast about her home for any form of distraction. Her diversion quest was interrupted by a knock at the front door.

Without even thinking, she spun around and opened it, revealing a startled Tanya.

"What the fuck! Were you just standing at the door waiting to scare the shit outta me?" she gasped.

Hannah chuckled as she stepped aside to let her friend in. "Sorry, I was just coming out of the office when you knocked."

"Yeah, right," Tanya said as she strolled by, purposely avoiding eye contact, and headed for the kitchen. "And here I was, innocently coming over to help you with the whores-duerves."

Hannah followed in step. "I was wondering why you're here so early."

"Okay, full disclosure, I used this as an excuse to get out of a production meeting."

Hannah laughed again. "I told them the same thing. I had this big event where I had an opportunity to promote the series finale that I needed to prepare for."

"Great minds and all that," Tanya said as she opened the fridge, surveyed it for a moment, then scooped up a bottle of coconut water. She whirled around to face Hannah. "Are those sun-dried tomato basil roll-ups?"

"You know they are," Hannah said playfully.

"I forgive you for trying to scare me white," Tanya said, then took a long drink.

"I told you, it wasn't intentional. It was just a happy little accident."

"Since it looks like the pinwheels are done, I take it my work here is too."

Hannah leaned forward onto the white granite countertop of her island. She crinkled up the side of her mouth and said, "I'm glad you're here. I was kinda in a bad place."

"What, your office? You just need a few candles, a lighter paint color, some recessed lighting, modern built-ins, and, well, I guess what I'm saying is, a complete renovation."

When Hannah looked away, Tanya's tone changed. "Van?"

Looking down, Hannah just nodded. "I just needed something to get my mind off of… well, you know."

"Gotcha. Is there anything else we need to prepare for this party? I mean, not to brag, but I do have my own baking show."

"No, we should be okay. I doubt Jenna will even need or notice the pinwheels."

Tanya glanced back at the fridge. "Her loss just means more for us. So, what time is Malibu Barbie's thing anyway?"

Hannah cracked a smile. "Who knows? She said seven, but in Jenna speak that either means six or eight, depending on your prestige. Since I fall into more of the help category, I think she'll want me there earlier."

"And what's the occasion? Did her husband go a whole year without an affair?"

Hannah smiled again. She always envied Tanya's acerbic wit, along with the fact that she could gleefully say things that were verboten for most. "It's just a party for the sake of a party."

"It should be a party to celebrate us going to pilot. I'm not one to brag—" Hannah gave her a sharp side-eye that made Tanya correct herself. "Okay, maybe I am, but still, we crushed that shit. I could see them drooling all over your pitch, like a sneakerhead at the newest Air Jordans release."

"It did go pretty well, didn't it?" Hannah recalled the lively back and forth, then immediately sought to temper any expectations. "But let's not get ahead of ourselves. We still have an uphill climb." She felt something deep inside of her wanting to cling to the status quo like a child desperately holding on to an outgrown toy.

Tanya arched her eyebrows. "Whatever. Just take the win. I plan on celebrating, even if I have to do it at one of Jenna's get-togethers. Plus, I get to meet your mystery mate, right?" She intoned the word "right" with the same teasing playfulness as if they were still in high school.

Again, Hannah had to suppress a stab of guilt. "He texted me this morning and RSVP'd yes. I gave him the address and said any time after seven. So, we better hang around near the door."

Tanya sidled up to her friend and said, "Are you nervous? Excited? Queasy?"

"To be honest, I haven't had the chance to be anything about it. I've been..." she trailed off. Finally, she whispered, "Preoccupied."

Tanya put an arm around her shoulder and squeezed. "I get that, honey. You've got a lot going on right now. But I really think this is a nice little step in the right direction. You're finally leaving this sanctuary to do something other than work, visit your mom, or mourn. I know attending your sister's party isn't any sane person's definition of living la dolce vita, but it's a start."

Hannah wrapped her arms around Tanya and hugged her tightly. "Thanks. Thanks for going with me, for putting up with me, and for, you know, everything else. I don't know what I would have done without you. I owe you so much."

"You don't owe me anything. It's what hetero life partners are for," Tanya said, then added, "Well, you do owe me for tonight. A Saturday night at your sister's goes above and beyond the bounds of a BFF."

Hannah released her embrace. "I know. You win major points for that."

"You did say he was bringing his roommate. Maybe I will get something out of tonight besides good food and drinks after all," Tanya said mischievously.

"I don't know if that's the train you want to take. I get the impression the roommate's more of your basic piece of coal, not a diamond in the rough."

"Oh, so it's back to black means bad and white means good, huh?"

"You know that's not what I'm saying," Hannah said with a frown. "And anyway, diamonds come in lots of different colors, including black."

"I'm just fucking with you; no need to go all Claudia Alexander on me," Tanya shot back.

"Who?"

"Jesus, pick up a book. She's a famous geoscientist for NASA. I met her at a women's conference a couple of years ago. She's wicked smart and surprisingly funny. For a nerd."

"Don't play egghead with me just 'cause you get invited to all the cool events, and I'm relegated to familial ones," Hannah said. She couldn't help but think, *I bet Van would know who she is.*

Tanya said nothing for a moment, then pushed herself away from the kitchen island and said, "Let's go get you ready for tonight. We can't have you looking like Rumpled Shabbyskin."

"What?" Hannah objected, then glanced down at her frumpy, yet comfy, lounge clothes and followed her friend into the bedroom.

Chapter Thirteen

"I can't believe we're going to our first big LA party," Nolan said excitedly. He was studying his reflection in the bathroom mirror, almost like a jewelry appraiser regarding a rare stone. He rotated his head around, then decisively added more product to his hair.

"Hannah warned me that it's not going to be like what you're thinking. There won't be any celebrities or anything like that," Greyson called from his bedroom. "It's just a little get-together with some of her sister's friends." He was also examining himself in a second-hand, full-length mirror he'd bought from a thrift store.

"Who gives a shit about celebrities? You said her friends were Hollywood players, right? That's who I need to schmooze with! I don't want to wait tables forever, dude," Nolan yelled as he lathered on shaving cream.

"I didn't say players, just, I dunno, people in the business," Greyson replied, trying to sound nonchalant about the affair. He then yanked off the white Oxford dress shirt, tossed it into a growing pile, and switched to a gray one.

"People better mean women. If I'm not going to further my career, I damn sure better further my sexcapades."

Even though Nolan was in the hallway bathroom and couldn't see him, Greyson shook his head at his friend's boorishness. It had become an almost knee-jerk reaction. "You'd have made an excellent Neanderthal," he mumbled.

Greyson paused for a beat, awaiting some form of comeback. When nothing came, he smiled to himself, believing he actually got away with the rejoinder and returned to buttoning up the shirt. But before he could finish, Nolan suddenly filled his doorway, wearing only a sagging towel with specks of white foam dotting his face.

"Don't play Mr. Sensitive with me, dude. You like to act all fancy, like a sophisticated gentleman, and think it will give you an edge with the ladies. But which one of us has nailed the most chicks?" Nolan asked rhetorically as he leaned against the door frame.

"I was with Ansley for like nine years. So, you had an unfair advantage," Greyson defended.

"That's your own fault. Who the fuck gets married in high school anyway?"

"We weren't married," Greyson said, getting flustered at the mere mention of their relationship. It was the one button Nolan knew how to push, and he pushed it like someone impatiently waiting for an elevator.

"You might as well have been. But fine, let's throw out those nine years," Nolan said, then mimicked adding up numbers on an invisible calculator. "Do I have to reveal the score? 'Cause it's a touchdown for team Nolan to a big fat donut for team you."

Greyson knew that, even if he'd been single during that time, it still would have been no contest. Nolan boldly collected sex partners like hipsters collect vinyl. Sure, he was an attractive guy who lived at the gym, but he was still just a waiter with a Napoleon complex and a few college credits to his name.

What confounded Greyson was that Nolan never bothered to hide his antediluvian demeanor. It wasn't the typical Dr. Jekyll and Mr. Hyde situation, like with most men. Nolan was unabashedly Mr. Hyde, right from the initial introduction. And more often than not, Nolan was always in the company of a woman.

"Even if we completely level the playing field and just start counting from our time here in La La Land, it's two zip," Nolan continued, then quickly corrected himself, "Wait, three zip."

"That's not fair either. You work at a restaurant, which is a notorious hookup venue. I work for a Fortune 500 company, where we have to fill out a Consensual Relationship Agreement before we can even have lunch together."

To anyone else, this off-the-cuff employment comparison would also function as a career and status dig. But Nolan cared little for distinction. In his mind, he was one meeting, audition, or random encounter away from illustriousness. The roadmap to his dream required serving time in menial jobs as if it were an internship to stardom.

Nolan shook his head slowly. "Again, not my fault, dude. You're just an excuse factory. You don't want to face the ugly truth—most women don't give a shit about decorum. They care about this," he said, pointing to his square face, then flexed and nodded to his bulging bicep, "this," and finally waved a hand over his washboard abs, "and this."

Greyson instinctively took a step back, as if Nolan's assertion were literally toxic. He avoided mentally comparing his friend's chiseled physique to his own borderline dad bod and muttered, "That's not my experience."

"Which we just established is severely lacking. Sure, women like to play the whole 'what I really want is a refined man with a great sense of humor' card," Nolan said, with the last part in a falsetto voice, "but in truth, they just want a man. A guy. A bro. Not some wolf in women's clothing. There has to be a distinct difference between the two genders. Otherwise, you're just a lesbian with a permanent strap-on."

"You heard that one on NPR, didn't you?" Greyson joked, trying to lighten the mood in order to escape from this digressive lecture.

"Seriously, man, stop trying to pretend you're on their team and start playing by the rules nature established, like, forever ago," Nolan said, then added proudly, "It's worked like a charm for me."

Greyson briefly considered his friend's point of view. *There's no point in mentioning that he's never once been in a serious relationship. He always dismisses that by saying he's not looking for one. Also, I know most of the girls he's slept with, and they aren't going to win any Nobel Prizes. Or any game show prizes, for that matter.* As he internally dissected Nolan's slant, a smile escaped his lips.

Nolan noticed the grin and barked, "What?"

"Nothing," Greyson said, still looking for a way out of this futile conversation.

As Nolan uttered the inane response, "I'm just saying..." Greyson remembered his mother, and his smile faded.

When he was old enough, she taught him about the mechanics of relationships, an advantage Nolan could never understand. Her experience and wisdom had helped shape the man he'd become. She would always encapsulate her view into one sentence: "Always try to be kind, honest, and respectful."

"Since we've established that you're the noob, and I'm the nookie Jedi master, you need to listen to the sexpert," Nolan teased. "Look, I'm not trying to criticize you; I'm trying to encourage you."

As if waiting for a cue to return to his grooming, Nolan stood up straight and shot him a "you feel me, dog" expression. Greyson nodded and said, "I know," which acted like a class dismissal bell, allowing Nolan to get back to the more important task of primping.

Relieved to have Nolan's pep talk over, Greyson turned back to the mirror and finished getting ready. "Now, to wear a tie or not to wear a tie, that is the question," he whispered to his reflection.

He'd spent the week unsuccessfully trying not to build up this party to anything more than Hannah's description of "an awkward and uncomfortable gathering." But now, on the eve of the event, he couldn't help but fantasize even more. He imagined her greeting him at the door in a sparkling black dress straight from the red carpet, then inviting him into a posh cliffside manor.

Yeah, I better tie one on, he thought, then strolled over to the closet. As he was straightening the knot on a tie fit for an A-lister, the doorbell rang.

"Can you get that? I'm in the middle of manscaping," Nolan yelled.

Greyson regarded himself in the mirror and remembered that this was the very outfit he wore to his last interview at Crastino. Realizing that "stodgy professional" was not the look he was going for, he whipped the tie off, followed quickly by the button-up shirt. He stood frozen in front of his suddenly inadequate closet, paralyzed by his lack of style, when the doorbell chimed again.

Frustrated that he was now back to fashion square one, Greyson left his room, wondering who could be at their door on a Saturday evening. *Nolan better not have invited a date,* he thought as he turned the deadbolt and opened the door.

He went slack-jawed when he saw Ansley standing in his doorway, framed by the amber glow of the setting sun.

Chapter Fourteen

"What the hell is she doing here?" Tanya asked, pointing over at a woman in the kitchen eagerly taking pictures with her phone. They were standing on the outskirts of the impressive and seldom used, at least by the homeowners, restaurant-grade kitchen. There was stainless steel, quartz, and copper as far as the eye could see.

Hannah followed the invisible contrail of Tanya's gesture through the crowd toward the documentarian in a white tube top and black pinstripe pants. She had dark hair with very unnatural streaks of red that called to Hannah's mind the term "buffalo plaid." "I have no idea who she is."

"That's Mandy Petty. She's a blogger and one of those social media influencers," Tanya said with disdain as if she were talking about mixing chocolate with cheese.

"Social media influencers?"

"Yeah. You know, those people who are kinda like radio personalities but with looks instead talent. She has a ton of followers who do and, more importantly, buy whatever she recommends. Basically just because she's attractive."

"Thanks to the internet, pretty people are finally getting their due," Hannah scoffed. "This world makes less and less sense."

"That's 'cause you're getting old, honey," Tanya teased as she elbowed her in the side. "The internet can make anyone a star."

"I guess. Wait, is her name really Mandy Petty?"

"Only her agent knows for sure," Tanya shot back.

"I guess a blogger by any other name wouldn't be as effete," Hannah said, then grabbed Tanya's elbow and tugged. "It's getting too crowded. Let's migrate toward the front."

They had arrived at 6:30, and now that it was well past eight, they'd already made the party rounds. Jenna and Christian paraded Hannah and Tanya to anyone of importance, mostly to show off Tanya. Everyone respectfully introduced themselves with a guise of well-rehearsed blasé.

With wine in hand, they both made their way through the bevy of sycophants, like salmon swimming upstream, until they reached the vestibule of the home. Once free of the party bubble, they sat on a ridiculously overpriced wooden bench that had been painstakingly designed to resemble an antique. A circular ivory staircase loomed next to them, looking more at home in a plantation estate than in a seaside villa.

"This place gets more extravagant every time I come," Tanya noted.

"My sister only knows one style, and that's expensive," Hannah said, then glanced back down the hallway to the kitchen. "What time is it?"

"Five minutes after the last time you asked. Just relax; he will get here when he gets here," Tanya assured. "He's probably lost. I mean, we are deep, deep in Malibu."

Hannah turned to the front double doors and studied them for a moment. They were two espresso-stained oak sentries, and as with everything else in the house, were designed to impress. "How can you get lost? It's right off PCH."

"He's a simple Southern boy, right? So, he's probably not used to how big and spread out everything is here."

Hannah shot her a look of irritation, causing Tanya to put up both hands in a mock surrender. "Oh, I'm sorry. I didn't mean to insult your country bumpkin."

Hannah said nothing and just continued to glare. "What's the big deal? I thought this wasn't a date."

Hannah shifted her gaze down to her onyx block heels. Even though Tanya was right and it wasn't an official date, she'd worn her favorite cap-sleeve black cocktail dress. She wanted to stand out without looking like she was trying to stand out. Plus, there was the unconscious yet perpetual need to not disappear next to Tanya, who was effortlessly decked out in an elegant, off-the-shoulder maroon gown.

"It's not... I'm just..." Hannah trailed off.

"You have his number, so text him."

Hannah quickly turned back to her, as if insulted. "I'm not going to text him because he's a couple of minutes late. That would... would make it sound like this is a—"

"A date?" Tanya finished.

Hannah looked back down. "And I don't want to be *that* girl."

"Oh my God, you are so smitten."

"I'm not smitten," Hannah protested. Then, when Tanya didn't reply, she backpedaled. "Okay, maybe I am pre-smitten."

Tanya suddenly clapped, which echoed into the foyer. "I knew it. Little Miss Cooler-than-Thou has caught feelings."

"Pre-feelings," Hannah corrected.

Tanya put an arm around her friend and said, "This is a good thing. It shows that you are waking from your grief coma. Stressing over seeing a boy is a positive step. Granted, it's nerve-racking and even a little terrifying, but it's still a step in the right direction."

Hannah shook her head. "I don't love it."

"No one does. You're not supposed to. But it proves you are still alive in here," Tanya said, pointing at Hannah's heart. "Don't worry. Like I said, I'm sure he's just lost or whatever. He'll be here."

Chapter Fifteen

"Uh, what are you doing here?" Greyson asked, after metaphorically picking up his jaw off the ground.

Ansley tried to smile, but it didn't quite fit the rest of her expression. Her visage was one of eagerness, shaded with apprehension and just a hint of exhaustion. Beads of sweat began rising on her forehead, partly from anxiety and partly due to her oversized tan cardigan. A sweater and jeans were perfectly fitting for a March night in Virginia but not always suitable for springtime in California.

"I just… just wanted to see you."

Greyson just stood there, gobsmacked. It was as if he ordered a margarita but received a Molotov cocktail instead. "But what are you doing *here*?" he repeated, simply because he couldn't think of anything else to say.

"I guess I wanted to say I'm sorry," Ansley said, then looked down. "I know I didn't act appropriately when you left, and that's not how I want things to be between us."

Seconds ticked by like water droplets leaking from a faucet. Finally, a car horn sounded off in the distance, waking Greyson from his stupor. "Do you wanna come in?" he asked as he took a step back.

Ansley raised her head, and the shadow of a genuine smile appeared. "Sure, okay," she replied, quickly moving forward as if the invitation might suddenly expire.

"Who the hell is—" Nolan started to say, then froze when he saw Ansley gliding in and whispered, "Shit."

She looked him over and said, "Oh, hi Nolan," then turned her attention to the rest of the apartment, as if she were a prospective buyer.

"I didn't know there was a mail-order psycho service," he said, then abruptly spun around and headed for the bathroom. "All of a sudden, I've gotta take a Jurassic shit."

Ansley frowned and said, "Charming as always. I can't imagine why you're still single."

"I know exactly why you are," he shot back.

"Don't forget to fuck off and die," Ansley snapped before the door slammed shut. She turned to Greyson. "Sorry, he just pisses me off sometimes."

"You wanna sit down?" Greyson said, nodding to the couch.

"Yeah, okay," she said, plopping down in the middle. Now, Greyson had a choice—either sit uncomfortably close to her, claim the beat-up green club chair, or continue to stand awkwardly. He chose the latter.

"You want anything?" he asked. "We have water and beer, and, well, I guess that's it right now."

"Water's fine."

He turned and headed for the kitchen, all the while questions caromed around in his head like billiard balls. *Why is she here? What am I going to say? And how the hell do I get rid of her?* He snatched a glass from the cabinet and rotely began to fill it with tap water.

As Greyson pondered his imbroglio, the glass started overflowing and jolted him out of his own head. He turned off the water and absently wiped his hand on a dish towel. He stared down at the inundated glass and shook his head, then picked it up and forced himself back into the befuddling scene.

He carefully handed the glass to Ansley. As she took it, she chirped, "No ice, you remembered."

He couldn't tell if she was being sentimental or condescending and let out an uncomfortable laugh, thinking that pretty much summed up their entire relationship.

"What's so funny?" she inquired suspiciously.

"Nothing, I just…" He paused for a moment as he considered telling her the truth. He quickly dismissed it and said, "Just can't believe you're sitting in my apartment."

She glanced around for a few seconds as if confirming his statement, then said, "I know, right? I still can't believe you actually moved to California."

I bet you can't. I'd only been talking about it for the last year of grad school. Of course, you didn't want to hear about it, he thought as he nodded.

"This is a nice place," she said, the incredulity of her tone filling the room like a bug fogger. Then she rearranged the coffee table, stacking the scattered magazines to find a spot for her glass. "Although it could use a woman's touch."

He looked over the room and, as if suddenly seeing it through objective eyes, realized it was shambolic. "Yeah, sorry, we weren't expecting company."

"I can tell," she half teased. It was almost a Sherlockian moment, where she confirmed that, yes, Greyson was not dating anyone.

Do I press the issue or let it happen naturally? He felt a bit like an inexperienced paramour, wondering how long he'd have to endure this verbal foreplay before diving into the main attraction.

"Don't just stand there like a goon; sit down," she directed, patting the cushion beside her.

Unable to resist her command without starting an ancillary fight, he shuffled over and sat down next to her. "That's not so bad, is it?" she asked rhetorically.

Greyson stared blankly at the TV in front of him, imagining it was a massive hourglass. As the room grew still, he could feel the seconds piling up. Then Ansley put a hand on his knee and asked, "How have you been?"

He reflected on the routinely innocuous yet fully loaded question for a beat, then replied, "Okay, I guess. You?"

Ansley exhaled emphatically, which was her way of warning the listener that something dramatic was imminent. "To be honest, not so good."

She paused as her head slowly drooped. Greyson, being inherently familiar with the rhythm of an Ansley proclamation, knew to stay silent. "I haven't been the same since we went on hiatus. Really, even before that. You were right; we haven't been 'us' in a long time. And I realized that's partially my fault."

When she hesitated again, Greyson wondered, *Where is this going?* He got his answer almost at once.

"I just wanted to say I'm sorry," she said, then turned to face him. Greyson saw the tears welling in her eyes, and his involuntary reaction was to put his arm around her like he'd done hundreds of times.

She buried her face in his shoulder as a muffled sob escaped. They sat like that for a few moments, until she lifted her head up and said, "And not just for all the contention around you moving here. I'm sorry for not supporting your career decision. I know I was being selfish and stubborn."

Had this confession come six months ago, hell, maybe even six weeks ago, Greyson might have heard it with an open heart. But now he cynically wondered where this was all coming from, and why now?

"I just had this fixed idea of us and our future together," she continued. "And it was you working for my uncle as we started our family. I get now that it was insensitive to what you wanted, but it really was from a place of love."

Greyson didn't need an Ansley translator app to suss out her hidden meaning. Since his first year at UVA, she'd been planning their future together. He was to get either a bachelor's or master's degree and then proceed to ignore it as he worked for her family's investment company. It was a guaranteed six-figure job that he was guaranteed to loathe.

"I get now that you'd rather do science stuff and that the financial world wouldn't appeal to you. Back then, I assumed that you'd eventually change your mind. I just don't know anyone who would turn down a chance for a secure and lucrative career to chase a hobby."

Greyson recoiled as if she'd struck him. She immediately backtracked. "Sorry, I meant a passion, not a hobby. I'm saying I was wrong, and I can see that now. You turned your passion into a great job at a Fortune 500 company."

Finally, Greyson interjected, "You're making it sound more than it is. I'm at the bottom rung of the career ladder, so it's not like I'm rolling in the dough. I probably make just a little more than Nolan." Greyson purposely omitted all the other benefits, such as health insurance, paid time off, stock options, and matching 401(k) contributions.

That seemed to nudge Ansley off course just a bit. "That's just because you're new, right? There's potential to grow this into a lu—"

"Lucrative career," he interrupted. *Same old Ansley; it always comes back to the superficialities of life.*

"That's not what I was going to say," she scoffed. "I was going to say lucrative profession."

Her weak attempt at humor landed flatter than a pancake underneath a steamroller. "Listen, nothing's changed. I am still never going to pursue a high-paying job like you've always pushed me toward. I want to do something that makes me excited to get out of bed in the morning, not something that simply affords me a more extravagant bed."

She quickly donned her all-too-familiar expression, which was a combination of wounded and annoyed. "I didn't push you; I just explained the advantages of the different paths. You make it sound like I was some dominating maternal figure, and you were this innocent, naive little boy. I just played the role of a pragmatist to your idealist."

He could detect her anger seething beneath her composed facade like water slowly coming to a boil. "Did you really come all the way here to reprise this old argument?"

She glared at him for just a moment, and then her indignation seemed to evaporate behind a faint yet weary smile. "No, I didn't. I guess it's just easy to slip back into our old patterns."

Which is the perfect illustration of why we can never go back to how we were.

"I came here to show you how dedicated I am to making things work between us. I'm not going to give up on nine years simply because we fell into a rut."

He opened his mouth to object, but she cut him off with, "Okay, it was more than a rut. Way more. But I'm willing to change. To try and be more compassionate, open-minded, and, you know, not so domineering," she said with a smirk in her voice.

Greyson leaned forward as he considered her words. *If she had said this a year ago, we'd probably still be together. And it still wouldn't work. How can I make her understand that?*

"I know what you're thinking," she said. "You are wondering if I truly mean what I'm saying."

Not exactly, Greyson mused but allowed her to chase this verbal snipe while he organized his thoughts and feelings. He had to resist the part of him that longed to believe her, due to their shared past, their comfort with each other, and mostly because, for so long, she was his source of self-esteem.

"I wouldn't have come 3000 miles if I didn't mean what I'm saying. We have too much history together to throw it all away over immature notions. I admit, I was hung up on my own expectations of what our life together should look like based on my parents. I grew up with this whole assumption that I was going to marry a prosperity-driven man like my dad. The guy who works eighty hours a week so his family can live in the nicest house, drive the finest cars, and socialize with the other Richie Riches."

"I think we both know that ain't me."

"I do know that. And I lost sight of the very reason I fell in love with you in the first place. You weren't like all the men I'd grown up around. You were so different."

Before he could even make a snarky riposte, she said, "I mean different in a good way. A wonderfully amazing way."

Shit, I need to stop the praise train before it's too far gone. Her spiel was intoxicating, almost like a siren's song. He had to force himself to focus on the perilous rocks underneath her dulcet words.

"I'm here to tell you I'm going to change. And we can get back to the way things used to be. You know, when we were happy."

Greyson slowly exhaled, then turned to face her. "You have to understand that people can't go backward. We are constantly changing, growing, and evolving."

"Not Nolan," she countered, pointing at the bathroom.

"There's always one exception to the rule. But you know what I mean. You can't ever go back and recapture something from your past because, even if it is the same, you're not. It's why they say you can never go home again."

"This is what I'm trying to say. I want to work on not being that selfish and demanding girl who puts her idea of how things should be ahead of what's best for us as a couple."

"And I appreciate that, but like I said back in Virginia, we have just grown apart. We both want different things, and that's not anyone's fault. We aren't the same people we were when we first got together."

"So, you're saying you don't need me anymore?" she asked with a scowl.

He shook his head, still wondering how he was going to keep tiptoeing around this event horizon without getting sucked into the black hole. "No, I'm saying you shouldn't change who you are just to make someone else happy. That's a big, flashing sign saying you're not compatible and that it's time to start looking for someone else."

She looked away and sneered, "Oh, so that's it. You're trying to say you found someone else."

A mental image of Hannah briefly flashed in his head, but he pushed it aside. "I'm saying—"

Before he could finish, the bathroom door swung open, and Nolan said, "Dude, you said you were going to drop me off at that thing."

Greyson quickly turned to his fully dressed-to-impress roommate and uttered, "Huh?"

"You know, that Hollywood event with all those talent scouts. You promised you'd take me."

Ansley glared rays of disdain through him. "Why can't you drive yourself like a big boy?"

"Drinking and driving is so last century," he shot back.

"Can't you take a cab or something?"

"It's not like I make as much as Greyson," Nolan said while pointing knowingly at his suddenly florid friend.

Greyson finally caught on and turned back to Ansley. "Sorry, I did promise him I would." This entire gambit hinged on whether she'd ask to tag along or not. Greyson and Nolan both held their collective breaths as she pondered the situation.

Ansley abruptly shot up from the couch like an inflatable air dancer and said, "Fine, I need to check into my hotel anyway."

Greyson silently exhaled and followed her. She reached the door, then whispered, "Call me later; we still have a lot to discuss."

He nodded and closed the door behind her. After staring at the back of the door for several seconds, he sighed, "Fuck me."

Chapter Sixteen

Jenna escorted Hester to the door. As she approached, Hannah and Tanya shot to their feet like a pair of low-ranking soldiers, as if a general were passing by, and quickly exchanged awkward hugs with her.

"You look stunning," Hester whispered to Tanya, who replied with a shrug. Then she turned to Hannah and said, "Goodbye, dear. I'll see you on Monday."

"Bye, Mom," Hannah replied, then sank back down on the bench.

A few minutes later, Christian led a small troop of party guests to the front door. "Thanks for coming, everyone," he bid farewell, then shut the door. This was the signal of the beginning of the end of the event. Once the first group broke the party seal, others slowly began taking their leave. And soon, the trickle turned into a torrent.

Tanya and Hannah watched the parade of primarily average-looking men, accompanied by women far out of their league, with a mix of amusement and pity. After the third group left, Hannah casually asked, "What time is it, anyway?"

"You didn't notice Big Ben over there?" Tanya said, gesturing over to the mammoth grandfather clock across from them.

Without looking, Hannah said, "That's one of those showpieces that's so ostentatious you don't even see it."

"How long do you want to give him before calling it? I *can't* be one of the last people at Jenna's party," Tanya declared.

Hannah waited as Jenna led a very short, balding man walking next to a very tall woman out the door, then, after a long moment, stood and reluctantly declared, "I guess we can go now." She didn't bother masking the defeat in her voice.

Tanya followed and grabbed her friend's hand. "Hey, maybe something came—"

She was cut off by a thunderous knock on the door. Hannah and Tanya briefly exchanged confused looks. "Maybe discount Danny DeVito forgot something," Tanya suggested.

"Should we answer it?" Hannah asked, turning back and scanning for Jenna or Christian.

Tanya shrugged and opened the door. "Can I help you?"

Hannah turned her attention back to the cracked door but was blocked by Tanya. "Um, we're guests of Hannah's," a meek voice answered.

"Hannah? There's no Hannah here," Tanya barked, then started to close the door.

Hannah leaned past her friend and spied Greyson standing uncomfortably on the porch. She could see the relief wash over his face when he saw her. "Hey!" he beamed.

"Oh, you meant that Hannah," Tanya said as she opened the door all the way.

"Glad you could make it," Hannah greeted Greyson as he stepped inside. A shorter fellow quickly followed, whom she guessed was his infamous roommate.

Once inside the foyer, Greyson turned and said, "This is my friend, Nolan."

"And this is Tanya," Hannah introduced.

"Pleased to meet you," Greyson smiled. The mere sight of Hannah appeared to transform his mood completely, like spotting the lamp of a lighthouse in the middle of a raging tempest.

Nolan stared at Tanya for just a moment, then said, "Aren't you that mod—"

"Nope," Tanya cut him off.

"But you look just like her."

"I guess we all look the same to you?"

Nolan took a step back as if hit by a sharp gust of wind. "That's not what I'm saying."

"I'm just messing with you. Yes, I am she," Tanya said. That statement was followed by her well-rehearsed thousand-watt smile.

A gaggle of departing party guests promenaded by. Everyone smooshed against the wall as Christian and Jenna herded the flock out. Greyson took the opportunity to survey the magnificent entrance. "This is like something out of *Cribs*."

"Why is everyone leaving? It's only like nine something," Nolan asked in a failed attempt at discretion.

"It's after ten," Tanya corrected, "and Jenna's events are more like a shooting star; they shine brilliantly but burn out quickly."

"Sorry about being so late. Something came up while we were getting ready," Greyson whispered to Hannah.

Nolan chuckled with contempt. "You mean *someone.*"

"What happened?" Hannah asked as her tone perked up while trying not to sound too curious.

Greyson sighed and said, "Ansley happened."

Another exodus intruded upon their conversation. Over the din of farewells, Hannah said, "Why don't we change venues? There's a cozy bar not too far from here."

Greyson turned to his roommate and asked, "That okay with you?"

Nolan craned his neck down the long hallway of the house, hoping to spot at least one other celebrity, then quickly gave up. "I guess so," he said resignedly.

As they walked down the path to the driveway, Greyson sidled up next to Hannah and whispered, "You look very nice." She grimaced, causing him to ask, "What?"

"Sorry, nothing, just a reflex to that word."

"What, nice? Does it mean something bad out here on the left coast?"

"No, it's just a pet peeve of mine. I should just say thank you," she replied with a forced smile.

"Do you mind telling me why it bothers you?"

She sighed, then said, "Not to rant or anything."

"Of course not."

"But it's just lazy. It's like you can't think of a sincere compliment, so you fall back on a stock platitude."

"Duly noted, down with nice," he said, then, after a beat, added, "You look breathtaking."

She blushed and said, "Don't overcompensate or anything."

"It's not overcompensating if it's true," he said with a winsome smile as they reached their cars.

* * *

Greyson followed Hannah down the long and winding Malibu roads until they reached their destination. Mary's Spot was a single-story, beach-worn bar that looked both old and new at the same time. It was the same for most beach structures; it only takes a couple of years for a building to achieve that universally mature seaside look.

They spilled out of their cars onto the gravel parking lot and marched single file into the dimly lit cantina. Greyson spied an empty booth in the back and led the way through the middling crowd. He poured into the alcove first, with Nolan right behind him. Hannah and Tanya sat across from them. After everyone got comfortable, a waitress quickly followed, and their drink orders were promptly in the pipeline.

"Too bad we couldn't get a table with a view," Nolan said, longingly staring out the nearly wall-sized back window.

"It's too dark to see much anyway," Greyson replied.

A few moments of awkward silence passed to the beat of Lady Gaga's "Poker Face" playing in the background. Finally, Hannah broke the noisy muteness with, "So, what were you saying about Ansley happening?"

Nolan and Greyson exchanged quick side glances. Then Greyson exhaled and recounted, "We were both getting ready when, bang, there was this knock at the door. I opened it, and there stood Ansley like a ghost from Christmas past."

"Who's this Ansley chica? Ex-girlfriend, I'm assuming?" Tanya asked while simultaneously scoping out the bar scene.

"Ex-con is more like it," Nolan scoffed.

"What'd she do, destroy your microbrewery?" Tanya said.

Nolan laughed without truly understanding the jab, which wasn't out of the norm for him. He had a definite ear for a joke, just not always the discernment. "Naw, but she's definitely cray-cray."

When no one responded, he dug his hole a little deeper. "You know, those psycho women who are sweet and nice one minute, then change into a raging lunachick the next."

Greyson immediately hung his head as his friend continued, "I always said, 'If you don't like Ansley's personality now, just wait a few minutes.'" He then beamed proudly, as if he'd coined the tired phrase.

"You're holding that 'crazy woman' card close to your chest, huh?" Tanya asked. Her attention was now fully on the man-child directly across from her.

"You know what I mean, sometimes bitches be crazy," Nolan said, then quickly qualified it with, "Not all of them, but some."

"Let's unpack the whole bitches be crazy parochialism. What kind of crazy things did she do?" Tanya asked.

"Like she'd show up at Grey's work and make a scene, text him day and night, and stalk his Facebook page, posting all this drama shit. You know, typical crazy behavior," Nolan explained while twirling his finger around the side of his head.

Tanya grinned and nodded, as if she and Nolan were in total accord. "I do know. I've even known some bitches that stole their sweetheart's car and totaled it. Who cheated on them with their best friends. Who shoved a loaded gun in their boo's face and threatened to blow their head off. Who beat them into a hospital bed with a tactical flashlight," Tanya said nonchalantly, but Hannah recognized her simmering indignation. "Of course, these bitches were all men. But yeah, women be the crazy ones."

Her words hung in the air for just a moment as the drinks arrived, like a boxing bell signifying the end of one round. Greyson lifted his mojito and said, "Not sure how to follow all that. How about we drink to feminism?"

Hannah and Tanya giggled as they raised their glasses. "To feminism," everyone toasted in unison.

"Back to tonight, what did you say to her?" Hannah asked before taking a sip.

Greyson briefly glanced up at the TV showing highlights from an earlier college basketball game, then said, "I just asked her what she was doing here."

"And did she come bearing Hasenpfeffer?" Tanya said.

"Not exactly. She wanted to talk about us," he said, then added, "Us getting back together."

Hannah felt her stomach drop like she had just passed the zenith of a roller coaster's lift hill. Then, as if she were reading her mind, Tanya asked, "What did you tell this alleged lunachick?" as she side-eyed Nolan.

"I rehashed all the reasons why we..." Greyson paused for a beat, then continued, "You know, broke up in the first place."

"Did she take a selfie with you and then put a voodoo curse on it?" Tanya asked flippantly.

"I actually saved him," Nolan bragged, reentering the conversation. "I told her he had to take me somewhere. Which wasn't a lie. She left to go check into the Ritz-Carlton or wherever."

Relieved to hear she was staying elsewhere, Hannah asked, "What are you going to do?"

"Figure out a way to send her back home," Greyson said, shifting in his seat. "Hopefully, without loss of life or limb."

Nolan scanned the bar, then said, "What we need to do is find her a good replacement. What about imitation Ashton Kutcher over there?"

"I think he's with ersatz Kat Von D," Tanya replied.

Nolan shook his head. "No guy is with a girl like that for long. She's probably just his prey for the night. See, when a dude spots a girl with all those piercings and tattoos, it's like she's wearing a target. It tells every guy that you're a wounded, broken person. You know, easy prey."

"Wow," Tanya said, shaking her head. "Sounds like you've done your research on this, Dr. Freud."

"It's not just me; all guys know this. Defacing your body to that degree is almost the same as wearing a neon sign saying, 'Please use me.' It's like when a lion spots a limping gazelle on the plains of the Serengeti."

"I would like to state, for the record, that I don't know this," Greyson interjected.

"That's why I said all guys," Nolan teased, emphasizing the word *guys*.

"You should be a writer for the internet," Hannah said, causing Greyson to giggle.

Nolan ignored the jab and said, "All I'm saying is that dating is survival of the fittest. And I mean that literally and figuratively."

"Okay, now that is the first thing you've said all night that I can agree with," Tanya announced as she slapped her hand on the table.

Hannah took another sip of her drink, then asked, "Let me get this straight; you think dating is all about how someone looks?"

Nolan gave her a Venus flytrap smile. "I mean, if you want it straight, without all that namby-pamby bullshit about finding someone to love you for who you really are as a person, then yes, looks are primo. It's the gateway to a relationship."

Hannah raised a hand to cut him off, but Nolan was already on a roll, like a tiny snowball gorging its way downhill. "Sure, I concede that there are a few unicorns out there who don't give a fuck about physical appearance, just like there are a few employers that could care less about one's criminal record."

"*Couldn't* care less," Greyson corrected, partly to show off his grammar skills and partly to disrupt Nolan's diatribe.

Nolan ignored the rectification and continued, "So, putting the exceptions to the norm aside, one's appearance absolutely matters. I know this might make me a piranha, but at least I have the guts to say it."

"I think you mean pariah," Greyson said with an uncomfortable chuckle.

Nolan swatted the second verbal emendation away with his hand. "What I'm talking about is the five keys to physical attraction: face, hair, body, hygiene, and clothes. And what the lazy, love-me-for-who-I-am delusionist ignores is that you have a degree of control over these keys."

He gave everyone a moment to chew on his wildly superficial thesis and took a swig of his beer. Hannah looked at Tanya and could tell her friend was intrigued. She then dared a glance at Greyson, and he offered her an apologetic shrug. She guessed that he was all too familiar with this rant. So she figured that, like an astute attorney, instead of objecting, she would allow him to weave more rope.

When Nolan put his glass down, he quickly glanced around the table as if surprised to see that the floor was still his. "Dating is just like selling a house. Sure, there are things outside your control, like location and property size, but there's a lot you can change. We learned that from watching *Extreme Home Makeover*. Maybe you can't do anything about your height and facial structure, but you can influence all the other keys. You wouldn't dream of selling your house without at least cleaning it first, right?"

Hannah and Tanya gave him a courtesy nod. "So, in the dating world, you are selling yourself. Going out without a deep clean and a fresh coat of paint reduces the odds of finding a prospective buyer. It's really just simple math."

Hannah turned to Greyson. "Does his math check out?"

"Wait, are you asking if all guys think this way?" Greyson replied with a smile.

Hannah returned the grin. "In a manner of speaking."

"It's not a male chauvinistic idea here. If it were, Chippendales and John Stamos would be out of business," Nolan cut in.

"Why John Stamos?" Tanya asked with arched eyebrows.

Nolan looked at her with confusion and said, "Huh?"

"Like, you have an entire world of attractive men to pick from to help make your point, and you decide to go with John Stamos? I'm just saying it's an odd choice."

Nolan rolled his eyes. "Oh my God, like you wouldn't sleep with John Stamos."

"I think you mean you wouldn't sleep with John Stamos again," Hannah clarified.

Both Nolan and Greyson's eyes widened like male characters in a 1940s cartoon. "Whahuh?" Nolan intoned.

"That's neither here nor there," Tanya said with a wry smile. "I would just go with a more rich man's version. Like maybe Rob Lowe."

"Did you bone him too?" Nolan asked, with awe practically dripping from his voice.

"We're not here to play star shag," Tanya said with a coy glance.

"I'd watch the hell outta that show, though," Greyson joked.

There was a short pause as everyone took a sip of their drink, and then Tanya said, "Can we please get back to your muddled metaphor?"

Nolan tilted his head and asked, "Sure, where was I?"

"You were giving us deep insight into the paleolithic mind," Hannah teased.

"Chippendales and John Stamos are the last things I remember," Greyson said.

Hannah looked at him sideways and said, "I'd watch the hell outta that show, though."

"Touché," he replied with a grin.

For a moment, Nolan looked perplexed, like he was trying to find the start of a roll of tape. Then his eyes lit up, and he said, "Oh yeah, I got it. Women like to pretend looks aren't all that important, but I think history shows that they are just as shallow as men. Otherwise, Playgirl wouldn't exist."

Tanya turned to Hannah and said, "That reminds me; I need my April issue back, please." Hannah responded with an elbow to her friend's side.

"If you want to be more successful at dating, then you will work out, eat right, and get a haircut that costs more than a caramel Frappuccino," Nolan declared as he cut a glance over to Greyson, whose eyebrows curved upwards and jaw opened as if to say, "Who me?"

Nolan turned back to the ladies and continued, "Practice good hygiene, care about your health, and dress appropriately. It's actually not that complicated."

Tanya nodded. "You're not exactly wrong. Of course, the better you look, the more dates you go on. I don't think that theory is blazing any new trails. But how long do you want to keep dating around?" Nolan furrowed his brow as if he'd been asked to recite the newest tax codes.

"The question she's asking is, to what end?" Hannah translated.

Nolan put both elbows on the table and rested his chin on top of his hands as if playing in the Chess World Cup. "What do you mean?"

"If your goal is to keep finding different dating partners, then yeah, you're right. Just keep painting the house, mowing the lawn, and pressure washing the driveway. But if your goal is to find someone to spend the rest of your life with, that's where you run into a problem," Hannah said.

"How can expanding your dating pool be a problem?" Nolan asked with bewilderment in his voice.

"Because dating is merely the precursor to a relationship. It's like the appetizer. You're talking about just ordering one appetizer after another but never getting to the main course," Hannah explained.

Nolan slowly gazed around the bar as he pondered her suggestion. "Well, what's wrong with making a meal outta appetizers? It's like eating at a tapas restaurant."

"I'm not saying there's a right or wrong. If all you want to do is date, as long as you are upfront about it in the beginning, go ahead and tapas out. But most people eventually need that main course. So yeah, your attitude is fine for the short term but terrible for the long. And anyone looking for a serious relationship has to weed through all you serial daters."

"That's part of my problem, having to comb through all the players in chic clothing," Tanya sighed.

"My whole idea is to get more options to find the perfect match," Nolan said, ending his sentence with a measure of exasperation.

"No, we get that," Tanya replied. "Your fatal flaw is that you think someone who puts all the effort into being attractive will automatically have all these other outstanding qualities."

Nolan rolled his eyes. "This coming from a model."

"Just call me an expert witness. I know tons of the kinds of people you are describing, and there's not a whole lot more to them beyond what you see on the outside. What I have learned is that genuine people don't have endless energy and resources to continually funnel into their physical appearance. For some, it's a minor victory to put on their makeup and get dressed up. Or whatever the male equivalent of that is. You're speaking of a world where everything is equal—everyone is perpetually twenty-five, in great physical and mental health, and has an abundance of time and money to pour into themselves. Unfortunately, circumstances in the real world aren't quite as immaculate."

Hannah grabbed her friend's hand under the table and squeezed. It was an amazing relief to have a best friend who not only understood you but also the world in which you resided. Being a famous model and TV personality meant her world was a bit different from Hannah's, but she was not a product of that environment.

"Sure, everyone has flaws to overcome," Nolan said, trying to sound discerning.

"Look, I get what you're saying, and I thought similarly when I was younger. But as you mature, you realize what's truly important and how little physical appearance matters. Sure, attraction is one of the keys, but what attracts you to someone is not universal. And it changes over time, at least for some. It's called maturing," Tanya said.

Nolan rolled his eyes again. "Sounds more like settling."

Tanya shook her head vigorously. "That's a term someone in their twenties uses to describe a circumstance they lack the experience to understand. Think of it this way: your wants and needs have evolved since high school, right?" After a brief moment of quiet, she added, "Please say 'right.'"

"I mean, for some things, sure," Nolan reluctantly conceded.

"Hopefully, that continues through your life. And as you grow and change as a person, so do your aspirations."

"You are also forgetting one of the key components of a relationship, which isn't as controllable as, say, your diet and exercise," Greyson interjected.

Nolan quickly turned to him as if already betrayed and huffed, "What?"

"Love. You don't get to pick who you have feelings for. Love is like a quantum fluctuation," he said. When everyone at the table looked at him in collective bafflement, he added, "I just mean it's unpredictable. You don't get to choose who you'll fall in love with. Sometimes, there's no rhyme or reason to it."

Hannah nodded. "The man has a point. You can meet someone who checks off every single item on your soulmate wish list, but the one thing you can't account for is chemistry."

"Okay, but the odds are you'll have that chemistry with someone who's, you know, more like you," Nolan said almost exasperatedly.

"I don't know, man, they say opposites attract for a reason," Tanya said.

"I'm sure there are some people who are so narcissistic that they just want to date a mirror version of themselves, but most of us want a partner whose strengths are our weaknesses. Who makes us better. Makes us whole," Hannah said as she swirled the thin red straw around in her drink.

Greyson made brief eye contact with Hannah as he agreed, "Exactly. A strong relationship has a good balance between shared interests and traits along with individual differences."

"Jesus, y'all are talking happily ever after, and I'm just talking about seeing a movie and hopefully getting laid," Nolan said, then promptly took another swig of his beer.

"You started it with the whole selling the house analogy," Tanya pointed out. "Whereas the endgame is to find a buyer instead of another renter and avoid perpetuating an endless cycle of showings."

"What I'm trying to say—" Nolan protested but was cut off by Greyson raising his hand.

It was obvious to the table that Nolan had no "off" switch when it came to arguing, as Greyson said, "Let's let this subject die a natural death, please." He then glanced over to Hannah, who gave him an appreciative smile.

Tanya caught Nolan leering across the room at a diminutive woman in a black leather jacket sporting a slicked-back bob and asked, "You checking out her wraparound porch?"

Nolan quickly turned to her as if caught peeping through a bedroom window and said, "What, lesbian Joe Pesci? No way! I was seeing if she was done playing pool."

Now the entire table glanced over and watched the woman place a cue back on a rack. "Do you play pool?" Hannah asked Greyson.

"I've been known to smack some balls around," he replied, trying to sound like a pool shark but coming off more like a guppy. As Nolan snorted, he attempted to course correct. "I mean, I can stroke a stick."

This made the group giggle, and Tanya said, "Well, this I gotta see."

As they filed out of the booth, Nolan whispered, "Smooth. I bet she'll set you up with her brother now."

"Shut up. You know how bad I am at pool. Why'd you have to suggest it?"

Nolan slapped him on the back and replied, "Just trying to liven up the night."

Tanya led the way over to the vacant table. Greyson trotted behind Hannah and said, "Sorry about the unintentional innuendos. Truth is, yes, I've played pool. But not very well, I'm afraid. I can do the geometry on paper, but in practice, I'm probably going to embarrass myself."

Hannah couldn't explain it, but there was something endearing about his lack of billiard skills. It was almost as if there was an unwritten rule that the better a guy was at pool, the worse he was at relationships. "Don't worry, I'm not making the Olympic billiards team either," she assured.

"Is there one?"

"If there's badminton, then who the hell knows what else there is?"

"Wait, badminton's an Olympic sport?" Greyson exclaimed louder than he intended.

"You better concentrate on this game," Nolan warned as he dropped in four quarters and then handed Greyson the wooden rack.

As Greyson dug out the balls, Tanya said, "What are the teams?"

"How about me and you versus them?" Nolan suggested, nodding to Greyson and Hannah.

"Not sure if that's fair, but why not?" she shrugged.

When Greyson finished organizing the balls into the rack, Nolan handed Tanya a cue and said, "You wanna break?"

"You bet your ass," she said, then sailed to the opposite end of the table. She quickly lined up the cue ball, then deftly struck the triangle of balls, knocking two in.

"Fuck me," Nolan blurted out in amazement.

Greyson turned to Hannah and said, "It's gonna be a long game."

"I think you mean it's gonna be a short game," Tanya corrected as she glided by and swiftly knocked in another ball.

"Boom, we're solids!" Nolan cheered gleefully.

Hannah and Greyson settled into a pair of raised spectator chairs that seemed to only be found around pool tables. "So, if pool's not your game, what is?" Hannah asked.

"Honestly, I'm rubbish at most games and practically all sports. Well, I'm decent at a few video games. I got so into *Call of Duty* in college that I considered becoming a vet."

"Which branch of the military would you have gone into?"

Greyson shook his head. "Oh no, I mean veterinarian. *Call of Duty 4* has these adorable attack dogs that just make your heart swell."

Hannah lightly shoved him, and he nodded over to Nolan. "Seriously though, he's the one that's aces at pretty much any game, sport, or competition. Well, maybe not spelling."

On cue, Nolan shouted, "Someone get this woman a fin! She's running the table," after Tanya sank another ball.

"I know what you mean. Tanya quickly becomes an expert at everything she sets her mind to," Hannah said, then leaned over and whispered, "It's kinda annoying."

Greyson smiled. "Right? The nerve of these people. Why can't you be awkward, clumsy, and inadequate like the rest of us?"

Tanya finally missed a shot, then glared over at Greyson. "Happy?"

"Maybe not happy. More like relieved," he shot back, then put his hand out to Hannah and said, "After you."

She hopped down and selected a cue stick from the wall, then lined up a shot. After a short pause, she slammed a striped ball into the corner pocket. Then she slowly strutted by Tanya, grinning, causing her to warn, "Oh, you don't want none of this."

As Hannah studied the table, Nolan asked Tanya, "Does it bother you that nowadays, with social media, anyone can be a model?"

"I wouldn't call taking pictures with your cell phone in a parking garage being a model," she replied, then paused for a moment and added, "That sounded snarky. Honestly, do whatever makes you happy and helps you feel good about yourself. Social media has a dark side, though. From pathetic trolls to stalky psychopaths, girls have to be especially careful now. But I've always said anyone can be a model."

Nolan scoffed, "Yeah, right." Then, after Hannah dropped another ball in, he proclaimed, "Damn, we got two hustlers here."

Tanya nodded to Hannah and said, "Okay, that was a good shot," then turned to Nolan and continued, "No, seriously. It's less about looks and more about how you carry yourself and exude confidence. When done right, the camera can see through all the bullshit of hair and makeup to capture your essence. That's why it's more than just looking pretty and posing. I'd rather see a million pictures of someone just as they opened their dream birthday present than a statuesque woman selling a car or whatever."

After Hannah narrowly missed her next shot, Nolan took the cue and joked, "Yeah, but it's a lot easier to wank it to the statuesque woman."

As he leaned over the table to take his shot, Greyson's gaze followed Hannah as she climbed into the chair beside him. "Nice shooting, Tex. I thought you said you weren't any good?"

"I think I said I wasn't going to make the Olympic team. But I can hold my own."

"Well, I think you're going to have to hold my own too," he said, then quickly added, "Sorry, that sounded way dirtier than I intended."

"So, you intended it to sound a little dirty?"

Greyson vigorously shook his head. "No, no, not even a—"

Nolan cut him off with, "Your shot, dude."

"I hate this game," Greyson muttered as he stepped down on the floor. Hannah offered him the stick with an encouraging smile. He nearly tripped before taking his shot and missing wildly.

As he walked back, he overheard Nolan mumbling, "Told ya." He looked up at Hannah and just shrugged.

She smiled again. "At least it stayed on the table. I think the important thing is that no one got hurt."

"Tell that to my pride."

Tanya went on another run, which quickly ended the game. Everyone huddled around the pool table and went quiet for a moment as if hearing an invisible end-of-the-night countdown clock emphatically ticking away.

Greyson caught Hannah looking down at her watch and sighed.

"Well, it's getting kind of late. We've got a forty-five-minute drive home, so better call it a night," she said, giving voice to Greyson's fear.

After a minor quarrel over paying for the drinks, they quickly found themselves in the parking lot. "Thanks for coming tonight," Hannah said as she hovered near the passenger door of Tanya's silver BMW.

Greyson stood a couple of feet across from her at the driver's side door of his white Honda Civic. With sagging shoulders, he said, "Thanks for inviting me. Sorry we were so late."

Hannah stepped over and hugged him. Their quick embrace was like an adrenaline rush, and she whispered sanguinely, "Maybe I'll see you at the park tomorrow?"

His face went flush. "Um, okay, yeah. I'll bring the badminton set." A smile widened his reddened face as he watched her get into the car and pull away.

His blitheness was interrupted by Nolan declaring, "I think Tanya kinda liked me."

Chapter Seventeen

Greyson woke the next morning earlier than usual, still piqued from the prior night's get-together. He ambled to the kitchen and rotely made oatmeal while trying desperately not to overanalyze every interaction with Hannah.

"What are you going to do about Ansley?" Nolan asked, lumbering into the kitchen and grabbing a container of Greek yogurt.

The question jarred Greyson out of his basking in the glow of last night's quasi-date, like a blaring car horn snapping one's highway hypnosis. They took opposite seats at the tiny kitchen table with their respective breakfasts. Nolan had asked the same question as they drove home last night, and Greyson gave him the same answer: "I don't know."

"You better figure it out ASAP. I was surprised she wasn't waiting for us when we got home," he said, then added, "with a butcher's knife."

That same thought had crossed Greyson's mind, minus the knife part, when he pulled up to their apartment complex. He was relieved when they trundled up the stairs to a vacant doorway. "You wanna know the truth?" he asked.

"Probably not but go ahead."

"The thought of getting back together with her did cross my mind. It was very fleeting, like a squirrel scampering across a road, but I did entertain the notion. Then, when we got to the party and I saw Hannah, I knew I could never go back," Greyson said, then spooned oatmeal into his mouth.

Nolan sat up straight and pushed away from the table. "Are you fucking mental? Why the hell would you even consider getting back with Ansley?"

"I don't know. Seeing her suddenly at the door like that, I guess I didn't realize how much I missed her. And home, of course. She actually said she was sorry. That's something I've only heard her say maybe two or three times in our whole relationship."

Nolan nodded. "Well, you never actually broke up with her. Just sort of left the relationship on pause."

"No, I told her we should take this opportunity to figure our lives out independently of each other. Then I moved across the country. You don't need a psychic to figure it out."

"What the fuck does that even mean?" Nolan scoffed. "You didn't have the balls to completely end things, so you figured, what? You'd move away, and it would die out like an abandoned campfire? Jokes on you, 'cause that campfire turned into a raging forest fire."

Greyson opened his mouth to object, but he realized his friend was not entirely wrong. "Things had been so bad during that last year; I just figured she'd relish us being apart and come to realize that it's for the better. But you're right, I should have at least ended it before leaving."

"Instead of leaving her hanging," Nolan added.

"I guess she deserved better than that."

Nolan shook his head. "I still think she's a succubus, but no one deserves to be ghosted like that. Plus, it would have been better for you to get that full disclosure."

"I think you mean closure," Greyson corrected. "I tried to end it last night, but I messed that up too. Suddenly seeing her after several months like that just threw me for a loop."

"I know what you're saying. You haven't been laid in so long that you weren't thinking straight. I get that, man."

Greyson chuckled at his friend's interpretation of his admission. For Nolan, all relationship discourse revolved around intercourse. To him, a cigar was always a penis. "I guess—" Greyson started to say.

A buzz from his phone interrupted him. Nolan glanced down at the vibrating mobile and said, “Speak of the fucking devil.”

Greyson knew who it must be even before Nolan’s confirmation. He reached down, scooped up his phone, and said, “Hello,” with a sense of dread in the pit of his stomach.

Ansley said, “Hey, I hope it’s not too early.”

“No, it’s fine.”

“I’m sorry about just showing up out of the blue like that yesterday. It’s always such a demonstrative and romantic gesture in the movies, but I guess in real life it’s more awkward and jarring.”

He noticed that Nolan had already absconded to his room and was grateful to be without an audience for this heavy undertaking. He sighed softly, knowing this would not be a short or easy conversation. An image of Hannah smiling across from him in the booth last night flashed into his mind, acting like a mental shot of espresso, giving him the energy to proceed.

Chapter Eighteen

I love this time of year. Each weekend seems to get a little bit lovelier than the last, Hannah thought as she gazed across the pond. A polite breeze blew across her face, almost like a delicate kiss on the cheek, saying *thanks for noticing.*

The sun soared overhead, hugging everything in its radiant glow, or at least that's how Hannah's mood perceived it. Nature seemed to be serenading her with a song of encouragement. A majestic spring day prophesying the coming of summer. It was the first time she'd sat on this bench and felt serenity since before her husband's death.

I can finally remember why I love this place so much. Immediately after the thought occurred, she felt a pang of guilt. There was an innate darkness still buried deep inside her that resisted any desire for joy.

"I do deserve to be happy," she whispered. It was an adolescent mantra abandoned over the years, but now it seemed more apropos than ever. She turned her thoughts to Greyson and recognized an emerging feeling. A familiar sentiment that both thrilled and, at the same time, terrified her.

He's a lot like Van, yet so very different. He could almost be his younger brother, minus the confidence and self-reliance. And, of course, the background and upbringing. As she mused, her gaze was drawn to a raft of ducks waddling down to the shore below.

Van had grown up all over the country and had come to LA for a job. He'd lost both parents to illness—his mother to cancer and his father to heart disease—and didn't have many friends. He was the old-school definition of an introvert, and Hannah always felt a sense of distinction to be the one that he'd finally let into his life.

Although Greyson was similar in appearance and demeanor, he was what her mother would call a "mangenue." She was certainly the authority on young, inexperienced men. Two of her former husbands were intimacy novices that ended up being just too much effort for her to handle.

"You look pensive," a voice breezed in from beside her.

She turned and had to fight back a beaming smile that desperately wanted to shine. "I'm always pensive. This place just magnifies it."

She glided across the bench in an inviting gesture, and Greyson sat down. He was wearing an old 17th Street Surf Shop T-shirt and a newer pair of jeans. "I like your, uh, shoes," he said.

Hannah reflexively looked down at her worn Nikes and wondered what that was supposed to mean. Was it a swipe at her lack of style, even though it was wholly appropriate for their setting? Or was he just one of those sneakerheads who turned an appreciation for what she grew up calling tennis shoes into an elaborate obsession?

"I forgot to tell you that last night, so this is my weak attempt to make up for that. And it wasn't just the shoes; you looked fantabulous," he said with a faint blush.

"Fantabulous, that's much better than nice," she replied.

"I always thought it was a made-up word. Like slang or something. Kinda like ginormous. But it's in the dictionary, so it must be legit."

Hannah, who'd never bothered to ponder it, said, "It probably started off as slang. I read that they added 'chillax' to the dictionary. If that can make it, the door's open for anything."

"You mean cover," he said, miming opening a book. "But yeah, adding 'chillax' is like Joey Tribbiani getting into Harvard."

"Or Rose Nylund," she countered quickly.

"I say *Friends*; you say *Golden Girls*. Let's call the whole thing off," he intoned.

She smiled, and in that instant of their admittedly prosaic banter, she knew. Not that she knew she was in love; that was more of a movie or book trope. *In reality, love isn't so much an epiphany as it is a conclusion,* she realized. But she did know that she was now in the midst of an irresistible pull to Greyson Caden Squires. Together, they were entering the orbit of a nascent relationship.

The moment was interrupted by a reverberant sound emanating from Greyson's stomach. "I guess there's a rumble in my jungle," he said embarrassingly. "Sorry, I didn't have time for lunch."

She nodded and said, "You have to listen to your body. But now that your stomach has mentioned it, I could go for something to eat."

Greyson quickly pressed the opening. "Do you wanna go grab a bite somewhere?"

"Sure, what are you in the mood for?"

"Oh boy, the first compatibility test—food," he teased. "This is a big one. Do I go fast food or fine dining? Basic American or ethnic restaurant? Table seating or food truck?"

"Do I overthink it or go with my gut?"

"Don't mock. This is a watershed moment here," he said with an exaggerated sense of severity. "The options are Rubik's Cuban. My choice will be an indictment of my character."

"Look, I'm just a simple gal."

"In my experience, there's no such thing."

"Ten points to Gryffindor," she said with a sly smile. "But seriously, what does your stomach tell you?"

He scrunched his face and said, "Honestly, it's grumbling for a burger and fries."

"I could do that. Next question is inevitably 'where?'"

"Right. Do we go fast food or fine dining—" he repeated before being cut off.

"Have you been to In-N-Out yet?"

Greyson's eyes lit up like a child's on Christmas morning. "No! I have been meaning to, though."

"It's a rite of passage for all those who come to the Golden State. I personally recommend the Double-Double combo."

"You had me at combo," he grinned as he stood up. "Lead the way."

* * *

After he'd finished his meal, he wiped his mouth and declared, "It absolutely lived up to the hype."

"I'm glad you enjoyed it. Now, you are a true Angeleno," she said, then backpedaled. "Although no true Angeleno would use the term Angeleno."

"Good to know. So…" he said, then paused as he watched a mother trying to feed French fries to a recalcitrant child.

"So, where to next?" Hannah asked.

Greyson raised his eyebrows and said, "You're the de facto tour guide; what do you recommend?"

"Ever been to the Griffith Observatory?"

"That is literally the first thing on my LA bucket list," he gasped. "Okay, maybe second after the Jaws ride at Universal Studios."

"The observatory's one of…" She stopped herself before saying, "Van's favorite places." She felt an instant pang of anguish during her pause, then promptly buried it and said, "LA's most iconic and interesting places."

Greyson lifted both of their plastic trays as he stood up and said, "You had me at 'the.' Let's go."

"We're pretty close to my house; do you mind if we drop my car off and just ride together?" Hannah asked as she rose from the table.

"No, that would be great. It will give me an excuse to turn off NPR."

"Great. I'm less than ten minutes from here," she said, following him to the exit.

After dumping their trash in the receptacle, he turned and said, "But now arises the second compatibility test."

"What, temperature compatibility?" she asked.

"Nope, that's the sixth."

"It should really be higher. Is it chore compatibility?"

He gave her a quizzical look, and she explained, "You know, finding that special person who is willing to do the chores you abhor. Like taking out the trash or vacuuming."

He nodded. "Oh, yeah, that's number seven on the list. I'm talking about musical compatibility. Especially trapped in such a confined space as a car."

"I'm afraid it's either go 80s or go home," she teased.

He smiled as he opened the door for her. "I can definitely do 80s."

"Baby, have you got enough gas?" she sang as she passed him, then stepped out into the parking lot.

It took a moment for Greyson to process the reference to Prince's "Little Red Corvette," but when he finally did, he duly replied, "Oh yeah."

Chapter Nineteen

The drive was pleasant, or at least as pleasant as a Sunday drive in Los Angeles can be. LA may not have invented traffic, but it quickly imperfected it. As they pulled into the parking lot, the song "California Dreamin'" came on causing Greyson to quickly switch stations. He glanced over at Hannah and explained, "Sorry, that song's bad luck for me."

After they parked, Greyson rushed over to open Hannah's door. "Milady," he breathed.

"Why thank you, sir," she said as she stepped out.

As they hiked past the rows of cars, Greyson gazed up at the grand white building unfurling in front of them. "Jeez, it's bigger than I thought."

Did he really say, "Jeez?" Hannah mused as a smile cracked her lips. She led him up through the parking lot onto the walkway. "Let's walk around first. I want to take advantage of the sunlight so you can take in the city sprawl."

They headed to the left and strolled around one of the smaller copper domes. They moved through the undulating rabble of people like surfers paddling against the tide. "Is it always this crowded?" he whispered to her as they found an open spot on the back terrace.

"On a lovely, clear Sunday like this, everything's crowded," she replied, then nodded to the scenery before them.

"Wow, this view is magnificent!" Greyson exclaimed as he leaned against the barrier.

"It is, isn't it?" Hannah agreed, soaking in the panoramic view of downtown LA. It was almost the antithesis of her favorite spot, but still breathtaking nonetheless.

"I can see my apartment from here," he joked as he admired the cityscape.

She backed up from the stone barricade and turned to Greyson. "Wait till you see it at night. There's something—I don't know, magical sounds trite, but it's the best I can do."

"I bet."

She watched him survey the vastness below in wonderment. *Sometimes he seems so young. And I don't know why, but that makes me feel so—*

"Speaking of trite, the city looks so tiny from up here," he said, interrupting her thoughts.

As she regarded him, she realized that everyone probably seemed young whenever experiencing something truly awe-inspiring for the first time. *I bet this is why older folks love to travel to new places so much. New environments and experiences must help to rejuvenate the soul. Still, he has to be in his late twenties. What's he doing with a woman staring down forty?*

He turned and noticed her lost in thought. "Ruble for your ruminations," he said.

"Huh?" she whispered, as she was snapped back into the moment.

"Pound for your ponderings. Ostmark for your observations," he continued. "It just looked like you were in a galaxy far, far away."

"Oh, nothing really. Sometimes I get swept up in my own circumspection. It's like a mental undertow," she said, flustered. "I was just wondering... why me?"

"Why *you* what?"

Surprised by her statement, she quickly decided to follow her stream of superconsciousness. "I just mean, why did you stop and talk to me that day in the park?"

Confusion washed over his face, and she rushed to explain. "I don't mean it to come off as interrogating; I was just wondering why a cute, smart young man would want to strike up a conversation with..." She stopped herself from uttering "a broken-down old widower," and meekly finished with, "me."

He paused for a moment as he scanned the vista, then said, "Why wouldn't I stop to talk to you?"

"I can think of plenty of reasons."

"I can't," he quickly replied, then turned back and met her gaze. "It's not like I had any grand scheme or motive. I was just walking around, saw you sitting there, and this feeling came over me that said, 'She'd be interesting to talk to.' I know that sounds weird, but there was just something about you that seemed inviting."

Now it was her turn to look perplexed, so he clarified, "Inviting is probably a bad word choice. That makes it sound like you had this flashing sign that said, 'Come up and see me sometime.' I guess a better word would be intriguing. It was like I suddenly had to talk to you. I'm not sure how to explain it, but it somehow felt fated."

"Fated," she repeated softly.

"And for the record, I don't believe in fate. But it's the best way I can describe the pull I felt."

She smiled. "No, I like fated. It works in a situation where nothing makes sense. At least, nothing rational."

He casually leaned against the railing. "I could put you on the hot seat and ask, 'Why did you talk to me?' You could've easily dismissed me before I went all gimme relationship therapy on you."

"That's fair. I guess there was just this vibe I got from you that was… soothing, maybe? Even though you were a complete stranger, there was something calming about you."

"Like I'm human Xanax?"

She laughed. "That's one way to put it. But even now, being with you is almost preternaturally comfortable." She nearly added, "My first husband had a similar effect on me," but realized she didn't want to go down that prickly path.

"So now I'm like an old pair of shoes?"

She shook her head. "I mean relaxing, as in being around you puts me at ease. And I haven't felt that way in a very long time." She made eye contact with Greyson and continued, "It's like you said, there's just something here that defies prudence."

"That's probably the best way to put it. It's like they say, there's only one way to explain the unexplainable."

She squinted as she reluctantly asked, "How?"

"Unsuccessfully," he said with a huge grin.

She rolled her eyes, then turned around and said, "Let's go inside. If you think the view of the city is spectacular, wait until you see the universe."

They spent the better part of the day exploring the observatory. It was a cycle of Hannah asking questions and Greyson enthusiastically over-explaining. The way he'd get lost in exposition and then apologize for it just seemed to endear him more to her.

Although Hannah had been here before, experiencing it with Greyson for the first time made it all the more invigorating. Sharing in his passion gave her a new perspective on not just the stars and planets, but all the science behind our knowledge of them. He was a patient and interesting companion who never talked down to her and always looked to engage instead of lecture.

When they finally exited the building, a blanket of darkness had quickly fallen. "Now you have to check out that view again to appreciate how mere circumstance can change something familiar into something unexpected," Hannah said as she grabbed his hand and led him towards the back again. "It's beautiful during the day, but transcendent at night."

"Lead the way," he replied, happily drifting like a balloon on a string behind her.

Their spot was clear of rubberneckers, so they cozied back up against the short stone wall. Hannah stared out across the canyon. "And it's not just the glow of the city; it's all the houses and buildings that dot the landscape like distant stars that have fallen to Earth."

As she gazed out in reverence, Greyson stole a glance that, if caught, would've revealed how completely enamored he was with Hannah. He allowed himself to indulge in the moment as he studied the curve of her face. When the beat ended, he turned toward the much less inspiring view and smiled.

* * *

As Greyson drove Hannah home, the car was quiet, save for the sound of the occasional synthesizer. When he pulled up behind her car, she turned and said, "Thanks for a..." then paused.

"Nice—I mean, good time? Lovely time? Maybe even a stupendous time," he finished, hoping for more of the latter than the former.

"How about wonderful with a side of surprising?" she beamed.

He smiled back. "I'll take wonderful. As long as it's a good surprise and not a bad one, like getting socks for Christmas."

"Right now, all surprises tend to be good ones."

"Awesome, then I hope we can do this again," he said, then quickly added, "The sooner, the better." He immediately regretted the coda and blurted out, "I still like your shoes."

She couldn't help but smile at his nervous awkwardness. Then, without thinking, she leaned over and kissed him. It was a quick but passionate kiss. The kind that was like a perfect opening line to a novel, offering the promise of more eloquence to come.

When their lips parted, he simply breathed, "Whoa."

She opened the door and said, "Call me later?"

As she swung her legs around and stood up, he tilted his head quizzically, as if contemplating the definition of "later." Before he could speak, she glanced back and said, "Or sooner," then closed the car door.

He nodded and whispered, "Sooner sounds so much better than later," while watching her glide into her house.

Chapter Twenty

"What's with the permagrin?" Nolan hollered from the couch as Greyson breezed into the apartment.

The residue of the date clung to him like cologne, but he said nothing as he dropped his keys onto the console table beside the door. He lumbered into the living room like a sleepwalker, immersed in the most pleasant of dreams.

Nolan paused the action movie he'd been half watching, regarded his friend for a moment, then declared, "Wait, that's a look that says, 'I just got lucky.'"

"In a manner of speaking," Greyson replied as he melted into the old recliner.

"That means no," Nolan said disappointedly.

"It just depends on your definition of luck."

Nolan waved his arms over his head. "Oh, here we go."

Greyson ignored the histrionics and said, "I think having the greatest date of your life warrants the term 'lucky.'"

"And you just broke up with Ansley. Damn, you're faster than me."

Greyson shot him an exaggeratedly icy stare. "I didn't just break up with her. We haven't been together for almost six months."

"Don't try to play the relationship semantics game with me. You admitted that you were considering getting back together with her last night."

Greyson vehemently shook his head and said, "I said briefly, as in like a nanosecond."

"Sorry, bud, but even a brief contemplation resets the clock."

"Can you please stop pissing on my parade? Ansley is now and forever in the past."

"You're the one that's forever in the past," Nolan said, "Don't get me wrong, I'm glad she's gone and all, but I gotta admit, her tits are *the* tits. What's with her thumbs, though?"

"Huh?"

Nolan lifted his hand, wiggled his thumb around, and said, "I never noticed before, but she's got, like, big-toe thumbs."

"She's got clubbed thumbs. It's not that uncommon," Greyson said quietly as if they were suddenly in a library. It was a knee-jerk reaction to the one thing Ansley was self-conscious about.

"I bet she never loses at thumb wrestling with those Andre the Giant thumbs," Nolan snorted. When Greyson didn't respond, he switched conversation lanes and asked, "So, when do I have to go find a tux?"

Greyson paused for a beat, then said, "It's not like that. I just said it was a wonderful date. Who knows about the future? Anyway, her husband died not too long ago, so I don't think she's ready to rush into anything."

"How'd he die?"

Greyson grimaced and said, "I don't know; I didn't ask."

"Why the hell not?" Nolan said as if it were on the same introductory level as asking someone's name.

"You know I hate it whenever someone finds out my mother died, and the first thing they ask is how. Like it's my duty to feed their morbid curiosity."

Nolan shook his head. "It's not like that; it's more of a natural thing to follow up with. It's up there with saying, 'I'm sorry.'"

"That one bugs me too. How am I supposed to reply to, 'I'm sorry to hear your mother died'?" Greyson huffed. "Apology accepted?"

Nolan leaned back against the couch with a faraway look for several seconds. Finally, he said, "I think there's just nothing you can say when you hear that someone died. But you feel this overwhelming need to at least acknowledge it. They don't mean anything by it; they just wish it didn't happen. Of course, you can't say that exactly, but you have to say something, so you just say, 'I'm sorry.'"

"I guess," Greyson said, as he picked at a worn spot on the armrest.

"I don't think any date that doesn't end in sex can be classified as one of the greatest dates in your life," Nolan said with a smirk.

Greyson recognized his friend's not-so-subtle effort to try and steer the conversation back to more comfortable waters and said, "For you, maybe. But for the rest of us whose minds aren't controlled by our genitals, it damn sure can be."

Nolan swatted the dig away like it was a mosquito. "Okay, if it didn't end naked and sweaty, how did it end? Did y'all finish a crossword puzzle together or something?"

It ended with a sweet goodnight kiss and a promise of connecting later, he thought but knew Nolan wouldn't understand. "I dropped her off and told her I'd call her later." It might not have been the complete truth, but it wasn't a total lie either.

Nolan smiled like a proud father watching his son leg out a triple. "I have taught you well. Always leave 'em wanting more, but not knowing exactly when to expect it."

"Whatever the hell that means."

"So, do you have a plan?"

Greyson furrowed his brow. "What do you mean?"

"I know you, dude. You love these big romantic moments, but there's usually something that holds you back from moving forward."

Greyson dismissed the accusation. "You don't always need some grandiose plan. Sometimes it's okay to just live in the now."

"I call bullshit." Nolan snickered. "That's why you stayed with Ansley so long after the relationship expiration date. You had this shared history together, and you equated that with safety. Being with her meant you didn't have to face an undetermined future."

Greyson's jaw went slack at his friend's insight. Nolan did occasionally have these lightning-strike moments of astuteness. It was a result of nearly twenty years of familiarity, and primarily why he was Greyson's closest companion.

"I bet when you were banging Ansley, right before you climaxed, you thought back to how y'all first met," Nolan continued.

And he's back, Greyson thought as he shook his head. "Naw, I was too busy thinking about the laws of thermodynamics."

Nolan frowned and said, "What the hell?"

"You know how some guys think about baseball?" Greyson said, disappointed that he had to explain the joke.

It took half a beat, and then Nolan's face lit up like he'd just gotten the answer to final Jeopardy. "Oh, got it."

"Anyway, I'm not avoiding anything. I guess I'm just taking it slow and going with the flow," Greyson said. Nolan looked at him sideways until he continued, "Really. I mean, yes, I like her, and of course, I want to see her again, but this isn't the same as a college romance. It's like she's already lived a whole 'nother life. She's a widow, has a successful entertainment career, and—"

"Oh my god, she's got grandkids, doesn't she?" Nolan interrupted.

Greyson shook his head. "She doesn't have any kids." Then he glanced away as if he heard someone at the door and added, "At least, as far as I know."

"I mean, you're making it sound like she's a senior citizen. She didn't look that old. What is she, 35?" Nolan asked. After Greyson shrugged, he continued the inquisition. "What's her last name?"

"Dunno."

Nolan slapped the couch and said, "What the hell, man? You don't know anything about her. She could be a serial killer, and her late husband was her last victim."

"Why does it always go from ordinary person straight to serial killer? It's way more likely that she's an opioid addict, kleptomaniac, or cyberterrorist. But no, it's either you're a normal person or you're a mass murderer."

"Probably 'cause I'd still bone an opioid addict, a kleptomaniac, or a cyberterrorist."

"You probably have." Greyson chuckled. "But you'd draw the line at serial killer?"

Nolan tilted his head up, briefly inspected the popcorn ceiling, then said, "Guess it depends on what she looks like. Like, are we talking about Charlize

Theron from *Reindeer Games* or Charlize Theron from *Monster*?"

Before Greyson could reply, Nolan looked back at him and said, "I'm just playing. No way would I risk my life, even for Penthouse letter-worthy sex."

"That's a relief. I was about to go grab the phone book and search for the nearest psychiatrist."

"Do they still make phone books?"

Greyson nodded. "We got one in the mail a couple of weeks after moving in."

"Hmm, who knew?" Nolan hummed, then looked Greyson in the eyes and asked, "Seriously, what's your next step?"

Greyson started to shrug, then admitted, "I guess call her after work either tomorrow or Tuesday and see if she wants to go out again."

"For the love of your own sex organ, please make it Tuesday. The quickest way to scare off a girl is to be needy-over-easy."

"Fine, I'll call her Tuesday," Greyson acquiesced, then wondered if he'd be able to hold out that long. He viewed listening to Nolan as the classic lady or the tiger dilemma. The trick, of course, was figuring out which piece of advice was sage and which would lead straight into claws and fangs.

"You should text her; calling someone is so last decade," Nolan said, then added, "But since she's a grandma, you're right, you should probably call. She might not know how to text."

"She's already texted me, dumbass," Greyson snapped, then reached down to the coffee table, snatched up the closest *Entertainment Weekly*, and launched it at Nolan. He blocked it with his forearm, yelling, "Ninja!"

"I'm kind of starving; what do we have to eat?" Greyson asked as his attention once again turned to his stomach.

Chapter Twenty-One

Hannah exhaled a long breath as she glanced around her small workspace at the studio. *This could be one of the last times I'm here,* she thought wistfully. Then she looked at Tanya sitting across from her and asked, "What do you think about going international?"

Tanya looked up from her computer. "You know I'm always up for a trip. You thinking about taking the show on the road?"

"We're already planning to go on the road to different colleges. I mean going to culinary schools worldwide."

"I think they call them unis across the pond." Tanya chewed her bottom lip for a moment. "It's going to be expensive."

"True, but we'd only do it a couple times a year. Maybe during big events like Carnival in Spain. This way we could feature cultures, foods, and dishes from all over the world."

"It would definitely add spice to the show. But aren't we supposed to be working on the pilot? It's a little too early to be looking that far down the road." Before Hannah could reply, Tanya added, "Or sea or air. Whatever."

Hannah leaned back in her chair and stretched. "You're right, I guess I'm just fried. Is it okay if we call it a day? We got a lot done, and I can work on the rest later."

Tanya shrugged as she closed her laptop. "Alright then, spill the tea."

"What tea?"

"Honey, you really need to start watching *Ru Paul's Drag Race*. Tea means gossip. Like what happened when a certain best friend of mine went on a date with a certain science nerd."

"Oh, that," Hannah replied, playing coy. "Nothing to tell, really."

Tanya leaned in close as if waiting to hear a juicy secret. "I wanna hear everything, from A to Zee penetration." She said the last bit in a surprisingly spot-on Dr. Ruth impression.

Hannah couldn't help but laugh at her friend's directness. "What do you think? I brought him home and had wild sex?"

"No, you're way too classy for that," Tanya said, shaking her head. "I think you got a room at the Roosevelt and did the dirty there."

"It wasn't like that at all." Hannah paused for just a moment, reveling in the idea that she could have this torrid dalliance.

While she was busy pseudo-fantasizing, Tanya asked, "Then, what was it like?"

"It was, I don't know… pleasant."

Tanya let out a sudden and booming snoring sound. "Please tell me I didn't waste my entire day waiting to hear about 'pleasant.'"

"I thought you came here to, you know, work. Not to get some steamy tea."

Tanya twirled her chair away from Hannah. "Don't start using my word now."

"I'm just saying we got the whole pilot outlined. That should be enough of a reward. You don't *need* to hear the details of a beautifully brilliant date that ended with perhaps the sweetest kiss in the history of sweet kisses."

Tanya immediately spun back around and gaped at Hannah. "You serious? So pleasant suddenly turned into beautifully brilliant?"

"I had a little more time to reflect on it," Hannah said with a wide grin.

"Okay, then take it from the top."

Hannah recapped the date, concentrating more on how she felt than the prosaic details of the event. She described the scenes viscerally, like a play-by-play announcer tasked with conveying the emotions of the game instead of the literal action.

When she finished, Tanya whispered, "Beautifully brilliant."

Hannah replied with a buoyant smile. Tanya looked away and said, "You know, I hate you sometimes."

"Huh?"

"You're like a—what's the opposite of an asshole?" Tanya asked, then blurted out, "Saint. You're a saint magnet."

"What?" Hannah huffed. "You know damn well I've had my share of assholes too."

"Yeah, but you also tend to find the good ones just as easily. You know, guys that act like characters straight out of a romance novel. Written by a woman, of course. The rest of us are lucky to just find a halfway decent guy who isn't hiding a wife and kids somewhere in Utah or a criminal past or an addiction to drugs, gambling, or porn. But you—you attract saints like a thrift store attracts hipsters."

"Van was not a saint. There were plenty of things about him that annoyed me," she replied, then thought about her reflexive statement. To be completely honest with herself, outside of the few typical foibles, the only thing about Van that had bothered her was his reclusiveness. But she'd learned to handle that fairly early on in their relationship and hadn't dwelled on it since.

It was far too early in the courtship to call Greyson a saint. *He could be a serial killer for all I know,* she thought, then dismissed it. *Okay, maybe not a serial killer, but a scoundrel isn't out of the realm of possibilities.* Then she instantly felt a twinge of remorse for such a thought.

"If you compare Van to the average guy out there, the dude was a saint. And this new one sounds like he's cut from the same cloth. Unlike his friend—that Mark Wahlberg knockoff is a toxic masculinity dump," Tanya said while shaking her head. "I can see why Greyson reminded you of Van. There's some resemblance there, in that generic white-boy way. Like, he could be his younger, I don't know, cousin maybe."

Hannah's twinge of guilt suddenly became a throe as Tanya's words echoed in her mind. She'd done a very good job ignoring her constant companion for the last couple of days, but now it was back like a rash believed long since healed. Then, the guilt splintered into fear, and tears abruptly welled in her eyes.

Tanya noticed the sudden change, like ominous clouds hijacking a sunny day, and said, "I'm so sorry, honey, I wasn't thinking." Then, she reached over the desk and squeezed her friend's hand. "You know me; I don't always think before I speak. It's one of my fatal flaws. Right up there with impeccable style and grace."

Hannah wiped away the tears with the back of her other hand. "It's okay; it's not your fault. Sometimes the gloom just hits me outta the blue like that."

"It doesn't help when your best friend thoughtlessly runs her mouth off, either."

Hannah placed her hand on top of Tanya's. "Stop. You should be able to mention Van without me immediately falling to pieces. I promise you, I am getting better."

"I know you are. I can really tell these last couple of weeks."

Hannah considered the unspoken implication that her getting better coincided with her meeting Greyson. *There may be a kernel of truth to that, but correlation is not always causation. I have been doing the work, and I'm not about to surrender all the credit to some man.*

Tanya sprang up from her chair. "Let's put aside the tea and move on to some food and wine, shall we? We have a lot to celebrate, and you can't expect me to do that on a sober stomach."

Hannah rose and followed her out of the office. *Food and wine are good distractors and a tried and true way to quell suffering,* she thought and managed to put the pin back in the emotional hand grenade, at least for the rest of the day.

Chapter Twenty-Two

Greyson got home from work early Tuesday afternoon and had to forcibly stop himself from calling Hannah. *Maybe I will grab a bite to eat first,* he told himself as he laid his phone down on the kitchen counter, like a timed reward. *I can always reason better with a little food in me.*

It was only 4:00, too early for a full-blown dinner, so he made a sandwich. As he painted mustard onto the bread, he calculated what he would say. *The goal is to get another date on the books, so do I lead with that or start with small talk and slowly build up to it?*

He stacked lettuce and tomatoes on top of several slices of turkey and decided to open with "How have you been?" then instantly questioned himself. *That sounds like I haven't seen her since college. I need something more personal. Jesus, only being with Ansley since high school has really arrested my dating game.*

As he picked up the sandwich, his phone buzzed like an angry swarm of hornets, startling him. His heart jackrabbited when he glanced down and saw that it was Hannah calling. He dropped the sandwich, scooped up the phone, and breathed, "Hello?"

"Answering on the first ring, I like that; it's a good sign," she chirped.

The mere sound of her voice was like someone flooring his emotional accelerator, and his heart jumped from fifty to eighty mph. "To be honest, I answered out of fear."

"I'm sorry, what?"

He realized what he'd said sounded fairly rude and quickly explained, "I was making a sammy and the phone was sitting on the counter, and when it buzzed, it sounded like a transformer blowing up. I mean an electrical transformer, not a robot in disguise."

"I'm sorry—"

He quickly interrupted with, "Oh no, don't be. I'm glad you called."

"No, I mean, I didn't hear a word after you called your sandwich a sammy," she teased.

He laughed and said, "Oh yeah, sorry. Old habit." He considered explaining why he, as a twenty-eight-year-old professional, would use such adolescent slang, then thought maybe it was better to move the conversation forward with the ubiquitous "What's up?"

She gave the orthodox response, "Not much," then, after a beat, said, "I was just wondering if you were up for dinner tonight. But since you're making a sammy..." She left the invite hanging in the air like she was setting up a volleyball.

Greyson eagerly spiked her pass and replied, "Dinner sounds fantastic. Do you want to go out or eat in?"

"That's a good question," she said, then paused.

He considered his own question for a moment. Going out meant adding an extra layer to the getting ready process, followed by the additional discomfort of eating at a public restaurant amid a sea of strangers. There was considerably more intimacy in a relaxed and private setting. Greyson quickly tried to sweeten one side of the choice and said, "I could always make my world-famous spaghetti."

"Don't you mean pasghetti?" she quipped.

"No way, I haven't said pasghetti in nearly twenty..." he said, then paused for effect and finished with "days."

"Cute," she laughed and hesitated again. Greyson unconsciously held his breath until she said, "Spaghetti it is. What time should I come over?"

Greyson turned to scrutinize his surroundings. He edged over to the living room, which looked like someone had stepped on a man-mine, thanks primarily to Nolan. There was an old pizza box lying on top of the askew coffee table, surrounded by various types of beer and soda cans. Assorted remotes and game controllers were scattered about, and all the furniture was adorned in dirty clothes, from jackets to t-shirts to unmentionables. He glanced back to the bathroom at the end of the hall and shuddered.

Finally, he said, "I'll need at least an hour for meal prep and an hour for me prep, so how about around six?"

"An hour for meal prep?" she asked incredulously. "That better be some homemade pasta and sauce."

"I did say world-famous," he said as he opened the pantry door and grabbed a box of Barilla angel hair.

"World-famous, huh? I think your mouth's writing checks your culinary skills can't cash."

"I'm going to make you eat those words," he replied, with a generous helping of imitation smugness.

"Guess we'll find out at six."

"I guess we will. I'll text you my address."

"See you soon," she said, then ended the call.

Greyson scrambled to first clean the apartment, from kitchen to bathroom. He even christened their vacuum, which had been bought on their second day in the apartment and promptly forgotten about. It wasn't exactly a deep clean, but after ninety minutes of sweat and toil, Greyson was suitably impressed.

He used the remaining time to get himself ready for the impromptu date. After jumping in the shower to scrub off the remnants of apartment filth, he then shaved and sculpted his hair. He scanned his closet and quickly settled on jeans and a black polo shirt. As he was carefully tunneling his molded mane through the collar of the shirt, an insistent knock came from the front door.

He glided out of his room, then paused to close Nolan's bedroom door while saying a prayer of thanks that he was working the dinner shift. As he rounded the hallway corner, he took a moment to give the living room one last visual inspection. *It might not be ready for the cover of Better Homes and Gardens, but at least it's no longer a biohazard.*

He turned towards the kitchen, spied the unopened box of pasta and sauce on the counter, and whispered, "Shit." He'd planned to at least have the pans cooking on the stove before she arrived, to carry on the world-famous subterfuge for as long as he could. But the cleaning had taken longer than he imagined, which left him zero time to cover his tracks.

Maybe I shouldn't have set the bar quite so high. Regionally famous might've been wiser. Oh well, the bigger they lie, the harder they fall.

Another loud knock spurred him forward. As he opened the door, he said, "I guess someone's eager for that world-famous—" He cut his sentence short when he realized it was Ansley standing in front of him.

Chapter Twenty-Three

The shock of seeing Ansley standing there hit Greyson like a blast of heat after opening an oven door. She was wearing a very engaging, tight black dress that screamed "fancy date" and not "Pearl Harboring" an ex.

"Jesus, Grey, you look like you've seen a ghost," she said with a smirk.

When he failed to answer, she raised an eyebrow and asked, "World-famous what?"

"Huh," was all Greyson could mutter.

"You said 'eager for a world-famous something.'"

As if waking from a daydream, or more aptly a day terror, Greyson's faculties finally kicked in, and he came up with an excuse. "Oh, tip. I thought you were the pizza guy."

She shot him a confused expression, which he ignored. "What are you doing here, Ansley?"

"Uh-oh, you said my name. That can't mean you're happy to see me."

Greyson said nothing, so she continued, "I told you I was here for the week, and I figured you'd be off from work by now, so I thought I would stop by. You know, try and finish our conversation from yesterday."

"I thought we'd finished that conversation."

"Don't be silly. I'm not letting you go that easily. And not after a stupid phone call."

Surprise returned to his face as he uttered, "What?"

She took a step forward and was now invading not only his apartment entrance but also his personal space. "Can I come in, or do you want to do this here?"

He instinctively backed up, then stole a glance behind her as she assumed the invitation and marched by. He peered down and scanned the parking lot but saw neither movement nor car lights. A timer in his head started as he wondered how long he had till Hannah got there. And how in the hell could he get rid of Ansley before that?

"Wow, this place looks one hundred percent better," she declared as she surveyed the now tidied-up living room. "What, did the maid finally come?"

He followed behind her, cycling through excuses to escape his current predicament like he was switching channels on a TV. "Is Nolan here?" she asked, with more than a dollop of contempt in her voice.

"No, he's at work," Greyson said, then blurted out, "I'm actually on my way out too."

She reached the couch, spun around to face him, and said, "Really? It looks like you're getting ready to cook spaghetti."

Fuck, he screamed in his head, then calmly said, "That's for later. I have to go… go back to the office and get something I forgot."

She settled down on the couch and said, "I can just wait for you here. I'll even have the food ready when you get back."

Why am I so bad at lying? Nolan would have come up with a bulletproof excuse immediately after opening the door.

Ansley furrowed her brow, like she was working out a math problem, and said, "Wait, why would you order pizza if you were making spaghetti? And leaving? No, you opened the door expecting someone else, didn't you? That's why you said something about world-famous."

"What, no," Greyson hissed while vigorously shaking his head.

"You're cooking for someone, aren't you?" she declared, then her eyes widened. "Am I interrupting a date?"

Before he could respond, the answer came in a light knock from the front door. Greyson bowed his head and thought, *This is gonna be very, very bad.*

When he didn't move, Ansley looked over to the door and said, "You want to get it, or should I?" in a passive-aggressively threatening tone.

Greyson shook his head again and said, "I'll get it." As he trudged to the door, he tried formulating a plan to send Hannah away without damaging their nascent and vulnerable relationship. *Maybe I could say there's a dangerous gas leak, and she has to go. Wait, then why the hell would I be staying?*

He nearly reached the door, still plotting. *What if I say I suddenly came down with something? But then what would hit me so fast? The flu? Food poisoning?* He imagined himself explaining, "Sorry, Hannah, can we postpone dinner? I just got a bad case of explosive diarrhea."

After an ephemeral and futile brainstorm, he exhaled and reluctantly opened the door. Hannah was there in a square-neck. gray plaid shirt and a pair of dark jeans. She was standing cross-legged and holding a bottle of Merlot. "Since you're doing all the hard work, I thought I'd at least provide the beverage," she said, raising the bottle.

His heart sank to his toes as she smiled. "I'm so sorry—" he started to say but was interrupted from behind.

"Don't be rude, Grey, invite her in," Ansley chastised, strolling up after him.

Hannah's face dropped as she saw the blonde woman lurking behind Greyson. "What's going on?" she asked, slowly lowering the wine.

Ansley settled in beside Greyson, regarded Hannah for a long moment, then said, "I know you have a mother complex, but damn, Grey."

Hannah stepped back as if physically struck by the snark. She quickly recovered, looked her in the eyes, and said, "I guess this must be—"

Before she could finish, Ansley cut her off, "I'm Ansley; nice to meet you. I'm Grey's fiancé. Well, I guess you could say fiancé-in-waiting, but we're working on that part. And you are?"

Hannah ignored the question, turned to Greyson, and asked, "What's she doing here?"

"I could ask the same of you," Ansley snapped.

Greyson met Hannah's stinging gaze and said, "She just showed up out of the blue."

Ansley playfully swatted his arm and said, "Not just out of the blue. I mean, we said yesterday that we'd talk later about our future. Well, now is later."

Hannah's face went flush. "I thought you said that it was over?"

"It is—" Greyson started to say, but again, Ansley cut him off.

"What? Is that what he told you? Poor guy probably didn't want to hurt your feelings." Then she quickly looked Hannah up and down and continued, "But I'm sure you're experienced enough to understand that. You know how men are—they either mercilessly crush you outright or they give you a thousand cowardly cuts until you slowly bleed out."

Ansley's words appeared to hit Hannah like a winter draft as she momentarily quivered. "I should have seen this coming," she said, more to herself than to anyone present. "This is what I get when I don't listen to my instincts."

"It's not like that," Greyson protested, but now Hannah interrupted him.

"I don't have time for whatever's going on here," she said, pointing a finger and waving it from Ansley to Greyson. "You shouldn't have lied to me."

"I didn't," he started to say, but as he read the distress and embarrassment on Hannah's face, the rest of the words refused to come out. Something instinctual told him there was nothing he could do or say. At least, presently.

As her eyes started welling up, Hannah sighed, then turned and walked away. Greyson took a step forward to follow when he felt a hand grab his arm. He turned and looked at Ansley as she pulled him back inside.

"Jesus, I hope I didn't say anything to upset her," she said with a triumphant smile.

Chapter Twenty-Four

A bewildered and defeated Greyson slowly closed the door. Ansley said, "Sorry I ruined date night. But honestly, Grey, I don't see you with an older woman. You're too… naive."

Greyson turned to her and scowled as she continued, "That was a mature woman there. She wouldn't have the patience to deal with your, let's just say, youthful anxiousness."

He tried to calm himself before following an impulse to lash out at her. *I will be able to fix things with Hannah,* he told himself, then stormed past Ansley.

She immediately followed, saying, "Not like me. We pretty much grew up together, so I already know everything about you. The good, the bad, and the unfledged."

He stopped, spun around, and faced her. As if recognizing the fire in his eyes, she meekly asked, "What?"

"You didn't even talk to me until we were juniors, so we hardly grew up together," he said, emphasizing the last couple of words. "And you know everything you want to know about me, but it damn sure doesn't mean you know the person I truly am. You only know the version of me that you tried to shape, but that's not who I am anymore. I may have wanted to be that guy for you in the beginning, but I gave that up years ago."

She stepped back and said, "I get that you're angry. I didn't intend to come over and hit your life like some human tornado. But come on, we have too much history together to throw it all away. I'll admit that in the past, I may have tried to..." She paused for just a second, then continued, "Nudge you along, but it wasn't because I was hatching an evil scheme to control you and turn you into my very own Stepford husband. It was because I love you."

He fiercely shook his head and said, "You think adding 'because I love you' at the end of whatever selfish deed somehow makes it okay. Here's the thing: it doesn't. It actually makes it worse because it piles manipulation on top of egocentricity."

"So, this is devolving into a name-calling contest?"

"No," he said frustratedly, then exhaled. "I just don't get why you won't go find someone who already meets what you want in a partner."

She reached out and tried to grab his hand while saying, "Because I want you."

Now it was his turn to step back as he avoided her touch. "This is what I've been trying to tell you for months. You don't want me; you want your idea of me. And I'm not, nor will I ever be, that guy. So, I'm telling you right now to go find someone else because we are over. I don't love you anymore, at least not romantically."

Tears pooled in her eyes, but before she could answer, the door unlocked and swung open. Nolan stepped into the apartment, froze when he saw them blocking his path, and said, "I hope I'm interrupting something."

* * *

"What the hell was all that?" Nolan asked after Ansley charged by him and slammed their front door.

"I don't know where to begin," Greyson groaned. Surprisingly, as the seconds ticked by, relief started washing over him like a warm summer rain. This was the first time he'd actually told Ansley that they were definitely through. He'd tried breaking up with her for over six months, but in a vague and timorous manner, to avoid hurting her and completely severing their connection.

The calamity of the evening, along with a helpful boost from anger, forced him to finally take a forthright and explicit approach. He'd anticipated this moment but actively avoided the unpleasant task like one avoids cleaning out a closet. But with the deed done, it felt as if a stain had been scrubbed from his soul.

Nolan dropped his keys in a bowl and headed into the kitchen. "Start at what in the hell she was doing here? I feel like we need to get a priest to come and exercise this place now."

"I think you mean *exorcise*," Greyson corrected, stressing the *or*.

Nolan opened the fridge and said, "Oh yeah, guess it doesn't make sense for a priest to come here and do Pilates. So, back to why your demon lover was here. I thought you finally exorcized her." He accentuated the "or" mockingly.

Greyson sighed. "I kinda agreed we could finish our talk on the phone sometime this week. I guess she thought that was an open invitation for another unexpected visit."

"So once again you punted, and it came back to bite you, huh?"

Greyson just shrugged as he leaned against the entrance post. He didn't want to relive their conversation, so he changed the subject and asked, "What are you doing home so early?"

"We were dead, so they cut me," Nolan said as he scanned the barren shelves.

He finally slammed the door in disgust and yelled, "Why do we never have anything to eat?"

Greyson watched his roommate move on to the pantry. Nolan stopped when he noticed the box of pasta on the counter and asked, "Are you making spaghetti?"

The question jolted Greyson like a static shock, and he suddenly remembered Hannah and their dinner plan. "Oh shit," he muttered.

Nolan wheeled around and said, "What? There's enough here for two."

Greyson stared at the jar of sauce, which seemed to be taunting him. "I invited Hannah over to make her dinner. Ansley showed up first, and then when Hannah came, she answered the door with me and sort of ruined everything."

"Why the hell did you let her answer the fucking door?" Nolan gasped.

"It's not like I told her, 'Hey, can you get that?' She followed after me," Greyson said, then frantically reached into his pocket and pulled out his phone.

"Dude, you are so fucked," Nolan intoned as Greyson dialed Hannah's number.

It rang twice, and then her voicemail answered, which told Greyson that she probably saw him calling and declined it. *Rejected was more like it,* he thought as he heard the beep, then said almost desperately, "Hey Hannah, I am so sorry about that. She just showed up right before you got here. I... I'm sorry for how she acted. Right after you left, I told her, in no uncertain terms, that it was over. I mean, it was already over in my mind, but I made sure she understood it. I know I mentioned to you that we talked on Saturday, which was totally true, but I did tell her we'd continue the conversation later; I just didn't expect later would be so soon. I wanted more time to figure out a way to, I don't know, not hurt her, I guess. This whole thing looked and sounded way worse than it really is, and I'm so sorry, but I really planned—" The voicemail beeped again, cutting him off.

Greyson lowered the phone and met Nolan's scrutinizing gaze. "Smooth," he said mockingly while giving him a thumbs up. "You should have prepared something instead of winging it like a madman. You said 'I'm sorry' three times."

Greyson hung his head. "I know."

"You say it once, at the end, to show you truly mean it. But if you repeat it over and over like that, it comes off as desperate and disingenuous."

Greyson just nodded. "Don't make me take your phone away again," Nolan warned, referring to the time right after he initially tried to break up with Ansley.

"Was it that bad?" Greyson asked, then instantly regretted the question.

"Naw," Nolan hummed sarcastically. "I'm sure most girls love getting a voicemail that sounds like a rant from the Zodiac Killer. You know how psychosis gets them all wet."

"Fuck," Greyson moaned.

Nolan turned on the stove, then grabbed the steel pot and poured water into it. "Do you think your break-up with the demon seed will take this time?"

Greyson pondered the question for a moment, then said, "I don't know any other way to do it. I've tried the nice guy approach—"

"You mean the cowardly guy approach," Nolan interrupted.

"Whatever. This time, I tried the direct approach. There really isn't any other way."

Nolan dumped the sauce into the smaller pot and asked, "So, what are you going to do about Hannah? I mean, aside from leaving her deranged messages?"

Greyson lifted a hand to his head, quickly massaged his temples, and said, "I wish I knew."

"I'm sure you'll think of something," Nolan said, then turned his full attention to the meal prep, leaving Greyson to ponder a conundrum that had no perceivable solution.

Chapter Twenty-Five

The longer Hannah drove, the more her devastation palliated, almost as if it were a block of ice left out in the sun on a sweltering day. The shock of seeing Ansley next to a visibly disturbed Greyson incited her fight-or-flight response, and she was too tired for the former. She felt like such a fool for allowing her hopes to soar in anticipation of another date and instead crash straight into a melodrama. And what disappointed her the most was the fact that Greyson had lied to her.

She could appreciate the intricacies of a relationship, especially one's first, and would have understood the emotional minefield he was navigating through. She would also have been more cautious about allowing herself to indulge in the feelings that had manifested if only she had known the truth. Misleading her like that took away her emotional dominion.

She pulled up to her house in a fog of ambivalence. As she ambled up to the front door, her phone chimed. She pulled it out of her bag and saw it was Greyson. She stood frozen on her porch, staring down at the phone for a long moment, contemplating whether to answer. Finally, she pressed decline, like a judge banging her gavel, signifying "case closed."

She decided to compartmentalize the entire Greyson situation for the time being and focus on the other aspects of her life, mainly her career and self-care. *I don't have time for liars,* she told herself as she unlocked her door and instantly felt guilty for being so harsh.

But that's exactly what he is, and you deserve someone who's going to treat you with respect, she thought defiantly as she imagined a tiny angelic version of herself standing on her shoulder and nodding along.

She pictured another version on the opposite shoulder, dressed like a risqué devil, warning her, *If you don't give him another chance, you'll be alone for the rest of your life!*

The absurd tableau made her chuckle and helped diffuse the negative spiral. She decided to treat herself to her favorite takeout along with a hearty glass of red wine. Then, she vowed to repel the day's trauma with a new book she'd been eager to read.

* * *

The next morning, Hannah woke with a sense of urgency. She knew an idle mind was fertile ground for depression, so she planned out her week. For Tanya, unemployment was a gift of freedom, but for Hannah, it was a curse of apprehension. The Greyson situation had provided her with not only a welcome distraction from her grief but also from her career angst.

Now, with that situation tucked away in the attic of her mind, she was left staring down the barrel of her anxiety. Thankfully, she had years of self-improvement work and coping mechanisms to help manage her anxiousness. *If only I had been this strong years ago,* she thought, quietly hoping she wasn't overestimating her fortitude.

After plotting out a schedule, she checked her watch and figured it would be okay to turn lunch with her mother into brunch. While she was getting ready, her phone buzzed, almost as if warning her of impending doom. She checked it and saw that it was a text from Greyson. *It would be so much easier to repress the predicament if only he'd stop trying to remind me. Why do men have the worst timing? They're like cops—either never around when you need them or busting down your doors when you don't.*

She wasn't trying to punish him; she just needed time to think. At least that's what she told herself as she disregarded his text, then smirked at her own deception. *Well, I'll need time to think about it once I'm ready.* She put away the phone and finished getting dressed.

Then, without thinking, she did something that she hadn't done in months. She wandered into her office, sunk into the chair, and held her wedding photo. As she gazed down at the image of her younger self standing next to Van, she mentally unlocked the door to her constant companion. It was as if she were unconsciously submitting to the concept, "Better the devil that you know."

As the tears began to flow, she pulled the picture to her chest and hugged it tightly. Something deep inside her said, *At least this pain is earned. At least this misery is justified.*

Chapter Twenty-Six

The only thing Greyson could think of to do about the Hannah situation was basically a rinse and repeat method. Once a day, he'd either call and leave a voicemail explaining and apologizing, or, on the off chance she wasn't getting those, he'd send a backup text. He continued the pattern for the next few days.

The good news was that he hadn't heard back from Ansley. Of course, the catastrophe of losing any chance of a relationship with Hannah tempered that pyrrhic victory. Nolan tried to comfort him with the one-two punch of trite advice, saying, "You hardly knew her anyway," coupled with, "There are so many more nymphs in the sea."

While it was true that he had just met her, he didn't subscribe to the axiom that he barely knew her. He couldn't explain it to Nolan, but there was just something between them that defied logic. They had an instant, ethereal connection that surpassed any notion of time, and its loss haunted him.

He found himself hanging around work late on Friday, dreading going home to a paucity of diversion. At least here, he had a multitude of brain-twisting problems to occupy his consciousness. And the one he always came back to was his white whale—the 2001 conundrum. He could easily lose himself in the enigmatic challenge, like putting on a pair of personal life-cancelling headphones.

"What the hell are you still doing here?" Tsai asked after swinging open the door to their office.

"I could ask you the same thing," Greyson replied, barely looking up from his laptop.

"But you'd be deflecting my question, so you won't," she said as she folded her arms across her chest and leaned against the glass door.

Greyson lowered his head and sighed. "As I was getting ready to leave, I just had this idea that I wanted to check out. Then, I dunno, I got caught up in it."

"Let me guess; 'it' is the 2001 conundrum. You love that mystery more than white people love belting out *Sweet Caroline* in public."

"That's racist," he replied mutely. Then he looked up and met her gaze. "It's a potential game changer—"

"It's a distraction," she interrupted. "Look, I get it; you've had a rough week. But you're not going to fix it by fixating on something that no one's been able to solve. All you're doing is running away from your own shitstorm of a life." She said the last part with a playful grin.

"You say that like it's a bad thing. What's wrong with trying to escape a shitstorm?"

"Because you can't. It's just going to grow while you hide. Think of it like a toothache; the more you try to ignore it, the worse it's going to get."

Greyson paused as he soaked up her words. Finally, he said, "I know, but I've felt so worthless lately that I thought if I could just get this win—" He pointed at his laptop, then continued, "I could prove my significance. I know it sounds silly."

Tsai nodded. "No, I can understand that. But guess what? You prove your significance every single day. You don't need some monumental accomplishment to show that you belong here. All you need to do is keep performing at your usual high level. Listen, and you better never repeat this, but you've exceeded my expectations."

A smile slowly crept over Greyson's face. Before he could say anything, she said, "Don't even. We both know this is really about that fuck-up with your old and new girlfriends. Which, I'm still pissed you didn't at least record it.

I'd loved to have seen your face when they each knocked on your door."

"Sorry, I wasn't thinking about your schadenfreude at the time."

She shrugged as she lifted her jacket from the back of her chair. "Apology accepted, this time. But don't lose hope yet; just give her more time and space. How about this, instead of moping back to the scene of the crime, why don't you come out with me, and you can buy me a drink? I'm not meeting Sarah until later anyway."

He rubbed his eyes as he considered her offer. "I don't think—"

She cut him off with, "Just come on, dude. I'll even listen to your tale of woe without making fun of you… too much. Wine pairs well with whining."

Greyson closed his laptop in surrender and stood up. "I don't whine," he protested as he followed her out of the office.

"Oh my God—you're whining about not whining. This is going to be a two-drink minimum conversation," she teased as she closed the door.

Chapter Twenty-Seven

Hannah stared at her computer screen trying to conjure inspiration for the new show like a spiritualist trying to summon an apparition. Unfortunately, her creative ideation was currently an empty well. She let out a harsh breath as she wondered if she was all out of good ideas.

Her body twitched when her phone buzzed, disrupting her trance. As she reached down, part of her wanted it to be Greyson. So, she was both relieved and disappointed when she saw it was Tanya.

"Hey."

"How's my favorite producer?" Tanya chirped. "Working hard so I don't have to?"

Hannah silently cursed her laptop as she closed it. "To be honest, I'm in a bit of a rut at the moment."

"Why come?"

Hannah sighed. "You ever think that you've… I don't know, used up all your creative resources? That you peaked and now it's all downhill?"

"Wait, I thought going downhill was a good thing? Like you've struggled to make it and once you do it's all downhill from here."

"I mean downhill as in decline," Hannah replied, leaning back in her chair. "I just feel like I'm fading."

Tanya exhaled loudly as if in protest. "Are you kidding me? You're the most brilliant person I've ever met, and you just keep getting better. It's actually kinda annoying."

"Really?" Hannah uttered in disbelief.

"Yes really. That's why you're my ride or die babe."

Hannah closed her eyes and whispered, "Thanks."

"I'm the one that should thank you. I mean, you made me a star. Well, bigger star. And don't worry about the new show, whatever you decide on will be fire."

"Whatever we decide on," Hannah softly corrected.

After a slight pause, Tanya asked, "You want me to come over?"

Hannah gazed around her office for a moment, then answered, "No, it's okay. I'm going to take a mental break and grab a snack. Then I'll get back to building this fire."

"Please stop using slang like a grandma. Let me know if there's anything I can do."

"Just keep being you."

"Like I have a choice. Love you, babe."

"Love you too." Hannah set the phone down with a smile and headed into the kitchen.

* * *

Even though the call and food brightened her mood, Hannah couldn't escape her unproductive doldrums. As she swiveled back and forth in her chair, her mind wandered to Greyson and the incident with Ansley, wondering if it had started a crisis of confidence chain reaction. She caught herself glancing down at her muted phone almost willing it to vibrate. At first, she was irritated by his daily texts and voicemails but as the days went on, her aggravation waned, and her mood softened.

She remembered the helpless look on his face at his apartment as if he was hanging off the side of a cliff waiting for someone to throw him a rope. She was too angry to recognize it at the time but in retrospect, she began to see it from his point of view. *He probably did believe they were over,* she told herself.

Or maybe hoped was more accurate. And she certainly knew how an ex showing up unannounced was a shock to the system.

Hannah raked her fingers through her hair as she thought, *I'm still not ready to speak to him just yet...* But she knew in her heart that she couldn't avoid it for too much longer. If only she could finish this pilot outline, then she'd have the energy to consider forgiving him.

She rubbed the bridge of her nose and turned her attention back to her laptop.

Chapter Twenty-Eight

When the weekend rolled in, Greyson's hopes were dimming like a campfire quickly running out of kindling. *I could just go to her house,* he pondered occasionally but quickly dismissed it as going from lovable loon to dangerous stalker.

Maybe I could just accidentally run into her at the park. If only I could talk to her in person. Then again, I'm sure that's what every stalker thinks when they break into someone's bedroom.

So, he spent the majority of the time idling around the apartment with his phone as his only companion. An unfortunately quiet companion. *Why did my phone pick this week to take a vow of silence?* he mused as he plugged it in to charge.

He was sitting listlessly in front of the TV, only paying half a mind to the mindless sci-fi movie playing, when his stomach rang the lunch bell in the form of a growl. *I guess I could finally have that turkey sammy,* he thought, then felt a different kind of pang in his heart.

He got up and lumbered to the kitchen, then U-turned towards his room to retrieve his phone. *I could try calling her again.* As he coasted across the room like a man underwater, he imagined a text from Hannah somehow escaping his detection and rapidly increased his pace.

He paused at the bedside table, soaking in that ephemeral moment of hope, then reached down for the phone. As it came alive in his hand, he was greeted by the time and background image of the Helix Nebula, glowering at him like a giant cosmic eye. *It was a good dream,* he thought disappointedly.

He returned to the kitchen and his lunch plan. But before he made it, his phone buzzed in his hand, startling him into nearly dropping it. He reflexively looked down and saw that the caller was indeed Hannah.

His first instinct was to pinch himself to ensure that it wasn't just a pleasant delusion, but he quickly banished that idea. His next thought was that, although he'd longed desperately to speak with her, he was woefully unprepared to actually talk to her. The babbling, almost incoherent message he'd initially left a week ago started to echo in his head, causing him to cringe. With an ecstatic yet anxious heart, he tapped "answer" and cautiously breathed, "Hello?

He first heard a gulp of breath, followed by, "I'm sorry for calling like this; I just… just didn't know who to call. I don't want to worry Tanya or my mom, and I tried calling my therapist, but she's unavailable," Hannah rambled on, sounding frantic.

"Are you okay?" he asked, his nervous excitement now transforming into concern.

"I don't know, I… I just need someone to talk to. Can you come over?" she whispered.

"Did something happen?" he asked, hoping it wasn't because of the whole Ansley event. Greyson ambled over to the front window and superstitiously peered down at the parking lot below.

He heard her exhale and softly say, "No… not really. I know this is sudden."

"No, it's fine," he assured. "I can be there in twenty minutes."

"Thank you," she breathed, and then the line went dead.

* * *

As Greyson drove, he cursed LA's ubiquitous traffic. "It's goddamn Sunday," he growled as he followed his GPS through the maze of streets. The twenty minutes he'd vowed was now inching closer to thirty.

His brain cycled through all the possibilities of what could be upsetting Hannah. *I don't think it has anything to do with Ansley. She sounded distraught, not angry or disappointed. Maybe it's some kind of family drama. I just don't know Hannah well enough to troubleshoot this. I hope my calling and texting didn't exacerbate our little predicament.*

He finally made it to her house and parked behind her car, quickly unfolded himself out of the car and jogged up to her door. Before he could knock, it swung open, and there stood Hannah. Her face was waxen, her eyes were puffy, and she was wheezing. His initial reaction, which he'd never speak out loud even if waterboarded, was that she looked like a hot mess. Which made him desperate to comfort her all the more.

"Come on in," she said, slowly panting.

Normally, he'd take in his new surroundings, checking for cues and clues about the resident. Decor, cleanliness, and organization can tell you a lot about someone, but he was too focused on Hannah to analyze her feng shui. "Are you okay?" he asked as he stepped into the foyer.

She closed the door and faced him. "Yeah, I'm doing a little better now." She looked almost defeated standing before him, and without thinking, he leaned over and pulled her against him.

She sank into the embrace as if it were a soothing bath. "Sorry I couldn't get here sooner," he whispered.

"It's okay," she said, hugging him fiercely.

They stood there quietly, holding each other for one of those frozen moments that seemed to linger much longer than any standard period of time. When he finally let go, she said, "I didn't mean to alarm you like that, but I was having a panic attack and couldn't think of what else to do. Tanya and my mother just seem so proud that I'm finally moving forward; I just didn't want them to worry that I was, I don't know… relapsing."

"I'm just glad you're feeling better."

The color was slowly trickling back into her face, and her voice was finding its tone. "They usually don't last more than five or ten minutes. I haven't had one since—" She paused a beat as she unconsciously glanced at the kitchen clock, then said, "God, since I can remember. I used to have them more frequently when I was younger."

"Did anything trigger it?" he asked, worrying that he held a measure of responsibility.

"If I had to guess, it was work-related," she said, then led him into the living room. "It's almost like a headache; sometimes I know exactly what causes it, and sometimes it's a complete mystery."

He instantly felt a sense of relief engulf him like stepping into a sauna on an icy day. *At least it wasn't my doing.*

"I was reviewing my outline for the pilot, identifying what I like and what we need to tweak, and it just snuck up on me like… I don't know, old age, I guess," she said with a halfhearted chuckle.

"Yeah, work can be both a blessing and a curse sometimes."

She moved over to the couch and sat down. Then she took a long breath and said, "I don't know how I would have gotten through this last year without it."

"I know what you mean. Whenever things are going rough, I tend to throw myself into my work," he said, as he followed and took a seat next to her.

"Yeah, me too," she agreed, giving him a weak smile. "We just need to make this pilot the best it can be, and hopefully it gets picked up. That will lead straight into a whole 'nother stress bomb, but one I'm more comfortable with."

"Always cut the red wire," he joked. "I guess the whole limbo thing is the hardest part."

"It's the not-being-in-control part that is so triggering. I like to think I can handle whatever life hurls at me as long as I have some agency," she said.

"I get that. I'm somewhat of a control freak myself. At least, when it comes to work."

She leaned back and said, "There are control freaks, and then there are control super freaks. Unfortunately, I'm part of the latter."

He laughed. "Well, super freak or not, you look a lot better now. Guess that's the magic of a good hug."

She smiled and asked, "Can I get you anything?"

A turkey sandwich, he thought as he remembered the once again abandoned meal, but just shook his head.

"Now that I'm…" She paused as she searched for a way to describe her current mood, then settled on, "recovering, I'm starting to feel more like myself."

"I'm really glad," he said earnestly.

She yawned, then looked over at the clock. It was only 1:30, but she suddenly felt exhausted. "I'm gonna make some coffee. You sure you don't want any?"

"I can't say no to a cup of Joe; I mean, I am a white male," he said, then quickly added, "for Peet's sake."

"I see what you did there," she said, then glided over to the coffee maker.

As he watched her from the couch, he wondered if he should address the elephant in his mind. He had so much to explain, most importantly, how he'd unequivocally ended things with Ansley. But he also didn't want to break the positive spirit in the room. *Maybe I'll just wait for her to bring it up.*

"I have French or blonde roast," she called out.

"Gentlemen prefer blonde," he replied, then instantly chastised himself for the lame joke. She shot him a long-distance side-eye, and he quickly followed up with, "Of course, I'm no gentleman. I much prefer an auburn brew."

"So, you're saying cretins prefer dark gingers?" she teased while pouring the grinds into a filter.

He nodded. "What I'm saying is that I don't know how to dig myself out of this hole."

"Dig out of a hole? Isn't that like pulling yourself up by your bootstraps?"

"You know, I guess it is. Another example of our stupid phrasing. There's a reason old white men always love that expression when talking to the poor and downtrodden. It's to give them false hope. But really, it's an impossible endeavor."

She hit the brew button and asked, "Is that social commentary I hear?"

"Sorry, I didn't mean to start soapboxing."

"No, I like it. Social justice is a good look on you."

He shrugged and said, "Thanks." Then his mind drifted back to the unresolved issue that was this week's fiasco. *Or was it last week's fiasco, since today is Sunday?* he mused. As she waited for the coffee to brew, he percolated ideas on how to make things right between them.

As if she could hear his thoughts, she said, "You know, I never got a chance to try that world-class spaghetti."

"World-famous," he corrected.

"My bad," she said, then opened the pantry.

I guess this is as good an opening as any, he thought and said, "I'm so sorry about all of that. I guess I kept trying to end it diplomatically, but that all just blew up in my face. Right after you left, I told Ansley we were absolutely never getting back together. Ever!"

"She was… something." Hannah said, then, after a pause, added, "It's fine. I know relationships are complicated. Even after they're over."

Greyson nodded as she continued, "I'm sorry I never returned your calls or texts. To be honest, it was partly due to anger and hurt, but mostly due to work. I threw myself into this pilot and kind of froze everything else out."

With those words, he could feel the possibility of a future together slowly rising as if it were a hot air balloon. All he had to do was release the metaphorical sandbags weighing them down. In the end, it wasn't much of a choice at all. "No, I get it. Sometimes, I find myself sucked into a project, and I forget about the world for a while. And depending on the circumstances, it's not always a bad thing."

She pulled out a jar of sauce, held it up, and said, "I think I have all the—what do you Southerners like to say—fixin's to make your world-famous spaghetti."

Greyson nearly jumped off the couch and quickly made his way around the island that separated the living room from the kitchen. "Do you have pasta?" he asked as he peeked behind her.

She crouched down, grabbed a container, and lifted it over her shoulder. "About half a box."

He took the box from her hand and shook it. "This should work."

"I hope multigrain is okay."

He nodded, and she said, "I think it's better for you. At least it is for now. Who knows if it'll still be in ten years."

"I'm going to need some pots." He glanced down toward the cabinets under the island and paused, honoring kitchen rule number one: never go scavenging through someone's cabinets without permission. So, he waited until she pointed to the door on the far left.

He bent over and retrieved a saucepan and pasta pot. As he banged them down on the counter, he said, "I'm just glad you called me. I was getting worried that I'd blown it."

"Blown what?" she teased with a smirk.

"You know, the chance to cook for you. Or ever see you again."

"Oh, I don't believe in that ghosting thing. It's too cowardly."

He turned on the water and started filling the pot. "Yeah, I guess it is. But in the social media age, it's so commonplace."

"Because it's so easy."

He nodded. "Yeah, everything's easier on one hand but so much harder on the other. I'm just thankful I didn't grow up with Facebook or Myspace. I was a pretty shy kid and would have found all that posturing exhausting and overwhelming. Not only that, but I probably would have posted insipid things like, 'Man, that last episode of *X-Files* was off the hook.'"

"Aw, you were a geek even back then?"

"Once a geek, always a geek. It's not like someone glows down. The cool kids in high school don't transform into nerds later in life."

Hannah thought for a moment, then said, "I know a few who turned into losers."

"Oh, so you equate geeks with losers?"

She shook her head. "That's not what I meant. I'm saying that being cool in high school doesn't necessarily mean you're destined to be cool all your life."

"True, but those losers are working part-time at Big Lots or something, not dressing like Mr. Spock and going to Comic-Con. No one suddenly develops the geek gene after adolescence."

"Well, I was just teasing; you are definitely not geeky-looking now."

To the devil her due. That's all thanks to Ansley, he thought but knew better than to verbalize. Instead, he said, "I joined a twelve-step program in college. The first step is always the hardest: to admit you're a geek."

She laughed as he proudly declared, "And now, I have a Facebook account with over fifty friends. Seriously, though, ain't nobody got time for that."

"I know what you mean," she agreed. "It's funny how quickly I became enthralled with my smartphone, though. Almost to the point where I probably can't live without it now. And it's only a couple of years old."

"That, I get. It's kinda like trying to remember a time before the internet."

She unconsciously glanced down at the phone warming in her pocket and said, "But I'm not like one of those cell phone zombies who have it fused to their hand."

He heaved the pot onto the stove and turned the burner to high. "I'm starting to notice that a large portion of the population is constantly peering down. I find myself having to pinball around 'em whenever I'm out walking anywhere."

She chuckled as if imagining him bouncing off of people to a cacophony of ringing bells and melodic chiming. "We'd better stop. We're coming dangerously close to sounding like a pair of 'get off my lawn' retirees."

"I'm just shooting from the artificial hip. But yeah, I guess we have a few more good years before we have to embrace that stereotype."

"Van used to say, 'It's not the years; it's the mileage.'"

"Ah, an Indiana Jones fan. He must have been a good guy."

The corners of Hannah's mouth slowly turned up. "I think you two have that in common."

A feeling of apprehension crept into Greyson's mind. But he knew that accepting someone into your life meant accepting all of them, so instead of ignoring the anxiety, he gave voice to it. "I hope my being here is okay."

Hannah leaned back against the counter as if weighing his words. Finally, she nodded. "It is. Van was a huge part of my life. A part of me. Still is really… and will always be."

He briefly pictured his mother smiling at him from their kitchen. "I think I understand."

"But I bet he'd have liked you. You remind me a lot of him," she said, then paused for a long moment. "In a positive way. A healthy way. I can't explain it, but you being here right now just feels… natural. Feels right."

He bobbed his head, then scooped the jar of sauce off the counter. She watched him struggle to open it, alternating between hands, before giving the lid a sharp knock against the countertop. Finally, there was an almost basso pop as he unsealed the lid, raised the jar up in victory, and announced, "I have the power!"

He caught her gaze and asked, "What?"

She shook her head. "Nothing. I was just thinking how cute you are."

He grinned and replied, "Just wait till you taste my noodles," and immediately went several shades of scarlet. "I didn't mean, uh, that sounded a lot dirtier in my mouth than in my head."

She laughed as he shook his head. "I need to shut up, 'cause, per usual, I'm only making this worse."

"I know a way to shut you up," she said as she stepped in front of him. He stood there for just a moment, wondering what was happening, until she leaned over and kissed him. It took a second for him to react, but when he did, he engulfed her in his arms and passionately returned her kiss.

After a couple of minutes, they both came up for air. She then turned and led him out of the kitchen and towards her bedroom. Before crossing the threshold, he scampered back and turned off the stove. By the time he returned, she was already out of her pants and shirt.

He watched her softly drift down onto her four-post bed like an autumn leaf and labored to remove his clothes. Nearly tripping as he kicked off his jeans, he met her at the foot of the bed and eased himself down on top of her. They quickly found each other's mouths and hungrily kissed again.

Greyson had a nagging splinter of a thought in the back of his head about how making love for the first time with someone new was usually awkward and uneasy. He'd only had one first time with someone, and since it was also his literal first time, that rang true. But he instantly found a comfortable rhythm with Hannah, which made it feel less like strangers and more like versed partners. His nervousness and unfamiliarity quickly advanced into relaxed satisfaction.

As they lay entangled in the postcoital glow, Greyson said, "I think this is the beginning of a beautiful—"

Hannah covered his mouth with her hand, then quickly replaced it with her lips.

Interlude

2021

Greyson rubbed his finger over the memorial plaque embedded into the backrest of the old wooden bench. As a tear shimmered in his eye, he turned to gaze out over the crystal blue water, looking at but not seeing the panorama. Spring was blossoming all around him, yet he was oblivious to its allure. In his mind, he was navigating a problem and had little time to devote to the idle wilds before him. The sad truth was that he had stopped seeing what was in front of him the day his wife passed away.

Hannah suffered a brain aneurysm while Greyson was at work during the winter of 2021. It was a sudden death with no warning or prior symptoms. So, just like that, her radiant light was extinguished in a world that had far too few. To Greyson, it felt like she'd been wrenched from his heart and soul.

Once again, the person he loved most died when he wasn't there.

Now, his thoughts were only of the past. Of Hannah, of their life together, and of their shared happiness. His grief—or his constant companion, as he appropriated—was there whenever he looked forward, like a reverse shadow. The only way to avoid it was to simply turn away and look behind.

He now wore glasses more often than not and had gained over thirty pounds, making him a far cry from the scrawny kid he'd always felt like until he'd gotten his first nine-to-five job at Crastino. He was close to forty and, after the last couple of months, appeared even older. His brown hair had slowly faded to salt and pepper, and he'd grown a short, mostly white beard, not to look stylish but more from neglect. Nolan called it his grief beard after dropping by on an impromptu welfare check. It was one of the few times he'd seen his former roommate since the funeral.

He thought about his oldest friend and the curious thing he'd said to him that day. Nolan had stopped by unannounced and quickly recognized the state Greyson was in. Not only because of his disheveled appearance and the wreckage he'd let his home slip into, but because he'd witnessed Greyson like this once before.

"You need closure," Nolan said as he cleared a place on the couch and sat down. "Hannah was taken from you so suddenly that you can't recover without some kind of resolution. Remember when we were kids and we tried contacting your mom using that Ouija board? If only something like that could actually work."

This offhand comment sparked something inside Greyson, like a wayward match being carelessly tossed into a dry forest. He soon became obsessed with the notion of somehow connecting with Hannah one more time. And being a physicist, he understood that time was the key.

"Do you know how many damn benches there are in this place?" a gruff voice called out, breaking his trance.

Greyson turned and watched Dr. Greene lumber up the walkway. "Sorry, I didn't think about that," he said as his boss settled down beside him.

"I'm far too old to go hiking around, even on a lovely day like this," Dr. Greene huffed.

It's a paved park, not exactly a mountainous trail, Greyson thought as he waited for his boss to catch his breath. Dr. Greene basically looked the same as the first day Greyson met him. He was a large man then, and if he was any larger now, Greyson couldn't tell.

As if reading his mind, Dr. Greene said, "The last time I was in shape was my senior year of high school. I was on the football team and a pretty good left guard, if I do say so."

"I didn't know you played sports," Greyson said. Dr. Greene was never one to talk much about himself, and Greyson learned something new about the man with almost every interaction. True to his word, Dr. Greene had stepped back from Project Gateway but was still a fixture at Crastino. Through the years, they formed a tenuous mentor-mentee bond, especially after Tsai's promotion.

Dr. Greene gave him a wry smile and said, "There's a lot about me you don't know."

Greyson nodded. After ten years of working for the man, his boss was still something of an enigma to him. Dr. Tyson Greene always seemed to play his cards close to his chest. As he stretched out his legs, he asked, "So, what's so important that you had me trek out here instead of telling me in the cozy confines of my office?"

Greyson paused and finally took notice of the world around him. He'd often come out to Hannah's spot almost involuntarily. They'd met here, then came back regularly as a couple during the length of their marriage. The unchanging bench, sidewalk, surrounding trees, and lake became their shared space.

And now that she was gone, this was the only place where he could still feel her presence. If only in his head. "Sorry again, I just..." Greyson paused as he peered over the smooth water. "I guess I just needed to be here when I told you this."

Dr. Greene patiently waited as Greyson took a deep breath, then said, "I think I know how to make the gateways work. That is, I know where to get the power to increase the wormhole's size."

Dr. Greene turned and met Greyson's gaze. With a suspicious yet intrigued tone, he said, "Do you really? Well, do tell."

"We're using negative matter to stabilize the wormhole, so I figured why not use negative energy to fuel it? That, combined with gravitational energy, should be enough to bulk up a microscopic wormhole to a functional size. Then, we keep feeding in the negative matter to keep our plus-sized wormhole open long enough to go through."

"This is not the first time I've heard this idea," Dr. Greene said flatly.

"I know, but I discovered a way not only to generate more negative matter but to harness the gravitational and negative energy needed. That energy signature is very close to the one experienced in 2001," Greyson explained.

"I had a feeling that you were working on that again."

"Once an obsession, always an obsession," Greyson said with a shrug. "Of course, with those kinds of energy levels, we might need to augment our equipment. As it is now, I doubt that it could hold up to these new kinds of forces."

"Actually, we'll be fine there. I ensured that all the machinery could handle the kind of energy you're suggesting, and then some, a long time ago," Dr. Greene reassured. He glanced down, as if replaying a memory, then asked, "When did you figure all this out?"

"I came up with the solution a couple of weeks ago."

Dr. Greene raised his eyebrows and asked, "So, why am I hearing about this idea now?"

"I, uh, needed more time for some extra calculations," Greyson said, shifting in his seat and looking away.

"What kind of extra calculations?"

The question hung in the air for a moment, like a vapor trail. Finally, Greyson said, "In order to find a location on Earth, you need two coordinates, right?"

"Of course, the latitude and longitude," Dr. Greene answered.

Still looking away, Greyson said, "And in a three-dimensional space, we use a spatial coordinate system needing three points of information."

"Four, if you include time."

Greyson turned back and nodded. "Exactly. That's what I had to figure out, factoring in the time aspect."

Dr. Greene folded his arms. "Please dispense with the Socratic method. Where are you going with this?"

Tears welled up in Greyson's eyes, and he said, "I just… need to see her again. One more time. She was gone so suddenly, I never even got to say goodbye." Then he looked down and whispered, "She's my soulmate."

Dr. Greene watched Greyson as he wiped away the now streaming tears. "I am truly sorry for your loss, but I'm not sure that I'm following your intent here."

Greyson sighed. "You know how you say everything is out there in the universe? All the matter and energy from the Big Bang are still with us in some form or another today."

"Yes, I don't subscribe to the nonsense that anything gets removed from the universe in something like a black hole. Information cannot be destroyed."

"That includes the past, present, and future. They are out there somewhere in the universe. Which means she's out there, too," Greyson declared as his voice started to shake.

"In theory," Dr. Greene warily agreed.

Greyson straightened up and asked, "Do you remember Hannah's funeral? What the pastor said?"

Dr. Greene shook his head, and Greyson continued, "He said Hannah lost her life. I remember thinking, 'What an odd phrasing—lost her life.' It's as if her life got misplaced somewhere—like missing car keys or something—and it was just waiting for someone to find it. Later on, I realized, maybe it is."

Greyson paused for a moment as a couple of joggers cruised by, then said, "Obviously not here and now, but it is out there somewhere in the past. Then I thought about Project Gateway and what its potential could mean. Not just moving an object through space in an instant, but through spacetime. And well, I think I figured out a way to create a wormhole to go back in time."

Now, Dr. Greene looked away as he asked, "How do you propose opening up the end of this tunnel in the past?"

"I can use the quantum entanglement between Lilith and Eve," Greyson stated. "You built Lilith in 1999. With that entanglement, I think I can remotely activate her from here when I turn on Eve. Rather than using the entanglement between them to move from point A to point B in current time, I'll add an antecedent coordinate that will allow me to go through Eve here and come out of Lilith in the past."

"Slow down," Dr. Greene said as he held up a hand like a cop halting traffic. "You want to activate Lilith in 1999?"

Greyson shook his head and said, "Actually, 2001. Before Hannah met her first husband. I figured I could go back, find her there, and talk to her one last time. You know, get my closure."

"Let me get this straight. You want to use Project Gateway, my multimillion-dollar project, to risk your life along with my invaluable equipment to go on an emotional journey seeking closure?"

"When you put it that way, it sounds ludicrous and self-indulgent," Greyson said. "But seriously, I have been calculating this for over a month, and I think it'll work. Experimentation is the key to a successful theory."

Dr. Greene said nothing, so Greyson continued, "So, in this experiment, we open the gateway, and I go through to find her."

"In the past. Specifically, the year 2001," Dr. Greene said.

Greyson nodded. "Yes. I know she's always loved this park and regularly visited this very spot. So, I will hang around here until I run into her."

"Once you run into her, what do you expect to happen?"

Greyson slowly exhaled, then rubbed his beard. After a prolonged moment, he replied in an unsteady voice, "I wasn't even there when she died. I just need to see her. To talk with her. One last time."

"You do realize that the her you'll be seeing and conversing with isn't the same one that—" Dr. Greene paused before saying "died" and quickly alternated it with "you knew and loved."

"I know that, but she'll still be Hannah. Maybe not my Hannah, but she'll always be that singularly remarkable woman. Things on the outside may slowly alter," Greyson said, pointing to his graying hair and beard, "but who we are at our core never changes."

"So, if this crazy idea works and you get your closure, what then?"

"After a couple of weeks, you activate Eve again, and I come back."

Dr. Greene shook his head. "You come back. Just like that. What about the butterfly effect? What if you change something in the past and the 'back' you come to isn't the same as the one you left?"

Greyson paused as he considered the question. He gazed over the park for a prolonged moment. "I don't think that's going to be the case. The butterfly effect might make for an interesting story, but it isn't a real thing. But just to be sure, I'll be careful."

"I don't believe in it either, but this is uncharted territory, and we don't know what we don't know," Dr. Greene said as he pushed his glasses higher on his nose, "Here be dragons."

"I'll be extra careful."

Dr. Greene paused as he met Greyson's gaze. "You don't have to do this. There are numerous other ways to handle your grief. Much safer alternatives, to be sure."

"Maybe for other people. But if there's even the slightest chance of this working, I have to try it," Greyson insisted. "Think of this as a two-birds-with-one-stone proposition. One, we get to finally experiment with the gateway—"

"We've been doing that on and off for over two decades," Dr. Greene interrupted.

"I know, but not on this level. I'm talking about an experiment with not only space but with time as well. Think of the possibilities."

"It was never my intent to do that—"

It was Greyson's turn to cut him off. "I know but think about penicillin. That was a serendipitous scientific discovery."

"Okay, what's the second bird?"

"I get to see Hannah again. I get to talk with her one more time."

"Why go all the way to 2001? Why not go back two or three years?"

Greyson sighed again, then said, "I've thought long and hard about that. I… I just don't want to take a chance on seeing her when she knew me. I don't want to risk saying or doing something that could possibly harm her. Plus, it would be too hard. If I saw that Hannah, the one who knows and loves me, I don't know if I could…" He went quiet as he wiped away another round of tears.

"You don't know if you could leave her," Dr. Greene concluded. "I think I understand. It would be like losing her all over again."

Greyson nodded and whispered, "Here be dragons."

"I suppose it would be a lot safer to see her before you knew her. For her sake as well as yours. But why fixate on 2001? Why not 2005? Or 1999, when

Lilith first went online?"

"I need to see her before she meets her first husband. I know that happened on Valentine's Day in 2001. So, I figured I'd go back sometime in January."

"Why does it have to be before she meets her first husband?"

"Maybe it's the guy side of me, but I'm not sure that I could take seeing her while she's mooning over some other man," Greyson reluctantly admitted.

"Relationships are complicated enough as they are. If you factor time travel into it, that's a whole new level of complexity," Dr. Greene said while shaking his head. "But still, you'd be cutting it pretty close."

Greyson took a deep breath, then exhaled slowly. "After I solved the power source problem, I thought about the 2001 conundrum. And that's what gave me the idea, or at least pointed me in that direction."

Dr. Greene held up his finger and said, "Wait a minute—you think the mysterious power surge we experienced with Lilith back in January 2001 is, what, a proverbial red X mark on some spacetime map?"

"More like a metaphorical spotlight."

"It's an interesting thought, I'll grant you that," Dr. Greene said as he rubbed his chin.

Greyson knew at that point that he had him hooked. Now, he just needed to slowly reel him in. "I would have gone to Tsai with this, but she'd just try and talk me out of it, saying it's too dangerous."

"She'd be right, of course."

"But most importantly, I'd be asking her to risk her career by doing an unauthorized experiment."

"So, you figured you'd go straight to the top and ask me to risk my reputation and legacy?" Dr. Greene said.

Greyson shook his head. "You're not risking your reputation and legacy. If it doesn't work, it just doesn't work."

"And if it doesn't work and your atoms are scattered across time and space? Do I simply reset the days without an accident sign to zero?"

"That's not going to happen," Greyson stated firmly. Then, Dr. Greene shot him a sideways glance, and he immediately backpedaled. "Okay, it could happen. But come on, this last year has been a shit sundae with extra nuts.

And not just for me personally but for the entire world. There's been a steady rise in hate, intolerance, and fascism not seen since the 1930s. The planet is going nuclear, both figuratively and literally, without any signs of leaders capable of stopping it. It's like there's a war on not just science but on rational thought. And the cherry on top is this global pandemic."

"When you put it like that, it makes me want to go with you."

Greyson cracked a smile for the first time in a long while. He knew not only had he sold his mentor on his admittedly unorthodox idea, but he now had one of the greatest minds in his corner. If there was anything he'd missed or made a mistake on, who better to help than Dr. Tyson Greene? The last domino between him and seeing Hannah again was slowly falling.

Dr. Greene continued, "It's times like this I understand the appeal of wanting to escape to the proverbial good old days. The only problem is, for a Black man like myself, when the hell was it truly better?"

"How did we get to where we are right now? I mean, most people are basically good, so how can so many bad leaders keep on winning?" Greyson pondered.

"Ah, the specious 'most people are good' delusion. If only that were true. In reality, most people are neither good nor evil, if you believe in those constructs. The majority are ethically neutral. They walk a morally gray line between the two, periodically wandering over to one side or the other. Very few people are truly virtuous. Or nefarious, for that matter. The majority are simply selfish beings, thus susceptible to manipulation. And we just happen to live in a time when exploitation has run rampant," Dr. Greene explained.

"You sure you don't wanna come with?"

Dr. Greene inched up his glasses and said, "If it wasn't for my age and the fact that I can't abandon this company I worked so hard to build, I might consider it. Of course, the other dealbreaker for me would be leaping back twenty years in technology and innovation."

"Yeah, but you'd bring twenty years of knowledge with you. You could be the next Archimedes, Edison, Berners-Lee, and, well, you combined."

"That's not even remotely funny, and don't go getting any reckless notions," Dr. Greene scolded. Greyson raised his eyebrows and pointed at himself in an innocent "who, me?" gesture.

"This is an intriguing venture," Dr. Greene admitted.

"So, you'll help me?" Greyson asked, his hopes dangling at the end of his simple plea like a tiny worm over a vast ocean.

Dr. Greene sighed as he put both hands on his knees. He slowly rose, then turned and faced Greyson. His large frame blocked the sun and created a halo effect around him. "I can't believe you lured me out to this idyllic setting only to ambush me with an irresponsible and, quite frankly, aberrant request."

Greyson was nonplussed as he stared up at the towering figure. His expectations sank faster than a boat made of solid gold. That is, until Dr. Greene finished, "That said, I can't believe I'm going to agree to help you."

In an emotional reversal of fortune, Greyson's eyes widened as he opened his mouth to thank his mentor. But before he could get the words out, Dr. Greene held up his palm and said, "On one condition: we do this my way."

Greyson vigorously nodded in agreement as he mentally watched that last domino topple.

* * *

Dr. Greene's way turned out to be both slow and methodical. They started with the math, as Dr. Greene checked and rechecked Greyson's calculations. Then, they moved on to computer simulations, running every conceivable option until exhausting all foreseeable possibilities. At least the ones they could think of.

What Greyson had envisioned as taking one to two months stretched into an agonizing half a year. With 2021 nearly over, they slowly approached the anniversary of Hannah's death. An anniversary Greyson was desperate to avoid.

They met several times a week, under the auspices of an energy conservation side project. Having the owner of the company write your work schedule had its perks. And having unfettered access to not only the two gateways but the entire building made Greyson feel like a child with full behind-the-scenes access to Disney World.

The only problem was that the man he viewed as his partner/savior was growing into more of an obstacle each day. Every time Greyson believed they were ready to go, it seemed like Dr. Greene needed to check one more equation, calculation, or component. It was almost as if he was stalling. Finally, with a measured resolve, Greyson decided to confront him.

He stood in front of the circular machine and admired its ingenuity. It was a simple, clean design. As Dr. Greene once said, "Humans tend to make things more complicated than they need to be. Nature is more efficient and straightforward." Eve was essentially a nine-foot-tall vertical hole. A shiny metal oval standing perpendicular on a flat copper base with dozens of tiny lasers affixed around the circumference of the device, all slightly angled and aimed towards a central point.

Greyson moved over to the left of the thin, steely oval and ran his fingers over the control console that operated her. When he got to the keyboard, he thought, *I could enter the coordinates for 2001 and turn her on right now. If only Dr. Greene would give the okay.*

As if on cue, Dr. Greene stepped into the lab. He passed Lilith, Eve's twin, and made his way over to Greyson. "Itching to give it a go?" he asked, as Greyson spun around in surprise, like a child caught planning to stick his hand inside the forbidden cookie jar.

"I do think we're ready."

Dr. Greene stopped in front of Lilith and regarded his creation. It had the potential to ignite the next technological revolution. And as with many breakthroughs, it also had the potential to do incalculable harm. "Now I am become Death, the destroyer of worlds," Dr. Greene whispered the famous Gita quote into the opening.

"What?" Greyson asked.

Dr. Greene shook his head and said, "Nothing, just reminding myself to always consider the consequences."

"Well, I think we have."

"And you think you're ready?"

Greyson turned and faced him. "Yeah, like I said, I think we are."

"I mean, are *you* ready?" Dr. Greene asked, pointing to Greyson.

"As ready as I can be," Greyson replied a little too eagerly.

"Got all your bags packed?" Dr. Greene asked as he looked back at the machine.

The casual question surprised Greyson. It was as if he were planning a business trip to San Francisco rather than traveling back in time twenty years. But logistically, it wasn't that far off. He'd need a few changes of clothes and other travel necessities, just as if he were going on vacation for a couple of weeks.

"I'll need cash," Greyson declared like he suddenly remembered the title of a song he'd heard a snippet of earlier in the day.

Dr. Greene nodded. "And it will have to have been printed no later than 2000. Same with your clothing. Your iPhone will have to stay here, of course. It's not like it'd do you much good anyway."

"Unless I wanted to sell it for millions of dollars to Samsung," Greyson joked. "You know, get them a twenty-year leg up on the competition."

"Don't even joke about that. You promised no *Back to the Future* shenanigans. You have to be very careful not to even hint about upcoming events to anyone. That means no history lessons on the future," Dr. Greene warned.

Greyson replied with a smile as he thought, *Please, not another TedTalk on the importance of not interfering with past events.*

Dr. Greene crossed his arms and continued, "I am serious; we don't know the implication this could have."

"It's funny. *Avengers Endgame* made such a big deal about how all the time travel movies were inaccurate because they broke the rules and ended up changing the past. Then they proceed to do the same damn thing."

"I must have missed that one," Dr. Greene replied with mild annoyance.

"Really, how have you not seen that?"

"Maybe because I am an adult," Dr. Greene sneered.

Greyson shrugged, taking the jab in stride. He was used to Dr. Greene's snark, as one becomes used to a salty uncle. He looked at his mentor and asked, "How can you be so unbelievably brilliant yet not be even the slightest bit geeky?"

Dr. Greene ignored the question like it was junk mail and said, "We really should focus on getting you ready for the journey. You are going to experience something no one else has, and we don't know exactly what to expect. So, you're going to need to be prepared for anything."

"I guess this will be kinda like a work trip. But instead of TSA rules, I have to worry about anachronisms."

"Only take what you need. And your little superhero movie is right; you can't change the past, so don't even think about it. Documented history cannot be altered. You can't go back and stop the 9/11 attacks. The space you will have to operate in is the undocumented part. There you are free to roam," Dr. Greene explained.

"So, I should only bring vintage clothes and cash that predates 2001. I guess I can just buy stuff like toothpaste and deodorant there."

Dr. Greene nodded. "Then, I guess we're good to go?" Greyson asked tentatively.

Dr. Greene glanced over at the looming gateway and sighed. After a long pause, he reluctantly agreed, "I suppose so."

"Wait, once I'm there, how will I get out? You know, out of the lab and then out of the building?" Greyson asked.

"I considered that. It makes the most sense to send you back late at night on a weekend when no one will be working. I can give you my personal code, which will open every door in the building."

Greyson nodded as he glanced past Dr. Greene and over to the pewter numerical keypad on the door. "You remember your code from 2001?"

"Sure, I've never changed it. It's 324034, the numbers of the three greatest running backs of all time: Jim Brown, Gayle Sayers, and Walter Payton," Dr. Greene stated.

Greyson repeated the code as he locked it into his memory bank. Then he said, "Guess all that's left to do is pack a bag—"

Dr. Greene cut him off with, "One made prior to 2001."

"Of course. And I'll get like a couple hundred dollars..." Greyson said, then reconsidered for a moment. "I'd better make it a couple of thousand. To cover hotel, food, transportation, and other unanticipated expenses. I can probably get all that by tomorrow afternoon."

"Don't forget our list of medications for motion sickness and other after-effects that you may encounter on the other side. I know we've analyzed all the possibilities and consequences you may experience going through the wormhole."

Overanalyzed is more like it, Greyson mused.

"But Semper Paratus," Dr. Greene said as if reading his mind.

"I'm ready," Greyson affirmed.

"Then I will meet you here after lunch," Dr. Greene said, and Greyson replied with a short salute as he hurried off. After he was gone, Dr. Greene walked over to the camera they'd set up in the corner and checked the battery. They agreed to document everything but to keep it off the official record, so Dr. Greene disabled the room's security cameras during their work.

He wandered over to the computer, then reached into his jacket pocket and took out a wrinkled, yellowing envelope that he received long ago and carried around like a memento. He held it up against the skylight and peered at the outline of the letter inside. Then he turned it over and dug a finger into the corner of the seal flap but stopped short of opening it. He paused for a few beats, then quickly tucked it back into his suit.

Part Two, Chapter Twenty-Nine

2001

"Are you crying?" Tanya asked, trotting up the sidewalk. She was decked out in her workout gear, which consisted of a thin, black track jacket and gray yoga pants. It was a typical January morning in LA, which meant there was tepidity in the air to the degree of sixty-two.

Hannah shook her head as she wiped away the nascent tears and lied, "No, it's just… my allergies." She was sitting on the park bench wearing her favorite light blue denim jacket and dark blue jeans.

Tanya collapsed next to her and said, "Yeah, LA winters are synonymous with allergy season." She took a swig of water and leaned over to catch her breath while scoping out the other Sunday wayfarers.

Hannah always felt somewhat invisible next to her best friend, even long before she became a famous model. Tanya had always been tall, athletically thin, and strikingly beautiful. "Effortlessly attractive," Hannah had always said, much to the chagrin of Tanya.

As her friend sat next to her, huffing and sweating, Hannah couldn't help but compare herself once again to the famous Azalea. And once again, in her own estimation, she came up short. Both literally and figuratively. *Why does seeing Tanya make me want to immediately run five miles on a treadmill? I think I'm in pretty good shape, at least until I'm juxtaposed with someone who looks like an Olympian goddess. Granted, I'm still in the process of losing those freshman fifteen. But I mean, it's only been what, ten years? God, I just feel like such a cow right now.*

Stop it, she chided herself, thwarting her shame spiral. *This is only because of the fight last night that you're back to doubting yourself like this.* And it didn't help matters that she was in a relationship with someone who passive-aggressively pushed her to continuously eat less and work out more. Always under the devious guise of "for her own health and well-being," of course.

"Are you going to the Country Music Awards later today?" Tanya teased, pointing to Hannah's outfit.

This broke Hannah's self-loathing trance. "Huh?"

"Honey, that outfit is a denim-on-denim fashion crime."

Hannah glanced down at her clothes, then lightly pushed her friend. "Shut it."

Tanya feigned almost falling over the side of the bench from the gentle shove. Once she straightened back up, she tentatively asked, "Is everything okay with you and your man?"

Hannah's hesitation nearly betrayed her as she nodded. "Can we please talk about something other than relationships?"

"Fine with me, since I haven't had one in a minute."

Hannah turned to her friend and said, "What about what's her name?"

"Freya? Yeah, that was more of a miscarriage than a relationship."

"Sorry," Hannah uttered, wincing at Tanya's phrasing.

"Don't be. I'm beginning to think my default might be single. But there's always more fish in the sea, especially when you cast a line in both ponds."

"I guess," Hannah agreed. "Anyway, the reason I wanted to talk was I got this idea. You're probably going to hate it at first, but please hear me out."

"Great salesmanship there."

Hannah ignored the jab. "You know how you love baking, right?"

Tanya shrugged and said, "It's more that I love eating, but yeah, I guess baking is a large part of the equation."

"Please, if it was just about the eating, you'd pay someone else to do it."

"True, thanks to my Bibi, I do enjoy the baking process," Tanya agreed. Her grandmother, affectionately called Bibi, was a legendary home baker in their neighborhood. She could go toe-to-toe, or more precisely, dough-to-dough, with any of the baking icons of her time.

"Remember when that guy pitched you a show about what really goes on behind the scenes for fashion shoots?"

"It was so fucking ridiculous. He wanted a show like *Melrose Place* but with models."

"*Melrose Place* is a show with models."

Tanya raised her eyebrows. "Yeah, I guess. But I have zero interest in doing another sleazy, pretty people show."

"Well, it got me thinking. You would be great on television."

"Of course," Tanya agreed, placing both hands palm down under her chin and smiling the most artificial smile in her repertoire.

Hannah grabbed her hands and pushed them down. "Stop, I'm serious. Obviously, you have the looks, but I'm talking about personality. I think you could host a TV show in your sleep."

"What do you mean host a show? Like Rosie O'Donnell?"

Hannah shook her head. "Not a talk show. I'm envisioning something akin to a game show but focused on baking. We'd have new contestants come on each week and have a bake-off in this massive kitchen. And you would be a host/judge. We'd need a couple other judges, like maybe Paula Deen or someone."

"Hold on," Tanya said, holding up a hand like a teacher silencing a rowdy class. "I'm not a professional cook or anything; I just dabble. There's no way they'd give a baking show to someone who's not known for, you know, baking. It'd be like asking Julia Child to host *America's Most Wanted*."

"That's where you're wrong. I think you'd be the perfect host for a baking game show. You're quick-witted."

"True," Tanya agreed.

"You're charismatic."

"Also true."

"And you're congenial," Hannah finished.

Tanya frowned. "I'm not sure about that one."

"Plus, you know your way around the kitchen. Sure, you may not be Irma Rombauer, but she's not freaking Azalea either. Television is first and foremost a visual medium."

"Oh God, now you sound like one of those libertine TV producers," Tanya sneered.

"I'm glad you mentioned that. Since this is my idea, I figured I could be the show's producer. At least one of them."

Tanya shot her friend a side smile. "I sec, this is all a way for you to get your foot in the door as a producer."

Hannah lifted her hands up as if checking to see if it was starting to rain and said, "I'm not gonna lie, kinda. But, really, it's a way for both of us to transition to the next phase of our careers."

Tanya sat still for a long moment, then murmured, "Maybe."

"You'd be a great TV personality," Hannah assured her.

Finally, Tanya said, "Okay, I will admit I'm a little intrigued. I'll tell you what; let me think about it." Then she got up from the bench and stretched like she was reaching for something high on an invisible shelf.

"No pressure. If you want to do it, great. If you don't, that's fine too." Hannah knew that her entire pitch hinged on bringing Azalea to the table, so to speak.

Tanya stepped back onto the pathway, then turned and said, "I'll sleep on it and let you know tomorrow, cool?"

"Cool," Hannah chirped, trying to sound casual. She paused when she noticed two male joggers suddenly halting.

"Hello there, ladies. It sure is a lovely day for two lovely girls," the closest one said with a smile that walked the line between charming and sinister. He was dressed in a sleeveless white shirt and far too short black running shorts.

"I know my day just got brighter," his wingman added. He was dressed similarly but in opposite colors. Together, they looked like yin and yang Lotharios.

Tanya turned and said, "Thanks for the unsolicited compliment, boys, but we're not interested. Continue to have a lovely day, though."

The wingman backed up as if hit by a gust of wind, but the instigator confidently stepped forward with his arms spread out and said, "Aw, come on. You don't have to be like that; we're just being friendly here."

"Look, I understand how your lizard brain works. You see two women talking, minding their own business, and you automatically think it's an invitation to put on your playa short pants. Well, you took your shot, and we politely blocked it, so now it's time to move along," Tanya said as she waved them on.

Rather than walking away, gigolo number one chose to double down. "Mhmm, I do like it when a girl plays hard to get."

Tanya glanced over at Hannah and said, "Look at the sleazeballs on this guy." Then she pointed down the sidewalk. "Alright, Casano means yes, you don't have to go home, but you do have to get the fuck out of my face."

Hannah fought back a smile as she admired her friend's fortitude in the face of unwelcome advances. *Thank God she's here, so I don't have to deal with this kind of shit alone.*

The wingman grabbed his friend's arm and said, "Fuck this. Let's go, man."

Prince Alarming finally retreated with the parting shot, "Wow, you don't have to be such a bitch about it. You're probably a couple of dykes anyway."

"Wow, eloquent and original, I bet you had it going on in middle school. Which is also where you peaked. Good night and good luck with all your future sexual harassment cases," Tanya called out as they trotted away. She turned back to Hannah and said, "That was fun."

"No, that was impressive. I wish you could handle all my pest control."

"I can eat douchebags like that for breakfast and still have room for crêpes," Tanya said, then turned in the opposite direction of the re-jocks. "I'll call you tomorrow."

Hannah nodded as she watched her friend jog away.

Chapter Thirty

Across the water, Greyson slowly rose from his bench. His legs were wobbly, so he took a long, deep breath to try and soothe his nerves. After temporarily calming his flustered emotional state, he strolled over to the other side of the park where Hannah sat.

As he walked, he tried to distract his agitated mind with the tantalizing environment around him. *This really is a beautiful area; it's just so tranquil and alluring. It's crazy how little it's changed, though. This could be yesterday instead of twenty years ago. I don't know what exactly I expected, but I can't distinguish any differences in the ambience of the past. I guess I thought the air would be fresher and the colors more vibrant, but everything looks and feels so normal.*

He passed a pair of joggers wearing neon tops and biker shorts and silently chuckled. *Well, maybe except for the fashion. That and, of course, the city's physical changes. It feels like I've gone from middle-aged Los Angeles to a younger adult LA. But this park is basically a time capsule.*

The closer he got to Hannah, the more his heart pounded. As she came into focus, Greyson found himself unprepared for what he saw. He immediately recognized her as he watched her talking with Tanya from across the pond. But up close, she was indistinguishable, yet divergent all the same.

It's like I'm seeing what her daughter would've looked like. If she could've had one, that is, he observed, all while trying to bury his astonishment underneath the mountain of sentimentality.

While he shuffled up the pathway, he scanned the area and was disappointed with the lack of other nature lovers around. *If ever I could use a gaggle of Jeep girls, it's now. This is going to be much harder than I anticipated.* As he grew closer to Hannah, he recognized an unmistakable look of distress on her face and felt a soft twinge in his chest.

Greyson's pace slowed as his mind raced, trying to settle on the best opening line, thinking that he couldn't just stroll up to her and comment on how it was such a nice day for January. Nearly parallel to her, his face suddenly turned ashen, and his breath became labored. *God, I hope I'm not about to have a heart—*

His panic was interrupted by, "Are you okay?" Hannah's expression suddenly changed to one of concern for the middle-aged man standing in front of her.

Greyson froze as if he had been caught by a helicopter spotlight during an attempt to flee from the police. He turned to Hannah and said, "Yeah, I think I overdid my morning walk. I'm not used to how mild the winter is here. I guess I didn't need this heavy of a jacket. Back home, this is more like late spring. Do you mind if I sit down for a moment and catch my breath?"

"Of course," she replied, scooting over.

"Thanks," he huffed as he folded himself down on the bench. His heart was still revving like an engine in a Formula One car, and he forced himself to take several deep breaths. *I can't believe I'm sitting next to her,* he marveled and hoped his body would cease involuntarily convulsing.

"Where's back home?" she asked.

Greyson's mind shuffled like a deck of cards as he suddenly realized how woefully unprepared he was for this moment. He'd rehearsed their meeting in his mind dozens, if not hundreds, of times in the past few months. Yet, all that planning was abruptly lost under an avalanche of unanticipated anxiety. *Just say the opposite of the truth,* he thought, then blurted out, "All over, really. I was a military brat, so we moved every couple years. However, most of the places had at least an echo of winter."

"Welcome to the Southland. I grew up here, so this is the only winter I know. But I have spent a Christmas or two in Tahoe, so I get what you mean."

As she spoke, he had to suppress the desperate urge to sweep her into his arms. *God, I've missed her so much. Now I totally get why Jimmy Stewart was so manic when he saw his wife and she didn't know who he was in that scene from* It's a Wonderful Life.

"What brings you to LA?"

The cadence and tone of her voice were a little different from what he remembered, but he wasn't sure if he could trust his judgment thanks to his disquietude. "Oh, I'm here for a few weeks working on a project," he said, this time leaning into the truth and remembering Dr. Greene's advice for any and every interaction: *Vagueness is essential.*

"And what do you do?" she asked, as if trying to help calm him.

What are you, a game show host? he mused, as he ironically felt more pressure from trying to dodge her barrage of questions. "I'm in the tech industry, but I'm contracting right now. I work on different projects for different companies," he explained, before feeling wretched from the deception. Even lying to this version of her felt anathema to him.

This is infinitely harder than I imagined, he thought, then said, "I've been a contractor for a couple of years, so I don't really have a home base. I just bounce around from place to place. I guess you could say I'm still trying to figure things out."

He couldn't help but smile at the unintended symmetry of their first meeting. *But to her, this is our first meeting,* he thought, then suppressed the notion, fearing it would quickly bake his noodle.

"You came to the right place for that. This is my favorite spot in the city. I come here to relax, read, or work out problems. That's why I call this my therapy bench," she said, patting the worn wooden planks. Then she motioned to the water and added, "And my reflecting spot."

"I can see why," he said, hearing another echo from his past.

"You seem much better now," she noted, then cast her gaze away so as not to appear inappropriate.

"I do feel much better," he agreed, then cupped his hand over his eyes and looked at the sky. "I guess the beautiful day got the better of me for a moment there. Who knew such hidden danger lurked in such picturesque scenery? I feel like I failed nature or something."

Hannah made a slight, asymmetric smile and said, "No, I get it. I'm not exactly sitting here basking in the glow of paradise myself."

"I'm sorry. Care to talk about it? You know, a little quid pro quo since you pretty much saved my life."

She exhaled slowly. "It's stupid, really. Just the stereotypical relationship bullshit that creeps up every now and again."

Greyson sat there with his mouth agape as he scrambled to think of anything remotely helpful to say. Instead, all he could think was, *Am I too late? Is she already with Van? Shit, I was sure they didn't meet for another couple of weeks.* Finally, he said, "Relationships and work are the two major stressors of adulting."

"Tell me about it," she huffed. "You see, I had this idea for a TV show, and of course, the first person I wanted to share it with was my fiancé."

The word fiancé pulsed in Greyson's mind like a neighbor's car alarm, and he could only nod. *I can't believe I'm too late.* He'd sometimes felt an irrational, yet inherent, rivalry toward her first husband. And it seemed he was destined to come in second once again.

"I hoped to get, I don't know, support maybe. Encouragement even. Or, at the very least, constructive criticism," she said, then looked at Greyson. "You see, he works for one of the television studios as a staff writer, so he knows the business pretty well."

"He's a writer?" Greyson asked, trying to mask his incredulity.

"Oh yeah. And he's slowly working on getting his master's degree. But poetry is his real passion. It's funny; he says he's a hack by day and a poet by night."

I had no idea Mr. Wonderful was once a TV writer. And a goddamn poet to boot, Greyson thought. After a few moments of silence, he recovered from the shock. "That makes him sound like a superhero. I am rhyme! I am the iambic pentameter! I am POETMAN!" he growled, in his best raspy, staccato Kevin Conroy impersonation.

Hannah smiled, getting the idea of the joke, if not entirely understanding the reference. "So, I pitched him my idea last night, and he just sat there for a minute, almost like he was trying to swallow a huge pill without any water. Finally, he said, 'I don't get it.'"

"What's the idea?" Greyson asked, assuming it was the genesis of her show, *Baking for Dough*.

She looked at him in an almost scrutinizing way, causing him to say, "I swear, I'm not going to steal it or anything. I'm not in the biz. As a matter of fact, I'm about as far from the biz as you can get without literally being in Timbuktu."

"It's basically a baking contest show where people are competing for a cash prize. You'll follow along with them as they try to whip up something in the allotted time. There'll be judges who taste their confections, then determine the winner," she explained.

Greyson's eyes widened as he said, "Are you kidding me? That's brilliant; I would watch the hell out of that."

Hannah's demeanor appeared to soften as she added, "And it would be hosted by my best friend Tanya. She's a model but also a wizard in the kitchen, and she'd make the perfect host. I literally just pitched her the idea, and she's thinking it over as we speak."

"I'm sure she'll agree to do it. And I don't know what Poetman's problem is, but it's a great idea. Wonderful even. If it were a stock, I would totally invest," he said, then mentally chastised himself. *What the hell are you doing? Dial down the over-aggrandizing.* But the exhilaration of simply being in her presence was intoxicating.

"Thanks," she replied as her cheeks bloomed.

"I'm just surprised your fiancé isn't more supportive."

"Well, he's got a lot on his plate right now with work and school," she defended as she looked down.

"Maybe so, but I still think you should always stand behind your significant other. Especially when she's got such a terrific idea," he said with a smile. It felt strangely exciting to criticize the revered Van.

"I don't know about terrific," Hannah said as she returned the smile. "It still needs some work."

He held her gaze and said, "Listen, if you truly believe in this idea, don't ever let anyone undermine your conviction, especially yourself. I think sometimes the hardest battle is convincing ourselves of our own ability."

"That sounds like it comes from personal experience."

"I guess it does. You see, I had this idea when I was a kid. Well, it was more of a fantasy, really. But I never forgot about it, and something..." Greyson paused briefly before continuing, "happened that made it relevant again. So, I worked my ass off and recently saw it come to fruition."

She nodded. "I was never terribly good at believing in myself. To be honest, I'm more comfortable with criticism or even indifference. I wish I could be one of those uber-confident people who never seem to doubt themselves. Even when they should."

"I know what you mean. My self-confidence is up and down, kinda like the weather. Not here, of course, more like the Pacific Northwest," he said with a smile, then thought about Nolan. "I have a friend whose self-confidence is unshakable. He's like a damn aplomb tree."

She giggled, and he said, "Sorry about the dad joke."

"Huh, what's a dad joke?"

"You know, the lame puns or one-line jokes a dad would make," he said, then instantly regretted it as he remembered that her father died in a car accident when she was only a child.

"Try having a supermodel for a best friend. Except that every ounce of her confidence is well deserved."

It's so unsettling talking with someone and knowing so much about them, yet they don't know you from Adam, he thought, as once again the urge to reach out and at least hold her hand was almost unbearable.

"She's so perfect that if I didn't love her so much, I'd have to hate her," Hannah said with a laugh.

Greyson started to speak, then paused. He had to consciously resist all their years of familiarity. *Beware of unearned wisdom, or in this case, unearned intimacy,* he told himself. Finally, he said, "Anything perceived to be perfect will always reveal its imperfections when examined up close. Whether it's the Mona Lisa, the Great Pyramid at Giza, or a loved one. The only exception to this rule is a stack of blueberry pancakes on a crisp autumn morning."

"Oh, so close," she grinned. "Now, if you had said blueberry waffles, then I'd have to agree with you."

He winced. "Waffles are for weirdos."

"You're a weirdo," she teased back.

"I'm sorry, but I'll have to ask you to leave," he said, motioning to the sidewalk.

Her mouth dropped open for a moment. "Are you kicking me off my own bench?"

"I'm afraid so if you're implying that waffles are superior to pancakes," he replied, pointing forward.

Hannah shook her head and said, "I'm not implying; I'm stating it as a fact." Then she glanced down at her watch. "You are lucky, though, I have to go anyway."

Greyson felt his heart sink as he watched her stand up. "Okay, fine, waffles… " He paused for dramatic effect, then said, "aren't that bad, I suppose. For like a six-year-old."

"Why is it that just when you think someone's a decent guy, they have to go and do something crazy like disparage a delicious breakfast food?"

He cupped a hand over his eyes to block out the sun and said, "Seriously, though, thanks for the chat."

Hannah took a step toward the pathway, then turned back. "I really enjoyed talking to you."

"Me too," he said, trying to stifle his emotional turbulence.

She nodded towards the bench. "This is kind of my home away from home, so if you're ever in the park again and I'm here, maybe stop by and say hi."

"Will do," he said with a weak smile. As he watched her walk away, he felt insufficiently replete, like someone dehydrated who'd only been given a sip of water.

"I have to see her again," he whispered desperately.

Chapter Thirty-One

As Hannah drove, she couldn't get the mysterious man she'd just met out of her mind. She thought of him as mysterious not only because she didn't know his name, but also because there was this sense of discordance, like seeing a bride at a funeral. It wasn't anything remotely negative, just confounding.

Her mind latched onto it like a paleontologist to a bone. The main question she kept asking herself was, *Why did I feel so comfortable around him?* She couldn't put her finger on it, but there was something familiar about him.

She was positive that she'd never seen him before. She would definitely have remembered meeting the quintessential professor type: a tall man with salt and pepper hair, tortoiseshell eyeglasses, and a neatly trimmed beard. Someone so distinguished-looking with such a calming presence would be hard to forget.

As she pondered the enigmatic stranger, guilt began seeping into her mind like a carbon monoxide gas leak. Her thoughts quickly pivoted to her fiancé, who was waiting for her. *I hope he's not still mad,* she thought as she pulled up to the restaurant and parked. She walked in with a familiar anxiety building in the pit of her stomach.

She was visibly startled when a voice came from behind, "I was starting to worry. It's not like you to make me wait this long."

She spun around and saw her fiancé leaning against the wall with his habitual look of discontent. “Sorry, I just lost track of time,” she sputtered.

“You sure this wasn't passive-aggressive payback for last night?”

No, that would be a page straight out of your script, she thought but just shook her head.

His smile broadened, and he said, “Good. Let's not ruin another day because your feelings got hurt by honesty. Like my father says, ‘Don't ask the question if you're afraid of the answer.’”

It was always a bad sign whenever he referenced his father, so Hannah just nodded. She learned early on in their relationship that certain subjects, mostly anything related to negative emotions, were verboten. At least they were for her.

“Where did you go?” he asked, as they found an empty booth.

She slid in across from him and said, “Just to the lake. It's such a lovely day; I didn't want to waste it.”

He picked up a menu and started scanning it. Without looking up, he said, “I guess, but I still don't see why you always have to go there. I mean, there are literally thousands of beautiful spots all over, and you just keep habitually returning to the same one. I'd understand it more if it were somewhere like Runyon Canyon, with legit hiking trails.”

“It's just always been my favorite spot since I was little. I feel a connection there that I can't explain,” she said. This wasn't the first time she felt forced to defend something that shouldn't need defending.

“But you just sit there like a bench potato, staring at the reservoir. You don't even break a sweat.”

“I told you I'll go with you anytime you want to go hiking at Runyon or Griffith Park,” she fired back.

As if recognizing the exasperation in her tone, he said, “Relax, I'm just kidding.” This was his fallback that magically nullified any slight, at least in his mind. He set the menu down and finally made eye contact. “It feels like you're still mad about last night. I already apologized for hurting your feelings. I don't know what more you want.”

Even though her brain knew this was classic misdirection, her emotions had already taken the bait. “I haven't even mentioned last night, but this is the second time you have. Sounds like *you* are not over it."

"You don't have to; I can just tell that it's still bothering you. That's the only reason I keep bringing it up. Listen, I want to get past it, but I need you to stop moping and trying to rain on this beautiful day," he said, then glanced past her and folded his menu.

Before she could respond, a voice behind her said, "Are we ready to order, or do you still need a minute?"

She picked up the untouched menu in front of her and rotely said, "Another minute, please."

"No problem. I'll go grab some water while you're deciding," the server said and vanished.

"I'm surprised you're not just getting a salad."

She didn't know if she was detecting annoyance in his voice or if her irritation was coloring everything red. Either way, she said nothing as she glanced over the menu. She quickly decided on a burger with fries, mostly to spite him. *So what if it's an immature gesture? At least it'll be a tasty one,* she thought with a measure of delight.

The server returned with two glasses of water, and they ordered. After he disappeared again, the uncomfortable silence enveloped them like humidity. That is until a familiar voice disrupted it.

"I was hoping to find you here," Tanya said, strolling up to the table.

Hannah turned in surprise and asked, "How did you know we'd be here?"

"Y'all are so routine; it's like you're an old married couple," she replied, then planted herself beside Hannah. "I had to find you. I started thinking about your idea and couldn't stop. And the more I thought about it, the more I liked it. And it didn't take long for me to fall in love with it, so I had to come tell you that I'm in."

Hannah felt her mood shift, like a rainy morning that rapidly transformed into a clear and sunny day. "Are you serious?"

"As serious as the look on your face before you saw me," Tanya said, then looked across the table and asked, "You think it's a great idea, right?"

"I'm probably not the person to ask. What do I know about food shows?" He shrugged, then edged off the seat. "I'm going to run to the restroom. I'll be right back."

After a brief pause, Hannah hugged Tanya and whispered emphatically, "Thank you."

"Don't thank me, girl; this is your million-dollar idea." Tanya craned her neck around and asked, "Okay, so who the hell was that distinguished gentleman you were talking to at the park?"

Hannah's eyes widened as she whispered, "What? You saw that?"

"I mean, I wasn't spying on you or anything, but I was finishing my run when I noticed you snuggled up on the bench with some older dude."

Hannah lightly elbowed her friend and said, "We were not snuggled up. And I don't know who he is—just some nice man who nearly passed out."

"Yeah, from overwhelming feelings of passion," Tanya teased. "Come on, you can tell me the truth. Sisters before misters. It's not like I'm going to tell you-know-who."

Hannah shook her head recalling the last conversation they had about her fiancée. It was more like a lecture that ended with Tanya vowing she would just stay out of it. "Shut up. He was struggling with the unseasonably warm day, you know, probably trying to get back into shape, but just overdid it. Something your skinny ass can't relate to." She purposely used Tanya's trigger word to distract her.

"I am not skinny and neither is my ass," Tanya protested. "All I am saying is that's the first time I've seen a strange dude make you smile like that. Normally, you're all weirded out by people you don't know and immediately go running off screaming, 'stranger danger, stranger danger,'" she said, flailing her arms all about.

"I am not that bad. I'm just nervous around unknown people—"

"Like a cat," Tanya interjected.

"Who's a cat?" a voice asked from behind.

Without missing a beat, Tanya answered, "I was just telling your fiancée that she's like a cat, and you're like a dog. Wait, that was way too fast. What, did you piss and run?"

He shook his head as he folded himself back into the booth. "There was too long a line. I can hold it."

Tanya turned to Hannah and said, "How about I come over tomorrow, and we can work on your idea together?"

Hannah nodded enthusiastically. A moment later, their server arrived, and Tanya begged off, leaving Hannah with her food and other notions to digest.

Chapter Thirty-Two

Greyson lingered on the bench for almost an hour, soaking in Hannah's residual presence. Their short conversation was the most alive he'd felt since before her death. He'd finally felt whole again and just needed one more encounter to fully complete the closure process.

He walked the park until he found a payphone and called for a taxi. He gave the driver the name of his hotel located in a more questionable part of town. It was necessary since he needed a place that took cash and wasn't concerned with proof of identity or a credit card for incidentals.

After folding himself into the back of the cab, he recounted Friday night's events. He pictured the lab with Dr. Greene standing in front of the computer. His mentor nodded to Greyson then powered up the machine. There was a brilliant shower of chromatic lights from the lasers surrounding Lilith's circumference followed by a silver bubble rapidly expanding out of the middle of the gateway. As he idled up to the pearl-like sphere, he turned and gave Dr. Greene a wink, then stepped into the mercurial orb.

Going into the wormhole was discombobulating and penetratingly cold. It must be similar to how those Polar Bear Club members feel when plunging into arctic water, but times a thousand. Then I felt pulled... no, more like swallowed by that evanescent void.

A post-traumatic shiver ran up his spine causing him to shift in his seat.

Everything else after that is a haze. I recall waking up on the floor of the now-darkened lab in front of Lilith, so disoriented that it was hard to even stand. Like I'd been on that astronaut training centrifuge. At least I inspected the equipment before hauling my butt out of there. And thank God I remembered Dr. Greene's code.

He absentmindedly watched older LA blur by as he thought, *Except for the power overload, I would say it's been an immensely successful experiment. Well, and the side effects of nausea, this lingering mental fogginess, and fatigue that caused me to sleep through Saturday. But all in all, I'd give the experience a four-star Tripadvisor rating.*

They passed an In-N-Out Burger, which made him think of Hannah. He ignored the brief twinge in his heart and concentrated on the present situation. *The main problem is that Lilith's power grid was completely fried. I knew there would be damage, but not to this extent. That's going to need more than a trip to Best Buy to repair. Or I guess RadioShack since that's still around now. I definitely need to get that fixed if I ever hope to return to 2021. Question is, how do I get it working in time? It's not like I can show up with a tool belt and tell them, "I'm here about the mysterious energy surge."*

As the cab pulled up to his seedy hotel, Greyson realized to get the gateway working again, he would need an inside man. And he only knew of one person on the planet who was qualified to offer that kind of help. *Looks like I'm going to need to visit Dr. Greene,* he thought as he slowly eased out of the cab.

* * *

Getting a meeting to see one of the world's most influential and esteemed CEOs wasn't like making a Genius Bar reservation. It was more akin to trying to get an appointment to see the President of the United States. Greyson needed a hook and figured he could use Friday night's incident to get Dr. Greene to take the bait.

So early the next morning, he called Dr. Greene's secretary and dangled the lure in his ear. "Yes, I have important information about Friday night's… uh, event and urgently need to speak to Dr. Greene about it," he sputtered to the young man who lackadaisically answered the phone. After laying back on the stiff hotel bed while waiting several moments in the ether of hold space, the secretary came back on the line and confirmed an 11 a.m. appointment.

"Damn, that's quick. And a hell of a lot easier than I expected," Greyson whispered as he returned the phone to its cradle.

Once again, he longed for his cell phone. It had only taken him the length of time he spent quietly slipping out of the Crastino building the other night to start missing his iPhone. He easily avoided the security guards as he lumbered around the nearly empty building, but once outside, he was automatically reaching for an empty pocket, hoping to order a late-night Uber.

How did we ever get along without a smartphone? he mused as he was forced to troll the dimly lit streets in search of a payphone.

Now he was filled with the bubbly excitement of once again meeting his idol for the first time. *I wonder how different he will be,* he contemplated as he rolled out of bed to get ready.

He took a white button-up shirt and dark gray slacks out of his bag. "I wish I'd brought fancier clothes," he mumbled to his reflection in the cloudy mirror. Now that he was forced to meet with Dr. Greene, he regretted his semi-casual clothing choice.

How did we not see this coming? Or at least, why didn't Dr. Greene? This was supposed to go a lot smoother. But now I'm about to break rule number one: no contact with anyone from my past, or, I guess, from my future, besides Hannah. Greyson exhaled, grabbed his money clip, and headed out of the dingy room to wait for another cab.

Inside the lobby, he couldn't help but stare at the younger man behind the counter reading the sports section of the newspaper. *If I didn't know better, I'd say that was my old middle school archenemy, Cameron Donovan. I should find his ass and pay him a ghost of Christmas future visit.* Greyson chuckled to himself as he turned to see the yellow taxi pull into the portico of the hotel.

* * *

I hope I don't look like some crazy person off the street, he thought as he sat nervously in Dr. Greene's office narthex.

He'd started sweating a couple of minutes after donning his clothes and hoped he didn't appear half of the hot mess he felt like. "Dr. Greene will see you now," the young man said as he opened the door to the office.

Greyson walked the familiar carpet and tried to project an image of calm and cool inside the sleekly modern office. This facade nearly crumbled when he saw the younger version of his mentor sitting across the cherry executive desk at the rear of the spacious office. Matching built-in bookshelves stood behind him like a pair of sentries, with an imposing array of scientific tomes.

Greyson quickly scanned the library until he spotted the seemingly out of place *Art of War* by Sun Tzu. Dr. Greene had teased that it was an original copy but was serious when he stated it held as much value as any other book on the shelf.

"Please have a seat," Dr. Greene said as he removed his thick glasses and motioned to the leather chair across from him. "I hear that you know something pertaining to the weekend's mystery."

His friend's welcoming demeanor immediately soothed Greyson. Dr. Greene still cut an impressive figure, even seated behind his desk. He was probably twenty pounds lighter, and the white patches in his hair were now merely a whisper. *It's going to be fine,* Greyson thought as he sank into the oversized chair. *I just need to figure out my flux capacitor moment.*

"Sorry, we should probably do introductions first," Dr. Greene said. "As you probably know, I'm Dr. Tyson Greene. And you are?"

Without thinking, Greyson blurted out, "I'm Cameron Donovan," then grimaced at his impetuous pseudonym.

"And who do you represent, Mr. Donovan?"

"I'm sorry, what?" Greyson asked with a touch of bewilderment.

"Who do you work for?" Dr. Greene said slowly.

You, Greyson thought, then said, "I don't."

Dr. Greene eyed him suspiciously and asked, "You don't work?"

"I mean, I do, but..." Greyson hesitated. "I'm kinda in between jobs right now."

"So, you're more of a free agent, kind of like Simeon Rice. And here to steal proprietary information from my company and sell it to the highest bidder?"

Greyson leaned back in his chair in surprise, almost as if pushed by Dr. Greene's words. "No, not like that at all."

"So, you do work for someone? Who is it?"

Greyson's mind started churning, and to buy a little time, he uttered, "Stark Industries."

Dr. Greene paused as if appraising the man in front of him, then said, "That sounds made up."

"Well, it's not. It's one of the leading tech companies in the world. Owned and run by the mega genius, Tony Stark," Greyson said, as he quickly found his footing in the fantastical lie.

"You're suggesting that, as the CEO of the top tech company in the world, I don't know every single one of my competitors? Do you know how utterly ridiculous that sounds?"

Greyson couldn't hold back a smile as he said, "Okay, fine. But really, you've never heard of Tony Stark?"

When Dr. Greene said nothing, Greyson continued, "He's Iron Man. How do you not know that Tony Stark is the alter ego of the comic book character Iron Man?"

"Because I'm an adult," Dr. Greene said bluntly.

Greyson glanced away and chuckled, "Déjà vu all over again." He looked back at Dr. Greene and asked, "What, were you born an adult? Did you wear a three-piece suit to kindergarten like Boss Baby?"

"Can we please get back to your attempt to steal my proprietary information?"

"I'm not trying to steal anything."

"That's the only explanation for how you know about Friday night's incident. I thought maybe you would come clean, but it appears you simply want to play games. I have neither the time nor the inclination to suffer this ruse, so I am afraid I must adjourn our meeting," Dr. Greene explained, then picked up the phone and said, "Tao, please send in security."

A few seconds later, two very large men in suits stormed into the office and headed directly for Greyson. "This isn't right," he protested, as they effortlessly lifted him off the chair.

"Maybe you'll be more inclined to speak to the police," Dr. Greene said.

As they dragged him off, Greyson turned his head and shouted, "I'm the reason the system overloaded. I turned Lilith on. And I did it from the future with your assistance. Now, I need your help to fix the power grid so I can get back there!"

"Oh, I'll agree that you certainly do need help," Dr. Greene mumbled, then spoke up, "Don't forget to explain to the cops how you got in and out of my lab."

"I got out because you told me the greatest NFL running backs were Jim Brown, Gayle King, and Walter Payton," Greyson yelled, desperately clinging to the doorway.

Dr. Greene scratched his chin as he watched Greyson be hauled out of his office.

Chapter Thirty-Three

Hannah was engrossed in refining her baking show brainchild when a pounding on the door startled her. She hopped up and shuffled to the front of her abode. When she checked the peephole, she smiled at the fish-eyed version of Tanya waving a bottle of wine in front of the lens.

As she opened the door, Hannah was greeted with, "I come bearing fermented juice of the grape," by her friend in a faux Italian dialect.

"Mama Mia!" Hannah teased, matching Tanya's over-the-top accent.

"Whatcha doing?" Tanya asked as she breezed into the apartment. It was a small, one-bedroom box with the kitchen and living room in the front and the bedroom and bathroom in the rear.

"Just refining my—" Hannah started to answer, then pivoted to, "I mean, *our* pitch for the show."

As Tanya moved past the kitchen, she paused at the compact desk housing a keyboard, CRT monitor, and computer tower and scanned the screen. "I see you're already working on the logistics." Then she turned to Hannah and said, "Someone's ready to graduate from production designer to producer."

"I don't want to do this forever," Hannah replied with a shrug. She'd gone straight from college into a career in television, with a minuscule assist from her mother. Her modicum of guilt from treading on her mother's fame quickly faded when she realized how widely used and abused the custom was.

She'd worked her butt off to get where she was today and wasn't content to rest on her laurels.

"Good for you," Tanya said, then remembered the bottle in her hand. As she U-turned into the kitchen, she asked, "So, is he here?"

Hannah shook her head. "He's working late again."

"Then, I guess it's girl's night out of the bottle," Tanya grinned, fetching two glasses from the cabinet. "Our choice tonight is a Two-Buck Chuck Cabernet Sauvignon." Despite the fact that they could easily afford the more bougie wines, both of their palates tended towards the proletariat side.

"Have you eaten yet?"

Tanya gave her the side-eye and said, "Do I look like my Bibi? It's way too early for dinner."

"It's almost six."

"And only the elderly eat before seven," Tanya said while overpouring a glass for each.

Hannah scooped hers off the counter. "I don't think either of us are going to wanna cook, so if we order now, it probably won't get here until closer to seven."

"That's why we make such a good team. You're always thinking two moves ahead, and I always benefit from it," Tanya said as she raised her cup. After they clinked glasses, she strolled into the living room and parked herself on the couch.

With her free hand, Hannah lifted the cordless phone off the charger and asked, "Chinese, sushi, Thai, or Indian?"

"They all pair well with red, so dealer's choice," Tanya said, then quickly added, "Wait, not sushi; I had that for lunch."

"Sushi it is," Hannah teased as she scanned over the takeout menus pinned to the refrigerator.

"Listen, Ackerman, don't think I won't take my wine and go home."

Hannah turned from the fridge and leaned against the edge of the kitchen counter. "Then I will call Naomi Campbell or Kate Moss and see if they want their own TV show."

"Kate Moss wouldn't know parchment paper from rolling paper," Tanya scoffed.

Hannah laughed as she dialed the number to the Thai restaurant. She ordered their usual, returned the phone to its stand, and joined Tanya on the couch. "They said it'll be here in about twenty minutes. Which, of course, means more like forty-five."

"They better hurry, 'cause now I'm starving."

Hannah's head whipped around as she stared at her friend. "What the hell? A minute ago, you lectured me on eating this early."

"You know that sometimes all it takes to get my stomach growling is the mere mention of food. It's like with sex; I could be dead tired, super bloated, and suffering from severe menstrual cramps, but kiss the back of my neck, and suddenly I'm as horny as a teenage boy."

Hannah held up a hand like a crossing guard and said, "TMI."

"You started it."

"I most certainly did not," Hannah protested.

"How about *Bake for Dough*?" Tanya asked.

"Whahuh?" Hannah asked in confusion.

"The title of our show. It is a baking competition, right? I assume there will be a cash prize for the winner."

"I guess you can't call it a competition if there's no money. I mean, this is America," Hannah said.

"Right, so *Bake for Dough* or *Baking for Dough*."

"I like *Baking for Dough*. It's clearer, if not lacking subtlety."

Tanya nodded. "Like you said, this is America. It's also television. Subtlety is lost on the casual viewer."

"I guess," Hannah agreed. Her mind suddenly drifted to the man she'd met in the park yesterday. *I wonder what he'd think of that name,* she pondered as her attention vacillated to the window across from them. Then, she questioned why this stranger could so easily breeze into her head like lyrics to a familiar jingle.

"Helloooo," Tanya intoned as she waved a hand in front of Hannah's face. "Where'd your beautiful mind wander off to?"

Hannah's attention snapped back to her friend. "Huh, nowhere. I… I just thought I might have heard the delivery guy."

"Five minutes after you called? Yeah, right. That was the look of yearning, and I don't mean for Tom Yum soup. I doubt it was about him either," Tanya said, pointing to the picture of Hannah and her fiancé on the end table. "You haven't made a pining expression over him since I can remember. So, I'm guessing it's about the man in the park."

"How in the hell do you do that?"

"It's a talent, honey. Plus, I know you better than anyone, including yourself. Psychics might be bullshit, but we definitely have a spiritual connection between us," Tanya said, motioning a finger from her head to Hannah's. "So, what were you thinking?"

"You tell me, Doctor X."

"Professor X," Tanya corrected. "And I said I can't read your mind, just your mood."

After a long moment, Hannah sighed and said, "It's nothing really. I told him about the idea for the show, and he seemed excited about it. He had this kind of enthusiasm that was, I don't know, encouraging. So, I just wondered what he'd think about the title, '*Baking for Dough*.'"

"He'd think it was fantastic unless he was a total douche clown."

"He's not a total douche clown," Hannah laughed. "At least, as far as I know."

"That's the problem with men. You never know if they're a douche clown until after you've bought a ticket to their circus," Tanya declared as she raised her glass.

They clinked glasses again, and Hannah said, "Amen, sister."

Chapter Thirty-Four

Greyson sat quietly in the empty room. Calling it a room might be a little generous; it was more like a closet with metal racks against blank white walls, storing all manner of cleaning and office supplies, along with a single folding chair. The two dapper security guards placed him inside with no word on what to expect save for Dr. Greene's threat of police engagement.

Well, I am royally fucked, Greyson thought as he stared at the wooden door. *How am I going to get back now? I don't have anyone to help me. Tsai's in Texas right now, and Nolan's probably hung over after some wild frat party back in Virginia. It's not like I can call him or his parents and explain that I'm Greyson from the future and need help with bail.*

He exhaled loudly and put his head down. *And my only potential ally here thinks I'm a corporate spy. This couldn't have gone more wrong if I'd planned it! On the brighter side, at least I'm seeing a new part of the building.*

As he waited for the cops to come busting through the door, he briefly considered calling Hannah. *And tell her what? Oh, I know your name and contact info because we'll be married in about eleven years. Then, after your sudden passing, I time-traveled to see you one last time. I needed to get something akin to closure because I was struggling to get over losing you.*

"Yeah, I'd go straight from jail right into the loony bin," he whispered. "I don't have any kind of ID, and there's no record of me, at least this version of me, anywhere. I literally materialized right out of thin air. I have less than a month to find a way to fix Lilith and go home. Or I'll be—"

The door squeaked open, cutting off his brooding. He looked up, expecting someone in a blue uniform, but was surprised to see Dr. Greene's imposing figure lingering in the entrance. "Who's Gayle King?" he asked as he adjusted his glasses.

"Huh?" Greyson muttered, then he remembered his frantic Hail Mary as he was being dragged away. "Oh, she's a TV journalist. I couldn't remember the second guy's last name."

"Gale Sayers," Dr. Greene replied. "So, how did you know my code was my top three running backs? I've never told anyone that."

"I know, but you told me. Or, at least, you will. It's how I got out of here the other night—by using your code."

"I know you used my code; I checked the log. What I don't know is how you figured it out."

Greyson paused as he tried to think of a way out of this current predicament. So far, the direct approach had been a total failure, and he needed a new angle. He realized this might be the first time in their shared history that he possessed knowledge that Dr. Greene did not and understood that was the key. "You built Lilith, what, last year?"

"Sixteen months ago, to be exact," Dr. Greene corrected.

"And you are currently trying to see if you can not only find a microscopic wormhole but inject it with enough energy that it's viable for use, right?"

Dr. Greene said nothing and just leaned against the door frame. "Once you've done that, then you'll move on to building another gateway. I'm sure you're working on the updated designs for Eve right now," Greyson said, trying to sound calm but speaking like he'd just shotgunned a 40-ounce espresso.

"Again, how can you possibly know all that? Do we have a mole?" Dr. Greene asked as he crossed his arms.

Greyson shook his head. "Even after you've built the second gateway, the main obstacle will be, of course, energy. If you can overcome that, then you can move objects through space in an instant. But really, it's incomplete because what's missing?"

"Time," Dr. Greene whispered. "Are you proposing that Lilith is also a time machine?"

Greyson put one index finger on his nose and pointed the other at Dr. Greene. He recalled a prior conversation they'd had about unintentionally changing the past and said, "I honestly didn't want to involve you in this, 'cause you know, the whole butterfly effect and all."

"I don't subscribe to the butterfly effect, at least when you're talking about time travel, because basically, it's not possible. At least, not in the direction you're claiming," Dr. Greene interrupted.

"Let's just put a pin in that for now. If you have two gateways, what prevents you from entering coordinates for all four dimensions?"

"The laws of physics," Dr. Greene answered abruptly.

"Which law says time travel is impossible?"

Dr. Greene frowned. "Again, we know due to Einstein's theory of special relativity that the faster we go, the slower time moves. So, time travel from the past to the future is indisputable. But that's merely going faster in the same direction that time naturally moves. Reversing time is a whole different ball game. Otherwise, we'd see some kind of evidence."

Hello, you are seeing evidence, Greyson thought, then said, "Not until the time machine first gets built. Or else I'd have gone back farther and stopped my mother from being murdered."

Dr. Greene said nothing as he took measure of Greyson. The stale air in the closet went still until he asked, "I'll indulge you for a moment. Why would you come back to this point?"

"You mean, why did I come back to 2001?"

"Yes. I assume you're not from next year. And I don't get the impression that this is merely an experiment to see if time travel is possible. There has to be a hidden agenda."

Greyson hesitated once more, wondering how truthful he should be. He'd already broken rules number one and two: don't interact with anyone you know except for Hannah, and don't tell anyone you're from the future. He looked down and said, "It's more of a personal reason."

"That leads me to believe this is about a woman," Dr. Greene said, then quickly added, "Or man. But definitely of an amorous nature."

"What makes you say that?"

Dr. Greene met his gaze. "You already mentioned it's not about your mother. You glanced down when you said it was personal, so that indicates something tragic, and judging by your age, it would mean the loss of a partner. And you have an overall despondent nature about you."

"Who are you, Dr. Phil?"

"Is that supposed to be some future scientist?" Dr. Greene scoffed.

"I'm pretty sure he's famous right now," Greyson chuckled. "He's a TV psychologist who deals with feelings and relationships. Kind of a love doctor."

"I must admit, I myself have little comprehension of or use for romantic entanglements."

"That explains why you never bought a greeting card company," Greyson joked.

"It just seems like an excuse for someone to lose control of themselves and act in ways contradictory to rational thinking. Apologies to Karl Marx, because religion is just a disguised form of government. Love is the real opiate of the masses. It's simply a social construct created to subjugate a population," Dr. Greene ranted, then cracked a half-smile and added, "I guess that's why my mother once said I was too rational to ever understand it."

Greyson tried to keep a poker face as he thought, *Holy shit, this is a side of Dr. Greene I never got to see. And it's the first time I can say with complete certainty that he is 100% wrong.*

"I suppose if I asked you for more proof, you'd tell me that we're best friends in the future and that you know personal details about me that no one else would know."

Greyson briefly considered his response, then figured the truth was the only thing that would set him free. "Honestly, yes, we do work together, and yes, I consider you a friend. Although I'm not completely confident that it's a two-way street. You're an extremely private person, and the only reason I know your personal code is out of necessity. I probably couldn't tell you anything that's not already on your Wikipedia page."

Dr. Greene paused for a moment as he rubbed his chin, then stood up straight and said, "Although I have no idea what a Wikipedia page is, that's the most believable thing you've said so far. Occam's Razor says this is more about corporate espionage than science fiction, but I can't completely discount your claim. As my favorite comedian Bill Cosby would say, 'The past is a ghost, the future a dream, and all we ever have is now.' So, I might as well keep my possible enemy close. At least for the time being."

Greyson visibly cringed at the Cosby reference and said, "You might want to stop quoting the Coz."

"Why?"

"Just trust me," Greyson replied, then pondered his mentor's one-eighty turn. *I bet there's a little bit of hubris behind his reversal. I'm sure he's reveling in the idea that not only has he invented a teleporter but a time machine to boot.*

"It's funny how strangers tend to say 'trust me' before they've earned it."

Greyson just shrugged, then asked dubiously, "So, are you going to help me?"

Dr. Greene shook his head. "It's more like you are going to help me."

Chapter Thirty-Five

Greyson was released from the closet prison with the promise to return tomorrow and meet with Dr. Greene to, in his words, "evaluate the entire situation." He wasn't exactly sure what that entailed, but he was eager to escape the claustrophobic room. So, he left his future stomping grounds, wondering what his next move should be.

Well, that sure as hell went a lot easier and, at the same time, harder than I'd expected. I hope the rest of this excursion isn't so roller coaster-y, he thought while patiently waiting for his cab. His mind turned to Hannah as he wondered what she was doing.

I could go stalk the park, but it was always less likely that she'd be there on a weekday. Unless there was something stressful going on or it was a particularly majestic day. Of course, running into her so soon would probably raise a red flag. He spied the yellow taxi pulling up to the front of the building and got up from the concrete bench.

As he got into the cab, he resigned himself to dwelling in his hotel room, at least until tomorrow's meeting with Dr. Greene. *I've already broken two rules, so I better keep a low profile. Even if it means slowly dying from heartache and boredom. Oh, the things I do for the stability of the spacetime continuum.*

* * *

He stayed true to his resolve as he spent the rest of Monday eating takeout and watching decades-old reruns, at least to him. The Tuesday morning meeting couldn't come quick enough, and he showered, shaved, and dressed with renewed vigor. Except for working with Dr. Greene, he'd lived a hermit's life for the last several months, so it wasn't exactly a change of pace. But now that he was occupying the same spacetime as Hannah, he was suddenly eager for human interaction. He felt like a bear awakened from a hibernation of depression.

Greyson cabbed back to the Crastino building, trying to anticipate what would be in store once he got there. "Expect the unexpected," Dr. Greene had warned him just before he stepped through the portal to the past. *That was pretty prophetic,* he thought as he hurried up to Dr. Greene's office.

Although the overall layout and decor of the building were pretty much the same as it had always been or would be, there were enough minuscule differences to make the experience almost surreal. Greyson was amazed at how subtle changes could make him feel discombobulated and wondered if there were some residual effects of the time jump.

Talk about jet lag; this is more like anachronous lag, he thought as he stepped up to Dr. Greene's assistant's desk.

"Go on in," Tao muttered, not looking up from his monitor.

I wonder what happened to him. Does he still work for us, did he jump ship to a rival, or did he follow the trend of starting up his own company? Greyson speculated as he tentatively strolled into Dr. Greene's office.

"Please, have a seat," Dr. Greene said, motioning to the chair across from him.

Greyson couldn't help but look back at the closing door, half expecting the three-piece suited Stormtroopers to come barreling in. "Relax, this isn't an ambush," Dr. Greene assured. "But all I have to do is press a button, and they'll be back within a minute."

"Paranoid much," Greyson teased as he dropped into the chair.

Dr. Greene folded his hands into a pyramid under his chin and said, "You clearly don't know what it's like to be a multimillionaire. Or a CEO. Or a minority."

"That is true, but I did stay at a Holiday Inn Express last night."

"How is that pertinent?"

I really am a man out of time and references, Greyson thought. "Just kidding. So, what are we going to do? You know, about the whole assisting me in returning to the present."

"This is the present," Dr. Greene replied, then tilted his head down. "But that is the question, isn't it? What are we going to do?"

He allowed silence to slowly fill the conversational vacuum until Greyson could no longer take it and blurted out, "I vote we fix Lilith's power grid."

Dr. Greene shot him a suspicious glance. "That would certainly give you an insider's view of the machinery."

Greyson maintained eye contact and said slowly, "I am not a spy. I already know the machinery at a blueprint level, okay." He paused, then mumbled almost to himself, "Hell, you could even say I know Lilith in the biblical sense."

Dr. Greene paused briefly as a faint smile dawned across his face. "If what you say is true, what power source did you use?"

"Wait, what?" Greyson exclaimed. "If I told you that, I would be giving you unearned knowledge of the future, which you emphatically said *not* to do." He punctuated his sentence by pointing at Dr. Greene.

"Maybe I was wrong," Dr. Greene said, then added, "Or will be. Bosons, this kind of thought experiment is so frustrating."

"So, are you admitting you might be wrong? I mean, in the future?" Greyson asked, pushing the only button he knew Dr. Greene had. In the entire time he'd known him, Greyson never once heard him say he was inexact, incorrect, or mistaken. The only speed Dr. Greene knew was certainty. In that way, he was a bit similar to Nolan.

Dr. Greene held up a hand and said, "Hold on there; I am not saying that."

Of course, you're not. I don't even think you're capable of saying that, Greyson thought as he fought back a smile.

"Maybe I didn't have enough information to make a hypothesis," he backpedaled. "We need to study this and experiment more before declaring any edicts."

Which version do I listen to? Greyson wondered. *Compared to the Dr. Greene*

I know, this one is almost like a rebel. An apostate without a cause.

"Maybe we should start with something more basic, such as why exactly did you pick this date to come back to?"

Greyson itched his beard as he leaned back in his chair. "To put it simply, my wife died suddenly nearly a year ago. I just wanted to see and talk to her one more time."

"And have you spoken to her yet?"

Greyson scrunched up the side of his face and said, "That's not an easy question to answer."

"I didn't ask you how life began. I asked you a simple yes or no question."

"I mean, kinda. We talked briefly on Sunday, but it wasn't anywhere near closure level. I guess I wasn't as prepared as I hoped; everything was so unexpected. I just need to see her again, one more time," Greyson explained as the conversation echoed in his memory.

"And then what? You'll be ready to go home?"

The very thought of losing Hannah again made his heart sink, but Greyson knew there was no other option, so he simply nodded.

"If you activated Lilith from another time period, I'm assuming the plan would be to do it again after a certain interval. How long did you give yourself—a week?"

"A couple of weeks," Greyson corrected.

"That seems risky; why so long?"

"We didn't know how long I would need to find Han… her and make contact, so we calculated on the side of caution."

Dr. Greene tapped on his desk. "It still seemed overly risky. My next and most important question is, can you fix Lilith? We've checked her over, and it's more than just the power converters; the energy surge you're claiming responsibility for fried a lot of her circuitry."

Greyson shrugged, then figured he'd better at least act like he knew what he was doing. So, he said, "I should be able to get her up and running before I'm scheduled to go back. With replacement parts and your help, of course."

"Of course." Dr. Greene nodded. Greyson couldn't tell if it was a mocking or arrogant agreement. Then, Dr. Greene shocked him with, "Cutting it kind of close there, McFly?"

Greyson's eyes widened. "Did you just make a pop culture reference?"

Dr. Greene just raised his eyebrows, so Greyson continued, "Yeah, it's a little close, but it shouldn't be a problem." The thought, *Why didn't future Dr. Greene warn me about any of this?* crept into his head.

"When exactly are you from?"

Greyson pondered the question for a moment, then said, "Probably best I don't reveal that."

Dr. Greene leaned back in his chair and stroked his beard. "In this ambiguous future, do we know what the universe is made of? As in any breakthroughs on what dark matter is?"

"Not much more than you know now."

"Any signals from extraterrestrial life?"

"Nope."

"Have we solved the unified theory of physics problem?"

As Greyson shook his head, Dr. Greene asked, "Have we advanced our understanding of black holes?"

Greyson thought about the fanfare from the first image of a black hole released a couple of years ago and tried to remember what exactly they knew back in 2001, then said, "I don't think so. Look, all these are very complicated questions. Kinda like asking if Ben Affleck and Jennifer Lopez are still together."

"I don't know who those people are. And don't talk to me about complicated things; there's nothing you could tell me that I wouldn't understand, even better than you. But it doesn't sound like there's been any significant progress in your so-called future."

"Hello, time travel," Greyson replied as he motioned to himself.

"Fair point. If this all isn't some devious stratagem," Dr. Greene said, then threw him a curveball with, "Have the Cubs won a World Series?"

"Spoilers," Greyson replied with a wry grin. "You should really stop asking questions about the future because, from now on, I'm just going to plead a fifth of Beethoven." As he watched Dr. Greene slowly swivel in his chair, he mused, *He's not exactly the man I knew and revered. Maybe I am in a parallel universe or some other dimension, and he isn't that same person.*

There was a sharp knock on the door, and Greyson turned just in time to see Dr. Aarón Vicario bounce into the office waving a print-out. "I got the report from Saturday's—" He paused when he saw Greyson. "I'm sorry, I didn't know you were with someone."

"Dr. Vicario," Greyson said in surprise. The short, distinguished, and handsome man was often described as the Wozniak to Dr. Greene's Steve Jobs.

"Yes, do I know you?"

Greyson shook his head as Dr. Greene said, "Thanks, Aarón. I need to finish this interview and work on some things, but I can meet with you later to go over it."

"No problem, Jefe; just give me a ring whenever you're free."

Greyson watched a more youthful version of the man he'd known for over a decade retreat back out the door and thought, *This is too freaking weird.*

As he turned back around, Dr. Greene said, "If we are going to work together, I should at least know your real name. And please don't say Bruce Wayne."

I guess it couldn't hurt to know my name, he thought and said, "I'm Greyson."

Dr. Greene stood up and said, "Nice to meet you, Greyson. Or, from your perspective, meet you again. Since I'm not going to get any spoilers out of you, we might as well head down to the lab and examine the full extent of the damage you did to my machine."

"Yeah, great," Greyson said, suspecting this would be a quasi-audition. As he followed him out of the office, the question that now plagued him was, *Did I actually go back in time, or did I jump to some alternate reality?*

Chapter Thirty-Six

It took Hannah the entire week to pull every string she had to get a meeting scheduled with a pair of executives at the Food Network. To even score an audience with such power brokers was a testament to her stellar reputation, tenacity, and fledgling clout. When she called Tanya to reveal the good news, her friend simply replied, "Took you long enough."

Her fiancé had a similarly short reaction: "Good for you." She tried not to take his passive-aggressively condescending lack of support personally. At least, not too much. He'd been under an ocean of pressure since slamming headfirst into a great wall of writer's block, which was interfering with both his work and graduate thesis.

When the weekend finally came, she eagerly made her pilgrimage to the park. Hannah sat there in a bubble of nervous energy as her mind focused on work, among other things. "This could either be the start of a new phase of my career or the end of it," she whispered as she gazed across the still lake.

All her life, she'd fought to keep her hopes from ever rising high enough that a subsequent fall could do any permanent damage. Hovering just below cloud level, her Icarus wings would never taste the rays of direct sunlight. She liked to think of it as the hallmark of a realist.

Almost unconsciously, her eyes left the blue waters and began scanning over the park. There was finally a chill in the air that was fitting for the beginning of February, topped off with a canopy of gray. The crisp morning breeze licked her face with a sharp tongue.

When she caught herself searching for the mystery park man, she immediately stopped, feeling a twinge of guilt. "I've got way too much to worry about right now. There's no need to conjure up some fantasy crush distraction," she said to herself as she forced her attention back to the reservoir and practiced the mindful meditation exercises her therapist taught her.

So, she closed her eyes and heedfully slowed her breathing. A few minutes later, a voice chirped up, "Please don't tell me I'm interrupting a moment of Zen."

Her head whipped around, and her eyes landed on the familiar stranger. She saw that this time he was dressed appropriately in jeans and a dark blue windbreaker. "I see someone finally watched the Weather Channel before going out."

He looked down at his clothing and laughed. "Yeah, I think I'm getting the hang of dressing for the temperature you have, not for the temperature you expect." When he peered back up at her, he had to squint hard to prevent any tears from escaping. *I can't believe I'm really seeing her again.*

"Good. I haven't practiced CPR since high school, and unfortunately, the patient didn't make it. I mean, she was a dummy, so there's that."

"Annie are you okay, are you okay Annie," Greyson sang.

"I can tell you're not here for a record contract," she said with a playful grin.

"Alright there, Simon Cowell. You don't have to vocally shame me," he replied, feigning offense.

She shot him a confused glance at his reference, so he quickly reversed the conversation. "I always wondered if that song was talking about Resusci Anne."

Hannah smiled as she scooted over in the universal gesture of "Please, have a seat." "You know, I never thought about it till now."

"It's not like I wrote my dissertation on it," he said as he bookended her on the bench.

"If I'm going to share my favorite spot, I should at least know your name."

"It's Gre..." He stopped as if an automatic danger alarm suddenly went off in his head and quickly recovered with, "A great question. You don't want to be sitting in the park beside a man with no name." He sang the last sentence to the tune of America's "A Horse with No Name" in an attempt to stall for time.

"You really need to stick to your day job, Mister…"

The second swipe at his singing unconsciously stirred pubescent memories, and he once again blurted out, "Cameron Donovan, at your service." He clenched his teeth as he recalled the menacing bully from his youth. Then he mentally kicked himself for being unprepared for something so obvious as an introduction. And for saddling himself with the very same moniker as his adolescent nemesis.

"Cameron, that's my fiancé's middle name," she said, which gave Greyson another mental kick, only several inches lower this time. She offered her hand. "Pleased to meet you, Cameron. I'm Hannah."

He took it and said, "Lovely to meet you, Hannah." Then quickly added, "Again." As the touch of her hand accelerated his heart rate, he turned to the lake and took a deep breath. *So the elusive Van's middle name was Cameron; what an unfortunate coincidence. I'm learning more about him than I ever cared to know.*

Hannah hadn't spoken much about her first husband, and Greyson was more than happy not to pry. Her romantic life before him was like an unopened tomb, and he'd always been wary of the curse that came from breaking that seal. It was easier on the ego not to know the details of her amorous life before him.

After a long moment, he turned back to her and asked, "So, did your model friend go for the idea?"

"Ah, as a matter of fact, she did."

He leaned over just a fraction and asked, "And?"

She couldn't contain her smile, which spread across her face like a sunrise. "She said yes."

"Congratulations."

"That part was easy compared to the next step. I spent all of last week calling in so many favors just to get a meeting with some TV execs that I'm now in favor-debt for life."

"I'm sure you'll win 'em over and earn that proverbial green light," he said knowingly.

She shook her head. "I wish I had your confidence. Getting a pilot produced is extremely difficult, even when you have experience. Getting one when you don't, well, that's like stepping off the bus and landing the lead role in a new Spielberg movie."

"I wouldn't go that far. You have plenty of experience," he said, then added, "I'm assuming. And you look like a hard worker; your communication skills seem to be more than adequate. I mean, you don't use no double negatives or any other egregious conversational faux pas. I'm sure if you go into the meeting and pitch your idea with confidence and verve, they'll recognize its brilliance. Just end it by telling them that this show will be a trailblazer and probably last at least a decade. It will be such an innovation that it'll inspire a cornucopia of baking competitions."

She went silent as she looked toward the shoreline. He watched a single tear stream down her cheek. "I'm sorry, I got a little too mansplainy there. I'm sure you have this and don't need any advice, especially from a guy not even qualified to have an opinion," he said, hoping to reverse any unintentional damage.

After a long pause, she said, "It's not that; it's just that I wasn't expecting so much encouragement. I've just been in such a negative mindset for so long that hearing anyone other than Tanya or my therapist boost me up like that is just… unexpected. Even my mother told me, 'I hope you're not counting on any help from me,' when I shared the news about the meeting."

An image of Hester, a martini in one hand and her own autobiography in the other, slipped into his mind. He'd known about their tumultuous relationship, but it was on the mend during their time together. *I guess I just never understood how fractured it was.* All he could say was, "I'm sorry."

She wiped her cheek and said, "It's fine." Then she let out a brief sigh and asked, "What's mansplainy?"

"Huh," he breathed, then remembered what he said. "Oh, you know, mansplaining is when a guy explains something to a woman in a condescending way." As he watched her smile once more, he teased, "And condescending means showing a patronizing or superior attitude toward others."

She softly nudged him. "Mansplaining, I like that. It perfectly describes a lot of my bosses."

Their second brief contact sent a charge of emotions through his body like a jolt of electricity, and again he had to fight the urge to throw his arms around her. Seeing and talking to Hannah was exhilarating and emotive. But it was also like suffering a death by a thousand fervent cuts.

"You okay?" she asked.

He breathed out slowly, hoping to steady his pounding heart, and nodded. "I'm fine. Once more, this unnatural heat is getting to me."

She glanced up at the ashen sky and said, "Yeah, it's practically torrid."

After finally composing himself, he realized their conversation was dying on the vine. "You said your mother refused to help you? What is she, the president of NBC or something?"

She laughed as she kicked away a small rock. "That would make more sense, right? No, she's…" Hannah hesitated. Greyson knew she never quite understood why it was embarrassing to talk about her renowned mother, but it always gave her pause. "She's a famous actress," she continued, then appeared to wait for the inevitable question, "What was she in?"

But that question never came. Instead, he said, "I bet that must have been tough, growing up with a celebrity mom."

Hannah shrugged. "It was more your stereotypical Hollywood family. But nothing provocative or scandalous. Hell, Lifetime wouldn't even bother to make a movie about it. My mother was always busy working or promoting. Every family has its issues, I suppose."

"It could be worse. You could be the daughter of a notorious serial killer. Or a politician. Or a mime. Imagine those Christmas mornings, having to pantomime opening presents," he said as he shuddered.

She laughed, "I'm sure they don't take their work home with them."

"I don't know, you ever heard of method miming?"

She shook her head and asked, "So, what do your parents do? And please don't tell me they are serial killers."

Shit, what do I tell her? I feel like a spy caught in a congenial interrogation. After a short pause, he said, "I wish. It's way worse than that."

Before he could finish, a man in a plaid flannel shirt and jeans strolled by with a yellow Labrador Retriever, who raced up and started barking at them. The dog stopped suddenly as a man tugged on its leash and said, "Stop it, Magic; calm down, boy."

"Anyone else having Cujo flashbacks?" Greyson said as he scooted back against the bench.

The man called out, "Don't worry, he's friendly. His bark is way worse than his bite." Then he dragged the dog back to the sidewalk, gave a friendly wave, and continued down the path.

Greyson couldn't shake the notion that he somehow knew the dog walker. He mulled over this while waiting until the man was out of earshot, then said, "They always say that right up until the dog's mouth is clamped down on your throat like the jaws of life. Or death, in this case."

"Someone's scared of a cutie poochie," Hannah teased.

"More cautious than scared. Have you seen the needle for a rabies shot? It's like an ice pick." As he intently watched the guy being pulled away by his hound, he blurted out, "Oh my God, that's Ron Swanson!"

"Who?"

"Uh, sorry. That dude looked just like a younger version of my old shop teacher back in high school, minus the mustache, of course."

"Of course," Hannah agreed as if pretending to know exactly what he was talking about.

The brief interlude gave him time to contrive a response to her inquiry. "Anyway, back to my parents—they're both teachers." He figured he could stick close to the truth by using Nolan's parents in lieu of his own.

"How is that worse than serial killers?"

"I would much rather explain getting a D in English to a pair of serial killers than to my parents. They took every missed assignment, bad grade, and dangling participle personally. Like I was doing it to spite them. A veritable rebel without a dependent clause."

"Must have been a rough childhood with all that grammatical bullying."

"You have no idea. Even when I moved away, I was still afraid to e—" He hesitated for a moment, trying to recall how prevalent emailing was twenty years ago, before deciding to keep it old school. "epistolize them. You know, fear of the letters being returned soaked in the dreaded red ink."

"Did you really just use the word epistolize?" she marveled.

"That's what happens when you grow up with teachers for parents."

"Do you talk to them a lot?"

He paused again, and the sudden urge to come clean and tell her the whole truth almost overwhelmed him. *God, I hate lying to her like this. It feels so unnatural.*

As if sensing his reluctance, she said, "I'm sorry, I don't mean to get all nosey."

"No, no, it's not that," he said, shaking his head, "They passed away last year. My father from heart disease, and then my mother from cancer not long after. Both happened so unexpectedly that I didn't even get the chance to say goodbye." The thought, *The best lies spring from a kernel of truth,* popped into his head like a text message alert.

Hannah put a hand up to her mouth and said, "I'm so sorry. I didn't mean…"

As her voice trailed off, he said, "It's okay, I know. They were older. Not that it makes it any better or easier, but to know they both lived full and happy lives does—"

Now, it was his turn to waver, so she finished his thought, "Give you peace?"

He looked at her, and suddenly, tears started rolling slowly down his cheeks. The ache to touch her, to hold her against him, and to feel her warmth nearly paralyzed him. *She is the most beautiful thing I've ever seen,* he thought as he wiped away the tears.

As if an unseen force of nature read his heart and decided to intervene, she reached out and placed her hand on his shoulder. The minor consolation was akin to an errant match being dropped in a dry bed of leaves. It reignited a long-suppressed passion in Greyson's core. In that quiet moment of solace, *I have to see her again* was the only thought he could conjure.

He finally exhaled audibly and said, "Sorry for ruining the mood. I guess their loss still feels kinda fresh."

"I know what you mean. You never got closure, so the wound doesn't quite heal properly. My father died in a car accident when I was very little, and it still haunts me, even to this day,"

Greyson thought of his own mother and his adolescent fantasy, or obsession at the time, of going back to prevent her death. A death he'd always blamed himself for, even though everyone, including the rational part of his mind, tried to assure him that it wasn't his fault. And even though the circumstances were completely different, he was now living out a variation of that fantasy. A fantasy he desperately wanted to preserve.

"Closure is a strange thing. It's kinda like a privilege: you can't truly understand what it means until it's taken away," he said, looking past her to the distant trees.

"Isn't a privilege something that you can earn, though?"

"I'm not talking about a privilege like a reward for good behavior. I mean something that makes a hard time easier. Like white privilege."

"White privilege?" she repeated.

"Oh yeah, that's the systemic benefits white people have over non-whites in our society."

"Are you sure you're not a sociologist?"

He met her gaze and snickered, "I mean, I did take a sociology class. But that was a different time and place. I do my best to be woke, though."

"Woke?"

"That just means being aware of racial prejudice and discrimination, along with other forms of oppression and injustice," he explained. *Damn it, I keep stepping on these anachronistic landmines. I didn't anticipate how hard talking with someone twenty years in the past would be. I guess this is what dating someone a generation younger than you feels like. They don't get your accustomed references.*

"I could see you being a sociology professor. Or maybe English; I mean, you did use the word epistolize. And you already have that scholarly appearance," she said, waving her finger at his beard and glasses. Then, without thinking, she added, "I know I would sign up for one of your classes."

Is she flirting with me? he thought hopefully, then blurted out, "You'd be my favorite student." He immediately regretted the desperately thirsty and artless retort, so he tried to walk it back by quickly adding, "To torture with my dreaded red pen."

"See, you're already thinking like an academic," she teased.

"Really, though, I'd be a terrible professor."

She shrugged. "For what it's worth, I'm learning new things whenever we talk. It's probably why I enjoy our conversations so much."

"Well, thank you. I do feel a unique comfort level with you." Then he switched to a faux-English accent. "It makes our dialogues positively intoxicating."

"If you talked like that, I would *definitely* take one of your classes," she cooed.

I can't believe I'm actually flirting with my wife. Well, her younger self. But regardless of that, it's her. I guess I still got it.

He was abruptly brought back down to Earth when she glanced down at her watch. "Sorry, but I have to end today's seminar. Gotta go meet the old ball and chain."

"Oh, going to add wedding gifts to your registry?" he asked, trying hard not to sound too bitter and deflated.

"Hardly. We've been engaged for over a year yet have done absolutely nothing on the wedding planning front. Tanya jokes that he's taking the rent-to-own route. We're planning a trip up to Napa Valley. Tanya is doing a shoot up there this week, and the network agreed to meet with us. I think they just want an excuse to go on a business trip to wine country. Same with Bryce; my idea might not have struck a chord with him, but the thought of bottomless wine tasting sure as hell did."

I can see why you married him, Greyson thought sardonically. Suddenly, the whole sentence registered in his brain. "Wait, who's Bryce?"

"That's my fiancé," she answered matter-of-factly.

"You mean Van," he said automatically, half expecting an explanation that Bryce is part of his first name, as in Van Bryce. He honestly didn't know Van's full name.

"Who's Van?" she asked.

Confusion washed over Greyson, and he tried to play it off, saying, "Sorry, I meant are you renting a van to go up north?" He knew it didn't make a lot of sense, but since nothing else did, he figured, *When in La La Land.*

"No, it's only a six-hour drive. And since we're not planning on bringing any furniture, we're just taking a car."

Like a boxer still reeling from an uppercut, he tried to find his bearings. "I'd wish you good luck, but I know you don't need it. And don't worry, I'm sure you'll be walking down that aisle before you know it."

"It's funny. When you say something like that or about my pitch meeting, you make it sound like you already know the outcome. Maybe instead of a teacher, you should be a fortune teller."

Maybe I am in an alternate universe, he considered, then gave her a rueful smile. "I wish. If that were true, I wouldn't be here; I'd be out buying a winning lottery ticket."

She took his hand once more and said, "I'm glad you're here."

Greyson stared down at their clasped hands in disbelief, and before he could say anything, she let go and promptly stood up. "It was great talking to you, Cameron. I really hope I see you again."

"You too," he muttered, and then, like a whiff of honeysuckle, she was gone.

Chapter Thirty-Seven

"So, where have you been?" Bryce asked before Hannah could even get the key out of the door lock.

She offered him a bemused smile and said, "Where I always go on Sunday mornings—to the park." In the space of a moment, her jubilant day suddenly turned sour.

"Maybe I should've asked who you were with instead," he said, flinging the magazine he was pretending to read onto the table next to his beer. He positioned the chair so that it was facing the door, waiting for her to get home, like a hungry dog.

"What are you talking about?" she asked nervously as she dropped her keys on the counter.

"Tug saw you talking with some guy. Said you looked all friendly and stuff," he said in an accusatory tone. He then took a long drink from the bottle of Corona.

I hope he's not drunk, she thought, then wondered why she never spotted Tug at the park. She hated to think she might've been so enraptured in her conversation with Cameron that she wouldn't have even noticed the Pope, let alone Tug. He was Bryce's childhood best friend, and their rivalry for his attention bordered on acrimonious.

Finally, she crossed her arms and said, "I don't really know him; he's just some guy I met at the park last week."

He slammed the bottle down. "Last week? Why didn't you mention anything about it? And what, you just so happened to run into the same guy today?"

She still couldn't tell if or how drunk he was, so she had to tread carefully. "I usually see a lot of the same people there on Sundays. And I didn't think to tell you about it because there's nothing to tell." A twinge of guilt topped off her resentment because, even though her last sentence was nothing but the truth, it still had the feel of a lie.

He fixed his gaze on her as he took another sip, then said, "I don't know. Tug said you both seemed all happy and giggly, like two long-lost lovers."

Did he see me grab his hand? Why did I even do that? she wondered as she watched him twirl the bottle and knew he was waiting for a reply. She'd grown accustomed to his rash allegations, which were always broad and hyperbolic. This usually forced her to overassure until she'd satisfied his suspicious insecurity.

She knew he learned this game from watching his father mentally manipulate and abuse his mother. The irony was that he'd vowed never to be like his old man, all while being willfully blind to their identical behavior. "We both know what Tug sees and what actually happened aren't always synonymous. Remember when he told you he saw me out with some man at the Santa Monica Pier? Funny thing was, he didn't know that you and I were in Pasadena that day."

"He said he saw someone that looked just like you," Bryce defended.

"Yeah, after you told him that I was with you that whole day."

He stopped and considered this for a moment, like a judge mulling over an objection, then said, "This is different. You were with another guy."

Hannah shook her head. "I wasn't *with* him. He stopped by, and we chatted for like five minutes. He's new to the area and doesn't know anyone."

Bryce finished the bottle with a triumphant gulp, then said, "Yeah, so he figured he'd stalk my fiancé? You're so naive. There's only one reason a strange man would want to talk to you, and it ain't for directions to Hollywood Boulevard."

"That's a pretty indicting generalization. Also, self-incriminating. I've watched you strike up conversations with women you don't know."

He shook his head as he quickly got back on defense. "I don't mean me. You know I'm not like most guys."

Do I? she wondered, then said, "Even if you're right about other men, I'm not about to do anything or let them get me into any situation where they can even try."

Once he got the reassurance he was seeking, his tone finally softened. "I know that, Hannabelle. It's just I'm trying to look out for you."

The use of his sobriquet for her indicated his anger had lapsed, so she just nodded as he stood up and moved over to her. He pulled her tight against him and stroked the back of her hair. "I love you so much, and I don't want anything bad to happen to you because of your innocent and trusting nature."

Again, she simply nodded. She could smell the overpowering scent of beer now as if he'd just lit a three-wick pale lager candle. She stood stiff against his embrace, and for the first time in their relationship, she could no longer suppress her ambivalence.

Chapter Thirty-Eight

Once again, Greyson lingered on the bench, pondering parallel universes and alternative dimensions as the thought, *Who the hell is Bryce*? kept echoing in his head.

He finally gave into the chilly, overcast day and headed to his hotel-in-the-wall. *I wish I could rent a car,* he thought as he waited for another cab. *And who knew how much I'd miss Uber.*

He spent the rest of the day at an internet café, scouring the incipient web for any signs that he was not in the same 2001 of his memories. *I don't know exactly what I'm looking for, but like a hubristic white male, I'm sure I'll know it when I see it.* At the end of the day, he wasn't sure if he was pleased or disappointed not to have found anything.

He woke the next day and headed to work with an additional problem to resolve. *Time to consult a higher power,* he thought as he strolled into the lab. So far, the cover story of Dr. Greene "hiring" him as a contractor to help get Lilith back online was working like a charm. It didn't hurt that, outside of Dr. Greene himself, Greyson knew more about Project Gateway than anyone else in the building.

Greyson worked through the day while, in his mind, he tried to conceive of the best way to broach the subject of parallel worlds with Dr. Greene. Finally, near the end of the shift, he headed over to his mentor and whispered, "Can we talk for a minute?"

Dr. Greene looked up from the exposed circuit board and nodded. He followed Greyson into an empty hallway and asked, "What's on your mind?"

Greyson scratched his beard for a moment, then said, "I've been thinking about alternate realities."

"Which is the purview of science fiction."

"So was space travel until we actually accomplished it."

Dr. Greene shook his head. "That's a false equivalence. Space travel was always possible; we just needed the technology to achieve it."

"Okay, fine, so was time travel until I DeLorean'ed my way here," Greyson said as he began to pace.

"Do you know what I believe in, even less than the possibility of time travel?"

"True love?"

Dr. Greene ignored his quip and said, "Alternate universes. So, what are you trying to say?"

"How do we know I really did go back in time? Maybe I went dimension hopping instead."

Dr. Greene tilted his head down and stared at Greyson above the rim of his glasses. "Why in Einstein's name would you think that?"

Still pacing, Greyson explained, "I talked to Hannah yesterday, and she's engaged, which shouldn't happen for at least several months. And the kicker is, it's not even to the same guy that she married." When Dr. Greene didn't react, he added, "Plus, there's some other weird stuff."

"You didn't know her during this time period, correct?"

Greyson nodded, and Dr. Greene continued, "So, you only know about her from what, her recollections to you?"

"Yeah, but—"

Dr. Greene held up his hand. "That's hardly proof of an alternate reality. Was Junior Bush the president in the 2001 you remember?"

"Yeah, and I know where you're going with this. I spent the better part of yesterday looking on the internet for, I don't know, timeline discrepancies."

"And did you find any?"

"No. But it's weird how things aren't exactly how I remember them. Like, I could have sworn the movie *Galaxy Quest* came out after 2000."

"Memory is an inexact faculty. Don't ever completely rely on it," Dr. Greene warned.

Greyson stopped roving, recalled the Mandela effect, and thought, *But what if I'm misremembering what that is? Wouldn't that be ironic? Or maybe here it's called the Mandalorian effect.* Finally, he said, "I guess you're right. Still, we can't be 100% sure."

"Parallel universes or alternate realities, or whatever you want to call them, is hokum."

"Quantum mechanics might disagree with you," Greyson mumbled.

"So, let's put your theory to the test."

Greyson furrowed his brow and asked, "What do you mean?"

"Let's experiment. Where are you right now?"

"Standing in front of you," Greyson replied as he held up both hands, palms up.

"No, I mean the other you here. This supposed younger version."

Greyson thought for a moment, then said, "In Virginia." He almost added, "At college" but that would give away too much information.

"Since we're going to be in a holding pattern here waiting for parts," Dr. Greene said, motioning to the lab, "Why don't you go meet yourself? See if that you is the same one you remember. It's the safest way to know since you both should share the exact same memories."

"Which you just said I can't trust."

"True, but this is as close as you're going to get to recognizing a difference. I assume you have no memory of meeting a future version of yourself, correct?"

Greyson nodded while regarding his mentor heedfully. *You see, this is exactly the reason I'm suspecting this. The Dr. Greene I knew would never have suggested this kind of gambit.*

"You can use my corporate jet since you don't have a proper ID. If you leave tomorrow morning, we'll get you there and back in a couple of days. Maybe even before the parts we need arrive."

"I guess I should determine if this Hannah is my Hannah. Or at least will be someday."

"And it will ease your mind about returning to the future you left versus some other alternative reality," Dr. Greene pointed out.

"Yes, of course," Greyson replied as his mind screamed, *Shit, I didn't even consider that possibility!* After his brief mental hysteria passed, he turned his focus back to the more immediate dilemma. "What would I even say to my other self?"

"I'm sure you'll think of something."

Greyson wasn't sure if he liked this more audacious and impetuous version of Dr. Greene, but he was right. If he could make contact with the younger version of himself, creating a memory that shouldn't exist, he may very well find his answer. He briefly thought about Hannah and how she was out on some romantic pre-honeymoon trip, and that sealed the deal. "If there's nothing for me to do here, I guess I'll see myself out." Then, a beat later, added, "On the East Coast."

Chapter Thirty-Nine

"Where's the fiancé?" Tanya asked as Hannah ambled to the table in the quaint coffee shop. She was dressed in a dark purple velour tracksuit with just a hint of post-workout sweat. It was early Tuesday morning, and Hannah marveled at her friend's dedication. Nothing came between Tanya's morning exercise routine, even a long road trip to Napa Valley.

"He's still in bed. Where are the rest of the Spice Girls?" Hannah replied as she claimed the chair across from her. As she sat, she laid a brown bag between her chair and the picture window.

Tanya took a quick drink of her tea, then asked, "Oh, 'cause I'm black, I gotta be Scary Spice?"

"Noooo," Hannah replied, waggling a finger at her friend. "It's because you're dressed like Sporty."

"Whatever happened to them anyway?"

"I don't know; I think they broke up."

"So much for friendship never ends. No wonder this world's gone to shit," Tanya said, then added, "Speaking of friendship," and nudged over a plain white cup.

"Oh my god, is this coffee?" Hannah asked, eagerly scooping up the drink.

"Yeah-feine."

"I knew there was a reason I love you," Hannah said, then took that first, glorious sip of the day.

Tanya turned her attention to the window beside them. "How is he still in bed? I mean, look at this gorgeous morning."

Hannah took another sip as she followed her friend's gaze. The fog was lifting over the rolling vineyard as the sun started breaking through, shining on the countryside with its golden beams. In the distance, the mountains dominated the skyline like a majestic bookend.

After drinking in the view, she said, "Well, he did have a little too much last night."

"Last night, or every night?"

"Don't go there, Holt," Hannah warned. "That's my soulmate you're talking about."

"You and that soulmate crap. That's just the media trying to sell movies, books, and, you know, misery due to impossible expectations."

Hannah looked at her friend and said, "You're way too young to be that cynical."

"And you're way too smart to be that naive," Tanya shot back. "Look, I was charmed by him too at first. But he's devolved into… I don't know, Mr. Imperfect. It's like you bought this amazing car that, like, a year later, is falling apart and giving you nothing but problems."

"Are you saying he's a lemon?"

Tanya nodded. "Mr. Lemon—that's a great way to describe him. A man who poses as Mr. Right until he locks you into a relationship lease."

Six months ago, hell, even one month ago, this kind of criticism would have immediately spun her down a defensive path. But something had recently changed, either in her relationship with Bryce or, more likely, within herself. Now, she simply absorbed the metaphor with a more discerning mind.

After a long moment of reflection, Hannah said, "I know he's under a lot of pressure with work and school, and I always wrote off his behavior to that. He always used the abusive relationship with his dad as an explanation, which also became a justification for his drinking. I didn't want to see it as a crutch. When you love someone, you desperately want to believe them, but more importantly, believe in them."

"Which is a dangerous thing because that can easily be taken advantage of, even if unintentionally."

Hannah nodded, then took a long drink of her coffee. "I don't know, lately things have just been piling up, and I do believe we need to have a serious talk about our future together."

"Ah, the old Tetris relationship wall. We've all been there," Tanya said, then reached across the table and took her friend's hand. "You know I'll support you whatever you do." Then, after a few seconds, chirped, "Even if you decided to marry the bastard. I'll be the very model of a modern maid of honor."

"Who said you'll be the maid of honor?"

Tanya snatched her hand back, feigning offense. "Who's your other option, Jenna? She'd take over your wedding and make it all about her within fifteen minutes."

"Or she'd fast-track whatever relationship of the month she was in just to beat me to the altar."

"Hanni, Hanni, Hanni," Tanya whined in her best Jan Brady impersonation, causing both of them to giggle.

"Can we talk about the elephant in the room?"

Tanya scanned the interior of the coffee shop and whispered, "You mean that old guy over there? He's not the most attractive man, but I wouldn't go so far as to call him the Elephant Man."

"God, no," Hannah said, then reached down and grabbed the brown paper bag. "I'm talking about this." Tanya watched as she slowly pulled a bottle of wine from the bag, revealing the label, which read, "White Elephant."

"Why does it have to be white elephant?"

Hannah looked down at the wine and said, "Because it's a white wine."

"Why does it have to be white wine? It's not exactly Sprite. It's more of a golden yellow."

"Okay, I'll give you that one," Hannah conceded. "Anyway, I picked this up when we got in yesterday. Figured we could pop this baby open after today's meeting. Either to celebrate or to drown away our sorrows."

"I'd ask if you're ready, but I know you. You've probably rehearsed your pitch every night since getting the meeting."

"Not *every* night," Hannah corrected, "but yeah, I think I'm prepared. And I brought my ace in the hole."

"Please tell me that's not a euphemism for your vibrator."

Hannah's eyes widened as she laughed. "You are so bad. I'm talking about you, dummy."

Tanya gave her a wry smile as she finished her tea. "Just checking." Then she glanced at her watch. "We have a few hours; wanna go touring and exploring?"

"Sure," Hannah said, then downed the rest of her drink. "When's your shoot?"

"That doesn't start until tomorrow," Tanya said, then pointed back to the hotel. "What about Mr. Lemon?"

Hannah returned the grin. "I left him a note."

"You devious little diva," Tanya said as she rose from the chair and led Hannah to the door.

Chapter Forty

Greyson leaned his white leather chair back, unconcerned about falling into the lap of the person behind him. He'd just boarded the plane and was still in awe of what he deemed first class plus. *So, this is how the 1% travel. I could get used to this. No baggage check, no flight delays, and no swimming through a wall of passengers waiting to break out into a line mob.*

As the plane queued up to take off, his mind drifted to his upcoming mission. He dubbed it "operation casual encounter," which triggered an eye roll from Dr. Greene. *What do I even say to myself?* he wondered, then doubted whether his younger doppelgänger would believe the truth. Most days, he didn't even recognize himself when he gazed into the mirror.

I look completely different now, with this salt and pepper hair that's way more salt than pepper. Along with the beard, glasses, and twenty-five extra pounds, I ain't exactly the man I used to be. At least physically. I guess it's true what they say—the body ages exponentially faster than the mind, he thought as he surveyed the tiny, vacant cabin.

He was reminded of the conversation with Dr. Greene just before departing. "I hate to admit it, but younger me will probably be disappointed in this," he said as he moved an index finger down from his head to his slightly bulging midsection.

"Don't be ridiculous. Unless the younger you is preparing for a career in modeling, what difference does it make how you look?" Dr. Greene asked pointedly.

Easy for you to say. You pretty much look identical to your older self, Greyson thought, then replied, "I mean, I always fancied myself being more the stud scientist. You know, like a Jeff Goldblum or Robert Downey Jr."

Dr. Greene started scrawling something on his notepad, prompting Greyson to ask, "What are you writing?"

"Just making a note *not* to hire you in the future."

Greyson chuckled and mused, *Joke's on you, 'cause you're not the one that hired me.*

The plane shot forward as it picked up speed. Greyson grabbed both armrests and squeezed. *I always hate this part,* he thought as the cabin tilted upward, and the plane ascended into the boundless sky.

* * *

When the plane finally touched down at the Charlottesville-Albemarle Airport, Greyson had the outline of a plan. *I might not know exactly where I was twenty years ago, but I do remember my routine. I can just wait in Corner Joe until I see me come in, then casually strike up a conversation.*

The similarity to his strategy with Hannah suddenly struck him, like a lyric to a beloved old tune, and caused him to laugh. *I guess if it ain't broke, don't fix it. Still, I better be careful; I don't wanna end up somehow fucking up my own life. Talk about being your own worst enemy.*

After deboarding, Greyson was greeted in the airport by a man holding up a handwritten sign that read "McFly." He smiled to himself and wondered how long Dr. Greene would continue to beat that joke into the ground.

"I guess I'm McFly," he said to the young man in the black suit. He was reminded of Argyle from the first *Die Hard* movie, although this gentleman was a little older and taller with a shaved head.

"I guess I'm your driver," the man said, then tossed the sign into the nearest trash can. "Seriously, is your name McFly?"

"No, that's just a joke between my boss and me," Greyson said. "My name's, uh, Cameron." He remembered Dr. Greene stressing not to use his real name, being so close to his younger version's stomping grounds.

"Like Diaz?"

More like Winklevoss, he thought, but knew that name wouldn't register for at least a couple of years, so he said, "I guess."

"Cool, I'm Elden. Like Elden Campbell, the basketball player."

Greyson had no idea who that was, but just nodded along. "I'll be your driver for as long as you're here," Elden said as he led him through the airport. "Which is going to be…"

"If we're lucky, maybe a day or two. If we're not, then probably till Friday."

"Copy that," Elden said, then reached into his jacket pocket and pulled out a business card. "This has my number on it for whenever you need me."

Thank God I don't have to rely on payphones and cabs, Greyson thought as he took the card, then said, "Alright, let's bounce."

Elden cut him a brief side glance, then said, "Where to, boss?"

Greyson glanced over at the digital clock on the arrival and departure board. The timing was nearly perfect because he knew he didn't have any late afternoon classes, so he said, "Let's go to The Corner Joe."

He gave Elden directions, even though he didn't seem to need them, and surprised himself with how well he remembered the area. Once inside Joe's, he scanned the bustling coffee shop for his younger variant. After coming up empty, he took the only vacant table near the front window.

This is completely bizarre, he thought as he took a sip of coffee. The familiar flavors danced across his tongue as they mixed with the intimate environment, intoxicating him with lucid nostalgia.

Apologies to Thomas Wolfe, but thanks to time travel, you can actually go home again, he thought and smiled to himself.

Then he glanced out the window and, as if Thomas Wolfe had refuted him, noticed his reflection. "Whatever," he mumbled, then looked past the older man in the glass to the winter vista.

It was a frigid, gray day that lingered on the edge of snowing, like being trapped on the verge of a sneeze. The streets and sidewalks were decorated with plumes of snow mixed with ice. *Now this is a proper winter,* Greyson mused as he watched the students scurry past. *I don't miss—*

A young girl's voice cut off his train of thought with, "Excuse me, do you mind if I sit here while I wait?"

He instantly recognized the voice even before turning to see its source and couldn't stop himself from uttering, "Ansley?"

Chapter Forty-One

The younger version of Ansley stood over him with a confounded expression. She had one hand on the empty chair across from the square table and released it while taking a step back as she asked, "How do you know my name?"

She was wearing a white, fur-lined jacket and looked stunning. His heart skipped more than a few beats as her question lingered in the air before finally registering. *Shit, what the hell do I say?* he thought, then heard one of the baristas call out a latte for "Lynne."

"Sorry, I overheard you give it to the guy," Greyson said as he nodded over to the counter. "It just... well, it reminded me of someone I used to know a long time ago."

He could see her instantly relax as she said, "Oh, neat. I've never met another Ansley."

Greyson motioned to the chair and said, "Please sit down."

"To tell you the truth, I used to hate my name when I was younger," she said as she pulled the chair back and flopped down. "But once I got a little older, I started to like it. The uniqueness of it."

I never knew that, Greyson thought, then said, "I've only known one, so you're right about that."

"I hope she's someone you liked. I can't have a woman out there besmirching my name."

What the hell are you doing using the word besmirching? This isn't an alternate reality—it's the goddamn Twilight Zone. And what the hell are you doing here? Then he remembered how she would, on occasion, visit him at school, often unexpectedly. He supposed the word "visit" was a softer way to say "checked up on."

After a couple of awkward moments of silence, he said, "Oh, don't worry. She was someone who meant a great deal to me."

"That's good; then I won't have to go hunt her down and kick her ass," she said with a devilish grin.

The thought, *Why is it my luck that I run into freaking Ansley?* screamed from the inner sanctum of his brain. He tried to ignore it and asked, "So, do you go here?"

She shook her head and laughed. "Me, no. My boyfriend does."

Then, he waited for her to say something like, "You actually remind me a lot of him," but instead she said, "I'm just here to see him. You know, since it's way too much trouble for him to come see me."

Greyson jerked back in his seat as her words dealt another surprising blow. "I'm sure he's just busy with school. Guys his age tend to get myopic about things."

Ansley shrugged, "Maybe. I guess it would just be nice to not have to be the one who's always, you know, trying."

"What do you mean?" Greyson asked, truly intrigued.

"It gets exhausting being the only one putting in any effort to make the relationship work," she said, then shook her head. "I'm sorry, I don't mean to unload all this on you."

"It's fine. And younger men often don't realize the negative impact they have on others, especially loved ones. That's not an excuse; it's more like a fault in their wiring."

"Tell me about it. Don't get me wrong, he's a great guy and all, but sometimes he makes me feel, I don't know, intellectually inferior. I know he doesn't mean to do it, but it makes me scared that I'm not smart enough for him. So, I tend to overcompensate in other ways," she said with a rueful smile.

Before Greyson could reply, the barista set two cups on the take-out counter and then called out, "Ashley."

She made a brief show of scanning the shop, then turned to Greyson and said, "I'm guessing that's me. It was nice chatting with you."

"You too," he replied as he watched her quickly rise and glide through the crowd to retrieve her order.

All this time, I've cast myself as the hero of our relationship. And every hero needs a villain. So that was the role I unfairly assigned, or better yet, mandated, to Ansley. But really, we were just two kids learning how to function in a relationship, he wistfully thought as he watched her exit the café.

Chapter Forty-Two

"Where've you been?" Bryce asked as Hannah stepped into their hotel room.

She pointed to the note on the table where he sat. "Tanya and I went out."

He picked up the folded note and then flicked it at her. "I know what it says, but it doesn't answer my question," he barked. Hannah recognized that his simmering outrage had started to boil.

"We toured a vineyard," she said plainly. "Had a girl's day out."

"Why did you even want me to come if you were just going to leave me at the hotel?" he snarled.

Coming was your idea, she thought, but there was no point in bringing that up. "You were asleep, and it was only for a couple of hours. I didn't think it would upset you like this."

"Of course, you didn't think. You never think about anyone but yourself," he said, then looked away from her in disgust, going all in with the victim card.

"That's not fair," she said, but before she could finish, he cut her off.

"What's not fair is me being stuck in this tiny hotel room waiting for my fiancée to come and spend time with me. What was I supposed to do about lunch?"

You sound more like a neglected child than a fully grown man, she thought. Then, like the sun scaling the horizon, it dawned on her that Bryce might be a twenty-nine-year-old male, but part of him would always be this paranoid child. It wasn't his fear of rejection that was the problem; it was how it manifested. And she could no longer stomach his adult tantrums.

"We need to talk," she said as she sank onto the edge of the bed across from him.

He turned back to her and said, "The four words no guy ever wants to hear." His tone softened, and like a child who had suddenly realized when they'd gone too far, he started walking back his indignation. "I'm just saying that I missed you, Hannabelle. I was hoping we'd go check out that restaurant we passed on the way here."

Hannah almost winced at his pet name for her. There was a time when his instantaneous emotional reversal might have defused this precarious situation. But now, she could no longer ignore the pattern. She was sick of the games and the constant assurance tests.

"It's no big deal. I guess we can always go there tomorrow," he said, offering her a weak smile. "Speaking of food, what do you want to do for dinner?"

As she listened to him deftly backpedal, she realized that she needed more than he could ever offer her. She wanted to be someone's partner, not his parent. The genie had slipped out of the bottle, and she couldn't unsee their toxic relationship for what it was. "Seriously, Bryce, we have to talk about us. This isn't working, and I can't go on pretending we have a future together," she said softly but firmly.

It was as blunt as she'd ever been with him. Perhaps with anyone. She watched him shrink in his chair as he absorbed her words, and she felt sorry for him. Not because he was going to be hurt by their breakup, but because he would never fully comprehend the reasons behind it. He didn't "know thyself" and would not understand the self-fulfilling prophecy that stemmed from his fear of rejection and abandonment.

Hannah would simply be another chick in his failed relationship wall that he built to hide behind. And that used to be one of her fears as well: to disappoint him and prove his insecurities. But now she was finally ready to unburden herself of his instability and paranoia.

I have enough anxiety of my own to shoulder someone else's load. Or maybe

I'm just too sick of all the bullshit to continue to go along to get along. That was something to explore in her next therapy session. Now was the time to write the final chapter of their relationship.

"After all I've done for you, you're done with me? You think 'cause you have this big opportunity that you no longer need me?" he accused, appearing both defeated and enraged.

"That's not—"

Before she could finish, he cut her off again. "You've finished using me, and now you think you can just throw me away, like some piece of trash?"

I guess there's no way this will end well, she realized and immediately understood that this was part of what had been holding her back. She sighed as she steeled herself for a long and arduous decoupling.

Chapter Forty-Three

"That was quick. Where to now?" Elden asked as Greyson piled into the back of the car.

"The hotel," Greyson muttered. The encounter with Ansley had left him shaken and stirred. He was in no condition to continue his current venture, so he decided to go back to his room and regroup while pondering the universe with all of its revelations and ironies.

He awoke the next day on unsure footing as if he were stepping on a freshly frozen lake. It was an extremely bleak and icy afternoon, and Greyson almost slipped as he gingerly walked to the car. "Back to Corner Joe's," he directed, embracing the warmth of the automobile.

"You're the boss," Elden replied, with an apparent underlying hint of, *Why the hell did you come all this way to hang out in a college coffee house?*

Or maybe that was Greyson projecting his own fear. Either way, it caused him to over-explain. "I'm looking to surprise an old colleague, and I know he frequents that place, so I'm hoping to run into him."

Elden just shrugged, as if wanting to remain a background player in whatever scheme Greyson was up to. The reasons of some random older stranger probably mattered not to him. So, Greyson just stared out the window and watched his past go by.

When they parked, Elden turned, pointed to the car phone, and said, "You know, I could call the guy and tell him I'm a student and maybe try to set up a meeting."

Greyson contemplated his offer a little too long, so Elden said, "Sorry, I just assumed he was a teacher here."

I must really be giving off some kind of professor pheromones, he thought. "Thanks for the offer, but he's actually a student." He quickly realized that a middle-aged man stalking an undergraduate might ring some alarm bells, so he added, "He's my nephew. We had a fight during Christmas, and I'm here trying to make amends."

Elden nodded, and Greyson thought, *Damn, I'm getting pretty good at this whole lying thing.* Then he was chagrined for being proud of this new deceptive skill set.

He exited the balmy sanctuary, and the wind immediately stung his face. He pushed on while the severe climate shift besieged him. Then, as if someone had dropped a quarter into his mental jukebox, the song "California Dreamin'" started playing in his head. "I've been for a walk, on a winter's day," he mumbled as he rounded the corner and joined the bundled-up throng on the sidewalk.

As he strolled up to the crosswalk, he was suddenly passed by a young man in a familiar royal blue coat wearing Walkman headphones. The thought, *I had a coat just like that,* started crossing his mind when he suddenly realized that it wasn't just like his old coat; it was his old coat.

The younger Greyson seemed oblivious to not only his older self but the entire world around him. When the light changed, he hurriedly stepped off the curb without bothering to check for oncoming vehicles. *What the fuck is he doing?* Greyson thought, then noticed a truck rumbling directly toward the kid.

Without thinking, Greyson grabbed his younger self by his collar and yanked him back. The younger Greyson's feet slid out from underneath him, almost like a cartoon character floating horizontally in midair. Then, gravity took over, and he smacked onto the sidewalk. As he landed, his head whipped back and slammed against the concrete, and he lost consciousness.

As if from the ether, a crowd materialized around the two Greysons. A second-year med student bent down and did a cursory examination of the junior version. "He's out. I think he might have a concussion. Quick, someone call 911," the med student implored.

The senior Greyson stepped back as the incident reverberated in his mind. Staring down at himself, he quickly recognized this juncture in his life and what it all meant. He'd always wondered who had saved his life that day, and now he knew. And that fresh knowledge discombobulated him, almost to the point of making him physically sick. Rattled and off-kilter, he sidled through the growing halo of onlookers and quickly headed away from the scene.

After ambling hazily back to the car, Greyson collapsed inside and instructed Elden to return him to the hotel. Elden drove away without hesitation. Safely on the road, he peered at Greyson in the rearview mirror and asked, "Everything alright?"

In between deep breaths, Greyson panted, "Yeah," and the car went quiet for the rest of the ride.

* * *

Thirty minutes later, Greyson was sitting on the edge of the hotel bed, holding a plastic phone receiver in his unsteady hand.

"Hello," the deep voice on the other end grumbled.

"Dr. Greene..." Greyson hesitated as he collected himself. He felt like he was slowly emerging from a dream.

"You're lucky you caught me; I was just heading out the door."

"I did it," Greyson huffed. The memory of that fateful day long ago had dimmed through the years like a faded picture in a photo album. But now, after witnessing the scene firsthand, it was as if someone had suddenly digitally restored a snapshot. Now all the revived colors and readjusted exposure levels were flooding his brain.

"Did what? Made contact with your younger self?"

You could say that, Greyson thought. For the last half hour, he'd been processing every little detail about the event, and the mere act of recounting it finally helped lift his thoughts out of the muddled brain stew. "Something happened to me a long time ago, back during my first year of college. I was rushing to get coffee, not paying attention, lost in my own little world of school assignments and relationship issues. I turned to cross the street just after the light changed and nearly walked right into oncoming traffic."

As he paused to take a gulp of oxygen, Dr. Greene hummed, "Okay," not fully grasping the point of the seemingly arbitrary narrative.

"Someone grabbed me from behind and pulled me back before I stepped into my own grave, so to speak. I slipped, and my head smacked down on the concrete pretty hard, and I blacked out. When I came to, the man who saved me had taken off. I'd always wondered about him, like, who this guardian angel was. I'd never even gotten the chance to say thank you."

After a long moment, Dr. Greene filled in the blank. "And it turned out that this mysterious benefactor was you all along."

Greyson breathed, "Yeah."

"Are you okay?" Dr. Greene asked after another long pause.

"What does this mean?" Greyson asked, directing the question more at the universe.

Since the universe was notoriously unresponsive, Dr. Greene replied, "It means you are and have always been an active participant during this time period. And I mean the you I'm speaking to."

"Right, but what does..." Greyson mumbled, searching for the words that could encapsulate his feelings, "I mean, I get the mechanics behind it, but not the meaning."

"We've been investigating causality. If you are searching for meaning, you're in the wrong field. That's the providence of philosophy. If you want my take on it, there is no meaning beyond what we personally ascribe."

Greyson exhaled loudly, then said, "I guess you're right."

"Of course I am. What's your plan now?"

"What do you mean?" Greyson asked, still trying to shake off the lingering feeling of disorientation.

"I mean, when am I getting my plane back?"

Greyson smiled and said, "Sorry, I guess there's no reason for me to stay here. No point in talking to myself now, and I don't remember any other near-death experiences I need to prevent. I can conclusively say I'm in the correct past."

"Good, the parts are due on Thursday. We should be able to get Lilith running soon and return you to your present."

"Could you please just say, 'send you back to the future' one time? For me," Greyson implored.

Dr. Greene responded by hanging up, causing Greyson to laugh as he dropped the receiver down to its plastic cradle. He collapsed back onto the bed, his mind swimming in a sea of existentialism.

Chapter Forty-Four

"Are you sure he's gone?" Tanya asked as she poured another glass of wine.

Hannah's eyes darted around the restaurant as if confirming, then said, "Yes, he left this afternoon. Speaking of, I'm going to need a ride home."

"Or a ride to the airport."

Hannah made a swatting motion as if the quip were an annoying gnat. "I knew I should've driven."

"So, what happened? You didn't have time to fill me in before the meeting. All I know is you talked, and it was all over."

"Well, 'talked' might be a bit of a euphemism, but that's the gist of it."

Tanya shook her head and said, "Oh no, you're going to have to do better than that. It's like escaping from a high-security prison and showing up at my door just saying, 'I got out.'"

"Look, it wasn't a very cheerful conversation to rehash," Hannah said, then poured more wine into her glass. "Why do men always think they can talk you out of breaking up? He was like a bad lawyer still arguing the case at the sentencing hearing."

"It's 'cause men think they run the world. Oh wait, they do," Tanya said in disdain.

After a long pause, Hannah attempted a conversational course correction. "Aren't we supposed to be celebrating?"

Tanya lifted her glass and toasted, "To us, the perfect pair."

"Hear, hear," Hannah said. "I still can't believe they agreed to shoot a pilot. Just like that."

"Your pitch was pretty damn strong. Hell, you had me ready for my close-up at the end."

Hannah blushed as she glanced down at the white tablecloth. "I think it's because you were there. They took one look at you and couldn't say no."

Tanya slammed her hand on the table and said, "Don't do that. You could have sold that show with Pee-wee Herman as the host. That was all you, babe."

Hannah offered her a weak smile. "Why is it when one part of your life starts going well, another turns to shit?"

"Don't think of it like that. Now you have an opportunity to make that other part of your life match the one going well. It's like when you're renovating a house—once you finish updating the kitchen, all the other areas immediately look dated. And since you can't live in the kitchen, it just means it's time to get to work on that outdated boudoir," Tanya said, then took a big sip of wine. "Or something like that. But me, I don't do reno—I just move and upgrade the entire crib."

"You just reminded me; where the hell am I going to live?"

"It was a metaphor," Tanya shot back. "Anyway, it's your apartment. You were there first."

"Yeah, but—" Hannah paused as her heart started pounding relentlessly. She could feel the sweat beading on her forehand and thought, *Oh, no, not now.*

After a few moments, Tanya asked, "Babe, you okay? Your face just went hella pale."

The room started spinning as Hannah suddenly had trouble breathing. Her body began trembling while her mind felt a complete loss of control as if the brakes on her reasoning suddenly failed. She was sure that nothing was going to work out—not the show, not finding a new place to live—and she was certain that she was going to die miserable and alone. Maybe even right now.

"Han, what can I do?" Tanya asked as if burying her alarm under a layer of attentiveness.

Hannah squeezed her eyes shut and tilted her head down as she tried to focus on her breathing. But it was difficult because her mind was screaming that she was a failure and not even worthy of the breath she was struggling to draw. She could feel the droplets of sweat racing down her forehead.

Tanya quickly glanced around, then she looked back at Hannah, whose head was bowed. "Honey…" she breathed.

Tears began to escape Hannah's closed eyes. The rational part of her recognized that she was only having a panic attack and was in no real danger. But anxiety had hijacked her brain, and, like a filibustering senator, it refused to surrender its control. The seconds that ticked by felt more like hours.

After a long moment, Tanya whispered, "Should I get some help?"

Hannah finally started to catch her breath and gasped in and out, like she'd just climbed several flights of stairs. She still couldn't talk, so she just held up an unsteady finger.

"Okay," Tanya said with a nod, then fell silent as she nervously waited.

After several excruciating minutes, the darkness that had seized her mind began to fade, and Hannah slowly became aware of her surroundings. *I hope everyone's not staring at me,* she thought, almost afraid to open her eyes. The overwhelming sense of dread that entombed her was gradually waning, like water swirling down a bathtub drain.

Finally, Hannah lifted her head and breathed, "I'm okay," as her heart rate slowed from its aerobic pace.

"Panic attack?" Tanya asked almost rhetorically.

Hannah just nodded.

"You scared the shit outta me."

"That's nothing compared to what I felt," Hannah replied as she forced a weak smile.

Still wearing an expression of concern, Tanya asked, "You gonna be alright?"

"I mean, I feel like I just hiked five miles through a suffocating tunnel. But other than that, I think I'll make it. That'll teach me not to forget my anxiety meds," Hannah said, then took a long drink of her water.

"I know what you mean. The heart-racing part, not forgetting the pills," Tanya said as she patted her chest. "When's the last time you had an attack?"

Hannah thought for a moment, then said, "God, it's been a few years. Maybe even several."

"I hope it wasn't 'cause of me. You know, prying about the breakup and everything."

Hannah shook her head. "Don't be silly. I think it was the combination of stress from all the work we've been doing for this meeting along with the issues I've been having with Bryce. It's just discombobulating to know it's over now."

"At the risk of instigating a relapse, we're just getting started. But this is going to be the fun part of the work. I'll always be here for you. And with this show, you're basically stuck with me. I'm like the cast-iron skillet of friends."

Hannah smiled genuinely and said, "I wouldn't have it any other way."

"Don't even worry about where you'll live. *Mi casa es su casa.*"

"Thanks. I guess I can figure it all out when I get back to reality," Hannah said, then an image of the view from her park bench blossomed into her foggy mind like a beacon from a lighthouse. As her breathing and pulse normalized, she couldn't help but wonder if she'd see Cameron there again. *Just to maybe share the big news with,* she told herself. That brief musing gave her a small measure of comfort, whispering to her that things might be alright after all.

"You are my soul sister, and I love you."

"Aw, thanks. I love you too," Hannah said as a server arrived with her pasta primavera. Suddenly starving, she dove into her meal with the glimmering hope of seeing Cameron soon germinating in the back of her mind.

Chapter Forty-Five

"Please sit down. Your pacing is making me qualmish," Dr. Greene ordered, pointing at the chair across from his desk.

It was the morning after the casual contact, or, as Dr. Greene called it, "the contingency." Greyson's mind had been on constant overdrive ever since, and he'd gotten little sleep. Now, fueled by speculation and caffeine, he was waltzing a hole into his mentor's carpet.

Finally, Greyson spun around and collapsed into the chair. "Sorry, this is all just, I don't know, inexplicable." His nervous energy now vibrated through his words.

Dr. Greene folded his hands into a pyramid under his chin and nodded once. "I can see that. We are sailing into uncharted territory. But try and approach it as a scientist; this confirms that you have indeed traveled to your past."

"So, you believe me?" Greyson asked, sounding more like an eager child than a scientist.

"I didn't say that. I spoke to Elden, and he backed up most of your story. Even though he didn't witness the event, he remarked how you were quite shaken up. So that, along with how you've acquitted yourself with Lilith's repair work, has expanded the benefit of the doubt program I placed you on."

Greyson frowned. "You were checking up on me?"

"Of course," Dr. Greene said as he rested his chin on top of his hands. "I just met you. Unlike most people, my trust must be earned."

Now there's the Dr. Greene I'm more familiar with, Greyson thought as he replayed the scene of him stumbling back into the town car. *I must have looked like I'd seen a ghost.* "How do you even know Elden?"

"He interns with us in the summer while working on getting his master's."

Greyson squinted for a moment, then, as if someone had given his brain a mental jump start, he made the connection and whispered, "Wait a minute. He must be Tsai's former mentor."

"I'm sorry, what?"

"Nothing," Greyson said, shaking his head. "It's just all sinking in, I guess. It's not every day that you save your own life."

"And you didn't say anything at all to the other you?"

"Nope, he marched past me on the sidewalk before I even knew who he was. Or who I was. Then, as I recognized him—I mean, me—it started to feel like an out-of-body anamnesis. When he stepped onto the street, it's like I knew what was going to happen and acted on something akin to muscle memory."

"Fascinating," was all Dr. Greene could say.

"Then, once everything registered, I got disoriented and nearly puked."

"Do you think that could have been a consequence of the physical contact?"

Greyson considered it, then said, "No, I just grabbed the back of his jacket. It's not like I ever touched bare skin or anything like that. Why would touching fabric from the past suddenly have an effect now?"

"It may have had your younger self's DNA on it, and you somehow reacted to that. Like how some chemicals react with themselves to produce energy."

"Maybe, but I don't think so. It just doesn't feel right. I think it was the combination of being back at UVA, talking to Ansley, and then re-experiencing that fateful day. That's enough to crack anyone's walnut."

Dr. Greene nodded. "I suppose. So, how are you feeling? Any lingering effects? If you need some time off, there's not a great deal that we can do today. Plus, I can't have any loose nuts around my equipment."

The notion of having a day off to process was surprisingly inviting. Greyson leaned back in the chair and surveyed the room for a moment, then asked, "Do you need me?"

"I'm not sure whether I've ever needed you," Dr. Greene scoffed, emphasizing the word *needed.*

Greyson couldn't help but wonder if Dr. Greene was joking. Like with many of his statements, Greyson couldn't distinguish between humor and brutal truth. As if reading his mind, Dr. Greene said, "Seriously, though, we are ahead of schedule. Go on, take a mental health day." Then he quickly added, "Just be back here first thing tomorrow morning."

"If you say so." Then, like a schoolboy being granted an early dismissal, Greyson sprang up from his chair and headed out into the crisp morning expanse.

* * *

Suddenly free, Greyson wasn't sure where to go or what to do, so he threw himself into the tides of fate and cabbed over to the Hollywood Reservoir. He strolled along the pathway, preparing what to say should he encounter Hannah, like an actor rehearsing a soliloquy.

"Piss nickel," he whispered when he saw her bench was vacant. *I knew it was a long shot. She's probably still up in Napa Valley,* he figured, then considered what to do. It was a typical mild winter morning in LA, with the sun shining on millions of dreams and aspirations. Just not his particular dreams and aspirations.

I could either stay here and enjoy the tame weather, especially compared to that abominable climate back in Virginia. Or I could go back to the hotel room and, what, slowly go crazy? God, I miss my friends, my house, my iPhone, and my car. Hell, I even miss stupid shit like tracking my steps on my smartwatch. He quickly decided to hang out and enjoy the ambiance, at least until lunch.

As he sat down on Hannah's bench, the irony of the situation struck his brain like a gong. *If I were back home, I would probably just be moping around the house anyway.* He laughed to himself as he looked down and shook his head. *As antiquated as this epoch is, at least it has Hannah.* The immediate thought of her warmed him like a glass of mulled wine.

I guess she's always on my mind, even if only indirectly. She's kind of my version of a cosmic microwave background, he thought as he watched a line of geese marching to the water.

"What are you smiling about?" a voice from above inquired.

He instantly recognized it, and his face turned flush. "Nothing, just enjoying the splendid morning," he white-lied as he glanced up to see Hannah. She was a pure vision, even just dressed in a gray sweatshirt with a giant white heart on the front and faded black jeans.

This might be the last time I see her, hc thought, trying to imbibe her presence, like a man stumbling into an oasis straight out of a scorching desert.

"And now you're blushing. It's like I caught you mentally masturbating or something."

He snorted at her joke. "If only my mind were that stimulating. No, my thoughts are more banal. My project is almost finished, and I was just thinking how much I'll miss it here. But enough about my chaste sentiments; how did your meeting go?"

Now, it was Hannah's turn to beam as she sat down. "Oh my God, it went better than I could've dreamed. They seemed to love the idea, and we're shooting the pilot soon."

"Love to say I told you so," he quipped.

She gently nudged him with her shoulder. "It's good to see you."

"Good to see you too."

"I was kind of hoping I would run into you. It's been a whirlwind of a week, and I guess I just wanted to talk with you about it," she said coyly.

"I'd be lying if I said I was only here for the squirrels and fish. Although I do enjoy the geese," he said, pointing to a couple at the edge of the water.

Hannah followed his gesture and said, "Ah, they are a big draw here, old mother goose and her gosling."

"Ryan," he pipped in.

"That's an oddly specific name," she said with a curious frown.

He just shrugged and said, "I guess," then mimed turning over an imaginary sign and declared, "The doctor is in."

"You don't know how super stressed I've been over this..." She trailed off, remembering her breakup with Bryce.

"I can imagine."

Even his platitudes were somehow soothing to her. "I broke up with Bryce, and I'm staying with a friend. So, yeah, I guess you could say I had a life-altering week."

"Wow, that's like a 6.4 on the lifequake scale. But I'm happy for you. Congratulations about the pilot and, you know, dropping Poetman like a bad sonnet," he said, thinking, *Guess old Van owes me one.*

She smiled as she shook her head. "I even had a panic attack in the middle of a restaurant. How's that for celebrating a career breakthrough?"

I nearly forgot about her panic attacks. He tried to remember the last time she'd had one. They were few and far between, so it must have been several years ago.

She glanced at the still water and said, "Thanks for nothing, anxiety disorder." She'd laid her most personal card on the table as if she somehow knew that he would accept this aspect of her without judgment or morphing into an armchair therapist like Bryce always did.

"I think my anxiety and your anxiety should get together and have a little angst party. Call it Club GAD."

"Yeah, then they could go home afterward and fret over every little detail."

He shrugged and said, "Why worry about the future when there's so much you can agonize over right now?"

After a long moment, Hannah asked, "Have you ever considered staying here?"

Her casual words struck Greyson's heart like a taser. His eyes widened as he tried to envision a path through this byzantine "mind" field. Her question was a mental Gordian knot, and he realized it had been like an itch in the back of his psyche since the moment he saw her. "I wish I could," he finally uttered.

He could almost feel the disappointment wafting from her as she asked, "Is there... someone waiting for you back from wherever you came?"

"No," he said quickly. "It's just that I don't really belong here."

She nodded, as if she understood, and said, "Well, at least let me take you out to dinner tomorrow night. You know, to both celebrate my new show and to mourn your passing... up on the opportunity to take up residence in the greatest city in the world."

"Sounds like a fun angst party," he snickered.

"How do you want to do this? Should we exchange numbers or what?"

He thought about his little hole-in-the-wall room and said, "I'm staying at a hotel. How about we meet here tomorrow, say around 5?"

Hannah considered it for a moment, then said, "That'll work."

"Just text me—" he started to say, then hesitated for a moment before blurting out, "Tex-Mex. Maybe we can get Tex-Mex."

"Sure, why not? It's a date," she said, offering her hand.

As he took her hand into his, he could feel their electric connectivity surge all through his body. The handshake lasted much longer than any typical one, almost to the point of holding hands. But before that transition could happen, Hannah let go and stood up. "I will see you tomorrow," she said with a smile that eclipsed the sun, then turned and slowly walked away.

After she left, Greyson turned his attention back to the geese as he considered her offer. *There's no way I can stay here. It's just too, too... I don't know, unnatural. Plus, there's the whole Van situation. I can't monkey around with their relationship. If I do that, I'll rob my past self of his chance to be with her. Talk about being your own worst future enemy.*

He tried to quell the conflict within him by burying the notion underneath a mountain of rationales. "It's not an option; I simply can't," he said to himself with manufactured resolve.

"Can't what, old man?" a voice coming from behind hissed, "Can't go out with Hannah?"

Chapter Forty-Six

Greyson whipped his head around and saw three men emerging from the shadows of the trees. They were all average-sized, in their late twenties, and the two that flanked the speaker were in jeans and sweatshirts. The one on the right had brown hair, and the one on the left was ginger. The man in the middle had short, platinum-blond hair stemming from darker roots. He was clearly the head of this Neapolitan mop top gang and was decked out in tight black pants with a white V-neck under a red and black flannel shirt.

He looks like a hipster. Do they even have those in 2001? Greyson wondered as he processed the scene.

"You're damn right you can't see my fiancée anymore," the flannel man hissed, thus revealing his identity.

"You must be the Poetman. Bryce Wayne, is it?" Greyson taunted.

Bryce didn't quite get the reference but recognized it was a dig at his expense, so he quickly led his crew around the bench. The three men filled Greyson's field of view, trying to appear menacing. "Bryce Scheck," he corrected, "Who the fuck are you?" His hostile tone was almost antithetical to his lax dress and demeanor, giving off a confusing vibe.

"Wait, your name is really Bryce Scheck?" Greyson asked, then quickly glanced at each goon to check if it even registered with them.

"You got more important things to worry about than my name, Pal," Bryce threatened. "Now, I asked you a question."

Greyson tried to look past the trio, but they were lined up shoulder to shoulder, looking down at him. "Me, I'm just a guy sitting here, minding his own business. You boys should try it," he said, nodding to the open benches to his right.

"Didn't look like you were minding your own business a couple minutes ago. Matter of fact, it looked like you were sticking your nose in *my* business."

The guy on the left chimed in with, "I bet he's trying to stick something else into your business."

Greyson scrunched his nose and said, "Huh?"

Bryce cut his friend a quick scowl, then looked back down at Greyson and said, "The poor, innocent man routine isn't gonna play here, Gramps."

"Kinda like this whole tough guy act?" Greyson said as he wiggled a finger back and forth. "You guys look more like community theater rejects from *West Side Story*."

"Fuck you, you geriatric ballsack," Lefty shot back.

"I'm only like ten years older than you," Greyson protested.

"You look thirty, dude," the guy on the right snorted.

"Well, thank you. I eat a diet rich in plants, try to keep hydrated, and, of course, moisturize daily. Plus, I avoid the sun like a vampire," Greyson replied, feigning sincerity. He then pointed to the ginger and said, "This guy gets it."

"I meant thirty years older than us," Righty clarified.

"Now you're just trying to be hurtful," Greyson said with an exaggerated frown.

"We're not here to just hurt your feelings, Santa," Bryce said, pointing at Greyson's beard.

"Hey, that's genetics; there's nothing I can do about it," Greyson replied, then nodded to Bryce and added, "I mean, I guess I could dye it, but then, after a week or so, the bottom half of my face would start to look like a black and white cookie."

"Shut it, *Just For Men*," Bryce snarled.

"I see what you did there," Greyson said with a smirk. "As much fun as this hasn't been, maybe you guys could take this harangue to Twitter or something, yeah?"

"What the hell's a Twitter?" Lefty asked.

"Sorry, I meant an AOL chat room. Isn't that where you trolls hang out these days?"

Bryce ignored the verbal fencing and said, "Hannah and I are getting back together, and I don't need any father figure getting in the way of that."

"Big George Michaels fan, are we?" Greyson asked.

Bryce waved a hand as if parrying the question and continued, "So, we're here to make sure you stop interfering."

"Okay, now it just sounds like you're auditioning for an episode of *Cobra Kai*," Greyson said. He figured the more they talked, the less likely there would be any commotion. Plus, what could they really do in the middle of a park in broad daylight?

"Things were fine until she started talking to your old ass," Bryce said in disgust.

"That's like a half dozen slurs about my age. Now, this can be considered a hate crime," Greyson said as he inched back on the bench.

Righty turned to Bryce and whispered, "Is that true?"

"No, you idiot," Bryce snapped, causing Greyson to smirk.

"Also, for the record, things were not fine, you puddle of toxic masculinity. Her realization of your gaslighting had nothing to do with me. I know you're not used to taking responsibility for anything in your life, but facts are facts, and you're nothing more than a sacrificial poet. Now, why don't you and the bro-chachos go find a real elder to abuse? I'm done playing poke the asshole," Greyson quipped, motioning them off with a backhanded wave.

"What the fuck you just say to me?" Bryce barked.

Both Righty and Lefty scanned around their sides of the park, and then Righty said, "If we're going to do this, we should do it now."

Greyson's eyes widened as his confidence drained. *I haven't been in a fight since, well, ever,* he thought. Not that three on one would be much of a fight unless he suddenly morphed into Jack Reacher.

"Get up!" Lefty demanded.

Greyson shook his head. "No, thank you. You know, on account of my gout and all."

Righty took that moment to step forward, grab Greyson by the shoulders, and yank him up off the bench. As Greyson faced the aggressor, Lefty sucker punched him on the side of his face. The blow caused him to see exploding stars in his retinas.

Bryce turned around, taking the opportunity to survey the park as his wingmen took turns pummeling Greyson. When he was certain no one was within view, he looked back just as Righty flung Greyson onto the dirt in front of the bench. He paused for just a moment, as if insipidly considering which brand of toothpaste to purchase, then swiftly punted Greyson in the stomach.

The fight, or more appropriately, the ambush, was over almost as quickly as it started. Bryce leaned over Greyson's curled-up body and asked, "How does that feel, funny man? Guess you're nothing more than a sacrificial lamb."

"I bet we broke his hip," Lefty joked as he slapped Bryce on the back.

The searing pain was racing up and down Greyson's body, like cars on the Autobahn. His stomach and head were engaged in a screaming match of excruciation. *What the hell am I going to do?* he thought in between stabs of agony. The only thing he could physically do was lie motionless in a fetal position.

There was a sudden stillness around the group as if no one knew what came next. Apparently, they had haphazardly strategized the assault but failed to formulate any sort of endgame. "What now?" Lefty asked.

Bryce shrugged as they stood over Greyson's curled-up body. The seconds ticked by slowly, and just as soon as he dared to hope the beating was over, Bryce delivered one last kick to Greyson's unprotected head, sending him into the twilight of unconsciousness.

Chapter Forty-Seven

Greyson slowly opened his eyes, and the blackness shifted to an almost bleached vista. As his vision adjusted, he recognized he was in a hospital room. He scanned his new, antiseptic environment and wondered how the hell he'd gotten there. His head was throbbing like a metronome, and he reached up and tried to massage it away.

A sharp snore came from behind the curtain to his left. *Guess I got a roommate,* he thought, then tried to recall the events that brought him here.

I remember talking to Hannah, he thought, and then suddenly, as with a whiff of smelling salts, his memories reawakened.

Oh shit, I got slammed by Poetman and his laureates. If Nolan were here, I'd never hear the end of it. God, I really should have learned how to fight.

He cast about the white room one more time as he checked his body, making fists and scrunching up his toes. He lifted each leg a couple of inches, then whispered, "Except for this massive headache, I guess everything's in working order. I wonder where the nurse—"

Before he could finish, an Indian man in a white coat opened the door and said, "Looks like Rip Van Winkle's awake."

Greyson groaned, "Et tu, docēre"

"How are you feeling?" the doctor asked as he headed over to check on Greyson.

"Like I got hit by a quatrain."

The doctor furrowed his brow in confusion and said, "It sounds like you got a concussion there. I'm Dr. Ramasamy. Can you remember your name?" He then pulled out a penlight from his pocket and flashed it in Greyson's eyes.

"Greyson," he answered while flinching back from the sudden light in his eyes. "How long have I been here?"

"Pupils are dilating," Dr. Ramasamy said more to himself. "Well, Greyson, you were brought in yesterday before noon. Follow my finger."

As Greyson tracked the doctor's index finger from side to side, he instinctively reached down to his hip for a phone that wasn't there. "It's Friday?" he asked incredulously.

Dr. Ramasamy nodded. "That's a good sign. Do you feel dizzy or nauseous?"

"No. Just have this pounding in my head like Ringo Starr's using my brain as a bass drum." Then, after inhaling, he added, "And my ribs hurt when I breathe. But other than that, I'm a blurry picture of health."

"Do you remember what happened?"

Greyson winced as if the memory of the beating intensified the pain. "I got jumped in the park by some hooligans."

"Hooligans, what are you, a time traveler?"

Greyson cut him a quick look and asked, "Why would you say that?"

"Because you sound like a 1930s beat cop," he replied, then, in a passable Edward G. Robinson imitation, said, "These ruffians must have pinched your wallet, see, 'cause you didn't have no ID when they brought you in, see."

"Not bad," Greyson chuckled.

Dr. Ramasamy dropped the 30s gangster accent and asked, "Is there someone we can call for you?"

Greyson's mind immediately pictured Hannah, and he said, "I actually have to get going. What time is it?"

Dr. Ramasamy glanced down at his watch and said, "5:45. You came in with a pretty big knot on your head. Your CT scan came back negative, but that doesn't necessarily mean you're out of the woods. You may still have a concussion."

Greyson leaned up, tossed his legs over the side of the bed, and said, "I don't think so. My head's starting to feel better, and there's somewhere I really need to be." He hoped mixing the lie in with the truth would make his statement go down more smoothly.

"Well, you're the doctor here… oh no, wait, that's me," Dr. Ramasamy said, as he took a step back and watched Greyson grab his clothes off the chair beside his bed and scramble to get dressed.

As he pulled on his jeans, a wave of relief washed over him when he felt his cash still in his pocket. "I know, but I am late for a very important date."

"And you're gonna end up right back in Wonderland if you have a brain injury. Why do so many patients think they know better than the one who actually went to med school?"

The thought, *Just wait till the pandemic,* crept into Greyson's head as he waved off the doctor's warning. "I'll be fine," he said, dragging his shirt over his head.

"We should at least get your information if you insist on checking yourself out," Dr. Ramasamy said as he drifted back to the door, then pointed at the desk down the hallway. "Lucky for you, the guy that brought you in is also picking up your bill."

"What?" Greyson huffed as he did one last brief inspection of his surroundings. "Yeah, I'll check out at the front desk."

"This isn't the Biltmore Hotel." Before he could continue his protest, Greyson breezed past the doctor and out of the hospital room.

Chapter Forty-Eight

Hannah checked her watch again, and this time she finally rose from the couch. "And where do you think you're going?" Tanya teased.

"I don't know; I figured I'd head to the park. I mean, it's such a lovely afternoon," she replied, glancing out the bay window behind them at the dreary day. Friday's forecast had called for a constant drizzle, and for once, the prognosticators were spot on.

Tanya muted the TV and asked, "I'm all for getting back on the horse sooner rather than later, but are you sure it's smart going out with some tourist you just met?"

"I know it may sound weird, but I trust him."

"Famous last words."

"No, seriously. I've never felt this kind of instant connection with anyone before. It's almost—"

"Harlequin romancesque?"

Hannah couldn't help but smile as she shook her head. "It's not like that at all. We just clicked. And it doesn't matter; he's leaving next week anyway."

"So, why are you going? Especially wearing that 'fuck me' grin?"

Hannah laughed. "I don't really know. But if this is my last chance to see him, I don't want to..." She trailed off, wondering what exactly she was hoping for.

"Alright, Nora Roberts, I feel ya. Be smart, though. And safe," Tanya said, then quickly added, "And don't stay out too late. I'll probably be waiting up for you, all worried and shit."

"Okay, Mom," Hannah teased as she scooped up her blue rain jacket draped over a bar stool.

"Oh, you're gonna need more protection than that. I don't want you bringing me back a niece or nephew."

Hannah shook her head once more and answered with a slam of the front door. As she strolled across the soggy path to her car, she couldn't help but think of Cameron. The butterflies in her stomach seemed to grow with each step, and she felt just like a freshman schoolgirl going on a first date with a senior.

When she got to her car, her flight of fancy was cut off by an all-too-familiar presence. She halted in her tracks and snapped, "What the hell are you doing here?"

Bryce, who was leaning against her passenger side door, smirked at her like he was simply waiting for a ride. "I just wanted to see you," he said nonchalantly.

He was still relatively dry, and she wondered how long he'd been there. Then, she noticed his car on the other side of hers and surmised he must have been waiting in it until she came out. "How did you know I was here?"

"Oh, come on, where else would you be staying?" he replied, gesturing to Tanya's house. "You haven't returned any of my calls, so what was I supposed to do?"

"I don't know, maybe move on? Like most normal people do after a breakup."

He stood up straight, then spread out his arms like he was conceding a point and said, "I'm sorry I've been kinda a dick lately. I get it; I should have been more supportive. I guess I've been too wrapped up in my own shit."

This was simply a variation of his argument against breaking up at the beginning of the week, and Hannah wondered if he'd even bothered writing any new material. "Look, Bryce, we've already been over this. I don't want to have the same debate that we just had the other day—"

"It's not the same," he interrupted. "I'm telling you, I get what you've been saying. You're right to be pissed at me for the way I've been acting."

"While I appreciate your condescending blessing, I don't need it."

Bryce waved away her words like they were merely sweat running down his brow. "I'm not saying that; stop twisting my words to suit whatever narrative you're trying to force us into. It's completely normal to take each other for granted every so often. And yeah, you rightfully called me on it. But we have a good thing, and sure, we've hit a rough patch, but that's no reason to just throw out the baby with the bathwater."

No, I'm throwing you out with the bathwater, she thought, then said, "Whatever we had, whatever was between us, has been gone for a while now. You know it, even if you can't admit it. That's why you've been so resentful."

"I've been resentful because you've been such a bitch," he snapped, then almost immediately tried to walk it back. "I'm sorry, but the stress of us being apart has made me a little nuts."

It was only a fleeting peek behind the curtain, but like a momentary glitch in a hologram, his true conviction had revealed itself. Hannah couldn't help but check her watch as she said, "I'm sorry, I don't have time for this right now."

The smirk reappeared on Bryce's face as he asked, "Oh, big date tonight?"

A little unnerved by his sudden change in demeanor, she replied, "I just… I've got things to do."

Bryce cupped his hand over his forehead and looked up. "Well, if one of them is a date with an older gentleman, I have a feeling it's going to be rained out."

Confusion quickly wormed its way into her mind, and she asked, "What do you mean by that?"

He glanced back at her and said, "I can see you're going to need more time, and being the understanding person that I am, I'm going to grant it to you." Then, surprisingly, he stepped away from her car and, like an usher bringing someone to their seat, gestured for her to get in.

Hannah gingerly moved around him, as if the water on the pavement had magically turned to ice. "Just the next time I call you, answer, okay?" he asked, then reluctantly added, "Please."

She said nothing as she opened her car door. "Have a good night. It's probably going to be a short one," he said, and it came out more like a warning.

She got into the car, then slowly backed down the driveway while not taking her eyes off of him. At first, he just menacingly stood there, watching her pull away. Then, when her back tires hit the road, he turned and headed for his car. Hannah shifted into drive with an ominous feeling of discomposure.

* * *

The bench was too damp to sit on, so Hannah stood over it with her umbrella like one of the Queen's Guard. Still feeling a twinge of agitation from the encounter with Bryce, she couldn't escape the thicket of apprehension that he had subtly planted. That, combined with the doubt that was a constant resident in her mind, made her expectations as bleak as her surroundings.

So, she wasn't entirely surprised when the man she knew as Cameron didn't show. Disappointed, yes, but something whispered to her that there was more to this story than merely being stood up. And she was certain that Bryce's fingerprints were all over whatever the reason was.

She waited in the rain for forty-five minutes before giving up. Had it been a more pleasant and Bryce-free day, she might've waited hours. But since the gloomy weather reflected her mood, she called it a night.

"I was just kidding about waiting up for you," Tanya greeted when Hannah walked in the door just over an hour later. Then she saw her face and asked, "What happened? You look like a sad and soaked little bunny."

"He didn't show," Hannah replied as she peeled off her coat.

"I'm sorry, babe."

"Did you see that Bryce was here?"

Tanya hopped up from the couch and darted to the front window. "Right now?" she asked as she craned her neck and scanned the driveway.

"No, when I left. He ambushed me at my car."

Tanya turned back to Hannah and crinkled her nose. "That little stalking piece of shit. What did he want?"

"Oh, just the usual tired song and dance about getting back together. The weird part was that he acted like he knew about the date and even hinted that it'd be canceled."

"How the fuck would he know…" Tanya started to say, then considered the situation for a moment. "Do you think he's following you? Or is having you followed?"

Hannah shook her head. "He doesn't have to. I mean, I am a fairly routine girl. I mostly go to work, home, and the park." With that last word, it was now her turn to pause and examine the circumstances.

As if reading her thoughts, Tanya asked, "You don't think he saw you at the park yesterday?"

"If not him, it definitely could have been Tug."

"That creepy redhead? He reminds me of the bully from *A Christmas Story*."

Hannah couldn't help but laugh. "It's funny 'cause it's true. He saw me there with Cameron last week, then ran and narced to Bryce. Men, can't live with 'em."

Tanya waited for a beat, then finished, "Can't live without 'em."

"Really? I never heard that part."

Tanya crossed over to the kitchen. "I will say, I have a lot of the same relationship problems with women. Maybe not to the same douchebaggery degree, but the fairer sex is not always fairer."

"Bryce definitely has a doctorate in douchebaggery."

Tanya opened the fridge. "But, you know, we could turn this chagrin day into a charcuterie night."

"I'm listening," Hannah said, as she came up from behind and hugged her friend tightly.

Tanya leaned back into the embrace. "I just went to the store yesterday and got all the makings for a blue-ribbon charcuterie board. I've got enough meats, cheeses, sauces, fruits, and vegetables to make Wolfgang Puck go 'Bam!'"

"You mean Emeril Lagassé," Hannah corrected as she let go and turned to the cabinet behind her. "If you're going to be a famous food celebrity, you better get to know the competition."

"Fuck that—they better get to know me!" Tanya declared, pulling out the deli drawer.

"You do realize this show could be a life changer, right?"

Tanya's brow wrinkled briefly, then she said, "I'm ready for a life changer. I've been doing the whole modeling gig long enough. I think it's time for the next phase of my career… of my life. Surprisingly, even my agent agreed. She said, 'It's a smart move 'cause in this business you gotta evolve or go extinct.' I'm excited to show the world a new side of Azalea. With the help of my BFF, of course."

Hannah gave her friend a lopsided grin. "Of course."

"What about you? Are you ready?"

"I think I've been ready for a while now. I just needed a little nudge from the universe."

"What about your new romantic parker?" Tanya asked while wagging a cured sausage.

Hannah snatched two wine glasses off the shelf. "You're always telling me to live in the moment, so right now, I'm going to pour us some wine and celebrate our new beginning. Everything else can be tomorrow's problem."

"I'll drink to that," Tanya said as she started pulling out the meats and cheeses.

"You'll drink to anything."

"You say that like it's a bad thing."

"Speaking of bad, let's make some bad decisions with some good food," Hannah stated as she opened the bottle. While they prepared their dinner, she was able to put the day's dread behind her, at least temporarily. But like a chronic migraine, it would be back with a vengeance.

Chapter Forty-Nine

By the time Greyson got to the park, it was almost seven, and he knew there'd be little chance of catching Hannah. But he hobbled around the lake for about as long as his body could stand it, then sulked back into the cab, feeling damp and dejected. Instead of going home, he took a shot in the dark and taxied to work.

If the younger version of Dr. Greene is anything like the older one, he might be burning the midnight oil, even on a Friday, he thought as he contemplated what to do about Hannah. He couldn't just leave things as they were. He owed it to her to at least explain why he flaked on their date. And maybe he owed her even more than that—maybe he owed her the truth. Repeatedly lying to her had been taking its toll on his psyche, and like a penitent man longing for absolution, he ached to be unburdened with the truth.

Greyson waited impatiently at the guard's desk as he called up to the top floor. *You owe me this one,* he silently prayed to the universe.

After several painstakingly long moments, the guard finally hung up the phone and said, "You can go on up," while motioning over to the elevator bank.

As Greyson limped over, he calculated when he should take his next round of ibuprofen. His ribs and head were mostly mute while he was still, but they sang a song of suffering whenever he moved. By the time he made it to the office, the throbbing was almost unbearable.

"Are you okay?" Dr. Greene asked as Greyson eased himself into the chair across from him.

"If you think I look bad, you should see the other guys..." Greyson said with a grimace, then continued, "hands and feet. I'm sure they're stained with my blood."

"I was worried about you when you didn't show up this morning. You want to talk about it?"

"You can't deny the fact that you like me. Right now, you like me," Greyson paraphrased as he rubbed his temple. "I got jumped in the park yesterday. Sometimes, when you're looking for a sign about what you should do, one comes out of nowhere and whacks you in the head. Repeatedly."

Dr. Greene studied Greyson for a moment, then suggested, "Maybe we should get you back to the hospital."

"I'm fine, just a little... ok, make that a lot sore. Wait, how'd you know I went to the hospital?"

Dr. Greene pointed to Greyson's patient wristband. He looked down at it, as if noticing it for the first time, and whispered, "Oh yeah," then tore it off. "Did I miss anything here?"

"No, remember, we got along for years without you, so I think we can survive a day. Now that we've installed the parts, it's just testing and retesting. If that goes smoothly, we should make your deadli—" Dr. Greene paused for a moment, then said, "Let's call it your 'launch window' without any issues."

Greyson tilted his head down and muttered, "That's nice, I guess."

Dr. Greene leaned forward and peered at Greyson over his glasses. "What am I missing here? You sound almost disappointed."

Greyson sighed as he looked back up. "I want to tell her everything. I feel like such—I don't know—a shit for lying to her this whole time. Do you know what it's like to have to hide something from the one person you love and trust the most?"

"No, I don't," Dr. Greene replied frankly. "You did consider all this before you decided to thrust yourself into her past life, right?"

The question stopped Greyson's guilt train in its tracks. After a long moment, he said, "Of course I did. But I didn't expect to get so involved in her life. Guess I never took into account just how damn hard it would be to see her again."

"Telling her the truth would be the most selfish thing you could possibly do."

Greyson arched his eyebrows and asked, "How so?"

"Coming into the past and trying to obtain closure creates a completely anomalous situation; you must see that. But if you were to ease your conscience, you would be transferring this burden onto her. Let's put the whole scientific aspect of it to the side. Inserting yourself into someone's life, then revealing to them that you're their future spouse coming back to see them after they've died, is invasive, to say the least. That kind of information could shatter a person. And there's no existing therapy to help put them back together."

"But I'm lying—"

"So," Dr. Greene interrupted. "Lying in and of itself is neither good nor bad, despite what the Christians will tell you. Which is ludicrously ironic since the whole of their religion is based on lies."

Greyson held up his hand like a telepath trying to deflect a psychic attack and said, "Please, let's not go there."

"As Stevie Wonder once appositely sang, 'When you believe in things that you don't understand, then you suffer.'"

"Okay, so no Midnight Mass for you," Greyson joked. "But you don't understand what deceiving the woman you love does to you. Even when you have a perfectly logical reason."

Dr. Greene shrugged and said, "Unless you want to destroy this woman's whole interpretation of reality, you will never divulge the truth." Then he added cheekily, "That is your cross to bear."

"I guess you're right," Greyson said, then sank back even deeper into the chair. His body felt a little better, but now his mind was agonizing.

"And I can say this from experience; I sincerely doubt she'd even believe you."

Greyson just nodded, knowing that he possessed intimate knowledge of

Hannah's past and future that could only be explained by his truth. But, to Dr. Greene's point, that might be too much for her or anyone outside a genius-level intellect to handle. The truth might set him free, but it would certainly put Hannah in an insufferable cage for the rest of her days.

Chapter Fifty

Sunday morning breezed in like a catchy song, and after two consecutive drizzly days, Hannah was eager to visit with the sun. At least, that's what she told herself as she parked on her bench and basked in its heartening rays. With the return of more cordial weather, Hannah leaned back, closed her eyes, and whispered, "If I see him, then I see him. And if I don't, well, it's his loss."

She would let fate take the wheel. That was the conclusion she came to yesterday, and it felt good to stop trying to micromanage every aspect of her life, especially the ones out of her control. And she was slowly accepting that others' actions and behaviors definitely fell outside her purview. Since the park was fairly empty, she was able to enjoy the serenity of the moment.

That is, until her brief mediation was interrupted with, "Please tell me we said Sunday morning and not Friday afternoon."

She gradually opened her eyes to find Cameron's smiling down at her. As she cupped her hand over her forehead, she noticed the fading bruises on his face. "Oh my God, are you okay?"

"It looks way worse than it feels," he said as he eased himself down beside her. His words weren't entirely false. Each day, the pain and discomfort waned. He still moved as if swimming in molasses, but his stamina had greatly improved.

"What... what happened?" she asked tentatively, as if afraid that she already knew the answer.

He'd contemplated lying to her, not wanting her to feel any sort of guilt or responsibility, but in the end, she needed to know what kind of man her ex was. Bryce was not only violent but cowardly. He was the textbook definition of a bully. One who only acted when he was positive that the deck was unequivocally stacked in his favor. "A couple guys jumped me after you left on Friday," he said, then added with a half grin, "I think one of them might have been Scott Farkus, sans the yellow eyes."

"Tug," she whispered as she looked down.

"I'm sorry, what?"

"I think it was my ex and his friend, Tug."

"Tug," Greyson said, as if interlocking a puzzle piece. "Yeah, that fits. The ringleader did mention you and how I needed to stay away from you, like he was your father."

"That's Bryce, alright," she replied with a frown. Then she looked away and sighed as a single tear slowly spilled down her cheek. "I am so sorry."

"Hey, it's not your fault," he said, trying to sound cavalier. "I've actually suffered worse after wandering into a mosh pit during a Limp Bizkit show," he added, recalling his first concert experience.

She offered a sullen smile and again asked, "You sure you're okay?"

"Right as rain," he said and inexplicably saluted her. "Speaking of, I'm glad all that cleared out, and today's a resplenday. I was fixin' to build an ark there for a minute." He used this as an excuse to survey their surroundings. Since the attack, he'd been periodically looking over his shoulder in a mild form of PTSD.

"Fixin'? First, you admit that you actually went to a Limp Bizkit concert, and then you follow that up by using the word fixin'. Who are you, Cameron Donovan?"

You can take the boy outta the South, but you can't completely take the South outta the boy, he thought. "I'm just a boy, sitting next to a girl, asking her to forgive him for missing their date."

"A movie fan, huh?" she said with a smile. "There's nothing to forgive. I'm the one who is sorry you got tangled up in my dysfunctional relationship." Then she quickly added, "Former relationship, I should say."

"Like I said, it's not your fault. It's all Poetman's responsibility."

"Did you call the cops?"

He thought about the potential ramifications of talking to the police and just shook his head. "You should," she insisted. "He can't be allowed to get away with going around and attacking innocent people like a damn wild dog."

"Like a Pitbully?" Greyson suggested.

"A Goonhound."

Greyson thought for a moment, then blurted out, "Boston Terrorist" and instantly regretted it.

Hannah snorted. "Or a Greyhooligan."

"Right? People still use that word," Greyson replied excitedly.

"Huh?"

"Oh nothing, the doctor just made fun of me when I described my attackers as hooligans."

Hannah's expression switched from jovial back to concerned like Greyson had just clicked the change lever on a View-Master. "You had to go to a hospital? Why didn't you tell me it was that bad?"

"Because it really wasn't. I just kinda sorta, you know, lost consciousness there for a minute," he said, then mumbled, "Or day."

"You were out for a whole day?" she exclaimed while gently shoving him.

"When you shout it like that, sure, it sounds pretty bad. But, if you factor in the jet lag and how tired I'd been from the whole week, the hospital visit was more like a spa day."

"Whatever, you should have called me," she said, turning away.

"I didn't have your number."

"And whose fault is that, Mr. Mysterioso?"

Greyson tilted his head and admitted, "Mine." Then he remembered that she was staying with Tanya and said, "But aren't you staying with a friend?"

Hannah sunk her hand into the bag opposite him and pulled out a gray Nokia phone. "I have a mobile phone," she said, waving it at him.

Oh my God, that thing is an antique, he thought, then asked, "Is it too late to get your digits?"

"I don't know, aren't you leaving anyway?"

"Yeah, but maybe I can get a do-over and make it up to you. Like, tonight, if you're not busy."

She appeared to stew in her pseudo-anger for a moment, just long enough to make him sweat, then said, "Of course. But no more hiding things, got it?"

Greyson nodded and thought, *If you only knew.*

"How about dinner and a movie?"

"There won't be anything new for at least twenty years," he mumbled automatically, then realized his blunder and added, "I mean, hasn't been anything. It's like Hollywood has given up on originality and just regurgitates sequels, remakes, and reboots."

"Okay, maybe you're not a movie fan. How about just dinner, then?"

"Yeah, but let's meet somewhere safer," he said, scanning the area again and seeing two guys off in the distance walking toward them. His heart picked up its rhythm until they got close enough for him to recognize that they were not a threat.

She followed his gaze and asked, "What do you mean?"

"Nothing. It's just that this place has gotten perilous of late. It's got me constantly looking over my shoulder now."

"I really am sorry about that," she said sincerely, then added, "I know it sucks to feel unsafe. It's how a lot of women feel pretty much anytime and everywhere."

He turned to her and said, "Yeah, I guess that's true."

"But don't worry; I'll protect you."

"If you'll be my bodyguard, I can be your long-lost pal," he sang.

"Just don't call me Betty," she smiled. "How about I pick you up at your hotel? Say, five?"

"That only gives me like eight hours to get ready, but okay."

"Such a diva," she teased. Then she rose and, with a grin, asked, "I have to meet Tanya for brunch; do you want me to escort you out of here?"

He offered her his hand, and she pulled him up. They stood face-to-face for a long moment as the personal electricity between them silently hummed.

Then, they simultaneously leaned forward until their lips met, sending waves of friction through both of their bodies. The kiss was brief yet enduring. Afterward, they silently walked hand in hand until they reached her car.

Chapter Fifty-One

As Greyson waited for Hannah in the lobby of his hotel, he was still soaring from that quasi-first kiss that was somehow both familiar and extraordinary at the same time. It consumed his reasoning and perspective. Most importantly, it awakened emotions he believed long extinguished.

Seeing and talking to her was one thing, he mused as he smiled ruefully. *But that kiss, that intimate reconnection—it's like it jump-started my heart.* Then he couldn't help but hum the old, similarly titled Mötley Crüe song, "Kickstart My Heart" as he stared out the window.

This got the attention of his childhood bully's doppelgänger behind the front desk, who threw up a sign of the horns hand gesture to show his approval. Embarrassed, Greyson just nodded. As his attention awkwardly turned back to the parking lot, he noticed Hannah's car pull up.

Saved by the Beetle, he thought as he popped up from the plastic chair and headed outside.

"What are you grinning about?" Hannah greeted as Greyson folded himself into the passenger seat.

He shook his head. "Nothing. Just had a little metal moment with the kid at the front desk." Then he gave her a quick once over and added, "You look very ni… fantastic."

"Did you just say I look nigh fantastic? Like, I almost look fantastic? What's the problem? Is it this dress?" she asked, pointing to her blue wrap dress. "I was on the fence about it, and now I'm starting to regret it."

"Nein!" he yelled, then dialed it down and continued, "I was going to say nice, but then remembered how…" He trailed off, thinking, *Shit, I can't reveal that I know how much she hates the word nice, and it's a trigger for her.*

"Remembered what?" she asked.

"That nice is such a vanilla descriptor."

She chuckled and said, "I must admit, I do hate that word. It's just so weak and trifling. It's what people resort to when they can't think of a genuine compliment."

"You're not the only one," he replied with a sly grin.

"Independent Women" by Destiny's Child came on the radio, and Hannah reached down to turn it up. "Do you mind?"

Greyson had to fight the urge to comment, "This is an oldie but a goodie," and instead just nodded. Several songs later, they were in Encino, parking next to the restaurant.

"I know it's a little cheesy, but I love this place," Hannah said, with more than a hint of embarrassment. "Have you ever been?"

Greyson opened the door for her and smiled. "To Buca di Beppo? I mean, who doesn't love a family-style Italian meal that feeds a whole basketball team?"

"At least you'll have lunch for the week."

Since it was a little after five, they were promptly seated at a booth in the back of the restaurant. The server quickly followed and delivered the standard pitch, then took their entire order. Greyson glanced around and marveled at how little the place had changed in twenty years. Then he chuckled at how that idiom was not meant to be applied in reverse.

"Don't judge me," Hannah defended as if misreading his amusement. "There's just something, I don't know, comfortable about this place. I've been coming here since they opened."

"I'm just wondering who their decorator is and how many garage sales they had to browse to find all these pictures."

"I do try to notice a new picture every time I come here. It's my personal scavenger hunt."

Greyson just nodded as the server returned with their drinks. After he left, Hannah asked, "How are you feeling?"

"Not as bad as you'd expect after getting pounded by three dudes. Wait, that doesn't sound right. After getting licked by three guys. No, that's not exactly what I'm going for either. Jumped by a trio of harangue bangers. Why do I make getting beat up sound more like filming a gay porno?"

"Three?" she exclaimed, as if not hearing anything after that. "You didn't tell me there were three guys?"

"Yeah, I guess you could say it was a three-body problem. But really, any more than one is unfair, especially for an unathletic academic like myself. Now, if they wanted to engage in a math melee, I would have given them what for."

She reached over the table and placed her hand on his. "I'm so sorry," she said softly.

"You have nothing to be sorry about," he reassured, as the spark from her touch coursed all the way to his soul.

She stared at his face for a long moment, then said, "You don't look so bad in this light."

"What can I say? The dimmer it gets, the better I look. You should see me in pitch black; if you squint hard enough, I look a little like George Clooney."

She giggled and said, "I meant, your bruises don't look that bad. At least from where I'm sitting."

"Right now, I don't even feel them because of where I'm sitting."

Hannah's face bloomed as she broke eye contact, so Greyson pointed to the Parmesan cheese shaker and added, "Sorry, guess there's already cheese on the table."

The salad arrived, disrupting their brief connection. As Hannah shoveled lettuce onto her plate, she asked, "Have you given any more thought to maybe sticking around?"

That's the million-dollar question, isn't it? What would happen if I stayed in the past? Greyson thought as he looked away.

"I didn't mean to…" Hannah started, then paused for a moment and continued, "It's just I enjoy spending time with you, and selfishly, I don't want it to end. But I understand that you have this whole other life to get back to."

"I enjoy spending time with you too," he replied, then finished the statement in his head. *More than you can ever know.*

"Maybe you could, I don't know, visit. Where are you going after LA?"

"That's not an easy question to answer."

"See, there you go being all mysterious," she said with a frown, "It shouldn't be that hard a question."

He nodded and said, "I don't mean to be vague, but I just don't have what you'd call a linear path like everyone else. When I leave here on Friday, I go back home and wait for the next job to—"

"And where is that again?" she interrupted.

He quickly took a bite of salad to buy some time. *Shit, obviously I can't say LA, but I can't tell her Virginia either,* he thought, then imagined a map of the US and split the difference by blurting out, "Oklahoma City."

"So, you're an Okie?"

"Gnocchi," he shot back while shaking his head. "I just mean that I have an apartment there since it's centrally located. That way, as long as it's in the continental U.S., I can pretty much get to wherever the next job is and back fairly quickly." He wasn't proud of how much easier the lies were rolling out now.

"Do you have one lined up?"

He held up a finger while he chewed his salad along with her question. *If I say no, then what's the hurry about getting back? If I say yes, she'd probably follow with, 'Where is it?' Man, lying is harder than working out. There goes any aspiration about being a politician.* Finally, he said, "I have a few offers on the table but still haven't decided."

"Since you travel so much, you should get a mobile phone. They're a bit on the expensive side, especially if you use it during peak hours, but they are hella handy."

"Who are you, Lily from AT&T?"

She scrunched up her nose and asked, "Who?"

"I'm just saying you'd make a great cell phone spokesperson," he said, then quickly changed the subject by asking, "How's your salad?"

"Delish," she said with a radiant smile.

A few moments later, their entrée arrived. As they switched plates, Greyson frowned, knowing that avoiding more future talk wouldn't be nearly as easy. *I doubt she's going to let this go. But what good reason could I have to just disappear? Do I tell her I've been lying the whole time, and I have a family back in OKC? That will pair well with her bad breakup,* he wondered as he scooped up the Macaroni Rosa.

As if sensing his consternation, Hannah asked, "What's the matter? You looked like you're handling toxic waste or something."

"Oh no, this looks, how you say, delish," he replied in a faux French accent. Then, in his normal voice, said, "I was just thinking about the world's greatest defective."

The expression of confusion returned to her face as she said, "I think I'm going to need a Cameron decoder ring. I swear I don't get half the references you make."

He chuckled, then said, "It's a play on one of Batman's nicknames, the world's greatest detective."

She arched her eyebrows, indicating his explanation was incomplete, so he continued, "I was just thinking about good old Poetman and how he's giving guys a bad name."

"Oh, that. Well, I'm not a simpleton who lets the actions of one guy," she said, then, after a pregnant pause, grinned, "Or even a few dozen, color my perception of an entire gender. I know there are a couple decent fellas out there."

At that moment, his desire to stay with her became almost overwhelming. He felt like a man who'd be adrift at sea indefinitely, finally spotting land. *Damn the repercussions, why can't I just be with her once more?*

With that question floating in his mind, the conversation hit a temporary break as they both enjoyed their meal.

* * *

Greyson was distracted throughout the rest of their date, wrestling with the dilemma of having to say goodbye to his one love, his soulmate, again. But this time, it wouldn't just be him that would suffer. Hurting Hannah would make this already impossible scenario infinitely more difficult.

The irony of the situation was not lost on him. His need for closure—need to ease his sorrow—had unintended consequences. He knew somewhere, or somewhen, the future Dr. Greene would be shaking his head at how poorly Greyson had followed his mandate.

"Ground control to Major Cam," Hannah intoned.

He smiled weakly and said, "Sorry, just mulling over how much I'm going to miss this place."

"What, Buca?" she teased playfully.

"Yes, Buca is the only thing I'm going to miss about this entire trip," he replied sarcastically. Then, more earnestly, said, "Seriously though, I'm going to miss you more than you can ever know."

Blushing, she said, "It's not like you're going to Mars or Antarctica or prison. It's just Oklahoma. Last I checked, they still had phones, mail service, internet, and airplanes."

He nodded. "That's true, although the service there is spottier than a leopard." *Guess Cameron will just have to be relegated to an asshole who ghosted her.*

"Where do you want to go next?" she asked cheerfully. When he didn't answer, she said, "Unless you're about to tell me that you have to get up early tomorrow, which is code for this date being a bigger flop than *Battlefield Earth*."

"Oh my God, I totally forgot that movie existed," he chuckled. "No, this isn't a flop. On the contrary, I'd say this date makes me want to jump up on a couch on *Oprah*."

"I'll never get your Midwestern references."

"Oh, you will someday," he hummed, then took another bite of the tiramisu. "You were right about this," he said, motioning to the half-empty round bowl with his spoon.

"I know, right?" she agreed.

After a long pause, he glanced around the now full room and asked, "You almost ready to go?"

She shrugged and said, "Sure." As they got up from the table, she asked, "I was thinking, since it's still kind of early, maybe we could go to the Griffith Observatory. It has the best view of the city. Have you been yet?"

The question was like a pang to his heart, causing him to grimace. After observing his reaction, she said, "Or not. We can go someplace else."

He swiftly buried the painful recollection and said, "No, it's not that; I think I overdid it with that last bite. I haven't binged like that since I first discovered Cicis' bottomless pizza buffet. I've been to the Observatory, but I'm game to go back."

She held out her hand and said, "Then, let's go."

He took her hand, and as she led him through the teeming kitchen, he thought wistfully, *Maybe this will be the perfect coda to our relationship. Our first date will also be our last.*

They stepped out of the artificial light of the restaurant and into the shadow of night. Greyson took a moment to marvel at how quickly the city had become shrouded in darkness. *It's like the sun is allergic to winter,* he mused while they strolled the parking lot.

Greyson was lost in thought as they reached the rear of her car, trying to figure out a clever way to open Hannah's driver's side door. Before he could enact his plan, he heard someone snarl, "Well, isn't that cute? A daddy-daughter date."

Chapter Fifty-Two

Both Greyson and Hannah spun around to find Bryce skulking from behind the SUV parked beside them. He was wearing a white and blue checkered button-up shirt, a pair of khakis, and a leather aviator jacket. Greyson's first thought was that he looked like a store mannequin from Banana Republic.

Before he could speak, Hannah asked, "What the hell? Have you been following me?"

Bryce shook his head and spat out, "No! I was just driving by and happened to spot your car. I know how much you love this place, so I thought maybe I'd stop by and say hi." Then he motioned to Greyson and added, "But I see you're busy trying to replace me with an older model. I know you have daddy issues, but come on, this is ridiculous."

Jesus, I'm not that old, Greyson thought, then had to tell himself to focus. So he surveyed the parking lot for Bryce's battery bros while Hannah said, "Poor Bryce, always playing the victim. You really do think that everything is about you. You just innocently drift through life while everyone's out to get you."

"Oh Hannah, little Miss Always Right," he scowled. "At least I don't pretend to be some kind of saint, all the while doing immoral deeds. You could have been honest about why you really wanted to break up—to go bang some senior citizen, instead of spouting some bullshit line about it being my fault."

Satisfied that there was no anti-cavalry lurking around, Greyson finally piped up, "Where's your little backup band? There's no way you have the guts to face anyone alone."

"Fuck you," Bryce growled. "I don't need anyone to deal with a vulture like you. A geezer that goes around preying on vulnerable women, hoping to weasel your way into their pants. Fucking pathetic loser."

"No, fuck you, Bryce," Hannah fired back.

Greyson just smiled and replied, "That actually says way more about you than me, tough guy." Then he glanced over at Hannah and continued, "You just see her as some vulnerable possession who needs your protection, don't you?"

"That's not what I said. Christ, man, you're twisting my words around worse than she does. No wonder you're the next branch she grabbed onto," Bryce hissed. The darkness contorted his face, enhancing his glower and making him appear even more menacing.

Hannah reached into her purse and pulled out her keys. "Look, I am done with this. We're leaving now, so you can go fuck off."

As she turned to her door, Bryce pulled a handgun from his coat pocket and said, "You may be done, but I'm just getting started."

Even in the shadows, Greyson saw the glint from the revolver and thought, *What the hell? I leave a gun-obsessed future only to end up getting shot in the past. The universe has a twisted sense of humor.*

Hannah froze as her indignation quickly transformed into fear and asked, "Where the hell did you get a gun?"

"It's LA. Places around here give 'em out as door prizes." When Hannah ignored his quip, Bryce confessed, "It's Tug's."

"Of course it is. So, what are you planning to do with it?" she asked, nodding toward the weapon as if it were simply a cordless drill.

"Oh, now you wanna talk," Bryce sneered.

"No, I still want to leave, but I don't want to get shot in the back while doing it," she said, still staring at the revolver in disbelief. In the space of a moment, the entire situation had turned from annoying to surreal.

I better say something here, even if it's a proverbial shot in the dark, Greyson thought, then cringed at his own gallows humor. "Look, you don't want to hurt anyone," he said, then stole a glance around, desperately hoping to see someone—anyone. But as luck would have it, the parking lot was deserted.

Bryce leveled the gun at Greyson and said, "Oh, you're going to tell me what I want now? I guess we hit you so hard that we must have given you delusions of grandeur to go along with your amnesia."

"Okay, maybe you want to hurt me, but not her," Greyson said, motioning to Hannah.

"You don't even know me, dude."

"But I do," Hannah interrupted. "And this isn't you. You aren't a violent person. At least, that's not the Bryce I fell in love with."

Bryce turned to her while still keeping the weapon trained on Greyson and said, "That Bryce was gone the minute you abandoned him."

Greyson watched Bryce's uneasy swaying from one leg to the other and guessed that he didn't really have any strategy here. He was simply acting on an irrational instinct. "What's your plan? Gun down two innocent people in a parking lot and then spend the rest of your life in jail?"

When Bryce hesitated, he pointed at him and continued, "You don't strike me as the kind of guy that would thrive in prison. There isn't a lot to draw inspiration from when you're sharing a cell with a 300-pound brute with bad hygiene." Greyson deftly played on what he knew would be most middle-class yuppies' biggest prison phobia.

Bryce extended his arm while cocking the revolver. "You wanna test that theory?"

With the handgun now only a few feet away, Greyson's eyes widened as he held his breath. He stood there frozen on the edge of an infinite moment wondering how fate led him to this juncture. Then the thought, *I can't let anything happen to Hannah* sounded in his head like a fire alarm.

Before Greyson had a chance to act, Hannah stepped in front of him. "I'm not going to let you hurt anyone else."

Like a child at the sunset of a furious tantrum, Bryce slowly lowered the gun and asked weakly, "How could you do this to me?"

And like a parent trying to negotiate a hysterical ceasefire, Hannah calmly replied, "I'm not doing anything to you, Bryce. You are taking my actions and assigning your own interpretation to them."

"But you're mine," Bryce softly murmured.

As if seeing red from his declaration of ownership, Hannah snapped, "And that's why we aren't together. You have this antiquated sense of how relationships work, and I want no part of it."

While Greyson contemplated how to de-escalate their predicament, a small group of people exited the restaurant, laughing loudly. Bryce reflexively pocketed the gun and stepped back into the shadow of the neighboring Cherokee. Hannah turned and looked at Greyson. He said with his eyes, *This might be the most opportune time to quit this awkwardly dangerous situation,* praying she could read his thoughts in the same fashion as when they were married.

Hannah may not have been able to read his mind, but she appeared to pick up on his inference and said, "Here's what's going to happen. We are going to get in my car and drive away. You are not going to contact me again. That means no more phone calls and no more pop-up appearances."

Greyson added, "If you abide by this, we will not go to the cops and report how you assaulted me in the park and how you threatened us with a deadly weapon. Do we have a deal?"

Bryce sunk his free hand into his jacket pocket, looking like a petulant child being called to the principal's office. He kicked a stray rock to the side as he mulled over the offer, then grudgingly agreed, "Fine."

Both Greyson and Hannah quickly made their way to the opposing doors and opened them in unison. Greyson quickly jumped in, but before Hannah could, Bryce took another step back and said, "I just… just wanted you to be happy."

He was like a matador waving his cape, and Hannah couldn't help but charge. She pounded on the roof of her car and said, "No, you just wanted you to be happy. You only wanted me to be happy for you."

Then she dropped into the driver's seat, backed out, and screeched off, leaving Bryce behind in a cloud of dust.

Silence enveloped the car as Hannah and Greyson said nothing for several miles. Both were lost in their own thoughts, trying to process the incident. As they drove on, an idea sparked in Greyson's mind that the passing streetlights seemed to fan.

This could be my way out, he realized, entranced by the city's ambient glow. *I think she'd understand if I was so unsettled by this whole ordeal that I needed to break things off between us. I just need to figure out how to express that without her blaming herself.*

Hannah finally disrupted the quiet and said, "I know I'm starting to sound like a broken record, but I'm sorry about all that."

When Greyson didn't reply, she asked, "Do you still want to go to the observatory? I'd completely understand if you didn't."

He sighed, then said, "Yeah, I think being held up at gunpoint is kind of a mood killer."

She just nodded solemnly and headed for his hotel. When they arrived, instead of pulling up to the front, she parked in the adjacent lot. After cutting the engine, she bowed her head and said, "I know you've been through a lot these last few days, and I can't help but feel responsible."

He had to fight against every fiber of his being not to reach over and try to console her. He was desperate to tell her that she doesn't even hold a shred of responsibility for that jackass's actions. Instead, he forced himself to just be quiet and do nothing.

"I swear, Bryce was never anything like this. I hope you don't think less of me because of his behavior," she said softly as tears trickled down her cheeks.

Seeing her cry and hearing the cracks in her voice broke his heart. *How did I ever think this was a good idea?* he wondered, regretting the whole escapade. Finally, he said, "I would never judge you based on his actions." After a long pause, he added, "But, I have to admit, this whole incident has me shaken up. I just don't think I can handle this right now."

Her tears became a steady stream as she just nodded. "I don't ever want you to think this is your fault, though. It's all just too much for me," he explained.

She nodded again, this time more intensely. He had to look away, not being able to bear her misery in addition to his own. After an extended moment, he said, "I still consider myself extremely lucky to have met you. You are such an incredible person. I don't think you really understand how amazing you are."

With her gaze still fixed on the steering wheel, he got out of the car and walked off into the opacity of the night. As he opened the lobby door, it dawned on him that he'd simply taken a different coward's way out. He recalled his conversation with Dr. Greene about the butterfly effect and how they debated the physical implications but never even bothered considering the psychological devastation one could wreak. He now questioned the ethical ramifications of this whole endeavor.

Chapter Fifty-Three

Greyson's final days before the return date passed slowly and uneventfully. He dedicated all his remaining time and energy to helping Dr. Greene prep the gateway for activation. The nights were much harder, as there was nothing to prevent him from sullenly pining for Hannah. It was a Herculean effort to suppress his yearning to contact her, either by phone or by strolling past her favorite spot in the park, but he managed it by reminding himself that it was all for her greater good.

When the departure day finally came, Greyson greeted it with a combination of relief and dolor. The relief came from removing the unbearable temptation of seeing Hannah one more time. But, this consolation was balanced with the anguish of never being able to spend another moment with her again. He spent his last day sulking around Crastino's like an inmate awaiting his execution.

As his final moments in 2001 drew to a close, he grabbed one last coffee from the kiosk in the lobby, then shuffled into Dr. Greene's office. It was nearly 10 p.m., and they were the only ones left in the building, aside from the security guards, who were instructed that Dr. Greene would be working late and to give them a wide latitude.

"It looks like everything's a go," Dr. Greene said after one final scan of the computer screen on his desk. He watched Greyson collapse into the chair opposite him and added, "All except you. What's wrong?"

"I don't think you'd understand," Greyson muttered, then took a drink of his coffee.

Dr. Greene pointed to the wall covered with framed degrees, honors, and distinctions on his right and declared, "Those beg to differ. Try me."

Greyson sighed, then said, "It's hard to explain, but somehow leaving doesn't feel right."

Dr. Greene glanced down at his watch and said, "Perhaps we should continue this discourse in the lab? We don't want to get entangled in a philosophical debate and miss your departure window."

Greyson shrugged, then lifted himself out of the chair and followed his mentor out of the office. As they marched abreast to the lab, Dr. Greene continued, "You said leaving doesn't feel right; expound."

"I'm trying not to let my emotions take the wheel, but damn it, maybe I shouldn't go back."

"The entire experiment was binary. One part was to see if one could visit the past and then return to the present. The second, more self-serving part was for you to come here, make your peace, then go back a renewed man, correct?"

Greyson nodded. "I know, but I had no idea it would be this hard. It's like I'm losing her all over again. But this time is worse because it's preventable. It feels like there is more for me here in the past than in the future."

"I know you think I'm some cold, soulless robot man—"

"I think the word you're looking for is android," Greyson interrupted.

Dr. Greene ignored him and went on. "But I can sympathize with your plight. Even though I attribute what you're experiencing more to a mental imbalance than rational thought, I do understand the dilemma that you face."

"I can't help but feel like you just called me a nutcase."

Dr. Greene waved his hand and explained, "Not at all. It's almost like you're caught in the pull of a fundamental force—let's call it emotional gravity. The only question is, do you possess the mental capacity to escape it?"

"You mean in more Hallmark-y terms, can my brain overcome my heart?"

"I suppose that's one way of framing it. You know the correct path, but it's not the easy one. It's a question of choosing what is prudent over your base desire."

As Greyson pondered the query, Dr. Greene added, "This introduces an interesting third element to the aforementioned experiment. A human element, if you will."

Finally, Greyson gave voice to his internal debate that started the moment he saw Hannah weeks ago. "I guess what I'm trying to ask is what if I stayed? Why would that be so bad? Would I break the spacetime continuum or ruin the future of humanity?"

Dr. Greene chuckled as if Greyson had shared a humorous anecdote. "Ah, the hubris of humans to believe they could affect something so much bigger than themselves."

"That's the go-to argument for climate change deniers. The fact is, we're wrecking our planet, our only home, on a cataclysmic level."

"Yes, we can impact our environment. But so can other species, from viruses to insects to bovines."

"Sure, on a microscale. But we're killing our planet," Greyson shot back.

"So? All planets die eventually," Dr. Greene responded with a shrug. "And there are eight other planets in our solar system devoid of life, at least as far as we know. That doesn't make them any lesser than the Earth."

"Seven," Greyson mumbled.

Dr. Greene stopped in front of the lab door, turned, and peered over his glasses down at Greyson, causing him to whisper, "Never mind."

He turned back to the door, punched in his passcode on the keypad lock, then pushed it open. After flipping the switch on the wall, the semi-darkened room quickly shone beneath the glow of fluorescent bulbs. Greyson's eyes were drawn to Lilith, who loomed over the lab like a mausoleum in a cemetery. At least, from his perspective.

"There are no laws that say we cannot alter our environment, for better or for worse. Even on a global scale. But break 'spacetime?'" Dr. Greene continued, adding air quotes around the last two words. "That, my friend, is not within our or any organism's abilities, regardless of what science fiction spouts. Might as well ask an ant to vaporize a black hole."

"Okay, fine, so what would happen if I remained in the past?"

"You mean logistically?"

"I guess," Greyson said, stepping forward and brushing his fingers over the control panel.

"You'd have to get a job."

The banal, almost parental reply took Greyson by surprise, and he laughed. "Yeah, I guess I would. I only have maybe a hundred bucks left."

He turned and regarded Dr. Greene for a moment as he considered his mentor's initial suspicion and skepticism during and even after their first meeting. Then, how those feelings slowly thawed into collaboration and trust. Other than demonstrating an adept understanding of the technicalities of Project Gateway, Greyson hadn't exactly proven his time travel story with any definitive eureka-type moments.

With that in mind, he asked, "So, you believe me now? That I'm from the future."

Dr. Greene turned on the power grid and hunched over the lab's computer to inspect the readout. After several keystrokes, he turned his attention back to Greyson and replied, "Let's just say I cannot deny the evidence."

"What evidence? My adept skill with this antique hardware," Greyson said, pointing at the bulky computer. "Or how my knowledge of Lilith is so inexplicable?"

"No," Dr. Greene stated plainly, then pointed to Lilith and said, "I will grant that you possess a nearly preternatural understanding of my work, but that could still be explained away by simple spying."

"So, what changed your mind?"

"Let's just say I vetted you."

As an expression of confusion washed over Greyson's face, he sagged down into one of the swivel chairs. "What do you mean you vetted me?"

"I vetted you," Dr. Greene repeated. "For one, I've had you followed since our initial meeting."

"Are you serious?"

"As far as I knew, you were a corporate spy. One with a grand imagination, I'll grant you. But it turned out that the only places you ever went were here, some seedy motel, and that park you're so fond of. We initially thought it might be to meet a contact, but soon realized that was not the case."

Greyson's mouth was agape as Dr. Greene continued, "Then there was your Virginia excursion. I know your first name is Greyson, and according to your story, the younger version of you is currently a student at the University of Virginia. So, I had Elden obtain a sample of his DNA, then I compared it to your DNA, and it was a match."

"But, what?" Greyson exclaimed. "How did you get my DNA?"

Dr. Greene tapped on the keys until Lilith began humming with power. "It wasn't hard. Since your arrival, you've haphazardly left your genetic fingerprints everywhere. And your younger self's DNA is scattered all over the campus."

Greyson couldn't help but equate that to bodily fluids and cringed, "Gross."

"Elden grabbed one of your cups from that coffee shop you frequent, and I matched it to one from here," Dr. Greene explained as he motioned to the paper cup in Greyson's hand.

"Betrayed by the thing I love most," Greyson scoffed as he held up the cup, then compulsively took one final sip.

"Back to your question, you would need to establish yourself in this time period. That means identification and credentials."

"Shit, that's true. It's like I'm a teenager all over again."

Dr. Greene shot him a quizzical expression, and Greyson explained, "You know, I need a fake ID. How would I do all that? And where would I work? It's not like I can work here." Then, looking for confirmation, he asked, "Right?"

"The counterfeit forms of identification are the easy part. But you're right, working here would be problematic. Are there any other fields of employment that interest you?"

Suddenly, Hannah's words, *I could see you being a sociology professor. You even have that scholarly appearance,* echoed in his mind. Then he thought about physics instead of sociology and said, "I mean, I wouldn't mind teaching. Maybe at the collegiate level."

Dr. Greene smiled. "You do know I'm on the board of trustees at UC Malibu."

"No, I didn't," Greyson replied, and then an epiphany jolted him out of his seat. It was the kind of notion that spirited him into jittery movement.

"What is it?" Dr. Greene asked as Greyson began to pace.

"I don't really know," he said excitedly as his mind tried to wrap itself around the concept taking root in his brain. "What if I did stay in the past?"

"That's what we're currently discussing."

Greyson raised his hand like a traffic cop and said, "No, I mean, what if I'd always stayed in the past?"

Dr. Greene nudged his glasses up, then said, "Are you suggesting that your future is this present?"

"I guess. When you mentioned UC Malibu, I remembered that that's where Van worked," he said, then stopped pacing and added, "As a physics professor."

"So you're postulating that you never went back to 2022, and you are in fact your wife's first husband?"

Without thinking, Greyson replied, "2021. Wait, how did you know when… "

As he trailed off, Dr. Greene replied, "Once I confirmed your identity in this time, it wasn't that difficult to ascertain your origination point."

Greyson absentmindedly nodded and returned to his proposal. He massaged his temple for a moment, as if the very conceptualization was straining his mind, then renewed pacing. As he did this, Dr. Greene asked, "What did he look like?"

There was only one photograph that Greyson had seen—the wedding photo in Hannah's office. He'd barely glanced at it before she packed it away. Hester had taken it shortly after the funeral when she and Jenna came to get a few of Hannah's personal items. "I only saw one picture, and that was several years ago," he said, "But I do remember he had a beard and glasses. I guess you could say he looked like your stereotypical college professor."

Dr. Greene pointed at Greyson as he roamed in front of Lilith and said, "You do realize that you have a beard and glasses. I could see someone categorizing you as a pedagogue. What else do you know about him?"

"That's a good question," Greyson thought, then answered, "Not much. Hannah didn't talk a lot about him, and, of course, I didn't ask. You know, the whole fear of not living up to the dead competition and all that. She'd pretty much given away all of his things by the time we'd met."

"How did he die?"

Greyson froze in place, then collapsed back into the chair. "Holy shit, I didn't even think about that. If I'm him, that means I'll die of a coronary in…" Greyson trailed off.

"There's one good reason to hope that you're not him."

Greyson just nodded as the weight of the potential revelation sank in. "Everyone knows they're going to die at some point, but to know almost exactly when and how? That's like having an expiration date tattooed on your arm."

"So, his name is Van, and he's a physics professor at UC Malibu," Dr. Greene confirmed as he lifted the black handset of the lab phone. As he dialed, he asked, "Last name?"

He shrugged. "I don't know. Hannah kept her maiden name."

As the phone rang, Dr. Greene corralled a stray chair and sat down. He swiveled back to the computer and said, "Good afternoon, Rebecca, it's Tyson. I'm doing well. How are you?"

Greyson inched forward, drawn in by the one-sided exchange, feeling like a tennis spectator who could only see one side of the court. Thoughts of conscious agency and predestination started fencing in his mind.

"I'm just calling to see if you have a physics professor there by the name of Van?"

"I guess we could've just checked their website," Greyson mumbled, more to himself.

"Sorry, I don't have a last name," Dr. Greene answered.

While Dr. Greene listened, Greyson studied his visage, hoping to spot some kind of tell that would clue him into what Rebecca was saying. Unfortunately, Dr. Greene's expression betrayed no hints. Greyson had always facetiously speculated that he only had two expressions: rumination and irritation. It had taken him several months of working together to distinguish between the two.

Finally, Dr. Greene said, "I see. Well, thank you for checking. I might be headed your way sometime next week. How does lunch sound?"

Greyson arched his eyebrows as he attempted to discern the conversation, then his jaw dropped when Dr. Greene chuckled. "I promise, nothing too spicy this time."

After he hung up the phone, Greyson asked, "Well?"

"There is a Van Singletary in the physics department. He's currently an associate professor."

Greyson sighed as his momentary bubble of hope was pierced. Then he tried to distract Dr. Greene and himself from his demoralization. "I was more talking about the lunch meet cute. If I didn't know better, I'd say you were flirting."

Dr. Greene dismissed his accusation with a wave of his hand. "Don't be juvenile. Rebecca is a friend."

"With benefits?"

"Of course," Dr. Greene stated matter-of-factly. "Every friendship is beneficial in some form or another."

Greyson offered him a strained smile, which drew an irritated look from Dr. Greene, so he tried to change the subject. "I guess that's that." Then he suddenly remembered another piece of information and shouted, "They met in the park on Valentine's Day!"

"Hmmm," Dr. Greene said as he glanced over at a wall calendar. "That's tomorrow."

"Are you serious?"

Dr. Greene replied by pointing to the date. Without looking, Greyson slapped his forehead and said, "Of course, that's why I set the return date for February 13th. I knew that would be my last chance to talk to her before she met him."

"So there's really no reason for you to stay."

"I know," Greyson dejectedly admitted as he looked down at the vinyl floor.

"It is all for the best. Now, we can focus on getting you home."

The word home sparked a reaction inside of Greyson's brain like a bolt of lightning igniting a wildfire. *What is home but a place that you love and are loved? The place where you belong? My home is where Hannah is, even if I can't be with her. Knowing she's here is enough.*

After a quiet moment, Dr. Greene punched several keys and declared, "Everything's ready on this end."

Greyson gazed over at the plain white clock on the wall that read 9:55. *I have five minutes. Five minutes to decide if I'm going to stay or go.* Suddenly, the tune "Should I Stay or Should I Go" by The Clash began playing in his head, as if a mental DJ were taunting him.

Finally, Greyson whispered somberly, "I have nothing in the future."

"You have even less here," Dr. Greene bluntly replied.

"Maybe, but at least Hannah's here. And even if I can't be with her, she's alive. That's enough for me." Greyson pointed toward the door and continued, "She's out there living her life, and she'll be happy. I'll take that world over one without her."

"Let's say you chose to stay here in the past. Do you even understand what that means?"

Greyson pondered the question for a moment, then said, "There'll be no new scientific or technological breakthroughs. All news will be old news. TV shows will basically be reruns. No point in getting hooked on *Lost* again. Plus, I'll have already seen most of the new movies and read most of the bestsellers." Then, after a brief pause, he added, "Oh, and pretty much all popular music will be oldies to me. No new Taylor Swift songs or new versions of her old ones."

"You really are a maven of pop culture," Dr. Greene said as he shook his head. "I'm talking about giving up your life."

Greyson shot back, "For me, a life without Hannah is not a life at all. Sure, we're not together here, but we're still sharing the same space… the same air. Just knowing that is all I really need. I will always choose a world with her, even if I can't be with her. That's what we, in the future, call a no-brainer."

"I think they say that here too," Dr. Greene mumbled, then checked his watch and said, "We only have a few moments before the gateway is set to open."

When Greyson nodded, he asked, "Are you positive you want to forgo your chance to return to where you belong?"

Before Greyson could answer, Lilith sparked to life. The electronic hum of the machine vibrated throughout the room. A silvery, reflective spheroid that resembled a mammoth droplet of mercury emerged from her center and quickly grew to encompass the once-empty space. The bubble slowly undulated, as if beckoning Greyson into it.

"It's now or never. 2021 is waiting," Dr. Greene announced.

As Greyson stared into the argentine orb, he recalled an old joke—*2021 called; it wants its Greyson back.* He sighed, then looked away from Lilith and turned to his friend. In that unspoken exchange, Dr. Greene appeared to recognize his resolve. Greyson's mind, like the laws of motion, had already been determined.

Greyson slowly rose, glanced back at the portal as if to say goodbye, and then plodded to the door. As he opened it, Dr. Greene asked, "Are you sure about this?"

Greyson turned and said, "I'm where I belong."

"Then, I wish you well," Dr. Greene said with a quick wave, then turned to the computer.

Chapter Fifty-Four

It was Valentine's Day afternoon, and Hannah sat in the park, dolefully reflecting on the fundamental events that had recently transpired. Never before had she experienced such a tumultuous week. The new career opportunity, the breakup, and her moving out all took a backseat to meeting and then losing Cameron. What perplexed her most was how he came to mean so much to her in such a short time.

Even with her week having more crests and chasms than a roller coaster at Six Flags, the one thing Hannah was surprised by—and proud of—was how she managed her anxiety. It had been a thorn in the back of her mind since her panic attack at the restaurant, which only increased the chances of another. But she had enough experience with worrying about her anxiety to understand that sometimes it became a self-fulfilling prophecy.

She used the tools her therapist taught her to great effect, and now, even in a melancholy state, she knew it was only temporary and things would get better. Of course, when talking about anxiety, knowing and believing are often worlds apart. But she was doing the work on the latter.

As she sat on the bench, she let the rays of the sun not only warm her skin but also remedy her pathos. She closed her eyes and thought, *It's such a beautiful day. Almost too beautiful to be glum.* Then, as she opened them, she whispered, "Almost."

She dipped in her bag for Barbara Kingsolver's *The Poisonwood Bible* and silently cursed when she couldn't find it. *I bet it fell out onto the floor of the car,* she speculated and weighed her next move. Was she to sit here and allow her thoughts to run amok, or would she trek back to the car and retrieve her distraction of choice?

Had it been a Grisham or Fielding novel, she probably would have taken —or not taken, as it were— the lazy road and just nature and people watched. But Kingsolver had quickly become one of her favorite authors, and although she was late to the literary party, she was desperate to finish this one.

She slowly rose, took a moment to stretch out, then headed for her car. By design, she liked to park as far away as possible to get a good walk to and from her spot. The only time she regretted that routine was on the occasional rainy or chilly day. And a particularly lethargic one like today. *I can't believe I forgot that damn book,* she brooded during her long march to the car.

* * *

Just as she arrived at the parking lot, she noticed a taxi speeding off. A moment later, she spotted its former occupant. Greyson stood frozen in the middle of the lot like a prisoner caught by the spotlight during an attempted jailbreak. "What the hell?" she whispered.

She continued forward towards him as he managed a pitiful wave. When she got close enough, he said, "I didn't expect to see you here."

She reacted to his greeting by arching her eyebrows, so he pointed to a row of cars and added, "I mean in the parking lot."

"What are you doing here? I thought you'd be back home by now," she said in a flat tone that seemed to purposely temper any expectations.

Fuck me! I just wanted to see her again. And maybe to observe this watershed moment in her life. Hell, I couldn't pass up the chance to finally scope out the esteemed Van. Besides, it's not stalking if your intentions are purely scientific. Of course, it's just my luck to have a close encounter with her in the damn parking lot, he thought as his surprise waned. "Yeah, I kind of missed my flight."

"I'm sure there'll be another," she said warily.

"You think?" he said with a half-smile, then backed out of the way of a slow-moving SUV. As it drove off, he glanced around, then suggested, "Maybe we should talk back inside the park. That is unless you're leaving."

She shook her head. "No, I was coming to get my book. I planned on using the rest of the daylight to read." He gave her a coy smile, and she turned and led him back to her bench.

As he followed, he thought, *What the hell am I supposed to do when Van shows up? I better make whatever I'm going to say quick. Maybe I should just turn around and run away.* He chuckled at the notion and realized part of him was glad she caught him. The halo of her presence was once again revitalizing. He knew spying on her while waiting for the love of her life—well, this part of her life—would be grueling. Almost like cruel and unusual self-punishment.

As he spotted the empty bench, he mused, *I half expected him to be sitting there, like a chump on a log. Now, I just need to... what? Explain to her as much of the truth as I can without ruining her chance with Van. How do I pull off that paradoxical tightrope walk?* He sighed as he let all the abstruse uncertainties go like a half-inflated balloon lazily drifting off into the sunset and turned this chance rendezvous over to his heart.

Hannah sat at one end of the bench and said nothing. It was as if, during the long walk over, she resolved to let him do most of the explaining.

As he perched down at the opposite end, Greyson said, "I'm sorry I freaked out the other night. I guess I just got scared. I mean, it was my first holdup at gunpoint, not counting *Call of Duty*."

"What's *Call of Duty*?" she asked.

"Oh, it's a video game." He knew her knowledge of video games was akin to his knowledge of sports, so he wouldn't have to worry about that anachronism.

He looked her in the eyes and said, "Honestly, the fear was less about being shot and more about how I am profoundly drawn to you. Physically, mentally, emotionally, and spiritually. Hell, even algorithmically. I realize we've only known each other for a short period of time, but I felt an instant connection the first moment we spoke." He hoped that mixing in small lies with greater truths would almost negate the transgression.

As ill-prepared as he was to talk to her, Greyson was almost impressed with himself. Then he realized that it had more to do with his comfort and familiarity with Hannah than any game he had. He sat there, gripping the edge of the bench, while he awaited her reply and had to remind himself that this was not his Hannah. These were uncharted waters, and he couldn't rely on her future feelings for him to help make her understand. Especially after the damage he'd already done.

The moment stretched out agonizingly long until finally Hannah smiled and said, "I can understand how you feel. That whole Bryce drama shook me up too."

In an almost Pavlovian response, he turned away and scanned the park. *Great, she understands, and there doesn't appear to be any permanent damage. Now, how do I extricate myself from this situation before I ruin not only Van's chance but my own future self's?* Greyson pondered, desperately trying not to conflate this Hannah with his version.

She caught him surveying the area and said, "I understand that you've had a volatile couple of days thanks to Bryce. But you just being here right now says a lot." Then she reached out and gently placed her hand on top of his. "Maybe we can start over."

The emotional electricity from her touch shorted out his intellect. "Sure," he said with an enthusiastic smile.

She lifted her hand from his, then offered it out as she said, "Pleased to meet you; I'm Hannah Ackerman."

He paused for just a snap and stared down at her hand as if not understanding the gesture. Then he took it into his own and said, "I'm Cameron Donovan, at your service." As he slowly shook her hand, he thought, *I still cannot believe that out of all the names I've encountered during my life, I had to blurt out my least favorite bully's. Guess I'll have to either change it or rebrand it.*

Still holding his hand, she asked, "How married are you to Cameron?" A quizzical expression appeared on his face, and she continued, "It's just that's Bryce's middle name, so it's kind of tainted."

His eyes widened as he said, "Oh, yeah. Honestly, I'm not attached to it at all. You might even say I loathe it. Call me anything, really. Just not late to dinner."

"What does that even mean?"

"I have no idea. It's just something my mom used to say."

Hannah regarded him for a moment, then asked, "Do you have any nicknames?"

People back home call me Grey, he thought, then replied, "Nope. At least none that I'm aware of."

She put a finger up to her bottom lip and said, "What about Donovan?"

Before he could answer, she said, "No, I'd feel like a gym teacher calling you by your last name." Then, her eyes lit up as she asked, "How about Van?"

Greyson felt like someone knocked the wind out of him as he slumped over. *What the shit?*

Hannah saw the astonishment wash over him and said, "Sorry, guess Van's a nonstarter."

It took a quiet moment for Greyson to recover his wits. Finally, he offered her a weak smile and said, "I didn't mean to give off a hard pass vibe. I just had a momentary feeling of, I don't know, cognitive dissonance. Van works for me."

She casually took his hand again and asked, "What about Oklahoma City?"

"I think I prefer Van," he teased as he slowly absorbed the magnitude of the revelation. *I am Van!* his brain cried out. He exhaled slowly, focusing on Hannah to center himself and keep from falling into the cerebral tempest currently whirling through his mind.

"I mean, what are you going to do about your whole life there?"

After another deep breath, he said, "It's not like there's much for me there. Just some cheap furniture and outdated clothes. I'm on a month-to-month lease, so cutting that cord won't be difficult."

"What about personal possessions? You know, like old photo albums, favorite books, treasured childhood belongings."

Shit, I can't exactly tell her all that stuff is currently sitting in the attic at Nolan's parent's house back in Virginia. Then he recalled the show *This Is Us* and said, "I lost all that stuff in a fire. While my parents were at work, there was an electrical short, and my house burned down. This was back during my second year of college."

"I'm so sorry," she said and squeezed his hand.

He shrugged and said, "No one was hurt. Ever since then, I've been living La Vida Spartan. I'll just need to get the basics here. You know—clothes, bed, car, job, PlayStation. Along with an apartment."

"I know this is going to sound ridiculously crazy, but I'm looking for a new place. It would be a lot easier with a roommate," she hinted as she wove her fingers into his.

"What a coincidence; I'm in the market for a place to live," he declared, then, with a wry smile, added, "This must be fate."

A motion in front of them drew his attention, and he spotted a spiky, blond-haired man walking by wearing a beige trench coat. The scruffy man gave him a slight nod as he passed, and Greyson noticed he was smoking a cigarette. The absurdity of the situation—a person getting their steps in while smoking—made him think of Nolan and a joke he'd often say when seeing something inane: "That's like wearing a thong diaper."

He snickered quietly, then realized he would never see his quasi-brother again. Or Tsai, or pretty much anyone from his past. And if he did, it's not like he could walk up and say hi. *I guess life is really all about trade-offs,* he solemnly reflected.

"What's so funny?" Hannah asked.

This snapped him out of his brief, melancholic daze, and he nodded at the man down the pathway. "Oh nothing, just the guy chain-smoking while exercising."

She craned her neck and spotted the swaying coat, then said with a grin, "Oh, you'll see a lot of that here. They don't call this place Lotusland for nothing."

He nodded as he stole a glance at her smiling face. *I can certainly understand why. From the moment I saw you, part of me must have known I could never leave you. There's a bond between us that defies probability, time, and even rationality. You are truly my soulmate.*

She caught him staring at her and blushed. "What is it now?"

"Just thinking how lucky I am to have met you," he said, then rose and offered her his other hand. "You want to get out of here and grab something to eat?"

She took his hand as he pulled her up., "You read my mind."

Then, they confidently walked off together, hand in hand, into the anticipation of a certain future.

Epilogue

2021

Dr. Greene checked his watch again, then tapped the command to shut Eve down. He'd allowed it to remain active for the agreed-upon twenty minutes, even though he knew the outcome. But he kept to his tenet—strive to always ensure that you do not influence the experiment in any unforeseen manner. So, even though he knew Greyson would stay in the past, he was not about to be the determinant.

He watched his machine power down with both reverence and gravity. In a sense, he'd been awaiting this moment for twenty years. Ever since Greyson strolled into his office the day after Valentine's Day back in 2001 and relayed everything that had happened in the park and how he figured out that Dr. Greene lied to him about the phone call to the university.

Over the next couple of days, Dr. Greene had procured all the identification Greyson would need, along with a job at the college and enough cash to begin his new life. "Consider this severance," Dr. Greene had told him when he first refused the gift.

Even though he'd grown quite fond of him, he didn't see much of Greyson, or Van, as he was now known, over the next ten years. Part of that was due to his acclimation to his new career as a professor, but mostly it was because of his intent on spending every available moment with Hannah.

And Dr. Greene ascertained from their brief time together that he didn't want to know any more about the future than he'd already inferred. The last time he saw Greyson, at least the older version, he'd handed Dr. Greene an envelope along with the instruction that he would know when it was the right time to open. Over the years, he'd been tempted to read the contents, but on each occasion, he spurned his inquisitiveness.

I did confirm that even though time travel is indeed possible, events in the past are immutable. Greyson's destiny would always lead him to the past, where he was meant to remain, he ruminated, then cringed at his own unmethodical word choice of "destiny" and "meant."

But now, the future was wholly unknown and unwritten. The only thing left to do was to dismantle both gateways. He came to that decision after meeting Greyson for the second time.

He exhaled loudly, then turned and headed out of the lab. On his way to the door, he grabbed his suit jacket off the back of the chair and stretched into it. He lingered in the doorway as he wistfully regarded his greatest achievement one final time, then reached into his jacket pocket and removed the yellowing envelope.

He turned it over in his hand and traced the back flap once before sinking his finger in and breaking the seal. After slowly removing the handwritten letter, he nudged his glasses up and read it.

Dear Tyson,

I didn't know how to tell you this in person, so I figured I would do it old-school style, knowing you'd appreciate it more. First, I must thank you for everything you've done for me, both now and in the future. I consider you a good friend and, even more than that, a great man. You have not only helped me, but you have helped shape the person I have become. You are truly a peerless and brilliant individual, but of that, I am sure you're already aware.

What you might not know is that you are also a kind and generous person who deserves not only accolades and recognition but also love and respect. I realize you do not value those traits as much as others, but try as you might to conceal them, you can't hide what's inside.

As you probably know, I didn't come back to 2021. It might sound hokey, but I guess I had to go into my past to find my future. I suspect you've known this all along, even as we met for the second time in 2011. Well, first time for me, second time for you. The whole time travel situation still breaks my brain sometimes.

I want you to know that I have zero regrets. I used to think love was like a quantum fluctuation, but now I know it's more like quantum entanglement. I got to live what turned out to be two lives with the one person who defined both of them. And if you think about it, as you move forward in time, I am forever with Hannah in an endless circle, or, as I call it, the ring eternal.

So, thank you, my friend, and I hope that you live a long and happy life.

Your friend through time,
Greyson

Dr. Greene refolded the letter, placed it back into the envelope, and wiped a single tear from his eye. Then he flicked the light switch on the wall and headed home, missing his friend but buoyant in the knowledge that he was out there somewhere in time and space, and he was happy.

Acknowledgment

It was quite the journey to get here, and many people helped me along the way. First and foremost, I must thank my wife, Lynne, who when everyone said I was too short, too slow, too basic, and too old to write this story… you still believed in me. You're always my first collaborator, reader, and editor. I'm *your* biggest fan.

I want to thank the rest of my family—my mom, sisters, children— and friends who inspire me every day.

Next up are my two write or die critique partners, (aka BBB4L) Christina and Ana, who made this book so much better than it has any right to be. Meeting both of you was better than any literary luck one could manifest.

Thank you to my editor, Leilani, and amazing cover artist, Leraynne S., who exceeded all my expectations and were a joy to work with.

Last but certainly not least, to my fan(s?). You make all this possible. For an indie author like myself, fan support is paramount. So if you like the story enough, please leave a review (on Amazon and/or Bookreads) and tell a friend… or twenty thousand (I'll be your virtual bestie). And don't forget to follow my socials and sign up for my newsletter on the next page.

If you don't enjoy it, well, like I repeatedly told my English teacher, Mrs. French, "I'll try and do better next time."

About the Author

When I'm not projecting my anxiety, humor, and romantic fantasies onto fictional characters, I'm an instructional designer. I also have a blog (see below) followed by scores of bots that have repeatedly hailed it as "The best ting write on internet in ever."

You can connect with me on:

https://www.siroutlier.com

https://www.facebook.com/F.G.keel.author

https://www.instagram.com/f.g.keel

Subscribe to my newsletter:

https://www.siroutlier.com/newsletter

Also by F.G. Keel

I have three other finished books just waiting to be published soon.

Family Rune

Family Rune is a cozy tale about a lost soul who returns to the hometown he ghosted to take care of his estranged father and gradually becomes embroiled in the town's infamous mystery.

Since his divorce, Griffin Burke has been drifting aimlessly through his own life until he gets a dreaded call informing him that his father has early-onset Alzheimer's. Reluctantly forced back to the provincial town he fled, he is suddenly steeped in wistful nostalgia while reconnecting with a life he shunned twelve years ago. While trying to support and reconcile with his stoic father, Griffin soon discovers that he has a dark secret that may be linked to the disappearance of a teenage girl thirty-five years ago.

With the help of his former high school sweetheart, Nikki, who is harboring her own tragic secret, Griffin must unlock the cryptic history his father is hiding while confronting his own. He soon discovers that to realize his future he must finally overcome the past.

Trimble Hollow

When a young boy from their neighborhood is murdered, Ryan Carter enacts a plan to safeguard his own children by uprooting the family to the sanctuary of a small town. His wife, Simone, wonders if he is doing the right thing or giving into fear—a fear of a diversifying community that has driven him to escape into his own monochromatic childhood.

Everything about their new neighborhood appears idyllic at first until a series of bizarre incidents begin to plague the family. Simone slowly realizes these incidents are all tied to a haunting stranger. All her life, she has surrendered authority to a patriarchal society. Now, Simone must overcome her own self-doubt and find the strength to protect her children from a threat that her husband refuses to acknowledge.

A Hero's Road Trip

What if you are not the hero of your own story? That is the dilemma facing Dover Knox, a millennial with a chronic case of ennui. But that is about to change as his sister locates their estranged father on the other side of the country, providing him with a coveted opportunity for a journey, along with the chance to finally add a little extra to his brand of ordinary.

Dover, his sister, and their diverse group of friends venture across America during the dumpster fire known as the summer of social distance. During their search for reconciliation, they attend an All Dollars Matter seminar, take part in a religious wrestling extravaganza, and discover the Lost Dutchman's gold mine, all while debating related sociopolitical issues. Their grandiose escapade through the bowels of Dixie must be read to be disbelieved.

Milton Keynes UK
Ingram Content Group UK Ltd.
UKHW010625080324
438959UK00001B/120